Capitol Punishment

2

For my parents, Joe and Beverley, my friend Peter Calabrese and my cousin and top cheerleader, Lori Johnson. Thank you all for your support, your ideas and your suggestions. I couldn't have done this without you.

All tyranny needs to gain a foothold is for men of good conscience to do nothing" – Thomas Jefferson

Chapter 1

The rearview mirror once again caught the glare of the approaching headlights. Temporarily blinded by the reflection, the driver looked away, returning his eyes to the treacherous road conditions, and then -- unable to resist – he cautiously checked the mirror once more. The vehicle was approaching fast; too fast for the icy road conditions.

Simon Deefer pressed down harder on the accelerator and tightened his already white- knuckled grip on the steering wheel. Fear had made his palms sweaty in spite of the cold, December evening. At the speed he was traveling, he could not risk his hands slipping on the wheel. It would, in fact, be disastrous. He cursed the car, one purchased neither for its speed nor its agility, but for its image. It projected an appearance of environmental consciousness. It didn't matter that he left every light on in his home, or that he drove a fully-loaded Hummer when he wasn't in Washington. This was the car the Washington Press Corps and, therefore, the American people, saw; a compact hybrid that was fuel efficient and economically responsible. It gave a distinct illustration of his first lesson -- the American press and the American people cared far more for appearances than for substantive actions. He could hear his mentor's voice now in its familiar refrain, "Show the people what they want to see, tell them what they want to hear, and then do exactly as you damn well please."

The bare trees and snow banks which lined the road were nothing but a blur as he pressed the accelerator all the way to the floor.

And still the SUV gained.

It was almost upon him now. Simon knew what was coming, and what's more, he knew he deserved it. Shame welled up inside of him. Shame for how easily he had been seduced by power, for how easily he had been diverted from his goals, and shame for how he had betrayed those he loved. His stomach roiled with self disgust as the enormity of his actions slammed hard into a conscience he had long thought exiled.

He had been shifting further towards the wrong side for months now, distancing himself more and more from his true goals. It had obviously been noticed. He had stood teetering on the edge of making his betrayal complete and destroying everything he had first worked for, and they must have suspected. Their suspicions were correct. To his increasing dismay, he realized that he had become what he had once been determined to fight against.

When the anticipated impact came at last, Simon dropped his hands from the steering wheel and fumbled for the seat belt clasp. His slick, damp fingers slid over the release button twice before connecting. With the wheel free, the fuel-efficient compact slid into a wild skid on the ice-covered road. The seat belt finally clicked free, just as the rear wheels of the car came in contact with the high bank of snow on the shoulder. Simon resisted the urge to brace himself as the high speed, abruptly slowed by the snow bank, flung the car high into the air. He was thrown against the passenger side window, his skull making contact with the glass with such force that it shattered them both. He felt nothing from that point on. He was dead before the car came to rest.

The SUV braked hard, still rocking from the impact of the collision. The tires slipped once, making the car shudder, but quickly regained their grip on the pavement. The driver quickly regained control and maneuvered his way to his exit for a clean getaway. Pulling himself together, he ran his sleeve across his forehead to remove the sweat now dripping into his eyes and turned hard at the exit ramp. "Keep it together," he told himself. "Just keep it together until you get home. You're not done yet." But already the grief was welling up inside of him. Grief, now coupled with anger. He told himself the anger was good; he could focus on that and suppress the grief, drive it down deep for a while longer.

"Those bastards," he thought, "those miserable, corrupt, manipulative bastards. They have it coming - every damn one of them." It wasn't enough that they had wrestled control of the country from the people and were driving it into the ground, turning it into a nation that would make the founding fathers weep --- no --- they had to take his friend as well. They would pay for their sins. He would ensure, if it was the very last thing he did in this life, that every last one of them would pay.

Maximilian Reginald Abernathy III parked the SUV next to a blue, late model Ford Taurus that sat as if abandoned behind an empty warehouse. He then reached his gloved hand under the dash, pulled out the ignition wires, and hotwired the car. With only a moment's fumbling, the truck engine fired back to life. This would ensure that their story that the car had been stolen would hold up under scrutiny. Next, he wiped down everything he could have possibly touched, both inside and out, put the key in his pocket and strode to the waiting Taurus.

Twenty minutes later, the grief and anger still seething under the surface, but cloaked under a thin veil of indifference, he pulled into the parking lot of another apparently abandoned warehouse. There was a smattering of other cars in the lot, but not many on such a dark and dreary evening. Max slid from the Taurus, weary to the bone and chilled from the inside out, and pulled the collar of his long, wool overcoat up around his ears. The dampness in the air only added to his chill, causing him to shiver violently. He strode purposefully across the lot, moving into and out of the darkness as motion-detecting security lights clicked on. Still shivering, he grasped the icy metal door handle and entered the warehouse.

The large brick building only appeared to be abandoned; an appearance that was contrived and deliberately deceptive. What once had been a warehouse was now a state-of-the-art conference facility; the headquarters for the N.A.C.R., the National Association for Congressional Reform. Max walked through the portion of the warehouse which had been preserved as such in order to keep inquisitive people at bay, and through a steel door into the main conference room. This resembled any other conference room found in any office building in corporate America, but the decisions made at this long table were far different than those of any board of directors. Here they did not discuss profit margins and marketing strategies, they discussed the fate of their country and how to save her.

Over two hundred faces greeted him; some in person, but most displayed on a wall of monitors via video conference. These were the national committee delegates, spanning not only all regions of the country, but all races, religions, age groups, socio-economic backgrounds and professions. They included everyone from a 25-year-old electrician to a 67-year-old world-renowned geneticist. They were bound together by one common goal: to restore the government of the United States of America to the American people. Max cast his gaze at the faces before him, pulled his coat tighter to fight off the pervading chill that still assailed him, and answered their unspoken question with one phrase: "It is done."

Daniel Callahan felt like hell and was pretty sure that he looked even worse. It had been a long night, following a long day, preceded by an even longer five years. All he wanted to do was put the latest ridiculously sensationalistic story behind him, crawl under the covers, and hibernate for three days. But that was not to be. He rounded the bend in the road and saw it.

The car had obviously hit a patch of black ice, causing the driver to lose control and the car to flip. Suddenly alert in spite of his weariness, Daniel quickly pulled the car over and was dialing 9-1-1 even as he was exiting his vehicle.

After two rings an overly chipper female voice came on the line, "9-1-1 dispatch, what is your emergency?"

Daniel gave the prodigiously perky operator his location and the circumstances, flipped the phone closed, clipped it back to his belt, and approached the car. With the cold mist clinging to his hair and trickling under his collar, he steeled himself against what he would see. He was fairly certain that this wasn't going to be pretty. He wasn't wrong.

The late night coffee and greasy hamburger he had consumed that evening fought to jump out of his stomach at the sight that greeted him. The car now rested on its roof and had most likely flipped more than once, based on the damage to both the exterior and interior of the car, and the remains of what had once been a wire fence now wrapped around it. The vehicle's sole passenger lay in an unnatural heap against the roof, one arm extended out of the smashed window, the head turned at an impossible angle, the wide, sightless eyes locked in a now dead stare, and the breeze ruffling what hair was not matted with blood.

The damp chill of the air pressed in on him, and the night, lit only by a sliver of the moon and its reflections, felt preternaturally still. His chest tightened, the blood pounded in his ears, bile rose up to burn his throat, and his hands shook, though not from the cold. He recognized this man.

This was Simon Deefer, aide to Daniel's personal antichrist: the instigator of the great "incident" that had ruined his journalistic career; the reason that he had been pursuing a story on an alien landing in Arlington, VA instead of reporting the happenings on Capitol Hill. The man who had ensured that every door to a legitimate journalistic job had not just been closed, but nailed, bolted, and welded shut.

Daniel was startled out of his introspective ruminations when the silence was pierced by a siren's wail. He hurried out of the way as the ambulance, which was far too late to save the congressional aide, rapidly approached.

The EMTs jumped from the ambulance and moved with humorless efficiency. They went through all of the motions, leaving nothing out, even though it was obvious that the driver was dead. Daniel respected their dedication and professionalism in a job he knew he could never do.

The police arrived right on the tail of the ambulance, a single car that pulled up behind the wrecked compact, parked, and left the lights flashing. The rotating lights of the police cruiser and ambulance lent a surreal feel to the dark night. Daniel glanced again at the wreck's victim, shocked at how the red strobes enhanced the macabre scene, as if Simon Deefer were forever caught in a dance club for the damned. He felt that hamburger trying to work its way back out of his stomach again. God, what a night.

"Are you the gentleman who called this in?" the officer asked. He was over forty, slightly paunchy, and was walking forward with his hand resting on the butt of his gun.

"Yes, sir," Daniel replied, eying the hand placement nervously. What about him could possibly appear threatening to this guy? After his career was destroyed, but before he hit rock bottom, he'd had a few run-ins with the DC police. There were a few times when approaching him in this manner had been prudent and absolutely justified, but not tonight. Tonight he was stone cold sober, as he had been for over two years now.

The officer lifted his right arm, held it out in front of himself, and then gestured to the shoulder of the road as he said, "Please stand off to the side, sir." He then made his way to the vehicle, crouched down to investigate, turned another suspicious look Daniel's way, and began speaking into his shoulder radio.

Daniel couldn't hear what was being said, and couldn't bear to even look in that direction again, so instead he shoved his hands in his front pockets, hunched up his shoulders and willed himself back under control. He would have preferred to get back in his car, out of the mist, and blast the heat, but he knew that wouldn't really help. He was so focused on his breathing that he did not hear the officer approach. As a result, he was shocked and nearly stupefied when he heard the officer say, "Sir, have you been drinking?"

Since he had given no indication of intoxication, he wasn't sure where this had come from. "No, I don't drink."

The officer made no attempt to hide his skepticism. "So you won't object to a sobriety test, then?"

Daniel sighed, resigned to the humiliating and unnecessary process. After standing on one leg, touching his finger to his nose, and walking a straight line, the police officer should have been satisfied. He wasn't. A breathalyzer was also required. Daniel blew into it without making any move, large or small, that could be interpreted as a refusal. The suspicions that had begun to grow in his mind were further solidified when the officer was disappointed, and slightly irritated, that the results showed no alcohol in his blood. But still it wasn't over.

"Sir," the officer said, "walk over and face your car, place your hands on the hood, and spread your legs."

What the bloody, blooming hell was going on here! Daniel just couldn't believe it. He suffered through the indignity of being patted down, and gasped as first one arm, and then the other, was jerked from its supportive position. His arms pulled tight behind him, Daniel was then forced down onto the cold, wet hood of his car, knocking the wind out of him in a whoosh. He was handled roughly, one hand placed on his head and smashing his face down onto the metal, his teeth cutting the inside of his cheek, the metallic taste of the blood blending with the scent of the vehicle under his nose.

He knew the officer was hoping he would protest; that he would fight; that he would make any move that would indicate resisting arrest. But Daniel made no move at all and said nothing, not even when he felt the cold steel of handcuffs snapped around his wrists. Jaw locked and shoulders stiff in anger and disbelief, he allowed himself to be forced, with little concern for his head, into the back of the police cruiser. He hadn't been read his Miranda rights so he was pretty sure he wasn't actually being arrested, but he also hadn't been told what this was all about either; though a strong suspicion had taken shape in his mind.

The impression grew in strength when Daniel noticed, first, that the dash cam had been deactivated and, second, that the computer screen showed his own face with a flag labeling him an enemy combatant; for the love of God.

Daniel was left to cool his heels in the back of the cruiser while both the congressional aide's car and his own were inspected. At least now he was out of the mist. Definitely a "be careful what you wish for" moment. He knew they wouldn't find any signs that he had caused the accident, but lack of evidence had never posed much of a problem for the police before.

The authorities had proven to him five years ago that when it came to anything involving the grand poobah of all corrupt politicians, if no evidence existed, then some could be easily and swiftly manufactured.

The paunchy officer climbed into the car, the seat creaking as his bulk was pressed against it, pulled the door closed with a slam, and started the engine. All of this was done without once looking at the passenger secured in the back. They had pulled off the shoulder and made a U-turn on the highway before Daniel spoke.

"I suppose it's too much to ask for an explanation as to why I am sitting handcuffed in your backseat?"

Silence.

"Is it customary to arrest all citizens who report an accident, or am I just special?"

"You haven't been arrested."

The officer said no more; did not even glance in the rearview at him. "So, you're just offering me a ride home then? How kind of you, but there was nothing wrong with my own car, as you should have seen from your meticulous inspection of it. I was fully capable of driving myself." He'd tried to keep the sarcastic tone from his voice, but if the look the officer shot at him was any indication, he had not been completely successful.

"Your vehicle is being impounded until the accident investigation is completed." There was a pause, "And you're not being taken home."

Daniel waited for a further explanation, such as an explanation of where exactly he was being taken. He was already fairly certain he was being taken in for additional questioning, yet failure to advise him of this was a blatant violation of his civil rights. He had learned the hard way that not everyone had civil rights, and he was one of the chosen who had none.

If you angered the wrong person, especially in this town, all of the rights listed in the Constitution and the Declaration of Independence no longer applied to you. You could be harassed, persecuted, and tried for pretended offenses with impunity, but this time he was not the naïve man he had once been. This time he knew what his enemy was capable of, and he would not make it easier for them.

He sat in the back of the cruiser with nothing but the radio and the passing darkness to occupy him. The radio was set on a 24-hour Christmas music station and Daniel could not help but see the irony, and the humor, of being handcuffed and hauled in, all to the tune of "Holly Jolly Christmas".

It was twenty minutes later when he was escorted, still in cuffs, to an interrogation room in the state-of- the-art police station. Daniel could not prevent the smile that spread across his face at his paradoxical surrounding. It had always amused him that this city, which had more laws on weapons and spent more money on police than any other city in the nation, still had the highest crime rate.

What was funny, but also sad, was that the politicians in control were so sure they were taking the correct approach that they flat out refused to acknowledge that they might be wrong. As a result, every time a new law was passed or more money was thrown at the problem, it expanded exponentially -- and no matter how state-of-the-art the facility was, it still smelled like old coffee, stale cigarettes, and junkies.

Daniel was oddly saddened by the total lack of holiday decorations inside the station. There was neither a Christmas card nor a menorah in sight. The first amendment had been more and more consistently interpreted as a freedom *from* religion instead of a freedom *of* religion. He missed the days of garland and colored balls everywhere you looked. Their absence made the holiday just a little bit depressing now.

The current situation rose to the forefront of his mind again as Officer Paunch -- as Daniel referred to him, since he hadn't had the courtesy to introduce himself -- released the cuff from one wrist. He thought he might be able to massage some feeling back into his hands, but instead of being left free, his wrists were re-cuffed in the front. This was done with so little care that the sleeve of his leather jacket was scratched by the metal. Daniel loved that jacket.

Officer Paunch forced Daniel into the chair facing the two-way mirror, which was standard in every interrogation room in the country, along with the dull gray paint and the aforementioned stink. The officer took his leave and Daniel was finally left in peace. More than half an hour later, he was still alone. His extended isolation was no doubt meant to intimidate him, but it if that was their intent, they had failed.

Pushing the chair far enough from the table so he could sprawl, legs outstretched and apart, head thrown back over the chair, Daniel pretended to sleep; but it had been a long day, and he was crashing from the adrenaline that had pumped through his veins when he first came upon that vehicle. In addition, since he was unable to remove his jacket over the cuffs at his wrists, he was now toasty warm. In no time at all, his pretense had become a reality.

Awakened a full two hours later by a rough, downright rude kick to his chair, Daniel opened his eyes but did not straighten his posture -- especially when he saw who had entered. Looming in a stance designed to illustrate his power was his own personal nemesis. However, instead of righting himself as would be the polite thing to do, as his mother would wish him to do, he let his disrespect for all those involved in this ridiculous farce clearly show. Slouching further into his chair, Daniel propped one elbow on the back, spread his legs, and grinned. Unfortunately, with his hands still cuffed before him, it wasn't quite the insolent posture he was going for. However, the message was clear enough.

"Hey, Sludge. Long time no see."

The Chief of Police, who had so graciously awakened Daniel, bristled at the further disrespect. "How dare you speak to him that way, you alcoholic, tabloid hack! Sit up straight and show the man the respect he deserves."

Daniel did not shift his gaze from its current battle of wills with the overblown politician. "I'd love to do that, sir, but it would be awkward to take a shit on his shoes while my hands are still confined." He raised his hands and jangled the cuffs to illustrate his point.

The chief's already florid face turned a particularly unappealing shade of purple, and for a moment, Daniel viewed the vein bulging at the side of his head and feared that the police chief was going to have a stroke. Sledgewater, ever the politician, turned on the charm.

An average looking man in his late fifties, jowls beginning to sag and close-cropped curly hair thinning on top, Clive Sledgewater managed to project and maintain a very commanding presence. He was every inch the smooth politician, from the top of his head to the tips of his buffed and polished toenails; able to hide his true self behind a pleasing façade. The best actor the country had yet produced; he should win an Academy Award for his near convincing portrayal of a human being. Daniel grinned to himself as he imaged Sledgewater thanking the Academy for his win as best actor in a horror flick. Inappropriate for the moment, perhaps, but still amusing.

Sledgewater's voice was smooth and well modulated, making him an excellent and commanding Speaker. "Now, John, there's no reason to speak so harshly to the gentleman. He has every right to speak to me how he chooses. This is still a free country, after all." Daniel snorted, Sledgewater ignored it. "But I don't have a lot of time, so we do need to get down to business."

"Does this mean I'm finally going to find out why my car was impounded, and why I was handcuffed and deposited here for no apparent reason, other than to await your illustrious presence?"

Sledgewater adopted a look of faint shock.

Daniel was unconvinced.

"Do you mean you weren't advised as to why you were brought in?" Turning back to the police chief he continued, "John, you need to speak to your officers about this. We can't have our peace officers violating the rights of our citizens. That goes against everything this country stands for."

Police Chief Jonathan Price looked confused for only the barest second. Daniel had to give him credit for that, especially since he knew full well that he was here, and had been given no explanation as to why, at the specific orders of good old Sludge. "Yes, sir, I'll speak to them as soon as we're done here."

Daniel watched the police chief fawn over this reptilian bastard, and was further disgusted as he saw the representative level a condescending smile on the chief. The man was so filled with his own superiority that it oozed from every pore. Like acne. Daniel didn't mean to speak, but the words were out of his mouth before they were fully formed in his head. "It's so obvious that you love kissing his ass, that I'm curious as to whether he has you sucking his dick as well?" Daniel watched as the chief's round face turned that florid purple again, and smiled in spite of himself. In for a penny, in for a pound, he decided. "Purple is a good color for you. It brings out the blue of your eyes."

The chief glared malevolently, his hands balled into fists. He turned to Sledgewater, but seeing the shake of his head, remained silent.

"There's really no need to get crude, Mr. Callahan." The voice was still smooth and controlled, nothing rattled him. It was that control that had steadily advanced him to the top of his profession and placed him, as the Speaker of the House, third in line for the Presidency. Daniel was still surprised that the President and Vice President had not yet met an untimely and suspicious death or been forced to resign due to some scandal, but was pretty confident that old Sludge had something in the works.

It was that ability to speak with a calm and civil voice when the other politicians were all screaming at each other, behaving more like two sisters fighting over the same man on Jerry Springer than leaders of our nation, which made him so appealing. "Since the officer on the scene so thoughtlessly neglected to tell you why you're here, why don't we just get to the point? I find it suspicious that my aide is killed in a motor vehicle accident and you are the one to find him."

Daniel just glared back. "And I find it damned inconvenient. Lord knows that, had I known the car belonged to your aide, I would have just kept driving."

Sledgewater smiled condescendingly, "Then you would have been guilty of leaving the scene of an accident. Not a good thing to have on your record."

"My record is shot to hell anyway, as you very well know since you're the one who manufactured all those charges, but I wouldn't be guilty of leaving the scene of an accident. I didn't see the accident, nor was I involved in it, so I would have been guilty of nothing more than driving by a person who may or may not have been in need of assistance. Not a very nice thing to do, I grant you, but certainly not illegal. It really is sad when the people elected to write our legislation can't even apply the laws that currently exist. But we know what actually happened, and the correct application of the laws doesn't really matter to you, does it?"

Sludge looked at him speculatively, "I still find it odd that a person who hates me . . ."

Daniel cut him off, "Last time I looked, the congressional approval rating was at 18%. That means there was an 82% probability that whoever stopped would have hated your guts."

Sledgewater's smile tightened. That approval rating was the one place he was vulnerable. "Thank God my reelection only depends on the people in my district and not the whole nation. And my personal job approval rating in my district is 92%; the highest of any incumbent." The politician actually preened.

Daniel was reminded of a feral cat dropping a rodent at your feet and expecting your adoration, although he was unsure whether Sledgewater was the cat or the rodent, so he just grinned back at him. "But that's the poll of likely voters and that's a pretty small sample, considering that your district also has the lowest voter turnout in the country."

"It is pitiful how little attention the American people pay to what's going on around them," Sledgewater sighed. "But I am still here as their voice."

"Pompous ass," Daniel thought to himself. Good old Sludge knew damn well that the reason people in his district didn't turn out to the polls was because they were disgusted with him.

The problem was that nobody would run against him, and he couldn't blame them, considering that the last guy who tried was suddenly accused of child molestation. Oddly enough, the charges were dropped after his candidacy was withdrawn. "I'm sure they know *exactly* how lucky they are to have someone of your level of integrity watching out for them."

There was a pause as Congressman Sledgewater allowed Daniel to remember that it was calling the congressman's integrity into question that led to the destruction of Daniel's career. Then, just to pour salt into the already gaping wound, the Speaker amused himself by saying, "Yes, well, unlike so many of my colleagues, my integrity has never been called into question; at least not by any *reputable* source."

Daniel smiled benignly and replied, "Nope. Just little ole me. The man your impeccable integrity caused to be hauled in to the police station for reporting an accident." Cocking his head to the side, he allowed his natural inquisitiveness that which had so benefited his career when he still had one -- and had also served to destroy it – to take over. "Why is it you're so sure that this wasn't an accident? Road conditions aren't great out there, so why are you so convinced that there was foul play? It can't be just because I called it in."

"But of course it is," Sledgewater said with a bland smile. "Had anyone else called it in, I would have seen the death of my aide as a tragic accident and nothing more, but your involvement, based on your criminal past coupled with your known abuse of alcohol, seemed too convenient. I lose my right hand man, and there you are. You wouldn't be trying to get to me through him, would you?"

Daniel sat up so rapidly that Sledgewater actually gave a revealing flinch. Disgust and anger were imprinted on Daniel's beard-shadowed countenance. "Unlike you, I don't get to people by hurting those around them. If I wanted to hurt you, which I don't, I would go to you -- nobody else -- just you."

Sledgewater smiled now in true amusement, reveling in the memory of what had finally brought Mr. Callahan to heel all those years ago. There was nothing like the power to have a man's parents investigated by the immigration services to remind him of what's important.

It was less than forty-eight hours after the INS showed up at the home of Robert and Margaret Callahan that Congressman Sledgewater was advised that Daniel's investigation had been dropped and his story buried. "Are you trying to tell me that you don't want revenge for what you believe I've done to you?"

Daniel snorted. Christ, even now, after all this time, after everything Daniel knew to be true, this guy was playing innocent. "I'm not *trying* to tell you anything. That would be an exercise in futility. I flat out said it. I believe you deserve to be punished for your crimes. And I believe that you will be punished, but it is not my place to do it. One of the things I learned as I was climbing my way back out of the bottle you helped me in to, was that vengeance is unproductive. Romans 12:19 says 'Vengeance is mine' and I've come to accept that God can punish you far more thoroughly than I ever could, and I'm happy to leave it up to Him."

Sledgewater threw back his head and laughed, laughed so hard that tears seeped from the corners of his eyes. "Oh, that's rich. You actually believe God will punish me?" He leaned in close, far closer than Daniel would have liked. Close enough that Daniel could smell the wine on his breath and see the small blood vessels that had burst in his nose -- and the scars from the recent facelift. "God doesn't exist."

Daniel smiled in return. "Oh, He exists. And it's His existence that keeps me going, that made me whole again.

And it's the thought of him banishing your black soul to Hell for all eternity that makes me feel all tingly inside. It'd almost be worth going to Hell myself just to see you suffer." Daniel sighed, "But, alas, I'm a believer and try my best to be a good man, so I'll make do with imagining your suffering while I reside safely and happily in Heaven."

"You'll be disappointed then, but you should be used to that by now, what with the way your life and career have worked out. So tragic." Sledgewater went so far as to shake his head and make that tsk, tsk noise, the universal sound of pity.

Knowing that good old Sludge was trying to get him to react in any way that would appear as a threat and thereby constitute grounds for real incarceration, Daniel gave no physical reaction, but simply said, "My disappointment sits mainly with the path of the country's leadership, but that's a disappointment that I share with most other Americans. It's one we've all dealt with for years and have learned to handle with equanimity. Don't you worry your balding head about me, I'll be fine with my disappointment in this life, but I know in my soul that I won't be disappointed in my next. You *will* be in Hell. Perhaps not the eighth circle that Dante envisioned for your kind, but you'll be there all the same. It doesn't matter that you don't believe. My comfort lies in my belief, not in yours."

Irritation flashed briefly across Sledgewater's face, so briefly that, had Daniel not been watching for it, he would have missed it entirely. The serene mask that had served the Representative so well slid immediately and firmly back into place.

"I suppose we must agree to disagree. These differing beliefs, ideals, and opinions are, of course, what make this country great. I would love to stay and debate these issues with you further, but I must take my leave to deal with the tragic loss of my aide. He was a great man with tremendous potential in politics. Such a shame." Sledgewater actually went so far as to drop his head and sigh in what anybody with less experience of the man would see as true grief and regret. Daniel, however, saw it for the staged performance that it was. "I thank you very much for your cooperation in this investigation."

An indelicate snort greeted this comment. "Of course, in the situation, I could do nothing else." He again held up his cuffed hands as an illustration. The words, and even the tone, were perfectly polite, but the underlying message was clear.

The worst part of this whole debacle was that Daniel would have been happy to cooperate if only he had been asked -- but he had not been asked. Instead of issuing a polite request to come to the station, give a statement, and answer a few questions, the police handcuffed him, bundled him into the back of a police cruiser, and deposited him unceremoniously into an interrogation room, leaving him waiting for hours.

Were he a man of color, or a Muslim, he could call the ACLU and file charges, but he wasn't. He was a white Christian male, so the ACLU couldn't give two shits about whether or not his rights were violated. Daniel sighed and shook his head at the sad state the country was in, the worse part being that nobody really seemed to care.

He was the original "forgotten man". Not the man that Roosevelt used in his famous speech, but the real forgotten man; he who is left to foot the bill and bear the cost for the benefits and liberties of others. He was the man whose rights were violated, yet there was no organization to stand up to defend him; the man forgotten by everyone except his persecutor. Being the forgotten man really sucked.

More than an hour after his visitor / persecutor had departed, Daniel still remained cuffed and locked in the interrogation room until, finally, an officer silently entered and removed his cuffs. The man opened the door to leave without as much as a glance in Daniel's direction, much less uttering a single word. Not wanting to risk a misinterpretation of his exit, Daniel finally asked if he was free to go and received a curt nod in response -- and that was it.

Rubbing his wrists at last in order to get the blood flowing again, Daniel pulled his weary body to his feet and headed out the door, only to remember that he didn't have his car. He checked at the desk and found that, to add insult to injury, he had to pay $827 to liberate his car from the impound lot. He was too disillusioned to be outraged and too tired to argue, especially since he knew it would do no good, accomplish nothing.

Feeling like death, eyes red and gritty with exhaustion, hands riddled with the pins and needles feeling of returning blood flow, Daniel rubbed his hand over the rasp of his perpetual beard stubble. He felt dirty, not just from the long day and even longer night, but more from his forced proximity to a man he viewed as akin to the devil. He felt tainted; soiled.

When he stepped out of the police precinct, he was bathed in the frigid night air. He stopped on the steps and closed his eyes, allowing the fresh air and cold breeze to wash over him, cleansing him as he sent up a prayer to heaven; a prayer for strength, patience and -- feeling guilty for even asking -- for freedom from this persecution. Taking a deep breath, he opened his eyes to find delicate crystals of ice dancing in the bright beam of a street light. It was beautiful, and he was in desperate need of some beauty at the moment.

Though his nose began to run and his eyes to water from the frigid night, he remained on the steps watching those dancing crystals of ice. Few cars drove by in the early morning hours, their sound adding to the beauty of the night instead of detracting from it, the motion of the passing cars stirring the crystals and expanding the patterns of their intricate ballet. They soothed him, the answer to his silent prayer.

A few years ago he would have been bitter about his treatment this night, but life had taught him a thing or two since then. His bitterness helped no one and hurt only himself.

As he walked the six blocks to the impound lot to recover his car, he allowed the hushed beauty of the night to restore him. He took comfort in those few buildings still decorated with bright lights and wreaths as a celebration of Christ, and by the time he arrived home and crawled into bed, his soul was at peace once more, his interaction with his nemesis all but forgotten. Justice would be served. He had faith, and that faith would see him through worse things than this night; of that he was sure. And soon, he would be proven right.

Chapter 2

Max hit the remote opener and slowly pulled in to his attached garage. Tired to his very bones and knowing his soul to be forever damaged by the events of this evening, he closed the garage door, but remained seated inside long after the automatic light had clicked off and the temporary warmth of the car had leeched out.

He sat until the chill registered in his bones, until he began to shiver and his teeth to chatter. This was not what he'd signed on for. It was not who he was. It was not what he believed; and yet it was necessary in order to achieve all of the above. Weary, and fearing he was becoming the evil he set out to fight, Max made his way across the dark garage and into his home.

His home, which had always been a place of warmth and love, now served as a sanctuary from the evils of the world. Making his way through the night-darkened rooms, the sound of his feet muffled by the plush carpeting, Max intended to go straight to bed. However, he instead felt himself drawn to another room; his daughter's room. He cracked open the door and peered inside.

The room was oddly absent of any frills or ruffles; the furniture functional and of good quality, but gender neutral;

the walls covered with posters promoting movies he had not seen and bands he had never heard. This was his daughter's room, and the sight of her sleeping peacefully was enough to reassert his resolve. She was the reason for his actions this night.

His only child was now just fifteen years old, but would soon be out in the world. It was his desire to ensure she had the same America he had known, the same freedoms, the same opportunities, which had initially driven him to seek congressional reform. That search had led him to the NACR; a small but quickly growing organization at the time.

He wanted his child to know the benefits of living in a country whose government is truly of the people, by the people, for the people. He wanted to protect her from a government moving from democracy to tyranny.

His gaze locked on her again. Long auburn hair spread across her pillow and draped across a face which appeared, in the peace of sleep, far younger than fifteen. What would she think of his actions of this night? Would she forgive him? Would she understand why he had done it? He did not think so. He had made a difficult decision and he forced himself to remember the reasons behind it.

Simon's betrayal had put the ultimate goal at risk; a goal that could not afford to be derailed; a goal that would save the country for his daughter and all the youth of this nation. A nation that was once great, and with their plan and the will of God, would be great again.

He consoled himself with the reminder that what was now the ultimate goal had begun as their last resort. The organization had tried to do things according to the American principles. They had spoken out as individuals, as the Constitution assured their right to do, but they found that right revoked. There was no law against free speech, that was true, but if you exercised the right which now existed in name only, the government would find a way to punish you for it. Three of the original members of the NACR were in jail for crimes they had not committed -- another was dead.

Founding member Paul Petkolakis had been the CEO of a small but successful company, a good and honest man whose integrity had never been called into question; not until his salary was released to the press – but with a few extra zeros added on to the end. Paul had attempted to correct the misunderstanding, but nobody cared about the truth, nobody would listen.

Outrage was whipped up by the press, who continued to print the lie over the truth, and by the government who insisted on pointing out that the CEO was paid half the proceeds of the company, breaking the backs of the working man with his greed. This was untrue, but the press printed what they were told to print, and organizations encouraged their people to protest at Paul's place of business and even at his home.

Still attempting to shine the light of truth, Paul went outside to speak to the protesters and was greeted with a barrage of obscenities first, and then of stones. One of those stones had connected with his temple, killing him immediately. As he lay dead on his own lawn, the shouting and the throwing not only continued, but escalated. As his wife ran from the house in fear for her husband, she was pelted with stones as well.

The thrower of the killing stone was not indicted on any charges, and yet nobody appeared to be in the least bit outraged or even upset that our country had resorted to stoning people who had committed no crime.

Max had no idea how long he remained in the hall gazing at his daughter before finally pulling the door silently closed and heading down the hall to his own bed. His wife of twenty-six years awoke when he entered; as she always did. He hated to wake her, but no matter how silent he was she always sensed his presence.

Smiling up at her husband from where her head lay on the pillow, Ellen Abernathy reached out for him, and said in a voice still heavy with sleep, "The bed is cold without you. Hurry up and get in here."

Quickly complying, Max shed his clothes, slid between the sheets, wrapped his arms around his wife, and drew her body as close to his as he could get it.

She was a perfect fit; always had been and he knew she always would be. He was a lucky man and he knew it.

Breathing the scent of her in deeply, he let it sooth him even further. He would never be the same after this night, and if the NACR succeeded in its ultimate goal and he was identified as a participant, he would lose her forever. This is what kept him careful, and why she knew nothing about his actions.

"Was it that rough a night, honey?" Ellen asked.

"Mmmmm," was his noncommittal reply.

Max was keeping a secret from her for the first time in their lives, but protecting his wife and his daughter was his main priority. Should he be caught and prosecuted, Ellen had to be clear of any charges and free to live her life, free to be there for their daughter. At times such as these, he asked himself why he was taking the risk of losing them, but the answer was always clear and immediate.

He truly believed that there were things far more important than he, and restoring the nation to what it was intended to be was definitely one of those things. Had the founding fathers not been willing to risk their lives, their fortunes, and their sacred honor in the pursuit of the dream of freedom, Max would now be speaking with an English accent.

Letting the earlier events of the night drift away, he concentrated on the woman in his arms and sank into a sleep he had thought himself unable to achieve.

Samantha Mallard let loose with a yawn so big that she actually heard her jaw crack. The reassuring hiss and pop of the coffee pot in action gave her some small comfort as she attempted to drag her brain into full consciousness. She never understood those people that popped up out of bed wide awake and perky. She was pretty sure that it was somehow unnatural to be that energetic first thing in the morning. Instead, she tended to resemble a pinball when she first awoke. She would stumble a couple of steps this way and bounce off the wall, stumble a few steps that way and bounce off a wall, and on really bad mornings, she would get stuck pinging back and forth from one door jamb to another. This had been one of those really bad mornings.

Yawning again and praying for the coffee to finish quickly, she sat at her kitchen table, cluttered with papers, notebooks, newspapers, and most importantly her computer, and powered up that most vital of all electronic devices; her link to the rest of the world. While the booting occurred, she glanced at the coffee pot again. Yippee! There was enough in there to pour her first cup. She rose slowly and padded barefoot across the cold, stone tile of the kitchen floor, pulled a coffee cup from the overstuffed and disorganized cupboard, then floated to the coffee as a spirit does to the light. Sending up a prayer of thanks to the brilliant individual who invented pause and poor, she filled her cup with the steaming brew, inhaled the intoxicating scent, and finally began to feel human.

With both hands wrapped around the warmth and security of her mug, an item that her friend, Sawyer, referred to as her blanky equivalent, Sam returned back to the now illuminated computer screen. Out of habit she launched Facebook and the Washington Post. The news came first, and then she'd check in and see what her friends were up to. She scanned the usual doom and gloom of the news that somehow managed to lavish praise upon the current idiots in Congress. She was on her third cup of coffee when the most important article of the day -- at least to her -- took its turn.

"4th Prisoner Dies Mysteriously" was the title of the article about four inmates who died unexpectedly of anaphylaxis within the penal system. No reason for the reaction could be found, but what really captured her attention were the names of the prisoners and a few particular sentences. "All prisoners were in different facilities; the only common link found was that all were patients of Dr. Samantha Mallard. Dr. Mallard was unable to be reached for comment on the mysterious deaths of her patients. Sources indicate that the prisoners, all convicted rapists, were part of a medical study being performed by Mallard."

Confused by the story, and troubled by the deaths of men who she believed were indeed part of a study, Sam rifled through her purse to find her cell phone. Not an easy task. When the entire contents of her handbag were scattered, along with four days of unopened mail, on the wing back chair sitting next to the front door, she finally flipped open the phone and checked for voicemails.

None.

Next she went to the answering machine for the land line. She had become so used to her cell phone that she usually forgot to check for any messages elsewhere. No messages there either. With increasing confusion and burgeoning concern, she fired up her e-mail, both personal and business. There were 42 messages but none of them from the newspaper. With now shaking hands she called her office phone to check the voicemail there. She had three messages; all from research staff.

Sam sat down hard in the kitchen chair. Nobody had attempted to contact her. Why? What was going on? She was pretty sure that those four men were part of the study, but decided that if the press finally *did* attempt to contact her it might be good to know for sure; and to have at least some idea of what the situation was.

Now wide awake, fingers flying across the keyboard of her laptop, Samantha Mallard navigated through all of the security necessary to protect the files in her genetic study. This was a routine navigation for Samantha, one she performed often, and yet her heart began to pound, her hands to shake, and her throat suddenly went dry when at the last security check her access was denied. She had been denied her own files. Something was going on - something bad - or at least something definitely not good.

"We have a problem." George Whitman spoke over his shoulder to his fellow watcher while pointing at the flashing warning on the computer screen before him.

Kali Jayachondran made no verbal reply, but nudged George away from the screen with her bony hip. She was not impressed with him or his capabilities and hated sharing this cramped space in the cavernous warehouse with him. He was competent in his role of the NACR but that's about all she could say. A short, scrawny, geek of a man with a stringy brown hair and waxy skin, he was made even less attractive by the green light of the numerous computers in the dark, cold room they shared. However, he did believe in the cause and she had to give him respect for that if for nothing else, but when it came to the computer, she felt better doing it herself. So she gave his chair a shove that sent it rolling across the concrete floor, pulled another chair over for herself, and after a review of the warning displayed, flipped open her cell phone and hit the speed dial.

George wasn't surprised at his treatment. He'd grown used to it. Besides, not only was Kali brilliant, she was beautiful. Far out of his league regardless of how much he admired her, and to be honest, she also scared him just a little bit. The fact that she'd confided, when asked, that she was named after the Hindu Goddess of Destruction, only served to increase that fear, but still he was drawn to her dark skin, large dark eyes, and silky coal black hair.

Knowing she would not bother to share the current conversation with him, George listened intently to her side in an attempt to stay as informed as he could, and more informed than he should be. This was not one of his better ideas, since the less he knew the better, but for some unknown reason it was something he could never resist.

No one person was allowed to know too much and, therefore, George always wanted to know more. The limited access to information was an attempt to protect the ultimate goal and the members of the NACR, should any of them ever be captured. But still he listened.

"She has attempted to access the file … Just now… Are you sure? … That could be risky… Does he agree? … Consider it done." Without casting even a glance in George's direction, Kali disconnected and dialed again. "Samantha Mallard has become a risk…. Yes… immediately….let me know when the risk has been eliminated." The phone closed with a decisive click and Kali returned to her own desk.

"God she's hot," George thought to himself.

Samantha was even more confused than ever. She tried again to get past that last level of security, hoping vainly that her shaking hands had caused her to type the incorrect password. Fat finger syndrome it was called. She hit enter, and again the "access denied" message flashed before her.

She sat in stupefied silence and stared at that bold message. How could this happen? This was definitely not shaping up to be a good day at all. She had two really big problems and no idea what to do about either. The denial of her access was not something she would normally have questioned, but would have instead called her IT tech and gone on with her day; but the newspaper article made it appear somehow sinister. So much so that she hesitated to call her tech as she normally would for fear of what she might hear.

She hated that about herself. That fear could immobilize her so completely; but she had always been a slave to her fears. She had entered the field of genetics, not because of a love for the science, but out of a fear of disappointing her father, and she worked tirelessly to succeed in her field for the very same reason. In her wildest fantasies she was actually a blues singer -- Billie Holliday, but without the heroin addiction. Though she admitted to herself, even had she been able to disappoint her father, the rejection which was part and parcel with a career in the entertainment field would have paralyzed her with fear as well, and she would still being doing something else.

All of this internal dialogue was an avoidance issue. If she had this running through her mind it kept her from thinking about what was scaring her to death. She forced her mind back to her problems, and immediately shied away once more.

Samantha's eyes strayed back to the hated "access denied" message, and finally she took action; she closed the window and sighed in relief. However, this relief was only temporary, for in place of the rude and disturbing message emerged the Washington Post article. Feeling quite decisive, she closed that one as well. "Excellent," she said to herself, "Crisis averted."

Sam sat at her cluttered kitchen table in her pajamas with bed head and a cup of coffee, and did her best to deny the fact that her career, if not her entire life, was on an express elevator to hell. She sat there in silence, afraid of turning on the television, afraid of what she'd hear on the radio. Finally, drawn back to the computer like a train wreck you don't want to see, but can't stop yourself from examining, she took another peek.

Facebook was the only application left open, and yet this only succeeded in depressing her more. The perfect illustration of just what she had given up. On the other hand, she was grateful to Facebook for allowing her to keep in touch with the people she didn't have time to develop face to face relationships with. She had only fourteen friends on Facebook and ten of those were co-workers. How sad was that? Not much of a distraction to be found there.

It was then she saw it; the "friend suggestion" that she had been ignoring for months. Ignoring out of fear. What if she sent him a friend request and he denied her? Could she take that kind of rejection? But he was a reporter, she argued with herself. At least that's what her friend, Sawyer, had said. And a reporter just might come in handy right now. He might at least be able to tell her why the papers printed an attempt to contact her, an attempt that had never happened. What if he was an investigative reporter? Somebody who could investigate this mess for her?

One hand left its death grip on the coffee cup and drifted to the mouse. She clicked on the friend suggestion, and there he was; still looking way too good; still able to make her knees weak and her heart pound with just a smile. It had been twenty-two years since she'd had any significant interaction with him, but looking at that picture she was thrust back into her adolescence. Not a fun place to go. This really was shaping up to be a bad day.

Should she contact him, she wondered? Debating with herself, she moved the mouse, the cursor hovering over the "Add as a friend" button.

Did she dare?

No, she didn't. She moved the cursor away and returned both hands to her now cold cup of coffee.

Allowing her coffee to cool to that point was proof positive of just how out of sorts she was. She couldn't believe she had done that. She rose from her cowering position at the kitchen table and poured herself some fresh coffee, but the heat of the cup could not penetrate the chill she felt. She glanced again at the computer. He could help her. She knew he could. But would he? That was the real question. What if he wouldn't help her? What if he wouldn't even see her? Oh my God, what if he didn't even remember her? How demoralizing would that be? There had to be another way. There had to be. She'd sit back down and think about it some more.

"Are you sure this order is right?" the dark haired woman in the passenger seat asked, "This seems a little extreme to me."

The driver of the nondescript dark sedan sighed. He had already answered this question. Three times in fact. "Yes, it's right. And you know damn good and well that we don't have all of the information, so what it seems to us is irrelevant."

The sedan turned off the highway and headed into the suburbs where the target lived. He didn't like this any better than his partner, but he knew it was necessary. The ultimate goal could not be risked. Therefore, any and all threats had to be eliminated. That didn't, however, prevent him from wishing this was not the case. She had been a key player to their cause no matter how unaware of it she had been; but if she started asking too many questions, as accessing her file on a test long since completed would indicate, then she was a risk they could no longer afford.

"I'm just saying…" the passenger replied.

"I know what you're just saying. But this has to end."

"This way though? Does it really have to end this way?"

"You know the answer to that already. Stop bugging me with questions you already know the answer to," he snapped.

The woman crossed her arms and hummphed.

The car fell into silence. The only sounds now that of the perpetual hum of rubber on the road as it moved closer and closer to the home of Samantha Mallard.

With no idea how long she had been sitting there avoiding reality, Sam suddenly heard a thump from her bedroom. The abrupt and unexpected noise caused her to jump so hard and so fast that the coffee that had again gone cold splashed all over her, the table, and the floor. Staring down the hall, eyes wide with fear she saw her three legged cat, Chloe, come limping down the hall to her. Knowing the source of the thud did not, however, alleviate her fear. Instead it galvanized her.

Things were seriously wrong and she was just sitting there on her bum paralyzed by fear yet again. This time she wouldn't submit. This time the fear would not get the best of her. She turned back to the computer, hit "send a message" and typed "I need help. I need you. Call me at…" typed her cell number and hit send. Taking one last longing look at his posted picture, she closed Facebook and started the shutdown process.

Finally incited to action, she all but ran to the bathroom, brushed her teeth with more speed than care, and hopped in the shower before the water had time to heat. She lived in an old home where, for some mysterious reason, the plumbing took forever to get water from the heater to the shower; at times she thought it might be routed through downtown Baltimore on its way from her utility room to the bathtub. The big front porch and large kitchen had charmed her into buying this house. She was feeling none of this charm now as she stood under the still cold spray and scrubbed furiously.

Just three minutes later, the water finally beginning to warm, she was out of the shower and running a towel over her body. She pulled her clothes on over still damp skin, something she usually avoided at all costs, ran a comb harshly through her hair, pulling out clumps of it along with the tangles, pulled the thick mass back and secured it with a serviceable clip. She didn't bother with make-up at the moment, but was vain enough to intend to be wearing it when she saw him again, so she threw her cosmetic case, along with clothes, shoes and various other sundries in her overnight bag. She wasted precious moments chasing Chloe, who could run quite well with only three legs, to get her into the cat carrier. Then she was ready. Picking up her suitcase and her cat she headed out the door to load them in her car.

The driver was beginning to feel the effects of his acid reflux as they wound their way through the residential area. The thirty mile per hour speed limit was grating on him. He wanted this over and done with so he didn't have to think about it anymore. He still hoped he could do it. His passenger was brought along in case his ingrained belief that you don't hurt a woman asserted itself. The glock 9mm felt heavy in its holster, but he was eternally grateful it was there. Killing from a distance would be far easier on him than something up close and personal. He knew with unwavering certainty that he would be unable to do this with a knife or his bare hands; but a gun? That was another story. Fast, clean -- sort of -- and clinical. Point and shoot. That's all he'd be doing. Just point and shoot.

He was oddly calmed by the neighborhood in which his target lived. The street was flanked on either side by mature trees whose limbs, bare now in winter, met above the road. The homes were modest but well kept and predominantly in the craftsman bungalow style. The majority of them were also decorated for the holidays, lending a festive air to this dark mission. The yards were a blanket of snow interrupted periodically by footprints and snowmen, but not by tire tracks.

No tracks because there were no driveways. "This neighborhood must have an alley access," he stated.

"Probably would have been better to go in the back way," the passenger replied.

"Yes, it would. But we'd have to be able to find the right house without a number, and I'm not sure we could do that."

Sure he was doing the right thing by approaching from the front, the driver still felt a trickle of unease down his spine, then cursed as he was forced to stop at a red light. Once through this light they would be on her block. He should be on his way back home, his target eliminated, in no longer than five minutes.

Hopefully less.

Samantha tossed her suitcase into the backseat of her Honda Civic and slammed the door closed. With Chloe's carrier under one arm, she rushed around to the passenger side, slipped twice on the snow she had never gotten around to shoveling and which was now packed into ice, opened the door and secured Chloe in the front passenger seat. She did this with more speed than tenderness and Chloe was making her displeasure loudly and assertively known.

Once the belt was secure, Sam headed back into the house, slipping on the ice again. For a brief moment she thought she was going to fall, but managed to grab the banister to the back stairs and keep herself on her feet. She wasn't done yet. The one thing she knew she was going to need was her computer. She'd shut it down but that was as far as she'd gotten with it.

Sprinting back up the steps and flinging the door open so hard that it hit the wall with a reverberating bang, she rushed through the kitchen to the spare room where her laptop bag was kept. She snatched it up and whirled around with such speed that the bag connected with a lamp, sending it sailing through the air and eventually to the floor. Luckily neither the lamp nor the light bulb broke, but she didn't stop to right it. Something was screaming in her head that there just wasn't time.

Her sneaker-clad feet slapping on the cold stone tile that led from the hall to the kitchen, she came to an abrupt halt, nearly losing her balance as she fought with wires and cords to detach the computer and get it, with all accoutrements, into the bag. When everything she needed was secured inside, she zipped the bag closed, wiped the accumulating sweat from her brow, and sighed in relief.

At that precise moment the telephone rang; her land line. Out of habit she reached over and picked it up. Had it rung just seconds before, while she was in her frenzy of fear, she would not have answered it, but in her single moment of inactivity the mundane activities of life had reasserted their control.

Their power was short lived, for nobody spoke on the other end of the phone.

Fear once again propelling her, Samantha slung the laptop bag over her shoulder, snatched up her coat, and turned toward the door.

The man clicked his cell phone closed. "She's still in there," he said and drew his gun from his holster.

The woman nodded and inserted the key that they had been supplied into the door and turned it as quietly as she could, which also meant turning it slowly. When the lock clicked open she turned the knob, thrust the door wide and both man and woman spilled into the house, the man with his gun drawn, finger on the trigger and ready to fire.

There was no cry of fear. No acknowledgement of the noise they made. The man strode forward and peeked into the hall -- nobody there. He took the few steps to the first door and looked inside. The bathroom was small, a bit cramped and cluttered, and empty of humanity although wet footprints still dotted the floor. A few more steps brought him to the bedroom, which was in entire disarray with clothes, shoes and bedding thrown every which way, but there was still no Samantha Mallard. There was just one more door to go. This was a small house. Just two bedrooms and one bathroom and the man was quite thankful for the home's modest size at the moment.

"Hey, look here," the woman called from the kitchen. "Her computer is gone. The keyboard and mouse are still here but the laptop isn't."

"Shit," he cursed under his breath. This was a bad sign. Turning away from the closed door, knowing that if she was in there cowering now she'd still be there in a few minutes, the man went back to the kitchen, kicking himself the whole way for not noticing the very important missing computer previously, but instead of going to the table, he went to the window and peered into the back. The garage door was closed but he was getting a really bad feeling.

The man made his way through the cluttered utility room, out the back door to the garage, and fearing what he'd find, peered through the window. This wasn't exactly what he had expected, but close enough. The garage was stacked floor to ceiling with junk. Obviously used more as a storage unit than an actual garage, but there was no car here either. She was gone. They had missed her. Damn!

  Sam struggled to regain control of the car on the slippery road. That phone call had unnerved her so much that she had literally flown out the back door to her car and left at a much higher rate of speed than the left turn and the narrow alley called for. Her hands, damp with sweat despite the chill of the car, slipped on the wheel. She removed first one, then the other, and rubbed them on her coat to dry, yet they remained clammy. She struggled to see out the small patch of windshield that the defroster had uncovered and, with shaking hands, hit the button for the wiper fluid to clear the frost on the outside. She repeated this process when the washer fluid itself froze on the windshield and kept repeating it until her view was unobstructed. Confident that she could see enough with this process, Sam pulled out of the alley and into the morning traffic.

  She needed to get to D.C. She needed to get to him. It would take her only an hour and a half to get from her home outside Baltimore to D.C. But once in D.C. she still had to find him. She'd have to call information and hope he was listed. Or call Sawyer and see if he had the number. But not now, definitely not now. She needed both hands and full concentration to keep the car on the road. She couldn't remember ever being this frightened in her life.

Chapter 3

Daniel was wide awake. Unfortunately. No matter what time he got to sleep, he woke up at 7:00 am -- even on the weekends -- and once awake there was no rolling back over and back to sleep for him, he was fully conscious. Groaning at the memories of the previous night, he strode down his hallway in his boxer shorts to his favorite household appliance, the coffee pot. Knowing exactly when he would wake every morning, he usually had the timer set and the coffee already brewed, but he'd gotten in so late last night-- or was it this morning -- that he hadn't bothered. He regretted that now as he was forced to wait for the nectar of the gods to manifest itself.

He used the time while he waited to fire up his computer. No matter what else had happened last evening, he still had an article to get in by the deadline, and said deadline was rapidly approaching. His computer fully fired and functional, Facebook, his home page, was now displayed. He had a message, but he didn't have time to get to it now. Instead he pulled up his e-mail, grabbed his notes, and started writing his article. Two hours and four cups of coffee later, Daniel hit the send button and said good-bye to the aliens in Arlington.

Still feeling a bit groggy, he decided that before anything else, he needed a shower and, running his hand over his chin stubble, decided probably a shave as well.

The driver flipped his phone closed and turned to the woman. "They've turned on the remote GPS in her car. They'll call us back in a few. Considering that she was home when we called and gone when we entered, she can't have gotten far."

"If only we'd noticed immediately that the laptop was gone, we may have been able to see which way she went."

The man ground his teeth in frustration. He'd been telling himself the same thing, but he didn't want to hear it from her. "Well, we didn't. So now we wait." Luckily the phone rang at that second. Relieved, the man flipped it open. "Where is she?" After a very brief conversation, he flipped the phone closed again. "We've got her. They'll be texting any changes in her direction to your cell."

"My phone?" the woman replied. "Why my phone?"

Grinding his teeth again, the man snarled, "Because I can't read text messages and drive at the same time, you freaking idiot. What the hell is the problem with them texting to your phone?"

The woman sighed, "I don't have free texting. It costs me ten cents every time I send or receive a text message."

"Well, you'd better hope she doesn't make many turns, because those messages are going to your phone." The driver started the car and headed after his target. He was just grateful that he wasn't that far behind her. He'd catch her, and kill her, and rid himself of his annoying passenger. Right now he thought murder would be worth it.

Daniel stared into his bloodshot eyes in his bathroom mirror. "Damn, I'm getting old" he thought, then brushed his teeth and stepped into the shower. The hot water beat down on him soothingly. Of all the things he had lost in the last five years, he was eternally grateful that the water pressure in the shower wasn't one of them. Oddly this was because he'd lost his nice apartment and moved into a bit of a dive. But the nice apartment had made all of the eco-friendly changes legislated by Congress, which included low flow shower heads, while his current landlord didn't give a rat's ass about code violations. So maybe his descent into career hell had been a good thing. God knew how he loved a long hot shower, but only with good water pressure. Those showers where water just trickled onto your head like Chinese water torture just pissed him off. The best shower he'd ever had, it felt like his skin was being beaten off his body. Now that had been glorious.

Clean but still unsatisfied, he stood with his face directly in the spray and let the water pound. Turning his head slowly from side to side, he let the force of the water ease all residual tension from his body.

Twenty minutes later, showered, dressed, shaved, and a plate of bacon, eggs and toast before him, Daniel returned to his e-mail. His editor had already replied with suggested "revisions" to his article. This pretty much meant that he needed to embellish things just a bit -- or more than a bit. Cursing luridly at the injustice, and then reminding himself to be thankful he had a job at all, Daniel set about making the requested modifications.

With that completed, he washed his breakfast dishes and debated whether to return to his computer, or to turn on his television and see what was happening in the world. He opted for the TV, and then wished he hadn't. The news of Simon Deefer's accident was all over the local D.C. coverage, and even some of the cable news stations. He flipped through for a bit, but the vast majority of the coverage was more sympathetic to Sledgewater than to Deefer's family. This love affair the media had with politicians in general, and that one in particular, was nauseating. He flipped over to FNB News to see what they said about it, hoping he'd get some actual reporting. He got some.

On the screen was Senator Fisk, known as Mara Fisk the Terrorist, and she was not happy, but when was she ever? She was usually on a tirade of one sort or another. Today it was about the coverage of the aide's death. She was condemning the press for focusing more on the man the deceased worked for than the deceased himself. Daniel thought to himself, "Go get 'em, tiger!"

It was then that he caught the ticker tape at the bottom of the screen. There he found the real news on this event; the news that this was Sledgewater's second aide to die in an accident in the last two years, and the fourteenth congressional aide to die in the same timeframe.

The ticker stated that being a congressional aide was rising to the top of the most dangerous jobs in the country. How could he have missed that? No wonder Sledgewater was suspicious. It took him a lot of time to corrupt his aides to the point that they would overlook what he did himself, and Sledgewater hated to waste time.

Daniel hurried over to his laptop once more and did a search for congressional aide deaths. Twenty minutes later he had to admit that FNB was right -- that was a hard thing for him to acknowledge -- but the congressional aides appeared to be dropping like flies. Closing the search engine window he noticed that he now had two messages on Facebook. He needed to take his mind off of the decline in his investigative reporting skills -- how could he possibly have missed that -- and have some face time with the faceless. He clicked on his inbox and got yet another shock. There were two messages, but only one name caught his attention; Samantha Mallard had sent him a message. He'd seen her on Facebook as he went through his high school graduating class and thought about sending her a friend request so many times, but he'd never done it, and now she'd contacted him. He opened the message and was sent reeling.

Sam was finally beginning to calm down from her scare and had begun to wonder if she was overreacting, but something had pushed her to hurry. Something had told her that she needed to go, and she believed it was more of a *who* than a what. She'd felt the hand of God in her life before, and she sincerely believed she had just felt it again. She knew she needed to stop questioning it just because she'd made it out alive, but she was now on 295-S quickly approaching the US-50 exit to Washington and, though things appeared calm, a whole new set of problems was coming in to play. She still didn't know how to contact Daniel. She'd left him that message but there was no guarantee he would get it and she needed help from somebody. She was thinking so hard about her situation that she nearly jumped out of her skin when her cell-phone rang.

Keeping one hand on the wheel and rummaging through her handbag with the other, she finally managed to extract her cell and flip it open. "Hello," she squeaked.

"Hello," said the deep, husky voice tinged with a very slight Scottish brogue. "Sammie?"

"Daniel? Oh, my God!"

"Sammie, are you okay? What's wrong? What's going on?" If he wasn't already concerned at her message, the crack in her voice would have done it.

Relieved beyond all reason, glad to have somebody to share her concerns with, coming down from her adrenaline high of the morning, Samantha Mallard burst into tears. "D-D-Daniel, its b-b-been such a ba- bad day." Sniffle. "I d-d-don't even know wh-wh-where to start."

"Shhhhh, baby. Just calm down. Where are you?"

"Did you ju-ju-just call me baby?" As soon as she said it, she was appalled. Hearing the chuckle on the other end of the line made her feel not a single bit better.

"Sorry, Sammie, automatic response to a hysterical woman. Now tell me where you are."

The bit of warmth that had begun to spread through her was abruptly doused. Taking a couple of deep breaths, she got herself under control and gave him her current location.

They agreed to meet at a diner around the corner from his apartment to have lunch and she would tell him everything. Well, at least everything about her morning. She didn't think she had the nerve to tell him everything, everything.

She stopped at a gas station to fill up and run to the ladies room for some basic grooming. Her hair had dried in the clip so there wasn't much she could do about that, but there was something she could do about her naked face. There was no time for full battle gear, but she could at least make herself feel better. Five minutes later, armed with powder, mascara and lipstick, she was back on the road. Thirty minutes later she was in the parking lot of a neighborhood diner in a lower middle class part of town. Now the only question was, did she have the courage to get out of the car?

"She's stopped," the woman said, and then thought, "Finally, that damn bitch cost me $2.80 in texting charges."
"Is it for good this time?"
"I hope so. Any more texting and I'll be in trouble. I'm not one of the rich people in this organization you know. I'm free to do this today because I'm unemployed. I'm lucky I still have my cell phone at all."
Frustrated nearly past the breaking point, the driver extracted his wallet from his back pocket, pulled out a ten dollar bill and threw it at her. He felt only slightly guilty for his outburst. Her story was all too common now and one of the main reasons for the NACR organization. Heavy regulation in the name of employee welfare had been levied on her employer. All non-union employers had been forced to pay an 'employee welfare' tax equal to half the difference between their employee's salary and that of the comparative union member. She'd been with the company for fifteen years when the new regulations had driven them out of business and they had been forced to shut their doors. The regulations had increased operating costs, thereby making it so expensive to do business with American-based companies that buyers went to the cheaper, unregulated companies overseas. An all too common story and what the administration referred to as 'growing pains'. The driver might buy that if the economy was actually growing, but it wasn't. The only thing that had grown in the last decade was the size and power of the Federal Government and, therefore, the labor unions. By forcing companies to hire union workers through this taxation, there were more union dues being paid and more politicians being bought.
"Thank you," said the woman, "I owe you $7.20 in change, but I think I'll hold the rest until this is over; just in case."
Now the driver really felt like a shit -- and he hated feeling that way -- but he assured himself that this would be over

soon. After that he'd have to see what the NACR was doing to take care of his partner. She was proud enough to not want a handout, but as she was actually working for them, some compensation had to be made.

There were several members like her. Supported by the NACR while they looked for work in an economy with a 16% unemployment rate, but adamant about working for what they received. Their organization was made up of people who truly believed in helping their fellow man, but helping with a hand up and not a hand out. They would see each other through this the best they could, and do it with their pride intact. They all knew one thing with absolute certainty, the longer you sucked off the government tit, the more palatable it became. Handouts had proven to be addictive and just as destructive to one's life as any narcotic. It was a drug they refused to take. They were bound and determined to free America from her current addiction and, as with any drug war, there would be casualties. One waited for them right now, completely unaware that she had no more than twenty-two minutes to live.

Samantha checked her make up in her rear-view mirror one last time before leaving the toasty car for the outside chill. Would he have changed? She didn't know how recent his Facebook picture had been taken. This wasn't where she would have expected him to be living after all these years, but then again, she hadn't heard anything about him in a while. Sawyer had mentioned he was struggling, but had said nothing else, and Sam had been afraid of revealing too much by asking. Would he recognize her? She hoped so. After hearing him call her Sammie, she thought so.

The time had come. She pulled open the door and scanned the bright diner. She was pleasantly surprised with the spot he had chosen. It was clean, homey, and busy while still affording privacy, and based on the smell, the food was going to be good. She was suddenly starving, but when she saw him a whole new hunger made itself known.

There he was, secured in a corner booth, the one with the most privacy. If anything the years had made him better looking, which was the very last thing she needed. Even from this distance she could see the wrinkles around eyes she knew to be a mossy green. Eyes that were now pinned on her. He slowly rose and she noticed that he'd grown, both in height and the breadth of his shoulders. How in the world was she ever going to get through this?

Well, at least one fear was averted. He recognized her. She smiled.

Daniel would have known her anywhere, but if he'd had any doubt of her identity at all, it was eliminated with that smile. She was what some people referred to as sturdy. She wasn't fat. She didn't carry extra weight, but she wasn't one of those waifs that many men found so appealing; and she was curved in all the right places. She wasn't any bigger than she had been in school, but she was shapelier. He could tell that even with her body enveloped in a red wool coat, with a giant purse slung over one shoulder, a laptop bag over the other, and dressed in clothes more comfortable than stylish. He opened his arms as she approached, and she extended her hand.

Not sure whether to shake hands or hug, they ended up in a rather awkward embrace when all he wanted to do was hold her close. Daniel assisted her into the booth and then, there they were, staring at each other in silence. The awkwardness of a long separation and an unusual circumstance prevailed.

Samantha fidgeted nervously and dropped her eyes. She was mortified to find that she was tongue tied in his presence still, and it wasn't helping her current situation one iota. It was probably best to get this ball rolling and see if he would help her. She cleared her throat twice, wished for a glass of water, and opened her mouth to speak. The waitress, a painfully thin, older woman with orthopedic shoes and hair dyed a brilliant shade of red made even brighter by the sun, chose that moment to appear.

"I'm Darlene, and I'll be your server today. What can I get you to drink?"

"Coffee," both Daniel and Sam replied simultaneously.

"And a glass of water, please," Samantha added.

When Darlene had taken her leave, Samantha cleared her throat again, sipped the scorching coffee, pulled on the last reserves of her pitiful courage -- which did not include meeting Daniel's eyes-- and spoke. "Thank you for agreeing to see me. I didn't know where to go or what to do."

Her fear disturbed Daniel greatly. She was wound so tight that he swore he could see the air vibrating around her. She hadn't even taken off her coat before sitting. He dipped his head in an attempt to catch her gaze, but she turned away. He did the only thing he could think of; he reached across the table and laid his hand on hers.

At the touch of his hand, Sam's head snapped up and her wide blue gaze met his. His hand was so warm, so reassuring. She was going to cry again if she wasn't careful.

With a tenderness that gave a slightly rough edge to his light brogue, Daniel said, "As happy as I was to hear from you, you've got me a bit worried. Tell me what's going on and we'll see what we can do about it together."

Well, damn, Sam thought as the tears began to spill over. Darlene picked that moment to return with their water and take their order. She put Daniel's glass in front of him with a bit more force than necessary and threw him a look that left no doubt as to her disapproval of any man who would make a woman cry. Sam gave a watery chuckle at that scathing glare and then looked up to Darlene and explained, "He's the cure, not the cause."

At this statement Darlene warmed significantly, even to the point of patting Daniel's shoulder and saying, "Good boy."

Since neither had yet even glanced at the menu, they asked Darlene for a few minutes, and when she left they were alone again, but without the tension.

"I'm glad you told her that. I thought she was going to cut out my heart with my spoon and serve it to you for lunch."

Samantha laughed. For the first time that day, she really laughed and her heart suddenly felt lighter. "Look, Daniel, I want to tell you what's going on. I need to tell you, but I also need to eat. How about we make our decisions, get Darlene back over here, and once ordering is out of the way I'll tell you my story."

The banality of reading a menu and placing an order helped calm Samantha's rattled nerves even more; so much, in fact, that by the time it was done she had begun to feel silly for reacting as she had. As a result, her confession to Daniel was a bit sheepish.

Daniel, on the other hand, didn't think it was silly at all. "So they printed that they'd attempted to contact you but no attempt was actually made?" At her nod he continued, "No reputable newspaper would do such a thing. Do you realize that they opened themselves up to a major law suit? You could sue the pants off of them if they said anything at all derogatory and gave you no chance at all to rebut."

Samantha wrinkled her brow. "Well....the only thing that wasn't true in the article was that they'd attempted to contact me. The fact that the men were part of my study......oh, my God....I just remembered." Sam leaned further across the table in her excitement. "The study was confidential. The press should not have had access to the study, or even be able to find out that those men were a part of it. Those men themselves didn't even know they were a part of it."

The driver pulled into a parking space, slid the car into park, and turned the key. "I'm going to go take care of this. I want you to cover her car just in case I don't succeed."

The woman turned to him in shock. "Cover her car? With what? I don't have a gun. I don't know how you have a gun, considering that anything but a hunting rifle is now illegal."

The driver sighed and stepped out of the car. The woman scrambled out her side, still asking how to cover the car, what she was supposed to do, how she was supposed to do it, and when she should react. The driver was beyond the end of his rope at this point; he wished he had the metaphoric rope in his hands and around his passenger's neck at this very moment.

Arriving at the back of his car, the driver opened the truck, rummaged around, pulled out the tire iron, and handed it to his passenger. "If she comes back to her car, wallop her in the head with this thing. That should take her out or at least incapacitate her. But be sure to hit her good and hard."

The woman took the weapon, feeling the weight of the cold metal bear down on her. She was a receptionist, not a killer -- a damn fine receptionist, too. She hoped that the driver would succeed with the gun and she would not be forced to bludgeon a woman to death. Just the idea of it made acid rise to the back of her throat. Her palms now sweaty on the cold metal, she swallowed the bile back down, not daring to show the driver this weakness. She knew he was unhappy with her, but this was her first assignment like this and she prayed it was her last.

Having no idea what it meant, Sam was still fairly humming with excitement at what she'd remembered long after they'd placed their orders. When Darlene returned with their food, Samantha got distracted from her ideas by the intoxicating smell of her grilled ham and cheese sandwich.

Daniel had ordered a big fat burger, but Sam had always preferred a plain old ordinary grilled sandwich. The fries were thick cut, crisp and piled high, spilling off the plate and scattering the table with their greasy, salty delight. But what were fries without ketchup? Sam had to stretch for the bottle at the end of the table, but was restricted by the coat she still had not removed and so leaned forward to grasp it.

As she wrapped her hand around the bottle, the sound of shattering glass assailed her ears and a searing, blinding pain spread across the back of her head. At the same time, Daniel grabbed her by the lapels of her coat, pulled her under the table, and slapped something against the source of her pain while forcing her nearly flat to the floor. That wasn't very nice. She thought, as she reached up to pull his hand away and realized she was still holding the ketchup bottle.

She dropped the bottle when two more shots rang out. Her head was still burning and Daniel kept pressing right where it hurt. "Daniel," she all but whined, "you're hurting me."

Terrified nearly out of his wits, Daniel pressed the napkin he'd grabbed from the table even harder against the wound. Her color didn't look good to him, and she obviously didn't understand what had happened. Hearing a call of all clear, Daniel pulled her gently from under the table and back to her feet. He threw $60 for their lunch down on the table, grabbed his coat and started pushing her towards the door, but Sam was having none of that. She wanted to know what had happened and she wanted to know now. Digging in her heels, she pulled Daniel to an abrupt halt.

Darlene showed up at that moment with a clean towel and a rolled apron. She handed them both to Daniel, then turned to Sam. "Don't you worry, sweetie. That no good bastard got what he deserved. You don't shoot one of my customers and walk away alive."

One word penetrated her shock. "Shoot one of your…. Shot! I've been shot!" Her knees started to give way. She hadn't had anywhere near enough coffee that day to deal with this. She wasn't sure there was enough coffee in the world to help her deal with this particular situation.

Daniel lowered her into a chair, folded the towel over the wound, held it in place with the apron, and dusted the shards of shattered glass from her hair and coat. "It's just a graze, but it is a scalp wound, so there's a lot of blood. Those fries saved your life." Daniel didn't even want to think about what would have happened if she ate her fries sans ketchup. He would have been staring across his burger at a corpse.

"I've been shot," Sam whispered. "Who shot me?" Louder this time. "Who shot me? Where is the miserable bastard who shot me?"

"Now that's the spirit," Daniel chuckled, "but you can simmer down. Darlene already got him."

"Oh. That's right. She did mention that, didn't she? I hope you left her a good tip."

Daniel smiled that full smile that crinkled his cheeks and scrunched up his eyes. One of the things she had always liked about him was how he smiled with more than just his lips. He smiled with his whole face. It was an infectious smile. "As a matter of fact, I did, but I have one question." Daniel turned to Darlene, his face now a mask of mock severity. "Exactly how did you manage to shoot him, Darlene? Aren't guns illegal within D.C. city limits?"

Darlene snorted and tossed her frizzy red hair in defiance. "That law went into effect and I got robbed four times in two months -- at gunpoint. Those criminals were so damn sure that those they robbed wouldn't be able to defend themselves. Well, all I can say is that the fifth asshole that walked in here with nefarious intent got one humdinger of a surprise. He went out with a bang." Darlene chuckled at her own bad joke, slapped Daniel on the shoulder, patted Sam on her knee, and then said, "I'm going to have to call the cops. You want to hang around for that or do you wanna scoot?"

"I think we'd better scoot," Daniel replied. "I don't know if that guy was alone and we probably shouldn't wait around to find out." He gently helped Sam to her feet. She was still a little unsteady, but he wasn't sure if it was from loss of blood or the residual shock. "Come on, honey, we'll take my car and get out of here."

Sam drew him up short again. "I need my car."

"But, Sam…"

"No. My suitcase is still in my car, and my cat."

"You brought your cat with you?"

"Of course I did. I didn't know how long I would be gone and I didn't exactly have time to put her in a kennel."

"OK, honey, we'll get your suitcase and your cat, but then we're taking my car and we're getting the hell out of here. I don't know how he found you, but your car is a definite possibility."

"Oh, okay, I see your point." They started out the door again, but didn't make it far before she stopped him again. "Damn! My purse and my laptop are still in the booth."

Daniel sighed. He really had had no idea what he was getting himself into. On the other hand, although he'd been scared to death, he'd also been having a good time. Sam had always been good for a laugh, even when she wasn't trying to be.

"Okay, wait here." Just seconds later he was back with her purse and her laptop slung over his shoulder. She did her best not to giggle at the sight of him carrying a purse. Instead she retrieved it and started the search for her keys.

The woman was starting to get really nervous. She'd heard the shots, and then nothing. Neither the man nor their target had returned. This wasn't good. How long should she wait? The police had to be on their way and her hands had cramped from the cold. She wasn't sure she could even peel her fingers off the cold metal; feared they were frozen to it, but still she waited. She didn't have the keys to the car anyway. He had them, but if she heard sirens, she was outta there. She couldn't get caught and questioned. She just couldn't.

Still rummaging in her purse, Sam walked out into the brisk wind and bright light of the afternoon sun, purposefully avoiding glancing in the direction of the dead man on the sidewalk, grateful to have Daniel at her side. She still couldn't believe he was there. Out of all the unbelievable and improbable things that had happened so far that day, Daniel had to be the most improbable.

"Where did you park?"

Face still buried in her purse -- she really needed to get one with pockets -- she replied, "I'm around back. The midnight blue Honda Civic."

Daniel stopped at the end of the building and peered around to see the parking lot. He didn't like what he saw. Not one little bit. "Would that be the midnight blue Honda Civic currently being guarded by a woman with a blunt instrument?"

Sam's fingers had just found the keychain and tightened convulsively around it as her head snapped up. Unfortunately, this caused the automatic unlock to activate and her car beeped out a welcome.

Daniel sighed, "Yes, I guess that would be the one." The car was being guarded, and they'd just given away any advantage they might have had with the element of surprise.

"If she hurt my cat, I'm going to kick her ass."

"When did you get so violent? What happened to the woman who burst into tears on the phone?"

"She got shot!" Sam replied belligerently. She even had her jaw clenched and chin thrust out. She was running on adrenaline at this point, but he was interested to see what was going to happen to her when she crashed. "Besides," she continued, "I have PMS so messing with me at this time of the month really wasn't a wise thing for them to do."

"Ah, that explains it."

"What exactly do you mean, that explains it?"

Daniel wasn't sure how to answer that. She had developed that tone. The tone that all men know. The tone that says no matter how you answer this question, you are going to be in big, big trouble. The tone that says just keep your mouth shut. He didn't follow the advice of the tone. "PMS perfectly explains why you'd be crying hysterically one minute and ready to commit murder the next. Those female hormones must be a bitch."

"Did you just call me a bitch?" she cried.

"No, of course I didn't," he replied, but she was already stalking away from him, right towards the woman with the lug wrench. "Well, shit."

Forgetting to be afraid for maybe the first time in her life, Sam marched towards the woman guarding her car; the woman who was now in a batter's stance and ready to swing a weapon that would do far more damage than a Louisville Slugger.

Sam strode purposely forward, and as the woman swung to the right, Sam ducked under and moved left, reaching out and grabbing the tire iron with her right hand, twisting it counter clockwise while stepping in and around so that they stood back to front. The woman cried out as her wrist was twisted at a painful angle and the tire iron ripped from her grasp. Sam released the weapon and grabbed the woman's wrist instead, continuing the already painful twist and expanding it to the woman's entire body so that she was driven down until she lay on her back on the cold asphalt. Sam didn't stop there; though the woman was already howling in pain, Sam was not deterred and kept up the pressure on the wrist while placing her other hand on the elbow. She then bent the elbow up and used the woman's own forearm to pin her head to the ground while placing her own knee on the woman's side, totally immobilizing her.

The woman was struggling against the restraints and Sam's strength was beginning to wane, she had recently been shot in the head after all, so when Daniel placed his hands beside hers and eased her away she allowed him to take over.

He had been so shocked as to be nearly petrified when he saw the action start. It would never have even occurred to him that she would know how to disarm somebody. And she'd done it quickly and efficiently. All he could say was, "Wow".

Finally crashing from the adrenaline high, the loss of blood, and the anxiety of seeing Daniel again, Sam sat crossed legged on the pavement, the cold seeping deep into her butt and her bones, her impromptu bandage dislodged from the struggle. "I took a self defense class for some exercise. I had a good teacher."

"I guess so." Daniel's attention was pulled away from Samantha as the woman beneath him started to struggle in earnest. This was possibly because of the sirens that could now be heard in the background. "Why were you here? Why were you trying to kill this woman?"

No response.

Daniel asked again, but there was still no response. "Okay, I guess I'll just let the cops get the answers out of you." Yep, the struggle was due to the sirens. "Look, you tell me what I want to know and I'll let you go."

The struggle stopped and the woman looked up at him with big pleading eyes. "Really? You'll really let me go?" Daniel nodded in response while Sam humphed in outrage.

The woman couldn't believe her luck. She had been sure she was going to jail and was not looking in the least forward to having to call her husband for bail. He knew what she was doing, as he was also a member of the NACR, but with her out of work and him not receiving a raise in three years, the legal fees would bankrupt them.

"I don't know much. All I can tell you is that some people didn't want her asking questions about her genetic study. I'm only here because she tried to access those files."

The sirens were getting closer. Too close. Both Daniel and the woman turned their heads to track the approaching sound. Daniel knew that he and Sam would have to get going, and soon. "What was so important about this study? Why was it worth putting a hit on her?"

"Please, you've got to let me go. I've got to get out of here. I don't know anything else. I really don't. I only know the study was important, not why. I only know that questions couldn't be asked about it. Please. Please let me go."

She had started to cry, and Daniel didn't think he was going to get any more out of her. He lifted his knee from her side and watched her scramble away, cradling her injured wrist. When he turned around, Sam was glaring at him. "Daniel, why did you let her go? What if she tries to kill me again? Don't you care if somebody is trying to kill me? Wait, of course you don't. You think I'm a bitch." Sam got up and put her key in the door and jerked it open. "To hell with you, I'll just do this on my own."

Daniel wrestled the car keys from her, dodging her slaps and scratches, and finally picked her up and set her bodily aside. Then he jerked out her suitcase from the back, and her cat from the front. He looked into the carrier for a moment to see a furry black face with big yellow accusatory eyes staring back at him. Damn, even the cat was mad at him. He threw her laptop bag over his shoulder, tucked the carrier under his arm, extended the pull handle of the suitcase, and started walking. Sam had no choice but to follow him, but she hurled accusations and insults at him the whole way.

Even as she was screaming at him, Samantha was shocked by her own behavior. She had never been a confrontational person and didn't know why this characteristic was manifesting itself in her now. Perhaps it was the shock of the day, but she suspected it was more of a defense mechanism. Exactly why she was defending herself against Daniel, though, she couldn't be sure; at least not without engaging in a level of introspection she had spent most of her adult life avoiding.

When Daniel reached his car he had to put everything down in order to pull his keys from his pocket. With his gaze concentrated on the lock and the door, he finally responded to Sam. "The D.C. cops and I don't get along well at all. I'll explain why a bit later, but we don't have time right this moment. If they find out that I'm part of what happened in that diner, we will get no information from them at all and they won't look any farther than me. We can't trust the cops."

He had tossed her things into the back seat and now turned to face her, grasped her by her upper arm, and steered her over to the passenger side. "I did not call you a bitch. I said that out-of-control hormones must be a bitch, not that you are, and you damn well know it. I understand you're under a lot of stress in this situation, but you came to me for help. I may not have realized that the help you were looking for was to have me to kick in your frustration, but I intend to give you a different type of help, whether you like it or not."

Sam's indignation started to wane as he forced her into the passenger seat, secured her belt, and slammed the door closed. Now she felt guilty. She hated feeling guilty. When he was in the car beside her, his own belt secured, she mumbled an apology. Daniel ignored her, which only made her feel worse. "I'm sorry, okay?" she all but screamed at him, but still received no response. "Where are we going anyway?"

"Away from here," he replied. "We don't know if there are more hit men coming, and the cops will be here any second. We need to get someplace where they can't find you."

Contrite, and trying to make up for her rudeness, Sam replied, "I don't know how they found me in the first place. Nobody knew I was coming to you. Even I wasn't sure where I was going until you called me."

"That reminds me," he said. "Turn off your cell phone. They can't trace it unless it's on."

Sam dug the phone out of her purse. "So you think that's how they found me? My phone?" There was a faint meow from the back seat. "Oh, I need to stop someplace and get some food and a litter box. Chloe's a good cat, but nature will take its course."

Daniel's mouth kicked up at one side in a sexy grin. "So we go from escaping to shopping. OK. That at least tells me which direction to turn. But no, I don't think it was your phone, not with that woman waiting at your car. Although I can't rule the phone out, it's more probable that it was the GPS system in your car that was tracked."

Sam was confused again. She was getting really tired of being confused. Being locked in a lab staring at genetic strings did not prepare her at all to be on the run from crazy psycho killers. "But I don't have a GPS system in my car. I should have, because I'm always getting lost, but I've never gotten around to getting one."

"That's not the kind of GPS I mean." Daniel turned left and headed away from the diner. He hadn't traveled more than a block when two police cars and an ambulance sped past in the opposite direction. "That was close."

"So what's with you and the cops anyway? Are you a criminal?"

Daniel laughed, "Well, according to some politicians I am. I wrote a story that a certain politician didn't want me to write. As a result, the story got buried, along with my career, and anything that I'm involved in has become suspect. The cops hauled me in last night for hours of questioning just because I called 9-1-1 to report a car accident. If they treated me that way for a car accident, I can't imagine what they would do for a shooting." Daniel shrugged, "So much for freedom of the press."

"Now you're starting to sound like my father. According to him, our freedoms are under targeted and escalating attacks from within." Sam didn't want to be reminded of her father. She loved him, but his love for her, his approval of her, had always hinged on her talents as a scientist more than her blood tie.

"He was forever explaining to me how each piece of legislation passed by Congress whittled away at our freedoms. He's the reason I don't follow politics. It became too depressing." Silence lingered for a while. "So why would the police pull you in for questioning for a car accident?"

Daniel had been mulling over what she said about her father. He wasn't sure if reminding her of her father was a good thing or a bad thing, but based on her tone, he didn't think it was good. "The victim of the accident was a congressional aide; the congressional aide for the subject of my career-ending story. So, since it was his aide and I found him, there had to be something suspect." Daniel was cut off by another meow from the back -- actually, this was much more of a yowl -- and the carrier was shuddering now as Chloe expressed her desire for some more leg room.

"How far to the store? Chloe's getting a bit restless."

That's putting it mildly, Daniel thought. "Not far. There's a Petland just a few blocks from here. We can run in, get what you need, and then head to my place."

"Your place?" Sam squeaked.

"You can't go home. That's obvious. And you shouldn't use your credit cards for a hotel. We'll try my place first and see how that goes. It will at least give us time to think and to see if we can figure out what's going on and where we go from here."

Less than an hour later, now laden with litter box, a 27 lb box of litter, a 20 lb bag of food, two dishes and some cat toys, they made their way into Daniel's apartment. Daniel, of course, carried the cat food and kitty litter. Not because he was the big strong man, Sam wouldn't have put up with that, but because she was still a little weak from her head wound. A wound whose hasty bandaging had drawn some interesting and interested looks in the pet store.

As soon as the door to the apartment was opened, Sam's curiosity got the best of her. The building itself had looked rundown and shabby, not what she had expected to see. The inside was small, sparsely furnished, less shabby than the outside, and obsessively neat. Once fully inside she set up the bowls, poured food and water, then got the litter box filled and opened the door to the cat carrier. Chloe came limping out and headed straight for the litter box.

"Does that cat only have three legs?" Daniel couldn't stop himself from asking.

"Yes, the poor baby disappeared for a few days and when she came back her leg was so broken it had to be amputated. I felt so sorry for her, but have to admit that giving her antibiotics and pain medication was almost too much of a challenge. Giving a cat a pill is not the easiest thing in the world to do. It's definitely a two person job and almost impossible to do by yourself; especially with an uncooperative cat."

Chloe finished her squat, covered it immaculately and then limped over to Sam all while keeping an analyzing stare on Daniel. She wasn't sure quite what to think yet, but that was set aside when Sam began to scratch her behind her ear, the one on the same side as the missing leg. Chloe let out a loud rumble, closed her eyes in bliss, and pressed her head into Sam's hand.

"So, what's the plan?" Sam asked.

"Well, first we need to pick up where we left off with your study. You said it was confidential and they shouldn't have been able to find out who the participants were."

"Right." Sam continued to scratch, an automatic response for her now. "I never went to see those men in the prisons. They were not under my care and I was not on their files. However, the court did give me copies of their DNA for analysis. They were all rapists, domestic abusers, serial killers, that kind of thing. Anybody who committed a crime whose basis was power over others. But in order to determine that these men were part of that study, you would have had to already know they were part of the study. A paradox. Nothing in their medical files would have told investigators that I was involved at all. It's bizarre."

"And what happened to these men? How did they die?"

"That's even more bizarre. They died of anaphylaxis, a strong allergic reaction, but according to the article, whose integrity is now in question, the source of the allergic reaction could not be determined. They weren't subjected to anything new and there were no allergies listed in their files, so they appeared to die of an allergic reaction to nothing."

Sam continued to scratch and Chloe continued to purr. She felt the action soothing in its very facileness. "What I want to know is, why, since the woman said questions couldn't be asked about my study, it was printed in the paper. Why bring attention to it at all?"

"Misdirection," Daniel promptly replied. "Questions may have been being asked about the deaths. They probably were considering the mysterious circumstances. So you were evidently offered up as a distraction. The focus will now be on you instead of the deaths."

"Oh, goody."

"I know. It really sucks to be the object of misdirection, being used as a scapegoat to distract people from the real issue. I've been there and I will do my very best to keep what happened to me from happening to you. We're going to get to the bottom of this and get it out there -- somehow."

"Thanks", Sam replied softly. She kept herself focused on Chloe. She found it was much easier to talk to him about emotional issues when she wasn't staring into those incredible green eyes. "It really helps a lot just to have somebody to talk to. I was feeling really, really alone this morning."

"You're not alone now. And you won't deal with this alone if I have anything to say about it at all.

Trust me on this one, nobody should have to go through this alone."

Chapter 4

"So what happened when you went through this?" There was a prolonged silence which had Sam rushing in to speech again. "You don't have to tell me if you don't want to, I understand." And then she promptly buried her face in Chloe's fur, embarrassed for prying into his personal life.

Daniel reached out to stroke Chloe as well. He'd always loved cats and this one was pretty interesting, quite willing to accept affection, and to give it. He wondered if that's why Sam was so reluctant to leave her behind. "It's okay; I just had to think about where to start. The story gets pretty ugly, and I don't want to scare you."

"Tell me. If you can take it, I can." She placed her hand over his as he scratched. She needed this. She needed to know what to expect, but even more, she needed to know this about him.

Daniel was sitting in a chair with knees spread. He withdrew his hand from Chloe and clasped his hands loosely, elbows on his thighs and dropped his head. It wasn't that he didn't want to look at Samantha, but he needed to look inward instead. He wanted to tell her the truth, at least to the best that he could remember it.

"I was arrogant and idealistic and believed in what I was doing" he began. "I had been very successful in my career and was part of the Washington Press Corps by the age of thirty. I believed it was my responsibility, as part of the press, to tell the truth to the American public. That's all I was trying to do, but nobody seemed to be interested in the truth -- most especially not the newspapers."

Daniel shifted in his seat and threw Sam a furtive glance. Her gaze was calm and sympathetic. He hadn't received much sympathy, not for a very long time. He took a deep breath and continued, "This happened five years ago when the economy was continuing downhill, before it stabilized into the horror show we have now. The politicians, refusing to accept any responsibility for their actions, cast the blame on the private industry instead. It was the greed of the private sector that had led to the economic downward spiral." Daniel laughed humorlessly. "Right. They were as much a scapegoat as I was. More so, at least on a grander scale. But one man in particular became a martyr for the private sector. He was speaking out against all of the accusations hurled at the businessmen by the government. He was explaining to the people, from a businessman's perspective, exactly what the problem was. He was explaining how the Federal Government's need to control everyone and everything was driving the economy into the ground -- and he was winning. People were starting to listen. Then his salary was leaked to the newspapers, along with the company's annual earnings. The article, in *my* newspaper, listed the man's salary as one half of the company's total earnings. This didn't seem right to me. No company could stay in operation that way."

Daniel was too restless. This was too hard to remember and to walk through, but it needed to be done. She needed to know what she was up against. And if he was honest, he wanted her to know. Other than his family, she would be the first person who knew the whole story. The price he had paid for his arrogance and idealism.

"I went to the company and asked for their records. They were more than happy to give them to me, which immediately set off warning bells in my head. They were almost grateful for me to ask. When I first saw the CEO's actual salary, I thought they must have cooked the books. It was only 1% of what my paper had reported. The man's salary was actually fairly low compared to the industry standard. Something was horribly wrong." He stood up and began to pace. Becoming more and more agitated, he ran his hands through his hair. Hair that was just a little too long and had started to curl, and due to its treatment would soon be standing up all over his head.

His apartment was small so he didn't have a whole lot of room to pace, but still he continued. "I thought this must be a mistake on the part of the paper. I went to the reporter who filed it and discussed it with her. She said the numbers were correct, that she had received them from a reliable source and that the company had obviously altered the files. So I took the books to a friend, a CPA who went over them with a level of detail only an anal-retentive number cruncher can achieve, and he assured me that they were legitimate. I didn't know what to do. The reporter was one of the top in the field and the whole idea that she would print something she knew to be false was inconceivable. So I went to her again. She still insisted that her facts were right and that the man deserved to have the country know what a hypocrite he was for speaking out against the government, calling them thieves, when was taking way more than they were. The man deserved to be exposed, she said."

Daniel stopped abruptly and turned to Sam, "Do you want coffee?"

The abrupt change of subject took her by surprise. She was engrossed in the story and it took her a minute to pull herself out of it. "Coffee? Yes, that would be nice."

"Is decaf ok? I drink it leaded in the mornings but I'm so high strung that if I drink it all day I never sleep, but I still want coffee. Decaf is my compromise." Then he smiled and said, "And of course since Congress put that tax on caffeine. The decaf is much, much cheaper."

Samantha grinned, "I actually do the same thing, so decaf will be perfect."

Daniel distracted himself with making the coffee, but picked the story back up. Having something to do with his hands really helped. "Shortly after my discussion with the reporter, I was called into my editor's office and told to drop my investigation. I tried to argue, I tried to point out the discrepancies, but he didn't want to hear it. The truth didn't matter. To an idealistic reporter who really believed we were the fourth branch of government, the one that served as checks and balances for others, the idea of being silenced on the truth and forced to let an incorrect story stand was a sucker punch in the gut. I couldn't help but believe the press was being controlled. The question was by whom? I kept digging on my own time and flying under the radar of my editor. What I found wasn't conclusive, but it was very, very suspect. Do you know who Clive Sledgewater is?"

Samantha shook her head, "I'm sorry. I told you I don't follow politics."

"That's okay," Daniel continued. "I just didn't know how much to tell you about him. Clive Sledgewater is the quintessential politician. He's been running for office since birth and has served in the House of Representatives for the last thirty years. He was made Speaker of the House just under five years ago. He was being considered for Speaker by his party at the time that I was doing my investigation, and what I had found out was that he met regularly with my editor. And worse, I found out that my editor was a large contributor to his campaign. The press hadn't been fully objective for years, but I still believed there were some ethics, some standards. I was naïve. But it only got worse from there."

"Oh, dear." Sam must have squeezed Chloe a little too hard because she objected and hopped down. Then she strolled, none too gracefully, over to Daniel and started rubbing her head against his calf. Unthinkingly Daniel reached down and scooped Chloe up. The cat did not object, but having made up her mind about him, curled up in his arms and started to purr. There is nothing like unconditional love.

Daniel began a methodical stroking of the cat in his arms, finally having something to do with his hands. The coffee was finished brewing, so he carried Chloe into the kitchen and cradled her while pouring them each a cup. He took one out and handed it to Sam and then returned for his own. Once that task was completed, he settled on the couch next to Sam and continued to gently stroke Chloe. "The meetings and the contributions weren't proof of anything, but I was really beginning to have some questions. Then the CEO, the subject of the incorrect article, was killed by protestors."

Samantha gasped in horror.

"They had been 'encouraged' to protest at his home and it got ugly. They started throwing stones at him and one hit him in just the right spot, or the wrong one I guess, and down he went. The protestor who threw the stone was pulled in for questioning, but he was never charged." Daniel turned to face Sam, "Want to hazard a guess as to why?"

"Sledgewater?" she whispered.

"Yes, I found out later that he put pressure on the police to keep charges from being filed. He was also the one who "encouraged" the protestors to show up at a private residence and picket an honest businessman. The point here is that the man had done nothing illegal. Even if the article had been correct, he still would have done nothing illegal; nothing worth stoning him for."

Samantha was disgusted with this story. What had the country come to when politicians wielded that kind of power? "Then what happened?"

"I was horrified by this. A man was basically killed because he spoke up and defended the principles on which the country was founded. He had his character defamed, his home violated, and his very life taken by the government, no matter how indirectly, for exercising his most basic civil right - the right to speak out against our government - the right that is supposed to ensure that we live in liberty and not under tyranny. I couldn't let this go. I just couldn't. I pursued the story and eventually dug up the information that linked Sledgewater to it all."

"But your story never got printed, did it?" Samantha was enthralled, yet she was ashamed of herself for paying so little attention. She couldn't delude herself into believing that she wasn't part of the current problem.

"I was fired for even turning it in," he turned a self-deprecating grin. "Being fired for writing that story was all the verification I needed that I was right. So I took the story to other papers. I just knew that somebody would print it and give me another job right away. I was wrong. Nobody wanted any part of it, at least not at the big papers. I was getting ready to go to the cable news networks with it, hoping somebody would take it and run, but I didn't get that far. Sledgewater himself showed up at my apartment and explained to me, in no uncertain terms, exactly why I would never print that story. He told me I would be blackballed from all reputable journalism jobs forever, but it appeared that had already been done, so what else did I have to lose? I was going full steam ahead. I figured I could take it, because once the story got out and people knew, I would be like Woodward and Bernstein breaking Watergate. Then the threats went beyond me."

Daniel's hand stilled on Chloe and she wriggled free and wobbled over to the food and water. Left empty handed again, Daniel struggled for a few seconds, until Sam reached out, squeezed his hand, and didn't let go.

"The next day, while I was still trying to make an appointment with the cable news networks, my parents called. The INS was at their house."

"Oh. My God! He turned the immigration service onto your parents?"

"Yes," Daniel choked up. "My father had taken his citizenship exam, so they couldn't do anything to him really, but Mom had hit one snag after another so she wasn't yet a citizen. But that threat ended my fight. I could risk my future, but I couldn't risk theirs. I'd never have forgiven myself if they'd deported Mom."

"I can't believe he used your parents against you like that. And you did the absolute right thing."

"They wanted me to fight," he replied, "My parents said they had all of their documentation and they could win, but I knew the rules wouldn't be obeyed and no matter the documentation they possessed, the government would find a way to deport her. I couldn't let it happen."

"Oh, Daniel, I'm so sorry. Nobody should have to make that choice. That was totally unfair. But I guess, based on his earlier behavior, not that surprising."

Daniel pulled away from her abruptly and started to pace again. His hands buried in his hair, making the curls stand up in disarray. "That's just it. You see it. Based on his earlier behavior, I should have expected this, but I just kept pushing. I was so arrogant I actually believed I could take a man like that on and win. How could I have not seen it? How could I have been that stupid? How could I have thrown away everything on a fight I couldn't win? And how could I drag my parents into it?"

Sam popped up off the couch in indignation. "You just stop it right there, Daniel Callahan. You will not, I repeat, Will Not, blame yourself for this. All you tried to do was the right thing. If nobody is willing to at least try to stand up to those assholes, then we might as well turn the country over to the power hungry bast…" Sam suddenly stopped talking, an arrested look on her face. "Power hungry bastards."

Daniel, a perplexed look on his face, replied, "Yes, Congress is stuffed full with a bunch of people only out for themselves. The only thing they care about is ensuring and expanding their own power, and their own pockets."

"That's it!" Sam cried. "Power!"

Daniel still looked puzzled.

"Don't you see?" she cried, "My research subjects were all criminals whose crimes had to do with obtaining power over another. There is a connection here. Power."

Daniel, worn out from his emotional retelling of the story, plopped back on the couch and leaned back, legs splayed. "Okay, I didn't get much sleep last night, so I may be a bit slow. I don't understand what your research has to do with my story."

In her agitation, Sam had dislodged the bandage on her head and it was starting to slip. She righted it as best she could and then plopped back down next to him. "My research was on genetics, to try to identify the genome that controls the pursuit of power. We studied those people, as well as many more, but we also had a control group so we could compare what genome was present in those who sought power and used it for criminal purposes, but was not present in others. Or who it might be dormant in. The woman in the parking lot said my study was important. I couldn't figure out why, because it's not like there's anything so exciting about genetics that it's worth killing over. We get our share of industrial espionage, but to try to kill me?"

Now with her, Daniel continued for her, "So somebody had to be planning to use your study for something, but on who? Who is it that would have that power genome that somebody would want to target? Congress is the obvious answer. But what ---"

"The anaphylaxis", she said. "They've figured out a way to attack that genome and cause an anaphylactic shock. I don't know how, and I don't know why, but something really tells me that this is the truth."

It was almost as if God had reached out and popped the idea straight into her head.

"What do you mean she got away?" The tone of his voice had the woman shaking in her shoes -- and this was just over the phone. She couldn't believe she was actually speaking with the commissioner of the NACR, a man whose name she didn't know, and who, to be frank, scared the shit out of her. He was the organizer of the ultimate goal. It was his brain child and he would sacrifice everything and everyone to see it come to pass. She really didn't want to get sacrificed.

"I heard shots and the driver" -- she hadn't known his name – "didn't come back. Then she came, but she wasn't alone." The woman continued with a rehash of the events in the parking lot, slightly modified of course so she didn't appear as big a wimp as she felt.

"She was with a man, you say?"

"Yes, he was tall with dark hair and spoke with a slight foreign accent. English or Irish or something." The obviously restrained tone of the commissioner's voice had her wracking her brain for any other information. "She called him Daniel."

The commissioner was rocked back on his heels a bit by this one. He had a strong suspicion who this Daniel person was, but he had no way of knowing whether or not he would be sympathetic to their cause; at least not yet. "Thank you for the information. It has been most helpful. We should be able to recover from your mistake shortly." And without so much as a good-bye, he terminated the call.

The woman flipped her phone closed, dropped her head between her knees and tried not to vomit. She had been afraid for a minute that she would pass out or disgrace herself. She wasn't cut out for this. She wanted to help save the country, to get it back on the right track, but this had been much harder, and much scarier than she had thought it would be. She had bitten off more than she could chew, and now she was choking on it.

But on the other hand, with her out of work, her previous employer bankrupt and no other jobs available, this would have been a very sparse Christmas for the children. The money she received for working for the NACR had enabled them to give the children a real Christmas instead of the ghost of one they had risked. She just hoped she lived to see them open their gifts on Christmas morning.

"Wait a minute," Daniel said. "You mean this is all a plot to take down the politicians? That seems to be a bit of a stretch."
Sam knew he was right, but she was also sick and tired of not being taken seriously. She'd always been too afraid to really fight back, finding it far easier to just keep her head down and let it slide. She was usually eventually proven right, but nobody seemed to remember that she had warned them. And the "I told you so" stance just wasn't her style.

Better not to make waves, she'd always thought. Well, this time she was going to generate a tsunami. She had somehow managed to grow a spine in the last eight hours, and it really felt good! "I know it's a bit of a stretch. I know how improbable it sounds. So improbable that nobody would ever suspect that kind of attack. I know it sounds crazy, but I also know that I'm right."

This was not the unsure, timid, even mousy girl he had known. It wasn't even the same woman he had met this morning. She was taking a stand, and that was significant enough to have Daniel giving her idea real consideration. "Okay, so let's say you're right. How do we prove it? And how do we make everybody else believe it?"

"You're a journalist, aren't you? Can't you write a story?"

"I work for a tabloid, Sammie. And I also have a reputation for being a drunk." At the look of shock that decorated her face, he continued, "That was the part of the story I hadn't gotten to yet. I told you it got ugly. Well once I had pissed away my career, I was mad at myself and mad at everybody else. In order to numb those feelings, I spent a lot of time with a drink in my hand. I've been sober now for two years, but that reputation is still out there."

"Oh, well, okay. Sorry."

Daniel felt like a total shit. "But, hey, what better place to print an unsubstantiated conspiracy theory than a tabloid? I'll give it a try." The joy on her face made the effort worthwhile. It was a charmingly childish expression and was only made more endearing by the bandage slipping on her head yet again. Daniel shook his own head. She was so easy to read. Everything she felt ran across her face and was there to see, at least to anybody paying attention. And he was beginning to suspect that nobody had ever paid attention. Or no one other than him, and that had been 22 years ago.

"Look, Sammie", he said, "Why don't you get in the shower and wash that head wound. Get the blood out of your hair and then we'll get you a better bandage."

"A shower?" she squeaked. Oh, no, it appeared the fear was back. A major conspiracy and gun shots she could handle, being naked with him in the next room was a whole other story. She reached up to straighten the bandage again. "Oh, okay, good idea. I'll do that."

Again, everything she was thinking ran across her face and Daniel did his best to hide his grin. He liked that fact that she was nervous around him. Having her naked in the next room wasn't exactly going to be easy on him either, but at least he could distract himself by working on the story he promised to write for her. "Come here and let me get this bandage off and have a look at that wound."

Samantha made herself walk over to him and tried her best to look indifferent. When she was within arm's reach of him, he placed his hands on her shoulders and turned her around. He then very gently unwrapped the apron and removed the towel. Releasing the clip and running his hands softly through her hair, he moved the mass of dark blond tresses aside and leaned in to get a better look. The bleeding had long ago stopped and the wound had scabbed over, but it was going to be tender for a while. It was very shallow, just a graze really, and if it had been anywhere but her scalp, there probably would have been very little blood, but scalp wounds really bled and he didn't want it reopened.

"Maybe I should wash your hair for you." He hadn't thought about how that would sound, but suddenly he was left holding nothing but air and a few strands of long blonde hair.

"That won't be necessary. I'm sure I can manage." She had quickly put as much distance between them as she could. An image of him standing behind her in the shower, massaging shampoo gently into her hair, brushing against her back with protruding parts of his anatomy had popped into her head. If she was honest with herself, in that image he was doing a lot more than that. Best to get away before she did something embarrassing, humiliating, or both.

She grabbed some pajamas, panties, and her toiletries out of her suitcase and headed to the bathroom to which Daniel had directed her. She allowed her long hair to fall forward and shield her face from him as she went. An old habit, but her newfound backbone didn't cover this.

Everything felt much better as soon as she was in the shower. The water heated delightfully fast, and the pressure was marvelous. Her shower this morning had been so cold and so abrupt that she couldn't resist just standing there and letting the water pound on her for a while. Her scalp was sore so she took great care in washing her hair, but the suds didn't turn pink and there was no blood on her hands so she figured she was in pretty good shape.

Once her hair was rinsed and her body clean, she stood in the spray and let her mind wander over the events of the day. How on earth could they ever prove what she knew in her bones to be the truth? The only way to conclusively prove it would be after it happened, and that of course would be far too late.

It would help tremendously if they knew –or even had a vague idea -- who was behind it, but based on the woman in the parking lot's response, that was a secret well guarded. Still, she had to try. She knew she had to try. She couldn't let her work be used like this. Would she be -- was she -- responsible for the deaths so far and all of those that might come? Could she live with that? She just didn't know.

Daniel was working away on the article, but the sound of the shower running kept distracting him. Was she okay in there? She'd been in the bathroom for quite a while, and she did have a head injury. Should he check on her? Should he knock? He was afraid if he did so, she'd be so startled that she would end up slipping in the shower, thereby making her head injury worse. If the water hadn't stopped in another three minutes, he'd check on her. That was a good compromise.

Pulling his brain back around to the computer – again -- he got back to work. He hadn't been sure if he should make it true tabloid or real news, so he'd settled for a combination, something that his editor might actually publish, but with enough facts tucked in there to make people wonder. If nothing else, the information behind the genetic study would be out there. Once that was in print, would there really be any need to make further attacks on Sam? He hoped it would mitigate the attacks instead of escalating them, but he had a feeling this wasn't over. Not by a long shot.

Two minutes and forty-two seconds later the water shut off and Daniel finally relaxed. He hadn't made much progress while she was gone, and the thought of her running one of his towels over her wet body wasn't helping him at all. He had to stop thinking about this or when she walked out of that bathroom she'd really be surprised. He didn't know how she'd react to his boner, or if she'd even notice. Now that would be demoralizing. Once again he reminded himself to focus. Pull his mind back around to the article. By the time she came marching out of the bathroom, armored in SpongeBob SquarePants pajamas and tube socks, her hair wet and her face clear of any make-up, he had himself back under control, but he did wonder why he suddenly found SpongeBob so sexy.

"How's your head feel?" he asked. "Do you need me to take a look at it? Put another bandage on it?"

Sam gently probed the wound with her hand. "I think it's okay. It's stopped bleeding, so I think I'm good for now. I probably ought to put something over it before I go to bed, though." Here she paused and hid behind her hair again. "Which reminds me, where will I be sleeping tonight? Do you have a spare room?"

Daniel nearly groaned. "I have a second bedroom, but it doesn't have a bed. I use it more for storage. You can take my room and I'll sleep out here on the couch."

Sam looked at the couch on which she sat, and then looked at him. There was no way he would fit on this thing and have any room at all to stretch out. "Don't be ridiculous," she replied. "I'm shorter than you are and I've slept on the couch in my lab often enough that this won't bother me. I'll be fine here."

"You do understand that if my mother ever found out that I took the bed while allowing a woman to sleep on the couch, I would have to go to the woods and cut my own switch." Sam chuckled at this. She had met his mother several times and she wouldn't put that past her.

"We wouldn't have to tell her, you know." Daniel just stared at her. "Okay, okay, I know. But I'd still feel really guilty chasing you out of your bed."

"What kind of man would I be if I couldn't give up my bed to a damsel in distress, and especially one who's been shot in the head? Is that really the kind of man you think I am?"

"Damn," she replied, "A guilt trip. That's just so not fair. Okay, I'll take the bed."

"Perfect", he replied, "Now I know exactly how to manipulate you. This should come in really handy."

Sam grabbed the throw pillow behind her and hurled it at his head. When he caught it and prepared to throw it back at her she scooped up her coffee cup and smiled tauntingly, "You wouldn't throw a pillow at a woman with coffee *and* a head wound, would you? What kind of man would you be?"

"Oh, man! Manipulation? I'm so disappointed in you."

Sam giggled and cradled her coffee. She was having fun. She couldn't believe it, but she was having fun. She was on the run with killers after her and a probable plot to assassinate some politician, but she was still having fun. Man, she was twisted.

"How's the article coming?"

Daniel frowned, his brow furrowing. "Not great, actually. I was too worried about you in the shower to concentrate. You should have let me wash your hair for you."

Sam reached across the couch, "I have another pillow here and I'm not afraid to use it."

That frown turned to a grin immediately. "Okay, okay, the problem is I don't really understand what your project was and what 'they' plan to do with it."

"Oh, well that's easy enough. What do you know about genetics?"

"I know I get my green eyes from my mum and my curly hair from my grandfather. I understand recessive and dominant genes, but that's about it."

"Sam tucked her legs up under her on the couch and made herself comfortable. "You get more than just your eyes and your hair from your parents. Your genetic code predetermines not just your physical characteristics, but nearly everything about you. You, of course, have the choices to make in your life which will take you down certain paths, but any tendencies you have may be genetically determined."

"Why do I suddenly feel like I'm in the matrix? Have I been reduced to nothing but code?" He was kidding. Sort of. "Do you see me in code?"

"Of course, I do. It makes it so much easier to deal with codes instead of people."

Daniel looked a bit taken aback, so she had to continue, "I'm kidding, of course. I can't see your code. Give me a strand of hair or a drop of blood and I could make a pretty good start on it, though." When he relaxed a bit she continued, "The identification of genomes has enabled science to identify people with a predisposition for certain things. For example, if a woman has the breast cancer genome, she would be monitored more closely than somebody who doesn't. That's not to say that a woman who doesn't have it won't get it, there are outside influences that cause it as well, but if we know a woman is predisposed to it, and we can catch it really early, her chances of survival are so much better."

"Okay, I think I'm following you so far. But hold on just a sec." Daniel rummaged around on his desk, came up with pen and paper, scratched some notes on what she had said so far, and then said, "Okay, shoot."

"I can get really, really technical, but I don't think you want me to, so I'll try to keep it in layman's terms. There are hundreds of thousands, potentially millions, of genomes and we've only started to identify them. But, by studying people with certain tendencies, such as a need for power over others, and comparing their genetic string to that of a control group, we can potentially identify the genome that controls that trait. That's what I did with my study. I identified the genome in those individuals that caused them to seek power or control over others."

"Okay," Daniel replied, "so you know they have that predisposition, so what can you do about it? Would you monitor them like you would somebody with the breast cancer genome? Wouldn't that be a violation of their rights? Being watched for some chance they might commit a crime?"

"Yes, that would be a violation of their rights, but that's not really what we intended. It was more of a rehabilitation situation. If they expressed that tendency to the detriment of others, we could attack that genome and eliminate it."

Daniels eyes opened wide in shock. "You could what!?"

"Well, that was the idea anyway. That wasn't part of my study, but I know that was the general idea. You see," Sam unfolded herself and leaned forward with her elbows on her knees. She was in her comfort zone now. "Genomes are split into quartiles. Historically we find that 25% of the population has a strong version, 25% has a moderate version, 25% have an inactive version, and 25% don't have it at all. The goal was to find a way to isolate that genome and introduce an agent that would attach to it and either lower its strength or eliminate it altogether. I was for lowering its strength, because you just can't know what would happen to the whole genetic sequence if you eliminate one genome. There is the potential that you could unravel it all."

"Okay, I think I can work with this. The need for power over another is as much in your genetic make-up as the color of your hair, your height and the size of your….nose. A study was done to identify and isolate this power hungry genome, and it was successful…" Daniel looked up from his notes. "How's that for a start?"

"I think it sounds wonderful. A really, really great start."

That little bit of encouragement made him feel amazingly good. He hadn't experienced that kind of blind support from anybody but family in a really long time. He decided that this would be the best article he had written, possibly ever. It was amazing what having somebody believe in you could do. "Look, Sammie, if I'm going to do this right ---"

"You need me to leave you alone. I totally understand. I'll just head to bed then. It's been a long day and I'm plum tuckered."

"If you're not quite ready for sleep, there is a television in there. Feel free to turn it on. I won't be able to hear it out here."

Samantha analyzed the situation for the appropriate good night response, and then decided to do exactly what she wanted and not what the data indicated as the appropriate response. She padded over to Daniel, wrapped her arms around his neck, hugged him tight and whispered her thanks. She started to pull back when the hug was not returned, but, as she withdrew, his arms wrapped around her and squeezed her tight for a few seconds. Her risk had been repaid.

"Dr Mallard's car was left in the parking lot of the diner, it has not moved. And we have verified that the man you sent was killed there."

"Thank you, Jack, but we already knew that." The commissioner sat behind the antique mahogany desk in his home office and contemplated his situation. He had retired several years ago and turned his full attention to the NACR. His office was now in his home and served him quite well. He had been very successful in his chosen field, and had been financially rewarded for that success. Of course, this was back when capitalism still ruled in this country. As a result, his house was large and spacious and could accommodate several members of the NACR as permanent residents.

The commissioner turned his soft, well padded leather office chair around so that he faced his window. The wide, nearly floor to ceiling window, draped in a midnight blue damask swag which hung all the way to the floor, opened out into the garden. There wasn't much inspiration to be found in the bare twigs and dead flowers that were currently displayed, but the very barrenness of the landscape allowed clarity of his mind. The Samantha issue had to be resolved, but they were also working up to their pilot, their test run. Maybe his initial decision to eliminate her had been rash. What did she really know anyway? She had no idea what her research would be used for. Since she didn't know the ultimate goal how could she alert anybody? Could the pilot be risked, should the pilot be risked, in order to eliminate a woman who may not even be a threat? The answer was no.

Edward Jackson, the commissioner's personal assistant, was not in the least surprised when the chair spun abruptly back around to face him. He had been working with or for the commissioner for years now and had learned the man's habits and his idiosyncrasies. Edward had been ideal for this particular duty, not because he was detail oriented and extremely well organized – though these traits were vitally important -- but because he was single, had no children, and had an employer who allowed him to work from home. This enabled Edward to live with the commissioner and be available to him twenty-four hours a day, seven days a week while still maintaining his own income.

Initially he had been thrilled with the assignment, but lately had started to wonder if the leader of their organization wasn't more dangerous than those they sought to remove. It wasn't yet enough of a question to make him give up their goal, that was much too important, nor was it strong enough to make him leave his current luxurious accommodations.

Though Edward made a decent living at his day job, the current tax rate compared with the still increasing cost of housing would send him from the palatial one hundred twenty acre Georgian Estate in Northern Missouri, to an apartment whose entire square footage would be less than his current bedroom. His concerns would have to become quite compelling to prompt him to make that switch. The call for the execution of Samantha Mallard had almost done it.

"I believe we can leave Dr Mallard be for now. Further attacks on her at this time might only raise more questions. We must focus on the pilot and then we can redirect to the good doctor."

Edward sighed in relief.

"However, we will need to watch her, and should she approach the authorities about this matter, we will have no choice but to eliminate her immediately. And in order to watch her, we have to know where she is."

"Are you sure you want to eliminate her, sir? After all, she is---"

"I know exactly who she is!" The commissioner had slammed his hands down on his desk, raised himself and leaned forward in the classic pose of intimidation. And it was working. "I would prefer not to kill her. You must know that. But I can't have her putting two and two together."

"But sir, if I may," Edward gulped, "Wouldn't her murder just raise more questions? The information about her was published in the Washington Post, and her sudden unnatural death could possibly raise even more questions when we need it least."

"And what, Mr. Jackson, would be your option?"

Edward ignored the condescension and derision in the tone. He had to do his best to protect Dr. Mallard. This was wrong and he knew it. She was not somebody who needed to be sacrificed for their cause, she was an innocent, and he was the only person in a position to save her. "What if we just took her out of the equation temporarily? You know, until the ultimate goal is achieved. She would still know nothing of who was involved."

"And then what? Just turn her loose to implicate us all? You assume that she is as much an idiot as you are yourself." The commissioner took in the man before him. Though obsessively efficient, he was the type of man you didn't notice on the street. A short man, too thick around the middle, the mouth in his round face a little too small, and the curly hair on his head a little too sparse, this was not a man whose advice you sought in troubling circumstances. "She *would* figure it out," he continued, "And then we'd both be in prison. Is that what you want?"

"N-n-no, sir."

"I didn't think so. So find her! And watch her! And then we may have to eliminate her. As unpalatable as we both may find it, if she contacts the authorities she will become a necessary martyr for the cause."

Edward wondered how unpalatable the commissioner actually found this. He was beginning to think that the man just wanted her dead. After all, it was the commissioner who had leaked her name to the Washington Post in the first place. It had been the commissioner who had created the situation which he now insisted called for her death.

Maybe he should start that search for a cheap apartment.

Sam entered Daniel's bedroom like a kid on Christmas morning. The rest of his house had been neat as a pin, though sparsely furnished and even more sparsely decorated except for the small Christmas tree in his front window, so she was anxious to see if it continued here as well. She opened the door and peered in, finding the relatively small space dominated by a king sized bed covered in a plaid duvet. The bed was immaculately made, not a wrinkle or a crease to be seen, and everything else was neat as well.

There was a minor bit of clutter, loose change and papers, on the top of his dresser, but the total lack of chaos in his room left her feeling totally inadequate. She herself was a bit of a slob – or more than a bit. She rarely took notice of her surroundings and managed to realize one day, much to her embarrassment, that things were such a disaster that it might be easier to move than to clean.

She had hoped that the sheets would smell like him, that she would be surrounded by his scent as she slept, but the pillows were completely smooth. Not a single wrinkle from where a head may have rested. Well, shoot.

It appeared that he had changed the sheets in preparation. Had he prepared the house and the room for her? The idea that he had done so stroked her pitifully small ego.

In addition to its neatness, the room smelled really good. Snooping shamelessly, she found the source of it; a bottle of Burberry cologne that smelled just heavenly and had her purring in pleasure. Sam located the remote control, snuggled under the covers and stretched. Oh, she felt so decadent being in his bed like this. She'd moan in delight but she was afraid he would hear her, and how humiliating would that be?

Finally satisfying her tactile needs, she propped her head up on the pillows and clicked on the television to see if the events of the day were in the news anywhere. What she discovered was that Darlene had done a great job of covering her own tracks. Nobody appeared to know who had shot her assailant with what would have to be an illegal gun.

There was, not surprisingly, more talk about the illegal gun that shot the assailant than there was about the illegal gun the assailant himself fired. Typical 'punish the innocent and protect the guilty' mentality that had ruled the nation for years. This is why she had stopped watching the news years ago. Crap, now she felt guilty again. She sighed heavily and made herself watch. She needed to be informed.

She wasn't sure how long she'd been watching when a tiny woman with dark, upswept hair, round glasses, and a big attitude came on the screen. She was not happy, that was obvious to even the casual observer, but she was also making sense, which was even more frightening.

The small woman was on a tirade about the focus on the gun that was used to protect, instead of the gun that was used to attack. She pointed out that, had it not been for that gun, outlawed by a blatant violation of the second amendment, everybody in that diner could have been killed. Sam found herself nodding in agreement. The woman went on to complain about how Congress is out of touch with the people, blind to what was happening around them. Sam laughed out loud when the woman said, "But it's no wonder they're in the dark. Not much light gets to you when your head's up your ass."

The woman's name was written across the bottom of the screen, but Sam couldn't make it out on the small television. She threw the covers back and crawled over to see it. Senator Mara Fisk. Sam liked this woman. If they could get more like her, then maybe the country would be okay.

Eventually the events of the day bore down on her, dragging at her consciousness and pulling her to the very edges of slumber, so she clicked off the TV, snuggled down into Daniel's bed, and dropped off to sleep. Her last thought was a hope that her head wound wouldn't bleed on his pristine pillowcases.

Daniel put the finishing touches on the article and hit print. Once that was completed, he pulled sheets and a blanket from the linen closet, stripped down to his boxers and settled in for a restless night. He lay for quite some time with a grin on his face. Samantha Mallard was finally in his bed. After twenty-four years of thinking about it, the event had finally occurred. And once this mess was over, he'd be in there with her. He was sure about that. The thoughts of what he would do once there kept him awake most of the night, but he didn't mind in the slightest.

He, of course, woke up at seven o'clock the next morning, Samantha still on his mind. He actually whistled while making his coffee. He hadn't whistled in the morning since …. he couldn't even remember when. His only problem now was keeping Sam alive long enough to convince her she couldn't live without him, but after everything else he'd been through, that should be easy.

Two hours later, Sam came stumbling out of the bedroom like she'd been on a bender. She shuffled and stumbled and wobbled her way down the hall. Her hair was sticking up all over her head and her SpongeBob pajamas were delightfully wrinkled. She gave a yawn so big he was surprised she didn't dislocate her jaw, and then rubbed her eyes, her head and her back. It was pretty obvious that she was not a morning person. Yawning again as she made her way into the kitchen, she smiled gratefully when he thrust a cup of coffee into her hand.

"Thank you. You might have guessed that I'm not quite human until I've had my coffee." Sam had been a bit self-conscious about appearing so rumpled in front of him, but he didn't seem the least bit put off by it. How nice to find a man who didn't need her to be always at her best in order to enjoy her company, but Daniel had always been that way.

In high school he had been one of the few boys who would speak to her, and he had always been kind. Which, coupled with his sexy accent and sexier – well -- everything, had been why she'd been infatuated with him. An infatuation she'd never quite shaken. And having him stand there in jeans slung low on his hips, bare chest sprinkled with just the right amount of hair boldly displayed to her devouring gaze, wasn't helping shake that infatuation in the slightest.

"I couldn't help but wonder if the wobbling was normal or the result of the head injury. How is your head this morning?" He reached up and cupped her chin, turning her head so he could see the back. "It appears to be healing nicely."

Sam took a few deep, ragged breaths to try to bring herself under control, and then pulled gently away. It was too early in the morning to deal with overwhelming sexual hunger, and she'd been too close to that bare chest while at the same time not close enough. Once she was at a safe distance she gulped her coffee, and then discovered it was still too hot for gulping. She really was not presenting herself well this morning. "How's the article?"

Daniel grinned at the change of subject. He'd heard the shattered breathing and now knew for sure that she was absolutely aware of him as a man; an excellent development. "I finished the article last night. I thought we could take it over to my editor today and see if we can convince him to publish it."

Sam's face lit up. "Oh, that will be wonderful. Do you think he will?'

Daniel wasn't sure, and he couldn't lie to her, not about this. "I really don't know. I never know what he is willing to publish and what he isn't, but we can at least give it a try. If not, we'll try something else, and we won't stop trying until somebody listens."

"Thank you so much, Daniel. You've gone so far above and beyond. You had no idea what you were getting into when you responded to my message, but here you are, being absolutely wonderful. I don't know where I'd be without you." Sam got suddenly more serious. "Probably dead - and that's the honest truth. You saved my life, Daniel."

"So you owe me big time. Don't think that I won't collect some day." His attempt to alleviate the tension was working. "So, other than dodging bullets and trying to inform the country of a subversive plot, what do you want to do today?"

"Hmmmm, well let me think about that. Well, once we've saved the world, how about a stroll through the Smithsonian? I really want to see Dorothy's slippers." Sam paused, "But, you know what? I think if I have the courage to save the world, I might finally work up the courage to sing."

"Sing? You want to be a singer?"

Sam grinned self-deprecatingly. "I always wanted to be a blues singer, but I never had the nerve. I've been afraid of everything my entire life." She shrugged her shoulders, "But I'm feeling braver than I have in a really long time, and if yesterday has taught me anything, it's that I can't keep telling myself I have plenty of time."

"I think we can arrange that. Save the world, sing Karaoke and go to the Smithsonian. Sounds like a plan to me." Daniel rubbed his hands together in anticipation and said, "So how does breakfast sound? Are you hungry?"

Sam smiled sheepishly, "I'm starving. I never did get to eat my grilled ham and cheese sandwich and we skipped dinner, so breakfast sounds heavenly. What have you got?"

"I have the standard bacon and eggs, or I could make pancakes or waffles. What sounds good?"

"Hmmmmm, how about waffles and bacon? Does that sound good to you?"

Daniel turned away and started rummaging through the cupboards, pulling out bowls, a frying pan, the waffle iron and pancake mix. "I had breakfast earlier. I wasn't sure how long you would sleep," he was crouched down in the fridge and threw her a sexy grin over his shoulder, "and I was starving myself. What I wanted wasn't available, so I settled for food."

Sam blushed to the roots of her hair and the soles of her feet. He couldn't possibly have meant what she thought he did, but that sexy grin stayed on his face. She looked away. She had to, for her own sanity. "Oh."

At his laugh she blushed again, and then looked around her at the immaculate kitchen. There was not a single sign that he had eaten that morning. Not a dirty dish in the sink, not a crumb on the counter.

"Are you sure you ate?"

Daniel followed her gaze and shrugged. "I got a little obsessive about cleaning when I was going through my bad spell. It seemed like my environment here, in my own home, was the only thing I could control. I took that control a little far, and then it became a habit. I was used to things being clean and organized." He shrugged again, "Clutter bothers me now."

"Well, it's a good thing we're at your house instead of mine then."

"Packrat are you?"

"I wouldn't say so much a packrat as a downright slob. I usually notice that I need to go through my mail when it slides off the chair I throw it on. I try to control everything else and let my environment slide."

"That's okay, I'd clean up after you." He winked. "If that wouldn't bother you too much."

He'd winked at her - this was surreal - and talked about cleaning her house. "If you cleaned out the litter box this morning, I may be in love."

A full blown smile spread across his face. That smile she loved so much. And although his eyes had been squeezed into near nonexistence, she could still see the mischievous sparkle that emanated from them.

"What woman in her right mind could possibly resist a man who saves her life, cleans, cooks, *and* scoops poop." She hadn't thought it was possible, but his grin got bigger. "Good thing I'm not in my right mind."

Daniel rolled his eyes so hard that he rolled his whole head, one of his more endearing idiosyncrasies, but the smile remained on his face. "That is so not fair. Really, really not fair. And I'll get you for that."

Sam giggled again. She was flirting. She couldn't believe it. She wasn't sure she'd ever flirted before, but she was enjoying it. She felt like she was in a protected bubble in his apartment. Just the two of them and Chloe, and nothing else could touch them. She was safe, and she was secure, and she didn't need to be afraid. Though in the back of her mind, in a place she refused to acknowledge at this moment, she knew that when they left the apartment the fear would set in again.

As it turned out, he was a really great cook. The bacon was perfectly crispy, the waffle light, golden and delicious; and when she had soaked up the last drop of syrup with the last bit of bacon, he even washed her dishes. She really was afraid she was falling in love.

Oh, who the hell was she trying to kid? She'd been in love with him for over two decades and just the sound of his voice on the phone was enough to send it into full flame again.

She was so screwed.

Chapter 5

That secure little bubble burst the second Sam stepped outside. She felt exposed, vulnerable, and the memories of yesterday's eventful lunch slammed back into her brain, causing her still tender head to throb. Even with Daniel at her side, she felt like her coat had been transformed into a giant target. Perhaps she shouldn't have worn red, but it was the only coat she had with her. She expected a shot to ring out with every nervous and slightly shaky step she took, and its absence did not alleviate her anxiety, it only increased it.

It was a beautiful day for late December. The sun was shining and, though the air was crisp, it wasn't a biting cold. It was a day she would have enjoyed were it not for her current situation. She kept scanning the horizon for suspicious characters and was still doing so when they arrived at Daniel's car. She had been too distracted the day before to realize its classic nature. The man drove a twenty-year-old Mercedes, immaculately restored. "Wow, nice car."

Daniel smiled, helped her in, and circled around to his own door. "Thanks, I'm surprised you didn't notice it yesterday."

Sam snorted, "I had a few other things on my mind."

"Right, you were too distracted yelling at me and trying to claw my eyes out to take notice of my vehicle's vintage nature." She snorted again. "But I forgive you."

"I didn't know that you were a gear head."

Daniel laughed as he turned the key and the engine started to purr. "I'm not. But I am a liberty head." At Sam's confused look he remembered that she didn't follow politics. "This car was manufactured before the government required a GPS tracking system be installed in every car sold in America. The older cars were not grandfathered in. I didn't want to be tracked by the government, so I drive an old car. But just because it's an old car doesn't mean it can't be a nice car."

Sam's brow was furrowed in thought. "Is that what you were talking about yesterday with the GPS in my car?" Daniel nodded as he pulled out into traffic. "I didn't even know my car had a system like that installed. Obviously."

"For the most part, something like that is good. It makes it easier for the police to find and track criminals, making a usually thankless job easier, but it also allows you to be tracked by people other than the police, as long as those others have the right connections. As with so many other regulations that the government has imposed, this one was rife with opportunity for abuse, and considering who I had after me, I didn't want to be easily tracked."

"Totally understandable. I just wish I'd known that when I took off yesterday."

'There's not much you could have done about it unless you were willing to steal a car, and for some reason, I just can't seem to picture you doing that."

Sam heaved a big sigh. "No. I'd have no idea at all how to steal a car. I'm so unprepared for this." She looked at him questioningly. "Is it wrong to feel inadequate for not knowing how to steal a car?"

Daniel chuckled again, "Yes, you should be totally ashamed of yourself. What kind of scientist can you be if you don't know how to hotwire a car? I'm so disappointed in you."

"Okay, I get your point." In the brief silence, Sam picked up the music on the radio. The volume had been turned way down, but she could still hear that it was her favorite Christmas song. "Can you turn up the radio?"

Daniel complied without a thought, and was then taken aback as she began to sing along. The song was "Do You Hear What I Hear?". One of his favorites, and yet one that was difficult to find recorded. To him, it really spoke of the meaning of Christmas and usually made him tear up just a bit, and it was made only better, more haunting, with her smooth, clear voice. She really was a beautiful singer. He couldn't wait to get her out to Karaoke.

As much as he wanted to forget what was going on, to put it from his mind permanently, he couldn't. He was repeatedly checking the mirrors to see if they were being followed, and he was beginning to suspect that they were.

There was a dark sedan maintaining a position two car lengths behind them. They hadn't moved up close, and they hadn't made an attempt to attack, so he was maintaining a watch and wait pattern now, but he really didn't want to let Sam know. She had been so tense when they stepped outside, and the music had helped her to relax. He wanted to avoid making her tense back up again. At least not until it became imperative.

Daniel checked the rearview again as they pulled into the parking garage that served the office building in which his paper was housed. The car that had been following them, either by coincidence or design, continued on past, but Daniel's anxiety was not eased in the least. Once they had parked, he started around the car to open the door for Sam and found that she was already out. Obviously not a woman used to chivalry. He'd be sure to change that.

Sam smiled as she came around the car, simply saying, "Ready?"

"As I'll ever be."

The building was one of those ultra-modern monstrosities that Daniel had always hated, all glass and steel and no real character. He really missed the old styles of architecture where detail and decoration had been a requirement. He'd taken a vacation to Scotland years ago, when his career was still in existence, and what he had loved most was the architecture. Comparing the buildings in "Old Town" Edinburgh to this modern office building was like comparing a rainbow to a funnel cloud. However, this appeared to be what people wanted in a building. He guessed there was no accounting for taste or style because this building lacked both.

They progressed through the unimaginative lobby with the curved reception desk to the side, the shiny tile floor and tinted windows to the elevator. The offices for his paper were on the sixth floor and the trip in the elevator went pretty quickly. Daniel hadn't seen anybody coming in as they were waiting, but he still couldn't shake the pervasive feeling that they were being followed.

The elevator dinged and the two stepped out and headed to the unimaginative curved desk, a twin to that in the main lobby, of the sixth floor's reception area. The man behind the desk was young, well groomed, and well dressed in a pale pink shirt with a matching tie which served as a beautiful contrast to his caramel colored skin. He smiled as they approached and, very professionally, called the editor and advised that his appointment had arrived. When the conversation was completed, the receptionist -- or administrative assistant as he preferred to be called -- directed them down the hall.

Sam followed along in Daniel's wake as he led the way. In the meantime she was taking in the whole environment. She had expected the offices to be a bit sleazy since this was a tabloid, but she realized now that this was prejudicial. They were a business just like any other, and from what she could see, they looked like any other. There were rows of cubicles with people working on computers, talking on the phone, or doing both simultaneously. This was not an environment she'd ever worked in and she was surprised how much it looked like the movie, "Office Space". She finally understood why people found that movie so funny.

"They're at the address listed as the man's place of employment. He's a reporter and the paper he works for is here."

The commissioner made no immediate response, but finally replied, "A newspaper or a tabloid? It was my understanding he was a tabloid hack, not a reporter."

Andrea SanGiacomo was a founding member of the NACR and a licensed Private Investigator, and she didn't find the distinction listed by the commissioner in the least amusing. "He is a legitimate reporter who works for a tabloid as the result of being blackballed by the current Speaker of the House. He is an excellent reporter. But yes, the paper is a tabloid. What would you like me to do?"

The commissioner, from the safety of his plush chair, behind his shiny desk, in his beautiful home, made a decision that he was finding easier and easier to make. "Did you attach the portable GPS to Callahan's car?"

"Of course I did." Andrea really didn't like the power trip the commissioner had been on lately. He appeared to have forgotten that she had been a member of the NACR years before he joined.

The commissioner communicated his instructions. Disgusted with the decision, but bound to carry them out just the same, Andrea exited the car and entered the building.

Before Sam knew it they were at the editor's office, and he was an even bigger surprise to her. The only newspaper editors she'd been exposed to were in the movies, and this guy was no movie star. He was a short, Hispanic man with pocked skin, a receding hairline and a prominent chin. All of this was minimized, however, by his pleasing smile, and when he shook her hand, he had a comfortingly warm and strong grip.

"Hello, Daniel, so what is this story you have for me? A story so fascinating that you couldn't describe it over e-mail?"

Daniel smiled at this down-to-business attitude. It's what made his editor so good at his job and what kept this paper successful. Daniel had worked for a bad editor or two, and this one may have his quirks, but he knew his market, knew his readers, and knew how to give them what they wanted; and he didn't waste time. Daniel saw Sam seated and took the other chair for himself, and jumped right in to the issue at hand.

Joseph Ruiz leaned back in his chair and listened to the pitch. The fact that Callahan wanted to talk about it face to face was a pretty good indication that it wasn't worthy of print, but he'd give it a chance. Daniel was one of the best, if not *the* best, reporter he had, and Joe knew how to treat his employees; but the more he listened, the less he liked it.

"So basically what you're telling me is that there is a plot to attack some unknown congressman's genetic make-up? But we don't know who, we don't know when, we don't know where, and we don't know how?"

"And we don't know how many." Sam had chimed in.

Joe's brow furrowed with this one. "So there could be a plan to take them all out in one fell swoop?"

"That's actually the most probable scenario," Daniel replied. "This is a lot of research and trouble to go through for one single individual."

Joe leaned back in his chair, propped his left ankle on his right knee, and linked his fingers behind his head. He thought about this for a minute and then a truly beautiful grin spread across his face. "Can you imagine if we could get all of those idiots out of office and just start fresh? That would be so beautiful."

"So you'll print it?" Sam asked, pleased.

"Not a chance." At her look of disappointment -- Joe hated to disappoint women -- he continued. "As much as people would love to hear that Congress is going to get wiped out, eliminated, booted out on their collective asses, write their very last piece of legislation or go to that big fund raising party in the sky, there has to be a certain believability to the story, and this just doesn't have it." When Sam opened her mouth to speak up, he cut her off. "You may understand all of that scientific research, but my readers won't. They need something they can understand and believe. Say the members of Congress are aliens and they'll believe that, but their genetic make-up won't really matter."

Daniel had been afraid of this, and the disappointment displayed in every cell of Samantha was exactly what he had been the most afraid of. "Is there any way to tweak it so we can get the gist of it out there? We can't ignore that there is enough to this story to have somebody trying to kill Dr Mallard."

Joe thought about this for another few minutes, taking a measure of Dr Mallard while he did so. He couldn't imagine anybody actually trying to kill this woman, and he couldn't imagine either of these two lying to him about it. "I don't see how. I kicked around a few headlines in my head while you were talking, but it always comes back to the genetic aspect of it. Either that, or it will discredit Dr. Mallard," Joe smiled reassuringly, "and we don't want to do that." He sat up, spread his arms slightly, and shrugged. "I'm sorry. Really I am. But this is much more of a legitimate story than I can print. If we had more information as to who was being targeted, I'd run it in a heartbeat, but we're just missing too much information." Here he looked directly at Sam. "I really am sorry, Dr. Mallard."

Sam sighed. "That's okay, sir, we knew it was a long shot."

Joe became suddenly very serious, even more so than as an editor. "If this is true, and I know you believe it is, you should be taking this to Homeland Security instead of to me. I appreciate the opportunity, but they're the ones who really need to know."

Daniel grimaced. "I know, but I've been avoiding them. For many of the same reasons that you won't print it, but also ---"

"Because of your past." Joe finished for him. He knew what Daniel had been through and he understood his reluctance. "You know, Callahan, if this was to succeed, Sledgewater would be history. You know that bastard has the power gene. Are you sure you want to save him?"

Daniel smiled with little humor, "If Sammie weren't involved in this, I might let them face the consequences of their actions, but I'm not willing to let her pay for their mistakes."

"Well said, my boy." Joe looked back and forth between the two and realized that his days of being able to send Daniel anywhere at any time were quickly coming to an end. "I'll expect an invitation to the wedding."

They both looked so surprised, so nervous, and so guilty, both rushing to deny that there was anything going on, that Joe couldn't help but laugh.

"Whatever you say. Whatever you say."

As Daniel and Sam made their way out of the offices, each was self-conscious, and each adopted a false air of indifference to what the editor had said, yet neither was thinking of anything else. They were both silent as they waited for the elevator.

There were four elevators total, two were going down, one was coming up, and one was sitting at the floor just below. The one to the right opened before the other had left the fifth floor where it appeared to be stuck, and they walked in and pressed the button for the lobby. As the doors to their elevator were closing, they heard the doors to the other one open with a ding.

Andrea was pissed, to put it quite bluntly. The commissioner had ticked her off, as he seemed to do more and more -- condescending asshole that he was -- and then she'd entered the elevator and, just as the doors were closing, a woman with three children threw out her arm to stop them. So Andrea had to wait. Then the little girl had pushed the buttons for every single floor, grinning up at Andrea with pride. It took everything Andrea had in her not to pull out her gun and shoot the snot-nosed brat, and put at least one bullet in the mother who had only smiled apologetically at her.

She was beginning to believe that Dr Spock had ruined the country. That and people rushing to accuse parents who discipline their children of child abuse. As a result, people were so worried about wounding the child's tender little psyche that they didn't bother to turn them into decent human beings, and then they had the gall to question why we had a whole generation of badly behaved adults and even more badly behaved children. Andrea was pretty sure it was because they no longer got their hides tanned for inconsiderate behavior such as what she'd just been subjected to.

In opposition to the views of Dr Spock, Andrea had long believed that we should all have the right to beat other people's children. If the kid had it coming and the parents weren't going to do it, then somebody needed to step up to the plate.

It really was tempting to pull out her gun.

When they finally arrived at the fifth floor, the woman prepared to herd the kids to exit. Unfortunately she wasn't very successful, as one of the children began throwing a fit, screaming at the top of his lungs in this confined space, and pulling against his mother's desperate grip. The door started to close, and was then reopened three times before the little boy could be successfully pulled from the cabin. Andrea was really in the mood to kill somebody now.

When, at long last, she arrived on the sixth floor, Andrea pasted a smile on her face and approached the reception desk. At least it was a man sitting there. Had it been a woman, she might have killed her on principle alone.

Andrea asked after Callahan and Mallard and gritted her teeth when she found she'd missed them. When she was finished here she was going back to the fifth floor, hunting down that woman, and putting two between her eyes.

She found out where the editor's office was and, after a brief call, was told the editor was free to see her.

Joe Ruiz stood as the woman entered his office. She was tall for a female; about two inches taller than he was himself, with very close-cropped dull brown hair, pale skin, and dark eyes. She looked like one tough broad, but his manners extended to tough broads as well.

"Hello, Mr. Ruiz, I hope you don't mind if I get right to business."

"No, of course not. Prefer it myself."

Andrea tried to paste a pleasant smile on her face. Judging from the tension she saw build in the editor, she failed. "Did Dr. Mallard by any chance try to convince you to print an article on her genetic study?"

"Yes, she did. She thinks they're going to try to take out congressmen by attacking their genetic make-up. Can you imagine if that were true?"

Joe had smiled again at the thought, but the smile immediately left his face, along with all of his blood, when the woman pulled out a 9mm handgun fitted with a silencer. Then she smiled, a real smile, and replied, "Yes, I can."

Andrea pulled the trigger twice, watched him slump to the floor, and made her way back out of the office. Not one of the workers even looked up. They had no idea that their boss now lay dead behind his closed office door. She made her way back to the elevator and, when the doors opened, she turned, fired two shots into the receptionist, walked in the elevator and pressed five.

They made the trip back to the car in silence, but once back inside, Sam finally broke the silence.

"So what now? Any ideas."

Daniel turned the key, backed the car up, and headed out of the parking garage. "We go to Homeland Security. I don't see that we really have any other choice."

"Okay, I think you're right. We should at least give it a try. Do you know where the office is?"

Daniel turned to her and lifted one brow in a question.

"Oh, right. Washington Press Corps. Of course you know where it is."

"I've also lived here for years. Have you ever been here before?" He was going to be disappointed if she said yes and had never looked him up.

"No. I never seemed to have the time. I have always wanted to come," but the fact that he lived here was one of the reasons she hadn't; too afraid of bumping into him on the street. "But I just couldn't seem to get it done."

"All righty then. We'll take the scenic route. As you may have guessed, I'm in no hurry to be suspected of probable treason, so I'll show you the sights instead."

For the next hour and a half they drove through heavy traffic packed with tourists and locals alike, and Sam sat with her nose pressed to her window checking out the historical monuments, statues and tourist traps. When he pointed out the Supreme Court building, he laughed at her exclamation of "That's it?" It was laden with so much surprise and disappointment that he couldn't contain his amusement.

"I know. It looks way more impressive in the pictures and movies doesn't it? Could be something about it sitting right up on the street that gets you. Plus, it looks much bigger in the movies."

On the other hand, she loved the Washington Monument and the Lincoln Memorial so much that he looked forward to bringing her here when the cherry blossoms were in bloom. When the air was heavy with their scent and the loose petals were carried on the wind, turning the whole park into a pink fairy land. Yes, he'd have to show that to her.

Eventually, unable to put it off any longer, they made it to the Homeland Security offices on Maryland Avenue. He found a place for them to park, and then they walked the block or so to the building, which was only slightly less ugly than the one they'd just left.

Sam was almost to the door when she realized that Daniel was no longer next to her. When she turned, she found he was several steps back, staring at the building with a bleak expression. She walked back to him and put her hand on his arm. "Is it going to be that bad?"

Daniel sighed, "Probably. I noticed that the police had my file flagged, so it's a pretty good bet that Homeland Security will as well. I just don't know...."

"Why don't you wait out here, or in the lobby? I can do this. I'm the one whose data is being used anyway. I don't want to put you through this if I don't have to."

Daniel felt relieved and guilty all at the same time. "I don't want you to have to go through this on your own. I can put up with it."

"I hate to say this because I don't want to hurt your feelings, but I probably have a better chance without you."

Daniel grimaced, but he knew she was right. "I'll wait. This is way more important than my ego."

Sam reached up and laid her hand across his cheek, smiled into his eyes, and left him.

Daniel had never felt so useless in his life.

Chapter 6

Samantha pulled open the heavy glass doors and entered the building. She was dreading this encounter and couldn't deny that she would have felt better, braver, if Daniel had still been at her side, but they couldn't afford their message being tainted by any prejudice against his past.

Steeling her spine, Sam tried to walk confidently to the main desk. She didn't quite accomplish her goal, but the woman behind the desk was still helpful. She was very professionally and seriously dressed, and appeared required to leave any humor or other human emotion outside. After only a short wait, another woman, this one even more severely and soberly attired, came out to escort her through the secured doors and into the heart of the agency.

Stripping off her coat and taking a seat, Sam waited as the severe woman, Agent Deckerd, took her seat behind the desk and the interview began.

It started off badly and spiraled downhill from there. Agent Deckerd wasn't interested at all once she found out that Sam didn't know who was targeted. In fact, she started speaking to Sam as if she were a toddler, or a mental patient. Sam thought the latter was far more probable than the former.

Agent Deckerd leaned her elbows on her desk and set out to explain something to the overly imaginative woman before her. "We, as an agency, have neither the time nor the resources to focus on every conspiracy theory that crosses our desks. We must focus our limited resources on what we deem are credible threats and, unfortunately, your theory does not meet that requirement. With no indication of who the target might be, or how it will be executed, we cannot view this threat as credible."

Sam sighed, rose from her chair and scooped up her coat. She started to turn and leave, but then had another thought. "So if somebody knows there is an attack brewing, but they don't know the details, you won't even investigate?"

"As I said before, Ms. Mallard, we have very limited resources."

Sam looked at rows of people sitting behind top of the line desks, in top of the line chairs, facing state of the art computer systems, and knew that this was just one of many offices. "So even though this is a situation that could only be executed by a very few people in the country -- the ability to develop an agent to attack a specific genome isn't your everyday knowledge, you know -- you will not investigate it? Your resources are so limited that unless a private citizen does all of the leg work for you, you will take no action?" Agent Deckerd pursed her lips in disapproval, but Sam continued, "And how much exactly does your ineffectual agency charge the American people for taking no action on the threats they bring to your attention?"

Agent Deckerd opted not to answer, and instead just leveled a quelling stare. Sam was not quelled. As she turned again to walk away, she threw over her shoulder, "And that's Dr. Mallard. I have PhDs in both genetics and biotechnology. I have an excellent memory and I will be sure, once this attack is executed, to share your name as the person who deemed it lacking in credibility. Should be good for your career." And with that parting shot, she flounced off.

It really was a good thing that Daniel hadn't come in with her. Getting so little attention as it was, she wondered how bad it would have been if they were discredited even before they started speaking. It was getting more and more difficult for her to justify spending her time and energy attempting to protect a government this broken.

Daniel hadn't lasted long outside. What had started out as a beautiful day was taking a harsh turn. Clouds had rolled in and the wind had started to whip up, cutting straight through his leather jacket and right down to his bones. It took no time at all for him to decide that he'd be better off waiting for Sam in the car. He justified this by telling himself he could move the car to a place where he could see her when she came out, thereby alleviating his fear that he would be leaving her unprotected. Shoving his hands into his pockets and burrowing his face into his collar, he walked the two blocks back to the car. He was sure that Sam was not in any danger as long as she was inside the federal building. Attacking her there would be far too big of a risk, so she'd be safe. She really would.

So engrossed was he in the internal battle which pitted his own warmth against Sam's safety, that he almost walked straight into his own execution.

Andrea pulled up behind Daniel's car in the parking lot. Damn, she'd missed them again. She probably shouldn't have taken that detour to the fifth floor, but it had felt really good to find that woman and her three children and let them know just how much their lack of consideration for others had cost them. It was that thought keeping her warm as the wind picked up and blew the cold air under her hair and down the back of her neck.

It wasn't too late. She could still deal with this. She knew that the trip to the Department of Homeland Security would serve them nothing and add no risk to the NACR. Homeland Security was just as incompetent as every other government agency. The American people ended up paying a lot more and getting next to nothing for it. No, the Department of Homeland Security was not a threat. She was the only real threat out there right now, and she intended to be lethal.

Quickly scanning the area for opportunities, she found a rooftop that was perfect and, in no time at all, was perched atop it, her Weatherby TRR feeling light and easy in her hands. She had chosen this particular weapon precisely because it was light and easy to handle, and she'd become frighteningly accurate with it. There was something about the feel of it as the bullet burst out of the twenty-two inch barrel that made her feel powerful and alive. She got it propped just right, facing in the perfect direction, at just the right angle to be able to pick them off as they got in the car, and then realized her bracelet was in danger of tangling with the bolt throw mechanism -- and she was going to need that mechanism free. She lifted her hand and shook the bracelet farther down her arm and out of danger, put the cheek press in its natural position and lined up her sight. She had them now. Not even the cold wind, whistling as it blew furiously at this elevation, could get to her now.

It was the glint of the weak sun on metal that captured his attention. He had just started to round the corner of the building and head across the parking area when something caught his eye. He looked up and around, seeking the source, and spotted the gun barrel protruding over the roof edge, made bold against the white cloudy sky. Shit. They were tracking his car now. They had to be.

He hadn't seen anybody tracking them this time. No car at a safe distance. Nothing at all, and yet still they'd been found.

Daniel backed slowly away from the open space, avoiding any fast movement that might alert whoever it was behind that rifle, and backed behind the shelter of the building. They couldn't go back to the car. He knew that now. But where were they going to go from here? He headed back to the Homeland Security building and went inside to wait for Sam out of the cold, very glad that he hadn't decided to take this option initially.

As he pulled the doors open hard and rushed inside, his agitation had the woman at the reception desk on high alert, but he told her who he was waiting for and she relaxed, though only slightly.

It was twenty minutes later when Sam came out those doors in such a huff that she almost missed him. She was focused internally on her anger and irritation, and if Daniel had not stepped into her path just as she was about to head out the door ,she would have stormed right past him. The receptionist relaxed more when she saw the welcoming smile flit across the woman's face. That smile was quickly replaced with a question. Something was wrong, and it was more than the expected, and realized, disbelief of the government agency they were leaving. As soon as they exited the building, Sam's anxiety escalated as Daniel grabbed her arm and steered her in the opposite direction from the car.

"Where are we going?"

"The Smithsonian" popped out of Daniel's mouth before he had even finished the thought. It would be safe there, and they'd be out of the cold while they figured out what to do.

"Why do I have the sneaking suspicion we are not going there because you think I succeeded in saving the world?"

Daniel quickly explained the situation to her as they walked the several blocks to the Smithsonian complex. On their walk they passed many of the great bastions of what the country once represented. The trees, absent of any greenery, aptly reflected how their current situation compared to where they had been. If this country were a tree, its early years would have been full of green leaves and ripe fruit. Now it reflected only these barren branches; but he maintained hope and faith that the tree of the U.S. spirit, economy, freedom, and liberty would flourish, thrive, and bear fruit once again. They just needed the right leader.

When they arrived at the desired museum within the massive complex, Daniel prepared to just walk right on in as he had the last time he'd visited, but that had been years ago, when the museums were still free. They had been under Federal Government ownership for nearly three years, along with most other museums and all other parks in the nation.

City and state parks were all now considered federal land and any proceeds went to the Federal Government while the maintenance costs were absorbed by the state. Not surprisingly, the quality of the parks and museums had deteriorated. The Federal Government had made the argument that with the entrance fees added on to the current donations, the museums could help to fund the Promotion of Higher Education Act. Considering that museums promoted education, it was only right that their admissions should pay for the higher education that Congress had deemed a right to all.

Daniel had initially supported the idea of the government paying for college for all students, but as with any government program, the costs had skyrocketed, the quality of the education had plummeted, and fraud and abuse of the system was rampant. The schools no longer had to be competitive and the costs just continued to rise. Since neither students nor their parents were spending their own money for this education, the cost of it no longer mattered. When the program was found to cost three times what was estimated, Congress turned to the parks and museums as a source of revenue.

Eminent domain is what they had used to simply take over all of these places, and they had based the revenue gain on the current volume of visitors. It had never occurred to them, not even for a moment, that attendance for the Smithsonian would decline when it was no longer free. The admission fees had started out fairly low, but were periodically raised as the powers that be realized that revenue fell far below projected, while the cost of the new program continued to rise. So they'd adjust the ticket price, and even fewer people would go, and the revenue generated would drop even further.

Now it cost them eighty-four dollars each to enter the Smithsonian, and that was for a single museum. They could have purchased an all access pass for the low, low bargain price of two hundred forty-nine bucks. What a deal.

Not having enough cash on them for even the single museum, they were forced to use Daniel's credit card. They knew they could not use Sam's, for it would surely have been tracked. By using Daniel's they at least had some chance that their whereabouts would not be identified and tracked, though Daniel didn't hold out much hope.

They had entered the museum from the National Mall, which put them on the second floor, and as soon as they entered they could see the Star Spangled Banner on display. An early flag, dirty, tattered and worn, and yet it remained a symbol of hope. It was the very same flag which had inspired the writing of the poem that would become the national anthem; written back when the flag still meant something to the people; when it could still inspire hope; and when it still meant freedom from tyranny and oppression. It showed so eloquently just what the country had been through, and what it was going through still.

Looking at that flag laid out in its climate-controlled, hermetically sealed enclosure, Sam felt the tears well up in her eyes. "The land of the free and the home of the brave. Are we really?" she asked. Were they still the home of the brave? She didn't feel very brave.

"Judging by the crowd surrounding that flag, maybe we are," Daniel replied.

Maybe there were enough Americans left who craved that freedom and were brave enough to fight for it. One could only hope and pray.

They walked on through the doors and Sam was even further overwhelmed with the great, white expanse of the museum before her. Not sure which way to go, she instinctively turned right and did her best to take it all in.

As nervous and edgy as she was, Sam still managed to enjoy herself as they made their way through everything they could in this massive, expansive museum. They had chosen the National Museum of American History; first, because it was actually the museum that housed Dorothy's slippers; but second, because it just seemed appropriate for their current situation. A reminder of what they were trying to save.

No matter how far the current leaders had strayed from the founding principles, those principles were still in the hearts and minds of the American citizenry. And one day, they would be restored. However, if this attack was allowed to succeed, there was no telling the chaos the country would be thrown into, and what it would resemble when it re-emerged.

Without Congress, the most powerful of all branches of government, the country would, in effect, have no government at all. And who would rise up to lead in that case? Would they be better or worse than those who had gone before? There was just no way to know for sure.

Even though she jumped in fear every time she was bumped by the crowd, and even though she kept looking over her shoulder to see if somebody was staring at her a bit too intently, she still managed to enjoy the museum. Once they had seen Jimmy Hendrix's guitar, replicas of the American Revolution uniforms, listened to the speeches on the civil rights movements, and finally saw Dorothy's ruby slippers, she and Daniel both knew they couldn't put this discussion off any longer. They had to figure out where to go next, and they still had to find a way to get the story out to the public.

It had been a long day already, and the waffle and bacon, as satisfying as they had been, were long gone. They were on the first floor, at Julia Child's kitchen when thoughts of food came immediately to mind. There was a small café here, so they decided to get some lunch and make a plan. This time Sam opted for some good old American barbeque, while Daniel ordered a pizza.

Sam dug into her food without thought of the mess she was making of herself with the barbeque sauce. When her hunger was abated, though not fully satisfied, she said, "So what do we do now? What's our next option?"

Daniel wiped the tomato sauce off of his chin, crumpled up the napkin, and grinned at the way Sam was devouring her barbeque. "I think our last hope is FNB News. The major newspapers and other news networks are so far up the government's ass, they wouldn't print anything that would show them in a negative light. Even though they would portray the plotters as crazy terrorists, it would still look bad for the leadership that somebody was so unhappy with their performance that they wanted to take them out. There are only two venues left open for the support and protection of the American principles. That is FNB News, which has survived against all attempts to bury it, probably to maintain the appearance of free speech and freedom of the press, and the blogosphere."

Sam perked up. "Do you know anybody in the blogosphere?"

"Unfortunately, no. I used to know some bloggers, but they were silenced in much the same way I was."

"Oh." Sam was getting more depressed the more she learned. Where had she been for the last several years? Encased in her own little cocoon, insulated from the outside world. Her work subsisted on government grants, but it was someone else who did all the work of requesting them and had the real interface with the government. All Sam had ever dealt with was the scientific side of it.

In this particular case, the scientific side of it was what they needed. "I guess if that doesn't work, I can always call my father."

The reluctance in her tone was evident. "I take it you really don't want to do that."

"No. I thought about calling him this morning, at least to see if we could find out who would have that kind of capability. I'd rather avoid it if at all possible, but my meeting with Homeland Security only reinforced the thought."

"So, what is it with you and your Dad?" The few times Daniel had met him, the man had appeared distant, and inconvenienced by his daughter. Daniel hadn't liked the man at all, more because of how he appeared to make Sammie feel about herself than because of his actual personality.

"Well, to begin with," Sam replied, "I'm a girl."

"I noticed that," Daniel replied with a slightly lecherous grin. "So since you can't pee standing up, you were automatically at a disadvantage?"

"Pretty much, although it goes much farther than that. My mom left us when I was really young, and I always got the feeling that he blamed me for that, maybe not so much for her leaving, but for her leaving him responsible for me. He couldn't be bothered really. The only thing he was interested in was whether or not I could carry on his genetic legacy. I was always afraid that if I didn't do things good enough, if I wasn't smart enough, if I didn't follow the path he laid out for me, that he would leave me, too."

Sam raised her gaze, hoping not to see sympathy there -- she hated to feel pathetic -- but what she found was that he wasn't looking at her at all. She was baring her soul to him and he wasn't even listening. He was staring out the window instead.

Andrea was freezing her ass off and she was now way beyond the realm of pissed and was knocking at the door of livid. She'd been on the rooftop for two hours now, in the cold and the wind, and it was starting to snow. She had begun to suspect that they had abandoned the car, and she couldn't ignore that hunch anymore. They must have spotted her, but she had no idea how that could have happened. Had she been smart, she would have brought her computer to this rooftop with her, but she hadn't been smart, she'd been cocky.

Packing up her rifle and stomping around to put the feeling back in not just her feet but her entire body, she let fly with some creative expletives. She strung these together in ways that it was possible nobody had ever tried before. At first she thought she was going to have to call the commissioner and tell him that she'd failed – again --but then decided that she would find them first. Depending on where they were, she might still be able to get them and avoid that call. And that was one call she was going to do everything in her power to avoid.

Tromping down the stairs and back to her car, she called herself every kind of stupid there was. There was no way that these two incompetent amateurs should have been able to escape her twice. Twice! She was a PI, but she had also been a Marine and a cop. She knew her stuff.

Somebody had to be helping these two. She was sure of that.

Back in her car, she turned the key and let the heat blast. She booted up the computer and let her fingers start flying over the keys. She entered the files for the credit card information that she had; an illegal, but very handy skill. She first ran the check on the woman's credit cards, but consistent with her previous checks, there had been no activity for days. Next, she ran the man's cards. On the third one she got a hit.

The card had been used for entry to the Smithsonian. She laughed to herself. How ironic that she now had that expansion of the Federal Government, that thing she was fighting so hard against, to thank for being able to track her prey. Had they not taken over the museum and started charging admission, she'd have no idea where the man and woman had gone. They'd have disappeared.

She was going to kill them slowly. They had put her to too much trouble to allow them a quick and painless death. Perhaps a shot to the knee to immobilize them, and then a shot to the gut. Those belly wounds took forever to kill you. Lost in the glorious fantasy of her prey laid out before her, bloody and dying, Andrea threw the car into reverse, backed out of her parking space, and took off for the Smithsonian with no regard at all for the speed limits.

She wasted precious time searching for a space, but finally located a place to park. She had to steal it from somebody who had been patiently waiting, but she felt no guilt over that and gave no acknowledgement to their honking protest.

She hated how this city was so unfriendly to drivers, some of that government behavior modification that they touted as climate change legislation. She left her evil gas guzzling vehicle in the lot and walked the few blocks down Constitution Avenue to the museum. The snow was still falling, melting as soon as it landed on her, sending rivulets of water down her face and her neck. She pulled the coat closer around her, but was careful not to pull it so tight that she couldn't easily reach the trusty 9mm in its holster, or the six inch serrated blade secured in a holster of its own.

She walked along Constitution Avenue with the massive museum on her right. Though beautiful in the sunshine, in today's cloud cover and snow, the stone seemed to absorb and reflect the gray sky above. She found this appropriate, as it was going to be a very dark day indeed for Dr. Samantha Mallard and Mr. Daniel Callahan.

As she turned onto the walk leading up to the wide museum entrance, she told herself that the hardest part was going to be finding them in the mass of people inside one of the most visited tourist attractions in the city, if not the country. Even the walkway was cluttered with people.

She didn't much care for people.

Andrea immediately started scanning the crowds going in and coming out, taking in everything. This was where her training really came into play - the honed ability to scan, really see, and catalogue all at the same time. To notice every little thing and determine how it can lead her to her prey.

She got lucky. Oh, so lucky. She thanked God, or whatever power there was, who made it a cloudy day, for there, on the opposite side of a window, a window made perfectly clear due to the gray outside and the bright light within, sat her prey; toasty warm and having lunch. Oh, she was going to enjoy killing them. She flipped her coat back and reached for her gun.

"Are you listening to me?" Sam was decidedly put out. Here she was pouring out her heart, baring her soul, talking about her father, which she hated to do, and Daniel wasn't even listening.

He didn't answer.

She opened her mouth to make a second attempt to gain his attention, but she didn't get a chance. Daniel half stood, half crouched, reached with his right hand across the table and grabbed it by its left side. He gave the table a heave that sent it toppling between them and the window, sending the remains of their lunch flying. At the same time he was yelling to the whole café, "Get down!"

The sounds of panic, of screaming people and pounding feet, could not mask the pop, pop, pop of the gunfire. The placement of the toppled table gave them some protection, but not much, and it wouldn't last for long. The underside was already beginning to splinter under the impact of the bullets that thudded into it.

Daniel reached up and snatched their coats from the backs of their chairs and started crawling out of the café, keeping low to use whatever small amount of protection there was. He assumed Samantha would follow him, and he wasn't wrong.

Sam crawled along the floor now riddled with spilled soda, plastic forks, half eaten sandwiches, and coleslaw. "This is disgusting," she mumbled to herself. Her hand landed in a pile of baked beans and slid out from under her, causing her to falter. She looked around momentarily for something to wipe her hand on, but a new barrage of gunfire brought her back to her senses.

She had lost Daniel in the crowd of pounding feet and was seeking him with growing desperation, when a man suddenly fell before her. She thought at first that he had slipped in the mess as well, but the blood pulsing from the wound on his neck and pooling on the floor beside him showed her differently.

She crawled faster, now disregarding the mess and trying her best to find Daniel again. Then she saw a flash of red, her coat clasped in Daniels hand up ahead, he was turning, and she hurried to follow before she lost him for good. She caught up to him again in Julia Child's kitchen as he reached out to pull her in, then they both hunkered down behind the wall of hanging pots and pans. The kitchen offered them some shelter, but not much, and probably not for long.

Andrea couldn't believe she had missed. She had caught the man's eye at the last second, just as she was pulling her gun free. She still managed to get off her shots, but he had reacted a little too quickly.

She really didn't like him at all.

Picking up speed, she ran into the museum. Pushing the panicking people aside, she continued to fire into the café, unconcerned as to how many innocent people were killed. Collateral damage in any war was to be expected. These people should be grateful to die for such a noble cause, and she was tempted to kill even more of them just to thin the crowd so she could locate her prey. Then she caught a glimpse of a red coat being dragged on the floor and around a corner, and trailing behind that coat was Dr. Mallard. Andrea aimed low and squeezed, but her leg was bumped by a running child and her shot went high. A man dropped, but the woman scrambled on.

Andrea continued to shove people aside with ever-increasing force in her attempt to get to the man and woman, but too many of those people didn't realize that she was the threat - proof positive of just how oblivious the American people had become. She raised her gaze to the escalator, but she didn't really think they'd try that. There was too much exposure, too little cover.

As her eyes were raised, two men decided to take advantage of her distraction and attempt to be heroes. She caught their movement out of her peripheral vision and quickly turned and fired. The first one was almost upon her, and when she hit him square in the chest he fell forward, throwing her off balance. She was still struggling to throw off the near dead weight -- he was still gurgling -- when the second man rushed her. She couldn't raise her arm to fire, so opted instead to slow him down. The bullet shattered his tibia and he went down hard, his momentum causing him to slide on the polished tile floor. Andrea stumbled as he came to rest against her.

The man was still determined to bring her down, to save the people in the museum, so he wrapped one arm around her leg and used the other to pull on her coat in an attempt to get to her gun hand and pull her to the floor.

Andrea was having none of that. Finally shoving the now dead man to the side, she raised her free leg and brought it down hard on the man's face. Blood splattered from his nose and she felt the cartilage give way beneath her boot. This was so much more satisfying than a bullet, but still he held on. The man was determined, she had to give him that, but she couldn't be further detained. She had to find the man and woman and end this once and for all. She was absolutely *not* going to call the commissioner and tell him she'd failed. She was not.

Another few well placed kicks and she was free. She made her way through the passage between the rest rooms into the west side exhibition area. Since they hadn't taken the stairs or the escalator, they had to be in one of these exhibits, and each had only one entrance. She had them now, all she needed was patience.

She entered the first, gun out in front of her, and turned from side to side just as she'd been trained. This exhibit was nothing but a bunch of book illustrations lining the walls. No place to hide here. She cast her gaze over the people huddled against the walls in fear, there were two security guards with their ineffectual tasers, but none of the others were her prey. She continued through to the next exhibition, but this one was just a bunch of old books and more frightened people.

Making her way back out of these exhibits, Andrea kept the gun trained on those who had sought shelter there, discouraging any potential heroic attempt, but these people just whimpered, cowered, and held tight to one another. There were no heroes here, just weak people, weak people who had abdicated their power to the politicians; the people who were ultimately responsible for the mess the country was in. She wished she had enough bullets to take out every last one of them, but alas, she had neither the ammunition nor the time. Once back out in the hall, she moved on to the next exhibit, and the next, and the next.

Chapter 7

Sam had heard the shots and wanted to leave their hiding place. She rose to do just that, but Daniel pulled her back down. "She's killing those people to get to me. To get to us. How can we let that happen?"

Daniel did not lessen his grip, but grabbed her shoulders and forced her to meet his gaze. "And if we go out there and let her kill us, then what? What will happen to the other people she's planning to kill? What will happen if they really are going to wipe out Congress? What will happen to these people when there is no government at all?"

"But --- "

"I know, Sammie. I don't want to wait here either, but we have to think about the bigger picture. We have to get the information out there. That's the most important thing. We're not protecting ourselves here, we're protecting the information."

Daniel looked around, taking in their situation, "But we're also sitting ducks here. There's no way out, and if she comes in here we're dead anyway." Daniel shifted and the pots and pans clanked behind him. He reached up to steady them; they couldn't risk the noise giving them away. One pan came loose of its hook and he caught it before it hit the floor with a resounding clatter. He met his own accusing glare in the reflection of the bright copper pan in his hand. The expression changed first to fear and then into one of dawning hope.

Daniel scanned the wall for another pan, a heavier pan, and his eyes finally found what they were searching for, a large, heavy iron skillet. Carefully he removed this from the pegboard wall, and slowly, silently, crab walked back over to the entrance. He felt frighteningly exposed, but there was no other option, this was their only chance. They couldn't just sit there and wait to be shot. Even hidden as they had been in the corner created by the stove wall, she would have eventually found them, and they'd have been dead soon after.

The copper saucepan was extended out with the shiny surface facing at an angle to reflect the hallway, and anyone in it. He could see her coming. She was doing what he feared most, methodically entering each exhibit and searching. They could seize an opportunity while she was in one of those rooms and run for it, but he didn't know how long she'd be in any single exhibit room. Validating this concern, she stayed in the current exhibit only a matter of seconds. He couldn't remember which one it was, but there must not have been many places to search.

They might be next. The entrance to the exhibit where they hid was directly across from the next exhibit in her line. It all depended on which way she turned.

The rounded edge of the copper pan distorted the image of the assassin, the gun expanded and the barrel elongated making the weapon look even more sinister than when it had been pulled from under her coat and pointed right at them.

The assassin was inching down the hall, her back pressed against the outside barrier of the exhibit in which Daniel and Samantha were concealed. Every few seconds she would look back and scan the building, and then return her focus to the front, verifying that they were not sneaking out and away behind her. His plan, as flawed as it might be, was their only chance at survival and escape, so he sent up a silent prayer to God and Julia Child for their help and support. They would need all they could get.

The prayers were answered, the woman moved away from the wall, training the gun at the doorway to the exhibit opposite them. As she stepped toward it, Daniel slowly straightened his legs until he reached his full height. Still using the copper pan as a mirror, he waited until she was nearly in the doorway, and then he stepped out, the copper pan slipping from his sweaty grasp and landing with the loud and resounding clatter on the hard tile floor.

Andrea had just stepped into a doorway and through a portal into Science of the Past, when she heard the cacophony of sound behind her. She pivoted on the balls of her feet and turned at lightning speed, pulling the trigger as she went. Bullets thudded into and through the wall of the exhibit, causing pans to crash to the floor on the other side. As she made the last bit of the turn to face her target, a blinding pain shot up her arm causing her to drop the gun, sending it skidding on the polished tile.

Daniel brought the iron skillet down with as much force as he could muster and when the gun was thrown from her hands and slid out of reach, he raised the skillet again. With both hands around the handle, he pulled it back as far as he could and swung like Babe Ruth going for a homer. The woman dodged, but not fast enough, causing the skillet to deliver a glancing blow to her forehead, dropping her to her knees, but unfortunately she was still conscious, still able to fight. He raised the skillet again, preparing to bring it down hard and fast on the top of her head, when a gunshot rang out and the woman's head jerked back, her body flopping lifelessly to the floor.

Andrea's last thought was that at least she would not have to make that call to the commissioner.

Daniel looked up in shock to find Samantha on her knees, the gun still clutched in her shaking hands, her finger still on the trigger. Her eyes were huge with fear and shock, but they didn't have time for comfort right now.

All Daniel could think about were the two people at the diner. Two people. This woman was probably not alone either, and they needed to get out and away before the other one came looking.

Sam stumbled along behind him, tripping over her feet as they ran up the stairs to the second floor and back out the exit to the National Mall. She paid no attention to where they were going. She didn't see the people along the walk as they rushed past, nor the trees or monuments. She didn't notice when Daniel took the gun from her hand and threw it in the reflecting pool, and she didn't feel the cold. She'd shot somebody. She'd been shot, and also shot another, all in the course of two days. What had happened to her life? She could have let Daniel smash that woman's head with the frying pan, but there was no guarantee that would have disabled her.

The woman had been going for the knife at her side, and she didn't want that woman to be able to hurt Daniel, or to hurt anybody else ever again. After finding Daniel again after all of these years, there was no way she was going to give him up to some psychotic bitch with a bad haircut -- no matter how big her gun was.

Sam returned to her senses as Daniel pulled her down some steps out of the weak light of the cloudy day into a dreary, dungeon darkness. Into a place of stale air and loud, echoing noises, when all she really wanted was peace.

Daniel reached into his pocket and pulled out his Metro pass, ran it through the machine, walked through the now open barrier and handed it over to Sam. She took it and looked at it blankly for a minute and then with stiff, robotic movement, copied his motion. Not until they were both on the other side of that barrier did Daniel relax even the slightest bit, but they were still far from safety. They needed to get the hell out of Washington and they needed to do it now.

It was becoming obvious that they could track them both by his car, which really ticked him off, and through his credit cards. He'd been afraid of that, but thought it worth the risk. He'd been wrong. Everything was far too expensive now to be able to carry enough cash for their expenses. They needed money; they needed a friend with money. Lots of it.

Suddenly he knew exactly where they'd go next.

By the time Sam came fully back to her senses, she was seated on the subway going she knew not where. She turned her head and saw that Daniel, his shoulders stiff with tension, was facing precisely forward. In an effort to ease that tension, she reached out and laid a hand on his knee. "Are you okay?"

Daniel released the breath he hadn't known he'd been holding, reached out his arm and pulled her in a close tight hug. He whispered into her hair, "I was so frightened for you. You were so closed off, so distant. You scared me so much." He released her, placed his hands on her shoulders, and held her while leaning in until their noses nearly touched. "Don't you ever do that to me again. Do you hear me, woman?"

Sam couldn't help but smile at that tone. Aggrieved and relieved all together, made even rougher by the slight accent. She just loved how he pronounced the word woman. "Yes, sir. I hear and I understand."

Daniel sighed and then pulled her in again for another hug, this one quicker and less desperate, though some desperation remained.

"So where are we headed?"

"To Union Station right now, and then I think a train to New York City. We should be able to catch one, but we're going to have to pay with the credit card again. We'll have to ditch those completely once we get to New York." Daniel gave her a long look. "This means that we need to go to somebody with money."

"Sawyer."

Daniel looked surprised, "Sawyer?"

"Yes, you remember Sawyer from high school, don't you? Sawyer Wayne Bellingham?"

This is exactly whom Daniel had been thinking of as well, so it knocked him back on his heels for a moment. "You've been in touch with Sawyer?"

Sam smiled, "Sure. He's one of the few people from school whom I remember fondly. You, of course, being one of those as well. He lives in New York now, has pretty much since graduation. He's got a house in the East Village."

"I know."

Sam cocked her head, "What do you mean, you know?"

Daniel grinned, "Sawyer was where I was planning to go. I've been in touch with him, too."

Of course Sam knew this, because Sawyer had been her source of information on Daniel over the years. However, she didn't want Daniel to know she'd been checking up on him. She hadn't realized that Daniel and Sawyer had stayed in such close contact. Sam herself had gone to visit Sawyer several times over the years. On her last trip they'd seen Mamma Mia on Broadway, and had the very best time singing along from the audience and dancing at the curtain call. Sam wasn't much of a dancer, but she did love ABBA and wasn't afraid to belt it out.

Sawyer was the perfect person for them to run to because: one, he had lots and lots of money; two, he was very generous with that money; three, he was a force to be reckoned with and would not be put off by attempted executions; and, finally, he was great company and tons of fun. He was everything they needed right now, and Sam was really looking forward to seeing him again.

"Now all we have to do," Daniel continued, "is get to him."

They rode the subway in companionable silence until they arrived at the Union Station stop. Sam was more than ready to get back above ground. She'd seen enough ugliness today, and the Washington Metro system was not a pretty sight. There were big recessed squares on the walls and ceilings, for soundproofing she was pretty sure, but they weren't very pretty. No attempt was made to make this appear as anything other than an underground. For all of the encouragement they gave the people to use it, they could have at least tried to make it more aesthetically pleasing.

Years ago, Sam had taken the Underground on a trip to London and noticed that many of the stations had tiles painted with historical events or even just beautiful pictures. But, this was Washington after all, and they would encourage you only with words to do what they thought you should; if that didn't work, they'd use regulations and legislation to make it too expensive for you to do anything else. Actually changing anything to make you want to do something, without that financial incentive, was not to be considered.

Daniel and Sam opted for the stairs instead of the escalator for the freedom of movement. Though by the time they reached the top, Sam was so out of breath, she wished she had opted for the confines of the escalator.

Finally she was out of the dungeon and stepping into the breathtaking beauty of Union Station. This was a building from back when train stations were as much form as function, before they changed them to squat, cinder block buildings with no style at all. From a time when taking the train was an event and an adventure. From a time before the government takeover and their monopoly of the passenger train system drove it straight into the shitter.

Union Station was a work of art. The arched ceilings with the circular insets, rising from wide, detailed doors with an arched window above created a spectacle her eyes could not resist. The tile floor reflected the same theme as the ceiling above, lending a beauty in every direction. The attention to detail given in the design and maintenance of this building made it a true national treasure and Sam wished that they still built stations like this. She might be more apt to ride the train if she could depart from and arrive in a place of such beauty.

But they weren't here for the view, no matter how lovely she found it. They needed to purchase tickets for any train that would stop in New York. One that continued past the city would actually be best. Their luck was still with them, as it turned out. The Northeast line ran from Newport News, Virginia, up to Boston and there was one leaving in roughly half an hour.

Daniel debated whether or not to buy the tickets now or wait until the last minute, but he feared that if he waited, either the tickets would sell out or they'd miss it. Conversely, he was also afraid if he bought them now, his card would be tracked again and a new assassin would be here before the train left the station.

He ended up compromising and waiting only ten minutes. This left them just enough time to get to the train platform, but not enough time for the assassin to get to them, unless they were already outside the doors of Union Station; Daniel didn't even want to think about that possibility.

Neither of them relaxed until they were safely seated on the train for the long trip to New York and the train was actually in motion. It was not a terribly scenic route; they didn't pass through the loveliest parts of the cities, so even though Sam began the trip by staring out the window, it wasn't long before she started to doze. It had been a long and trying day after all.

Daniel pulled her head from where it had come to rest against the window, bumping against the glass as the train rattled and rocked down the track, and laid it on his shoulder instead. In her sleep she sighed, rubbed her nose into his jacket, raised one hand up to curl against his chest, and settled into a heavy slumber.

It was a four-hour ride, stopping several places along the way, and Daniel let her sleep through it all. His legs began to cramp from inactivity and he really needed to use the men's room, but he didn't want to wake her, so he simply stroked her hair and let her sleep.

The commissioner was becoming impatient. SanGiacomo was supposed to have called hours ago with the confirmation that the targets had been removed, but he was still waiting for that call. He knew Dr. Mallard to be a timid scientist who lived her life in a lab because she was incapable of functioning in the outside world. How, then, could she be eluding the people he had sent after her? It had to be that Callahan character helping her, but he was a tabloid reporter, not a Navy SEAL; how could he be of any real assistance? The commissioner had thoroughly investigated his background in the last few hours, and the man had no skills in combat or evasion. The commissioner was totally baffled as to how this was happening. It was completely illogical, totally improbable.

Edward Jackson knocked on the office door and entered. He had a rather sick expression on his round face which did not bode well for the situation.

"Did you make contact with SanGiacomo?"

Edward grimaced, he wasn't looking forward to communicating this bit of information. "No, I was unable to speak with her."

The commissioner jumped up from his desk and stalked forward, the vein in his temple pulsing in his agitation. "I asked you to do one simple thing and you can't even do that? Why are you back in this office wasting my time if you did not do the one thing I directed you to do? Why?"

Edward cleared his throat and reminded himself to start apartment hunting. "I called her phone as you asked, and…well….you see, sir…."

"Just spit it out Jackson. What happened?" The commissioner was beginning to think he was surrounded by idiots. It appeared that even his simplest requests could no longer be executed. How were they going to succeed with the ultimate goal if they couldn't even make a phone call, and still Jackson stammered.

"Tell me! Now!"

"A police officer answered her phone." Edward rushed out. He then slowed his speech and continued, "When I called, her phone was answered by an officer with the Washington, D.C., Police Department. He asked how I was connected with the owner of the phone and what I knew about her actions of the day; he then informed me that she was dead." Edward gave the commissioner a moment to absorb this information. "The officer indicated that she had entered the Smithsonian American History Museum and opened fire on museum patrons, but was apparently taken down by a few of the museum goers and, it appears, eventually shot with her own weapon."

"Damn! Damn, damn, damn, damn, damn!" The commissioner paced his expansive and well-appointed office in agitation. "What did you tell them?"

"Sir?"

"You said they wanted to know how you knew her. What did you tell them?" This last was said slowly and precisely through clenched teeth.

"I told him that I had been given her name by a friend and that I had called to hire her. He asked for what specifically and I told him that it was a private matter, and as I would not be hiring her, none of his business."

The commissioner exhaled in relief. Maybe his staff wasn't as stupid as he had first thought. "Good. Well done."

Edward exhaled in relief. He was afraid that the commissioner was going to literally implode, but they always knew that the ultimate goal wasn't going to be easy. It was the Dr. Mallard situation that was causing all of the stress, but Edward was ashamedly relieved that Dr. Mallard had escaped again. He truly believed that killing her was wrong, and went against the principles the organization was supposed to support and encourage. However, just as Edward was about to relax, the commissioner refocused.

"So where is Dr. Mallard now? We need to have another team assigned to her."

Edward made a conscious effort not to fidget. Judging by the expression on the commissioner's face, he failed in that effort. "We don't know exactly where she is." He rushed to continue before the volcanic eruption preparing to spew forth from the commissioner was able to build up to full steam. "According to Callahan's credit card company, two train tickets to Boston were purchased, but we have no verification that they actually boarded the train."

"If they bought the tickets, why wouldn't they board the train? Send a team to Boston."

"Yes, sir, but I also believe that, due to SanGiacomo tracking them to the Smithsonian, they will at least suspect that we can track their cards. Therefore, they may have purchased the tickets as a decoy. It is just a theory, but based on how they have managed to elude or escape so far, it is something which should be considered."

"So if they aren't on their way to Boston, where would they be?" The commissioner raised his brows in question. "Any other ideas, or are you suggesting we throw up our hands in defeat?" When Edward made no response, the commissioner continued with a flat order. "Send a team to Boston."

Edward nodded and turned to leave, but he didn't get far.

"How are the plans for the pilot going?" the commissioner asked.

Edward slowly turned back around to face the commissioner; a man who sat in comfort and splendor and issued directives for others to carry out. A man who ordered others into danger while sitting safely at home in silk pajamas with a cut crystal cocktail glass filled with 18-year-old Glenlivit whiskey, the man who had become the leader solely because he was the man with the big idea -- the idea for the ultimate goal. That goal, and its execution, had transformed into an excuse to take over and run every aspect of the organization.

Initially Edward had been dazzled by his brilliance, but the glitter had started to fade, and Edward now saw that he'd been duped by the sparkle. He was akin to a miner with a pan full of iron sulfide, suddenly realizing that what he had been driven to seek so furiously, was nothing but fool's gold. Now Edward knew what he had, but was in the mine too deep and could not find a way out, and there was still the cause that he believed in so deeply, with all of his heart and soul. What he no longer believed in was the leader. The man still commanded the admiration and loyalty of the other members of the organization, but then again, those members didn't live with him day in and day out, and those other members hadn't watched him change.

The commissioner had slowly transformed from a man who accepted the responsibility of leadership, to a man who reveled in it. A man who would not, could not, be dissuaded from the path he had chosen for the event; which meant that he wasn't going to like what Edward had to say next.

"The pilot has all the pieces in place and is ready to go."

"But?" the commissioner asked. "I hear a but coming here."

"Pamela doesn't think the chosen target will be impacted." Edward held his breath.

"That woman is the perfect example of what's wrong. She stands up there, always bringing the focus of attention to herself, and talks about what a great country we are and how we need to fight for it, and then she does whatever she wants without regard for the people."

"But, sir, she has the voting record most compatible with our own beliefs. Are you sure she is the right subject for the pilot? What if it really won't impact her? How will we know if it works and what will we do for the organization of the culminating event?"

"It will work." The commissioner's tone brooked no argument. He had made up his mind. He walked over to Edward, standing so close that he made the shorter man uncomfortable, which was, of course, his intent. Invading the other man's personal space, towering over him, gave the commissioner the advantage in the conversation. "Tell Pamela that she *will* run the pilot. We are not dropping this now. We don't have time to set up another plan and I am not going into full attack mode without a test run and the perfect venue."

"But, sir, with all due respect, what will we do if it doesn't affect her? Do we assume she is one of the immune and attempt another target, or do we start over?"

The commissioner began pacing again. His hands locked behind his back and his head down, he took large sweeping steps around the spacious room. Maybe he had chosen the wrong target, but with a nickname like "the terrorist" how could it be wrong? There was another he would have preferred, but the target required a female aide, and his most desired target was a misogynist who allowed no women on his staff. Not officially, of course, because that would be discrimination and therefore illegal, but this was the man who knew his way around every law. This would work. It had to work. He was sure it would work. Sort of.

He couldn't believe how things were falling apart around him. He'd worked so many hours for so many years to see this happen. He knew this plan could work, but nothing was going according to schedule or according to his meticulous plan. Samantha was still out there and now she had help. Two of his people had perished in that attempt. Another had been added to the ranks of the corrupted, and he was beginning to fear that Edward was wavering. He just didn't know what he would do if Edward left. He couldn't do all the tasks that Edward performed, not without assistance, and it would take far too long to bring another person up to speed. He didn't have that kind of time.

The commissioner rubbed his hands over his face in frustration. Recognizing now how valuable Edward really was, he had to be more careful how he spoke to him. The last two days he had not been kind, and he needed to change that. Otherwise he would be made impotent and another would take over the leadership. It was his idea and he *would* get the credit. Not some backup schmuck who came in at the last moment and stole all the glory.

"Edward, I understand what you're saying, and I know your concern, but we have very little time. Congress is going to be leaving for their winter break in just four days. With the bills that are on the docket I do not want them coming back from the break and voting on those disastrous bills. Can you imagine subjecting us to the North American version of the European Union? But they nearly have the votes for that. We can't let it happen."

"As it is," he continued, "if there are any modifications that are required, we will be pushing the limit of the minimum time to get them completed. I am confident that the internal tests we've performed are sufficient, so if the terrorist is unaffected, we'll have to assume that our projections are correct and that the right people will be immune, but we'd still have the problem of the venue. The one we have chosen is perfect, but without a successful test, that venue will not exist."

The assistant looked at him questioningly. The tone had started out just right, with concern and understanding, but the condescension crept in more and more as he continued to speak. Edward was gracious enough to at least give him credit for trying. He was making the effort.

"I have a suggestion, sir." Edward hoped that since the commissioner appeared to be in a more conciliatory mood, he would be more disposed to hear his idea.

"Of course, Edward. Your input is always valued."

Okay, so maybe he was laying it on a little thick, but at least Edward was going to get to pitch his idea. "How about if she runs the pilot while the senator has another member of Congress in the office with her? Pamela could easily identify a backup target, as her senator has people in and out of the office all day. She's not really a well-liked woman on Capitol Hill and the other senators are always attempting to bring her to heel, which, of course, never works."

It's that exact reason which drove Edward to believe that they had chosen the wrong target. This was a woman who stood up against the corruption of the others and her vote could not be purchased with earmarks. In the last few years that was a rare thing. Since 2009, it had appeared that only one page out of every ten in a legislative bill was actually for the legislation itself. The other nine pages were filled with the bribes that had to be in there to buy the votes of the other congressmen. It was amazing what the senators and representatives would sign if there was enough money for their own district included in it. And it didn't seem to matter, to either the congressmen or the voters, that the money to pay for the legislation was coming from their district in the first place.

The commissioner thought about this suggestion, and he finally had to admit that it was a good one. It would be potentially problematic if both test subjects died, but it could still be explained away. Yes, Edward's idea would work perfectly.

"That's a wonderful solution, Edward. Good job. Please advise Pamela of the change in plan. And please remind her that the earlier this takes place, the better."

"Yes, sir. I will stress that the ideal situation is for you to hear about the death of at least one senator on the morning news as you have your traditional coffee and toast."

The commissioner raised a brow.

"That message will, of course, be coded. None of the current surveillance tools will generate even the smallest flag. We are secure, sir."

The commissioner waved him away with that circular wrist movement that the aristocracy had used to dismiss their servants for centuries.

Once again, Edward felt his place in the house established. Just a few more days and he would be free to leave. His plans were beginning to develop beyond just leaving the house, and progressed into leaving the commissioner all together.

Maybe, Edward thought, he'd go back to Georgia. He was ready for a small town in the south, and he could probably find a place he could afford on his salary, even with the fifty-six percent income tax that was slapped on it. It would really be nice to only work one job again. Maybe he'd even get a dog.

Chapter 8

Sam was rocking gently, but she wasn't sure where the motion was coming from. There was also a terrible noise that was inconsistent with her normal morning routine. However, most unusual was the hard surface beneath her cheek. Where was she? She burrowed her face into her hard pillow and inhaled deeply through her nose. The scent of leather and Burberry filled her head and made her moan in pleasure.

Daniel chuckled, which caused her head to bobble on his shoulder, and helped to bring her into full consciousness. When she opened her sleep-heavy eyes and stared up at him, he met her gaze with one of his full face smiles, then propped a finger under her chin in a teasing gesture.

"Time to wake up, sleepyhead. We're almost there."

Samantha placed both hands on his chest and used him to prop herself back up into a fully-seated position. She rubbed her eyes, shook her head and yawned, all in an attempt to force her tired body and sluggish mind awake. It was then that she caught her reflection in the train window and nearly shrieked in horror. Her hair was a tangled mess, puffed up high on one side and totally flat on the other, she had wrinkles pressed into her cheek from the leather jacket on which she had rested, and her mascara was now more on her skin than her lashes. She was glad she hadn't had a chance to touch up her lipstick after lunch, or there's no telling where it would have ended up.

Using the window to try to bring herself back into what would at least pass for presentable, she finger combed her hair, rubbed under her eyes, and removed most of the mascara. When she felt better groomed and better armed, she turned back to Daniel. "So, where are we exactly?"

She was so cute when she was embarrassed. "We just left the Newark Airport stop. We have one more stop in Newark and then we get to Penn Station. From there we just have to figure out how to get to Sawyer."

Suddenly Sam was wide awake and horrified, "Oh, my God!" She turned and grabbed Daniel by the lapels of his leather jacket. "Chloe! I left Chloe!"

Daniel placed his hands over hers and tried to pry her grip loose before she clawed the leather. "We couldn't exactly go back for her, Sammie."

She clutched tighter. "I know that, but she's still there alone. I can't believe that I didn't even think about it before now. I'm a terrible pet owner."

"Shhhhh, Sammie, loosen your grip please."

She suddenly uncurled her fingers and let go of the jacket as if it had suddenly grown horns and spit fire. "Of course, the dead animal you're wearing is way more important than my live animal in your apartment." She crossed her arms over her chest and turned away from him. She was in a huff and she wasn't afraid to let him know it.

"You know I don't believe that." Daniel couldn't keep the smile from his voice. "But damaging my favorite jacket won't do anything for Chloe."

Sam turned her head and glared at him with so much heat that he actually believed his hair would start smoking. "I already thought of Chloe. I thought about her while you were sleeping and decided that once we get to Sawyer's house, I'll use his phone to call my neighbor, Maddie. She gets my mail for me when I'm traveling, so she already has keys to the house and she loves animals, so Chloe will be well taken care of."

"Maddie?" The arms did not uncross, and now there were raised brows and an air of suspicion to go with them -- and if he wasn't entirely mistaken, a touch of jealousy as well.

"Yes, Maddie, short for Madeline. We're quite close, so I'm sure she won't mind doing me this teensy little favor." Another searing glare came hurling his way. "Your cat couldn't be in better hands. I know that for a fact."

Sam was getting more and more angry by the second, and she was building up to tears as well. She had started to believe that she might finally have a chance at getting what she wanted -- namely him-- if she made it out of this alive, that is. And now he springs this woman on her. A woman who he knows for a fact has good hands. The bastard. She was probably a masseuse or something like that. Thin with big boobs and not a speck of cellulite. She hated the woman on principle alone.

"I want my cat. I don't think I want your woman taking care of her. I don't trust her. The women you like are probably psychotic."

Daniel's smile spread wider, "I'm starting to believe that myself."

"And yet you'll trust my cat, the only thing on this earth that really loves me, with a psycho woman? You can leave me at Penn Station. I'll get to Sawyer myself and deal with the rest of this alone." She turned completely away, glared out the window, and tried really hard not to cry.

"You're adorable when you're jealous. Did you know that?" He got no response at all. "And Maddie isn't my woman. She's the retired veterinarian that lives in the next apartment. She's a sweet woman who needs somebody or something to take care of. So she'll be thrilled to take in Chloe, and as a vet, she'll be the best possible person to care for a gimpy feline."

"Oh," was the only reply he received. And then a grudging, "I wasn't jealous."

"Whatever you say, sweetie."

Sam kept her gaze focused on the darkening sky outside. The sun went down so early in the winter and they still had to get from Penn Station to the East Village. Although she had taken that long nap, she wasn't feeling very rested, and there was still so much yet to do. The problem of how to get the story out remained in the center of her mind. How were they going to accomplish that most important task, especially when they were so focused on simply staying alive? The task was beginning to feel insurmountable.

The train at last pulled in to Penn Station and Daniel and Sam took their exit with at least one hundred others. As Sam stepped out of the train and onto the platform, the first thing she noticed was the people. There were way too many of them. They were everywhere, and some of them were pretty darn interesting. One girl in particular had on green tights which made her legs look like they were dying or already dead, an orange miniskirt, a black and white striped shirt, and blue hair. She was a carnival of conflicting colors. It made Sam's eyes hurt to look at her, but at the same time, she couldn't seem to look away.

The pair made their way through the station, modernized of all of its previous character, pushing through the crowds of commuters while simultaneously scanning the crowd for potential attacks. The benefit of being in the crowd was that they were a harder target, but the drawback was that the attack could come from anywhere. Sam, already tense in crowds, was increasingly anxious with each new step. Her personal space was being violated at an astronomical rate, and every bump, brush or jostle was a potential attack. Were it not for Daniel's grip on her arm, Sam might have found herself literally paralyzed with fear. Being hunted was unnerving enough, but having no idea of whom your attacker might be made it even worse. Her mind was suddenly filled with images from The Matrix, where any person could suddenly become an agent. That's how she felt now, like the old lady in front of her could suddenly turn around and point a gun in her face. Sam shivered at the thought.

Daniel's mind was running in a similar direction and he just wanted to get to the relative safety of Sawyer's house. He fervently prayed that the man was at home. He didn't know what they would do if Sawyer was out of town, or even out *on* the town, which, with Sawyer, was a definite possibility.

Finally making their way through the crowds to the street outside, both Sam and Daniel pulled in deep breaths of the cool fresh air. They would have liked to think it was clean air, but this was New York, after all. Sam gazed longingly at the line of cabs that sat in front of the, and sighed.

"We can't afford to take a cab. We've precious little cash left as it is, and an ATM machine is out of the question."

Sam sighed again. "I know. Believe me, I know. I was just having a wild fantasy where we had a whole backseat to ourselves for the entire trip, as opposed to sharing another train with the unwashed masses." She sighed again, "But I know that it's much too far to walk, so the subway is what we have to do, no matter how unappealing it might be."

They headed back underground, checked the subway maps, and determined what route they would take to get from Penn Station to the East Village. Once the plans were made and the route identified, all they had to do was wait, but thankfully not for long.

Sam didn't really like New York City. It was a great place to visit, and she always enjoyed herself when she came, but she knew she couldn't live here. She needed wide open sky and room to breathe. The tall buildings sitting so close together made her a bit claustrophobic, and all the people, the hustle and bustle, just stressed her out. However, the one thing she had to give props for was the subway system. It was fairly easy to get from one place to another here. It may take a while, but it was still pretty easy; and it wasn't like driving would get you there any faster.

By the time they reached their stop in the East Village, it was completely dark, which made the view even more interesting. The village was eclectic, artistic, and pretty darn interesting overall. As they walked the five blocks from the subway stop to Sawyer's home, they passed tattoo parlors, record stores selling vintage vinyl albums, and art galleries for everything from traditional oil on canvas to sculptures of twisted metal that Sam could never picture in her own home. There were also many stores with their own niche market which appeared to be doing quite well, even in this depressed economy.

Window shopping in the East Village was like nowhere else in the world. The whole place screamed, "I'm artistic, trendy, and delightfully bohemian," and though Sam enjoyed it, the village always made her feel even more staid and dowdy than she actually was; like the village was pursing its lips in disapproval of her unfashionable self, tainting its image. There was even a moment where she wondered if property values plummeted when she crossed the village boundaries.

Added to the usual festivity of the elaborate neon signs in store windows were the requisite holiday decorations. Store fronts covered in garland, wreaths, and lights of red and green for Christmas competed with and enhanced the blue and silver of Hanukkah.

In recent years the agnostics and the atheists, never to be outdone by the Christians and the Jews, had created their own holiday decorations. For the agnostics, it was a celebration of whatever it is that's up there. The decorations held to no particular color scheme, but ranged all colors of the spectrum; a representation of the many possibilities that existed.

The atheists, on the other hand, had moved towards a return to the Winter Solstice and used the holiday time to celebrate science and Mother Earth. The color scheme tended to revolve around the colors of nature - jewel tones were the most popular, with windows decorated in refractive crystals rather than twinkle lights.

Many of these displays were breathtakingly beautiful, but Sam still preferred the decorations of her own Christian faith. There was much more to the holiday than the decorations, and Sam recognized the difference in decorations for the celebration of the birth of the Messiah versus the decorations for the celebration of nothingness. Even thinking about celebrating nothingness was making her depressed, and the last thing she needed was something else to depress her.

It was time to get out of the cold and the dark, and back into a false sense of security. They turned onto the street where Sawyer had his home and Sam was struck again with how lovely it was. It was nestled in a row of well-maintained, three-story brick townhouses; the individual architectural differences adding to the appeal of the iron rails flanking the five steps up to the front doors.

Some of these had been converted to multi-family units, but Sawyer's home was still a single residence. He did like his space. There were lights on in his home, but though this was reassuring, it was also no guarantee that he would be inside. Unlike the masses, those who had to be very careful with their electricity in order to keep the costs under control, Sawyer could leave every light on and still not bat an eye at the bill;, and he didn't give a shit about the regulations on conservation which made the cost of energy so high. Leaving the lights on was his own personal "screw you" to the Federal Government.

They walked up the few steps, pressed the door bell and waited. It was only a matter of seconds before the door was flung open, and a man who was definitely not Sawyer stood before them.

He was of average height, with dark blonde hair impeccably styled into artistic disarray, and a golden tan that made the most of his sapphire blue eyes. He was dressed in worn Levi's with holes strategically placed and riding low on his hips, and he was wearing no shirt at all, thereby leaving his chest bare. And what a chest it was - the muscle form and delineation, and the total absence of hair, presented an image that could make Michelangelo's David weep at his own inadequacy.

This paragon of masculine beauty gave Sam a cursory once-over and then turned his gaze on Daniel. The gaze lingered, and when the eyes of the surveyor met the eyes of the surveyed, they showed appreciation and interest. "Well, hello there," the paragon stated. "And what can I do for you?" There was a slight pause as he looked Daniel over again. "Or to you?"

Sam giggled as Daniel shifted uncomfortably. She knew Daniel was not homophobic by any stretch, but it was never easy dealing with unwanted sexual advances, no matter who they came from. And this one was blatant, making it even more uncomfortable.

Smiling again for the first time in what felt like forever, her heart lightened by the humorous situation, Sam pulled the young man's attention back from Daniel by saying, "You must be Jack, is Sawyer in?"

As she was speaking, she felt Daniel's arm snake around her waist and pull her close. Jack noticed this as well. As he was nodding in answer to Sam's question, he focused on the intimate movement of Daniel's embrace. Heaving a sigh, he focused on Daniel once more, shrugged his shoulders and said, "What a waste."

Jack then turned and walked away, leaving the open door as the only instruction they had as to whether or not they should follow.

Daniel squeezed Sam a little closer to his side as a shield. He knew Jack could have meant nothing by it, considering he was currently involved with Sawyer, but being flirted with always made him uncomfortable; and if the person flirting was already attached it made him even more uncomfortable, and if it was a guy, well, that made the situation just about as uncomfortable as it could possibly be. He just didn't know what to do or how to handle it, and with the current situation, his ideas on how to politely rebuff the advance without offering offense came up with a big fat zero.

While Daniel ruminated, Sam drank in the atmosphere of the house, loving what Sawyer had done with it. He had preserved the Old World architectural features inside, maintaining the character of the home, while decorating it with a mixture of the vintage and the modern. The pieces complimented each other instead of competing, and gave an overall feeling that was both warm and inviting. The furniture all had one common theme, and that was comfort. Sawyer wanted none of the trendy, stylish furniture that looked nice but nobody could sit on with any level of ease or relaxation. He liked to entertain, he wanted his guests to be comfortable, and he was a slave to his own comfort as well.

In the front parlor there was a vintage chaise that had been restuffed and reupholstered in a deep burgundy that worked well with the cherry trim. It was one of those elaborate pieces with the back that started low at the foot, arced up in an intricate pattern, and then sloped back down to the single arm. It was Sam's favorite piece in the house. It usually called out to her with a beckoning song that she was rarely able to resist. On most of her visits, she would eventually find herself stretched out on the chaise with her reading glasses and a good book.

The kitchen was the warmest room in the house, and it was there that they were currently headed. The heady aroma of chicken masala emanating from the kitchen convinced Sam that this is where God wanted them to be at this moment. Chicken masala was one of her favorite dishes of all time, and Sawyer's was the best she'd ever had. The scents of ginger, garlic, chili powder, and onions seeped out of the kitchen and worked its way straight to her nostrils. Like one of Pavlov's dogs, she started to salivate.

They entered the bright light of the kitchen and it was like stepping through a time warp. It was one of the large eat-in kitchens -- tragically absent from homes made after 1980 -- with a heavy table of distressed walnut dominating the large room. On the center of the table was an artistically displayed bowl of fresh fruit on a brick red table runner.

The cabinets were painted with a base of the same brick red with the doors a bright white in contrast. The vintage theme of the house was most obvious in this room with the red and white checkerboard tile pattern covering the floor, vintage door pulls on the cabinets, and porcelain faucet handles, but the most prominent vintage features were the appliances. These were actually state-of-the-art, modern appliances, but designed with a vintage feel. The refrigerator edges were rounded instead of sharp, the door had the long hinge connectors that wrapped around the side and the front, and the handles were highly polished chrome. The oven, obviously from the same supplier, was done in the same style. The room resembled a movie set more than it did a modern kitchen, but in the midst of the vintage feel were all the bells and whistles of a gourmet kitchen. This was because cooking, and sharing his creations, was a passion for Sawyer.

Sawyer Wayne Bellingham heard the footsteps coming down the hall and turned to see who had arrived. Unexpected guests were not an inconvenience for him unless it was somebody he didn't want to see. Although, if he was honest with himself, as he always tried to be, there were a lot of people he didn't want to see. The two people currently shuffling into his kitchen looking tired and bedraggled were not on that list. He smiled wide in greeting, held the hand holding the spatula out to Jack and instructed, "It's about ready for the chicken to go in. Keep stirring until it's ready; you know what it should look like. Then holler."

Jack nodded in response and took the spatula. Sam couldn't help but wonder how he was going to keep from burning his abdomen on the concoction with it popping as it was in the oil; but Jack and his bare belly were not her problem.

Sawyer took only a moment to note the possessive grip of Daniel's arm around Sam's waist and thought it was about damn time these two figured out what everybody else had known for decades. They'd wasted too much time already. Sawyer popped his hands on his hips as he perused them further, and then popped out with a welcoming statement of, "Damn, woman, you look like shit." Then he nodded a greeting to the now smiling Daniel.

"Gee, thanks, Sawyer, I can always count on you to boost my ego." This was said as Sam took the few remaining steps between them, leaned up and wrapped her arms around his broad shouldered 6'4" frame, and popped up on her toes to place a kiss on his cheek. "It's been a really rough couple of days and I guess it's beginning to show."

Sawyer pulled back with a pensive expression. "Okay, rough couple of days. But what exactly brings you here? Not that I'm not glad to see you and all, but what the hell?"

They both averted their gaze and looked embarrassed, and a truly horrifying thought came to Sawyer's mind. "Wait a minute, wait a minute. Don't tell me that after figuring out that each of you has the hots for the other, you've run into relationship trouble and come to me for counseling. Because, quite frankly, I don't know shit about how your messed up heterosexual relationships function. Too much drama."

Now they both really looked embarrassed. Daniel took the lead on getting through this moment, mainly because he was grateful for Sawyer for confirming what he himself had started to believe, though the confirmation process was not as discreet as it might have been, but that was Sawyer. He was going to tell you what he thought and if you didn't like it, well that was just too damn bad.

"No, Sawyer, we're not coming to you for relationship advice, mainly because we don't have a relationship."

Sawyer leveled an assessing gaze on the both of them and simply said, "Yeah, right. Tell yourselves whatever gets you through the day."

"Okay, to get past this issue, let me just say that Sammie and I have not discussed a relationship. Yet." Daniel grinned as Sam's head snapped up and her wide-eyed gaze met his. When she saw his grin, not quite the full-faced smile, but pretty darn close, the blush began spreading across her face. They'd discuss a relationship before he let her disappear out of his life again, of that he was certain.

"So what is going on?" Sawyer questioned. "As much as I love you visiting, you two are not the most spontaneous people in the world, so if you're here, together, and you didn't make extensive plans first, mail me the itinerary and notify the proper authorities of your plans, there has to be something going on. Please tell me before I expire right here from the suspense. I'm getting old and my heart just can't take it anymore."

Sam grinned at Sawyer's turn of phrase. It helped distract her from that "yet" comment Daniel had made.

Sawyer really did look intrigued, which worked to their advantage. He was a man they could count on to help as long as it piqued his interest. He would most likely help them anyway, he was just that kind of man, but the more interested he was, the better. Jack picked that moment to let him know the chicken needed to be added, so Sawyer moved back to the stove, added the chicken and some water to the frying pan, stirred a bit, placed the cover on the pan and adjusted the heat.

These two were an interesting couple, Sam thought. Sawyer was an average looking guy showing the passage of time in his thickening middle and his thinning hair. With his blonde hair and engaging smile, he was still an attractive man, though he was nowhere near as beautiful as his partner.

Jack had such fine features that he had an automatic effeminate air about him, accentuated by the way he moved and the way he spoke. There would be little doubt in the mind of anybody he met just exactly what his sexual orientation was. Sawyer was just the opposite. Most people would be hard pressed to pick up that Sawyer preferred the company of men to women, at least in his bed. He wasn't ashamed of his lifestyle, and he didn't actively try to hide it, he just was who he was. People simply assumed he was heterosexual, unless he gave them a reason to believe otherwise. If they weren't people that he wanted to know personally as well as professionally, or as more than just an acquaintance, his sexual orientation and whom he was screwing were none of their damn business.

The two men had been together for several months now, and it appeared to be working well. Sam was quite happy for how things were progressing for Sawyer. He'd had a relationship that had been quite serious for many years, but had ended badly when Sawyer's partner cheated on him with a woman -- an unforgivable betrayal.

Once the chicken was set to cook on a low heat, Sawyer knew they had at least some time to get the discussion going. He began setting the table to add a distraction. "So what's going on then? Come on, spill."

Sam said abruptly, "I'm in trouble."

Sawyer had the plates half out of the cupboard when she dropped this bombshell and he nearly sent them clattering to the floor, where they would splinter into a million shards of brick red stoneware. "You're pregnant? Why the hell would you come to me for that?" He turned his glare on Daniel, "And don't tell me that you have no relationship if you're the one that knocked her up."

Sam was shocked into silence, at first having no idea that he would take her statement in quite that way. That hadn't been a common phrase for pregnancy in years. Then she burst into laughter, "Oh, my God, Sawyer! Of course I'm not pregnant. Somebody's trying to kill me."

Sawyer was thankful that he had already set the plates on the counter when this new verbal bomb exploded. And the way she said it - she was actually laughing - laughing so hard she was holding her side.

Aw, shit, he thought to himself, she was getting hysterical. Sawyer moved to comfort her, but was pleased to see that Daniel got there first. Hmmm, there definitely was something going on there. Whatever trouble she was in, it would be worth it if these two finally hooked up. He was getting pretty darn tired of running interference for them. He knew each used him to keep up to date on the details of the other. Chicken shit, the both of them. And he'd been about to tell them both to deal with their own romantic shit, but here they were, bringing it to his doorstep. He'd never understand the mating habits of the heterosexual. They made it so much more complicated than it needed to be.

Daniel was stroking Sam's back and whispering reassuring nonsense to her in an attempt to bring her back from the hysterical laughter that had started, and which she appeared to be unable to stop. Finally, though, she did get it back under control. By the time Sawyer had the table set for four, the flatbread laid out and the chicken ready to serve, Sam was no longer laughing, but pulling in deep breaths to steady her breathing and her heart rate.

Jack poured them water and a glass of wine, which Daniel refused, and got everyone organized at the table. He sent a questioning gaze at Sawyer to see if he should leave, but Sawyer silently communicated for him to stay. Neither Sam nor Daniel had indicated in any way that this wasn't something Jack should hear, and he appreciated that.

Sometimes it was hard to get your friends to accept a new partner, but he wasn't having that problem with these two. Neither of them had ever been in the least judgmental about his men. As long as he was happy, they were disposed to like the guy. And when he was unhappy, they were prepared to hate the guy. The anger that Sam had expressed on his behalf when he'd received the devastating news that Justin was cheating on him had been a true blessing. She had actually suggested that she could modify his genetic makeup and turn him into a toad, and she didn't need a magic wand to do it, just a single strand of his hair. He'd laughed so hard at that one that he'd instantly felt better. Especially since Justin had a very deep voice that often resembled a croak. It was still soothing for him, when he thought about Justin, to hear the croak in his voice and picture him as a bloated bullfrog.

Once they were all seated, drinks poured, chicken masala served, and plates full, Sawyer could wait no longer. "Enough of the delays already. If somebody is trying to kill you, I want to know exactly what is going on."

While she all but inhaled the flavorful chicken, Sam explained to Sawyer what was happening and what they'd been through. Daniel interjected here and there, but left the communication mainly up to her. She became more and more steady and confident as she went along. Partly because of the food -- she hadn't realized how hungry she'd been -- partly because of the warm environment, but mainly because of the serious consideration that Sawyer gave to her every word.

He wasn't laughing and he wasn't brushing her off. He was prepared to believe whatever she said and she loved him for that. He'd always been an easy friend, even in high school. Once the story was complete, she sighed in relief, sat back and waited for his input. But it was Jack who spoke while Sawyer's jaw was still hanging open in shock.

"You need to get on the news. I think I can help you there. When would you like to appear?"

The other three sets of eyes turned to him in surprise, but Jack directed his response directly at Sawyer. "Hello! Producer of the Gary Bright show on FNB News."

Sam sent up a major thank you to God. If the chicken masala hadn't told her she was here by divine intervention, then eating that chicken masala with a network news show producer would have. And of all of them, the Gary Bright show was the most perfect. He'd been talking about an impending revolution for years now. He wouldn't be surprised to find that there was one, no matter how silently it was being waged.

Smiling brightly at Jack, Sam replied, "I think I love you. It would be wonderful to get on the news, but time is of the essence. Do you think he'd let us appear tomorrow?"

Jack batted his eyes at Sam in a playful manner. "Love you too, sugar pie, but I'm taken." After the laugh that this elicited, he continued, "Let me give him a call. I think he'll be okay with that, I don't see why not, but I don't want to spring it on him tomorrow either. We'll need some time to rearrange the format a bit and he'll have to change his opening and closing monologue and get the script to the teleprompter."

Jack left the table to retrieve his cell phone and was already talking when he returned. He gave a brief overview to Gary Bright, and then there was silence. After a few moments Jack held out the phone to Sam and said, "He wants to talk to you."

Sam took the phone with trembling fingers and in a voice shaky with fear and excitement said, "Hello, this is Dr. Samantha Mallard."

The other three people in the kitchen listened to her side of the conversation with rapt attention as she laid out her story on why she believed what she did about what was going on. She talked for twenty minutes, drinking glass after glass of water that Jack fetched for her in an attempt to moisten a mouth gone dry from anxiety. When she handed the phone back to Jack, she was physically and emotionally drained. She didn't even have the energy to answer the questions in the eyes of Daniel and Sawyer, but waited for Jack to get off the phone.

A few minutes later, Jack snapped the phone closed and grinned at the others. "It's all set. Not only does he want you on the FNB News show, he wants you on his radio program as well."

Daniel grinned and held up his hand for a high five, but Sam didn't have the energy to smack it. Sawyer was at no such loss. They were excited for her, and she could understand why, but her old sweeping fears were back. The radio? TV? How was she going to do that? Too many people listening to what she was saying. There would be callers.

What if they told her she was crazy? What if they yelled at her and called her an idiot? What if nobody called at all? Oh, God!

Sam pushed back from the table, put her head between her knees, and drew in deep breaths in an attempt to keep the fabulous chicken dish in her stomach where it belonged, instead of all over the floor.

Daniel leaned over and rubbed her back. "It's okay, baby, I'll be there with you. You know I wouldn't let you face the masses alone. There's no way I'm letting you out of my sight until this is over and I know you're safe. I'll protect you. You know I'll protect you."

Sam pulled in another deep, ragged breath. "There you go with that hysterical woman tone again. You're getting a lot of practice with it, aren't you?"

Lifting her head from between her knees but remaining in her hunched position, she looked up at him in resignation. She just kept making a fool of herself. She kept exhibiting the weakness that so disgusted her father. She hated needing somebody to take care of her in times like this, but no matter how hard she tried, she couldn't keep the fear at bay forever. Sooner or later it clawed its way to the forefront of her consciousness and sent her into panic mode. Then, to make matters worse, her brain couldn't decide on which physiological response to give in to. Fight or flight. So she ended up doing neither, but as ashamed as she might be of needing the help and support, she was not ashamed of showing her gratitude for it.

Reaching up and placing her hand against his cheek, Sam whispered, "Thank you."

Sawyer lightened the moment by saying, "You two need to cut that shit out. I feel like a voyeur."

Jack made his own contribution by asking, "So am I preparing two guest rooms, or only one. Looks like one to me, but just thought I'd check." When they both looked at each other, but neither responded, Jack continued. "Okay then, I'll prepare two beds and let you decide if they both get used."

Sawyer chimed in, "If either gets used at all. All I have to say is that if you have sex on my kitchen table, I don't want to know about it and I don't want to find any evidence of it. I'd never be able to eat at this table again, and I love this table. No stains on my bedroom carpets, either. I just had those cleaned."

Daniel busted out laughing, but Sam was absolutely mortified. She had a hard enough time even thinking about having sex, talking about it so nonchalantly was a complete impossibility, and she couldn't believe that Daniel was laughing like that himself. What did that mean? What should she do? More than anything else, she wanted to lie in his arms and feel safe that night. But did she dare? Could she dare? Probably not. If she did, would she be able to focus on anything other than that while she was on the radio and the television tomorrow?

No, she wouldn't.

Jack, expressing more discretion than Sawyer was capable of, rose from the table and held his hand out to his partner. "Come, help me make the beds." When Sawyer hesitated, Jack prodded him along. "Let's go and leave these two to talk." The two men left the kitchen, Sawyer's arm around Jack's waist and Jack's head resting on Sawyer's broad shoulder. The intimacy and affection of the relationship was clear, and Sam wanted that. She burned with wanting it, and she found herself angry at the two men for having what she herself desired. Ashamed of herself, she dropped her head and let her hair shield her again.

Seeing every thought reflected in the expressiveness of her face, Daniel brushed her hair from her eyes and gently lifted her face so her gaze would meet him. "I would love to spend the night with you, and eventually I will. You're not walking out of my life again, so let's just get that straight right here, but I understand that you'll need to concentrate tomorrow, so no sex tonight, no matter how much either of us wants it or how much you beg me for it." Her eyes were wide with shock and fear. Daniel brushed a finger lightly down the side of her face, tracing her lovingly. "Yes, I want you. I think I've always wanted you. From the first moment I saw you in the eighth grade, I wanted you. But you'll have to focus, and once I have you, it will take you at least four days to recover."

Sam's lids dropped, her breathing picked up, and her head turned of its own volition to press against his hand. The desire for him that she'd always kept buried, always feared would not be returned, suddenly flooded her. "I want you, too." She couldn't believe she'd finally said it. Of course, it helped tremendously that he said it first.

It helped even more when he smiled and replied, "I know."

Sam sighed in relief. At least that was settled. So now they both just had to stay alive so she could finally see him naked. And she was pretty sure that this was going to be one humdinger of a sight. Maybe even worth getting shot.

"But if I'm being honest here," Daniel continued, "You should know that I'll feel much better if you sleep with me tonight. I'm afraid if you were in another room I'd get no sleep at all. It was hard enough last night, but after the additional attack today, I just need to know you're there and you're safe."

Sam blew out the breath she didn't realize she'd been holding. "Thank God. I didn't know how I was going to ask if I could spend the night with you without sex. It just seemed selfish." As soon as those words were out of her mouth, Sam's head snapped up in horror. "I don't have a nightgown. I don't have any other clothes. What are we going to sleep in?"

Daniel waggled his brows lecherously. "We'll just have to sleep naked. Think you can keep your hands off of me?"

Sam let her eyes run over him, confident now that she knew he wanted her. "Nope. Not a chance. If you're naked, we'll never get any sleep."

Daniel threw back his head and guffawed. Then he yelled up the stairs, "Hey, Sawyer, we need an old t-shirt for Sam to sleep in. And if you have a chastity belt for me, that might come in handy, as well."

They both heard the two men laughing upstairs, and then Sawyer shouted back down, "The only chastity belt I have is really just for show. It's leather and open in the back for easy access. Still want it?"

Sam smacked Daniel on the shoulder and then shouted back, "That won't be necessary. Maybe a pair of old sweats for Daniel and the t-shirt for me should be enough. I think I can manage to keep my hands to myself."

They were all laughing already when they heard Jack comment, "Well, at least we don't have to make the second bed. I told you we should wait."

Chapter 9

Pamela McCormack checked her reflection in the mirror one last time before heading out the door to work. The day ahead of her loomed long and difficult, and she wasn't sure if she could effectively execute the task assigned to her, but she also knew she had to at least try. To that effect, she picked up the bottle of perfume that sat on her vanity, and tucked it into her handbag.

Dressed in a navy blue suit with ankle-strap pumps of the same exact shade, and jewelry which consisted of a basic set of pearls, Pamela's ensemble gave her both a competent and conservative air. No matter their politics, a politician wanted to at least appear conservative in their dress. The lies they told to the American people went so deep that even their clothes were a part of it.

The problem that Pamela was facing was not what she was going to do, but who she was going to do it to. She was pretty confident that the senator she worked for was one of the good guys; one of the few still working for the people and not for their own power, but she still might have the targeted genome and Pamela did not want her dead.

There were those that she knew needed to be eliminated; those who had spent their entire adult lives in Congress doing nothing for the people and continually getting reelected. The apathy, short attention span, and downright stupidity of the American people never failed to surprise her.

Pamela knew she was the front line of attack, and the attack absolutely needed to be waged. She was the reconnaissance mission, and her success would send out the battle cry. So she must succeed. She would succeed.

Tossing the handbag with the perfume bottle safely tucked inside over her shoulder, she grabbed her coat and headed out the door. She walked the few blocks to the Metro station with the sun shining down on her face. She was thankful for that, at least. It really would have been a bad day if it was dark, windy and snowing.

Fifteen minutes later she boarded the Metro for her normal commute. As a congressional aide, she was required to take mass transit to work; serving as an example to the people for energy conservation. Of course, the congressmen themselves didn't take mass transit. It was a security risk, they said, and Pamela could see their point. After all, she was planning to kill them, so other people probably would, too, if given the opportunity.

Pamela got off the Metro at Union Station and walked another few blocks to the Hart Senate Office Building, where her senator's office was located.

The Hart was designed in the 1970's and built in the 1980's, and it showed. Where the other buildings at least attempted to match the design and feel of the Capitol and the other major government buildings, the Hart was a modern monstrosity. Looking like a 1980's office building on the outside, meaning it had no real character, it carried that look to the inside.

The center area of the building was open to the top floor, so the poor suckers who were assigned offices in this building could look out a window into the lobby. This meant they had a perfect view of a hideously ugly metal sculpture which hung from the ceiling in pieces; pieces that reached down to meet more ugly pieces anchored to the floor.

Making her way past the wretched sculpture to take the elevator to the fourth floor, where her senator's office was located, Pamela did her best to look inconspicuous. She was here every day and nobody paid her any attention, but having that bottle of perfume in her purse made her feel like everybody was looking, and that they all knew what she was planning.

She pressed the button for the elevator and waited, trying hard to keep from looking over her shoulder. When the doors opened, she stepped in and was followed by Nebraska Senator Alan Highfall. Pamela pushed the button for four and scooted away as Alan leaned in far too closely to press the button for his own floor, taking the opportunity to brush against her.

Alan Highfall was a perfect example of why Pamela was involved with the NACR. He was out for his own power and never voted for anything that did not directly increase the power of Congress as a whole and his own individually. He was against capitalism and blamed the free market for everything that was wrong. According to him, nothing was the fault of government; it was all the fault of the private sector. He believed that government was the answer to all things, regardless of the fact that history showed the exact opposite to be true. He was one of those congressmen who created problems with his legislation, and then ran his reelection campaign on promises to fix the problem he acknowledged no responsibility in initiating. He was a politician down to his precise genetic makeup.

Pamela had originally sought a job as a congressional aide in order to identify, for the NACR, exactly what was occurring within the Congress. As the belief that the newspapers could no longer be trusted to tell the people what was actually happening had grown, the NACR had needed people on the inside to identify the legislation they should be working against.

Several of the aides placed by the NACR had been turned, but Pamela was proud that she was one of the first, and she remained uncorrupted and true to the cause. This was one of the reasons she had been chosen to perform the pilot, and, of course, the senator she worked for was the chosen target. This was her single regret, as she truly believed that Senator Fisk was working for the people, trying to change things from the inside. Why couldn't Senator Highfall be the target? It wouldn't take much for her to get him now. She could take out her perfume bottle, remove the top and wave it under his nose. Better yet, she could douse him with it. In an enclosed space this small, it would be sure to get to him. She could do it. She could say to hell with the plan and just do it. Nobody would even know. She stroked her purse as this idea solidified in her mind. She could reach in and just pull out that bottle and end the man right here and now.

Two things stopped her from taking this action. One, the commissioner would have the mother of all shit fits, since Senator Fisk was who he really wanted, and two, Pam could not be absolutely sure that there were no cameras in the elevators. There probably were surveillance cameras, and they would see her unscrew a bottle and the senator drop dead. Then the entire plan would be at risk. So, as tempting as it was to throw the perfume in his face like acid and then watch him writhe on the carpet, she resisted, and she ignored his appreciative gaze and suggestive comment of, "I'll see you later" as she exited the elevator.

Making her way through the maze of offices, she walked briskly to her desk. Her area was set up directly outside Senator Fisk's office, so she was close at hand. Pamela stowed her handbag in the lower desk drawer, fired up the computer, and checked her Blackberry for the day's schedule. Senator Fisk was not in yet, but that generally indicated that she'd started working early from her home office. This was confirmed when Pamela pulled up her e-mail and found fourteen messages from the senator beginning at 4:30 am.

Pamela read one of those e-mails and a broad smile spread across her face. Mara Fisk had set up a meeting with Alan Highfall for early this afternoon. This was perfect. She would get the target she wanted. Perhaps not as early as the commissioner would like, but she could make him wait. In order to get this senator, she could and she would make the commissioner wait.

"Oh, honey, no. That color is all wrong for you. You'll look like a combination between a Smurf and the Grinch in that thing, especially on a television screen." Sawyer gave a delicate shudder to emphasize his point.

Sam put the teal blouse back on the rack and sighed in frustration. When Sawyer had offered to take her and Daniel shopping, she'd jumped at the chance. She needed clothes to wear for the radio and television show today, but she also needed to take her mind off of the night she had spent wrapped up in Daniel's arms. However, this was proving to be a bit too much of a distraction. Sawyer's total lack of tact was very rough on the old ego while shopping. On the other hand, she wanted to look not just good - but also not like a crazy person - on the interview with Gary Bright.

So far they had picked up a pair of jeans and a few sweaters to tide her over until she could get back to her suitcase, but now they were looking for "the" outfit, and it had been torture. If prisoners were subjected to this kind of treatment, they'd sue, and they'd win. She was even pretty sure that this type of thing was prohibited under the Geneva Convention.

After this Sawyer intended to take her shopping for lingerie, and she could only imagine what he would deem appropriate. The big problem was that he was paying for it, since neither she nor Daniel could use their credit cards, and he was adamant about not buying anything he didn't personally approve of. He had exquisite taste, but most of what he wanted to see her in was not something she was comfortable wearing.

For example, the sweaters were a size smaller than she would normally purchase, and one displayed more of her breasts than she had ever shown in public. Daniel wasn't helping the situation, either. He was siding with Sawyer on everything, especially the sweaters.

When Sam had walked out of the dressing room in that sweater, feeling more exposed than Britney Spears getting out of a limo, Daniel had just smiled and said, "Oh, yeah."

Sam was wearing the jeans and one of the sweaters now, but not that one. This is what she would wear for the radio show, but they still had to find her that TV outfit and they were running out of time. Sawyer was going to have to settle for something soon or she'd be going on the Gary Bright show looking quite unprofessional.

Then, eureka! Sawyer held up a pale yellow suit that he deemed to be perfect. Sam grabbed it and stomped off to the dressing room. She hated shopping for clothes. There was just something cruel about putting mirrors on three walls of a tiny cubicle with fluorescent lighting and expecting you to strip. Every flaw was accentuated; every dimple created a shadow, and after finally sleeping in the arms of the man she had loved forever, Sam really didn't want to see her flaws. She was self-conscious enough about what would eventually happen without thinking about whether or not Daniel would look at her and be reminded of hail damage.

Stripping off her clothes without looking in the mirror, she'd seen enough of her body already that day, Sam pulled on the skirt and then the jacket. It was to be worn without a blouse underneath, which would save them time. Considering how long it had taken to find the suit, she didn't know if they'd ever find a blouse that lived up to Sawyer's standards.

With the last button through the last button hole, Sam turned around to finally look in the mirror and was pleasantly surprised with what she saw. Sawyer was right, damn him, it was a perfect color for her, working well with her blonde hair and slightly golden skin tone, and even flattering her figure. She looked respectable, intelligent, and serious, without looking forbidding or elitist. This was one instance where she was more than happy to walk out of the dressing room and spin for the approval of the man with the credit card.

Sawyer was sufficiently and discreetly appreciative, but Daniel let loose with a wolf whistle, building up her confidence and replacing the damage that had been done by the fluorescent lights and the three-way mirrors. She was feeling so good, she even curtsied.

Sawyer paid for the suit without batting an eye at the exorbitant price, turned to Sam and said, "Now for the shoes. Then the lingerie."

Sam looked at her watch with mock regret. "Gee, Sawyer, that sounds like so much fun, but we don't have time to do both before the radio show. So I guess it's off to the shoe store and the bras and panties will just have to wait for later."

"Chicken shit," Sawyer replied.

"Guilty."

"I have an idea," Daniel chipped in. "How about you give Sawyer your sizes and he does the shopping for you while you're on the radio."

"No way," Sam said at the same moment that Sawyer cried, "Perfect".

"No. no, no, no, no. There is no way that I am letting Sawyer shop for intimate apparel without some kind of supervision. There's no telling what he'll come back with."

"That's exactly what I find so appealing about the idea," Daniel commented. "Whatever it is he comes back with, I'm pretty confident it will be something I'll like. And Sam, don't you want to make me happy?"

Sam swung her shopping bag high and hard, connecting with Daniel's shoulder and knocking him off balance. "No guilt trip. You know I want to make you happy, but can't I do that while wearing modest white cotton?"

Sawyer drew in a breath in horror. "There will be no white cotton panties paid for with my credit card. They'd put me on a fraud alert!" Sawyer gave Daniel a wink and continued, "But Danny Boy here had the perfect idea," stepping back, Sawyer assessed her briefly, "so, size six panties and a 34 C bra?"

Sam's mouth hung open in wonder. "How on earth did you know that?"

"I've done a lot of shopping over the years. Not only for my own feminine attire, but I've helped other queens with theirs. I've just developed an eye for it."

"How could I have forgotten about Anna?"

Daniel was getting confused, "Who is Anna?"

Sawyer struck a pose of nonchalance and examined his immaculate manicure, but Sam knew this was one area where he was just a bit sensitive. "I have been known to dress in drag from time to time. I've even won a few competitions. My drag name is Anna M. Ossity, and she is a hottie if I do say so myself."

Daniel's face lit up with one of those full-face smiles of his. "I'll just bet she is. And with a name like that, how could you go wrong?"

"As a result of those times, I do have quite the eye for feminine fashion, and I also know that you feel best when you are completely coordinated. Therefore, we must have matching bra and panties for each outfit we have purchased. While you're on that television interview, you'll be wearing something beautiful under that suit. And something that matches it perfectly."

"Oh, all right," Sam finally agreed. "But I do have one stipulation."

"Any request will be completely disregarded unless I agree with it, but please, do go ahead and try."

"No thongs. I don't want to be sitting in the interview thinking about that string crawling up my butt."

Both men busted out laughing at this one, and even the woman walking by on the sidewalk chuckled.

"I think I can live with that," Sawyer conceded. "Let's go buy some shoes."

The day was dragging by for Pamela. She'd been busy with one request after another from her boss. She'd also been going over the highlights of a 3,000 page piece of legislation which would -- big surprise -- expand the role of the Federal Government by creating yet another government program that the people wouldn't need if they could just keep more of the money they earned. Included in this legislation were the bribes for votes that had become standard. Pamela wasn't even upset by them anymore, having become desensitized to the corruption.

Edward had called her that morning and she had explained her plan for the day. He had approved of her choice and promised to sooth the concerns of the commissioner for her. Now heading off to lunch, her excitement and anxiety were building so much that she wasn't sure she was going to be able to eat, but she would need to keep her energy up. The anticipation had already burned off her breakfast, and she didn't want her blood sugar to drop too low.

Pamela was actually becoming a little afraid of herself, considering how she had evaluated every visitor to the senator's office to decide if they were worth killing or not. She had contemplated their deaths and wondered whether, and how, they would react to her new perfume. She was feeling like a femme fatale, or a spider luring her prey into her web. As it turned out, none of the other senators held the appeal of Senator Highfall. That was one man worth waiting for, and his reaction would be worth the wait as well.

She had not a single doubt in her mind that he would react. He had to react, while Senator Fisk stayed safe; but the meeting was not until two o'clock, so there were still a few more hours to wait; a few more hours to keep up the appearance of normality. Nothing in her behavior could indicate that this day was other than what it appeared to be. It was critical that suspicion not be raised, either today or in the days to come. She could not jeopardize the full-scale implementation by screwing up the pilot. The authorities could not suspect.

Just two more hours to go and Senator Highfall would be trapped in her web.

Sam secured the microphone into position, fidgeted in her chair, and looked through the booth window at Daniel. He gave her one of those full-face smiles and the thumbs up signal for encouragement. She'd been introduced to Gary Bright just a few minutes previous, and they were preparing to go on the air. He had told her that he'd do his intro monologue, introduce her, let her give the rundown on what she knew and what she suspected, and then they would begin taking calls. She'd always thought he'd looked a little like Dilbert with his round face and short blonde hair, and this thought was only enhanced when she met him in person, but he was a good man who did his best to put her at ease. So she took a big breath, focused on Daniel to keep her fear under control, and prepared to dazzle the listening audience.

The producer ran the opening announcement, and then Gary started to speak. "Hello, America, this is Gary Bright and I have been telling you for years that we live in a time of revolution; that the American people will not tolerate the loss of their liberty forever, and that a grassroots movement will evolve to take the country back from the corrupt politicians. I have a lovely lady in the studio with me today who believes that this revolution has been building behind the scenes for years, and they are now preparing to strike. This is not your standard revolution, America. There will be no riots in the streets, no armed militias facing off against the military, no civil leaders inspiring the masses to rise up and take back the country. No, America, this revolution is to be a targeted strike using science as the weapon. Much as we now use drones and smart bomb technology to identify where we should hit so that we achieve the highest impact with the least amount of collateral damage, this revolution will be similarly targeted. When we return from our commercial break, I will introduce you to the lady with the information. She'll share what she knows and then we'll open the line for callers so we can find out what you, the American people, have to say."

Gary switched the microphone off and faced Sam. "As soon as we come back, I'll introduce you and then you can tell your tale."

Sam nodded, taking deep breaths in an attempt not to vomit. Maybe she should have let Daniel do this. She should have coached him on the science, and with that slight Scottish burr in his voice, the masses would be enthralled with whatever he had to say, especially the women, but then again, who was she kidding? She needed to do this. They didn't know who was listening and what kind of information they would have. She could receive some really technical questions and the people needed confident answers if they were going to believe the story. And she desperately needed them to believe.

What felt like only seconds later, Gary was throwing the audience her way. She kept her eyes locked on Daniel and pretended she was speaking only to him. "I'd first like to tell you a little bit about myself. I'll be asking you to believe the unbelievable, so you'll probably want to know a little bit about my credentials. My name is Dr. Samantha Mallard and I hold PhDs in both Genetics and Biotechnology. I have worked in the field of genetic research for nearly twenty years, and I'm darn good at it. My life has pretty much been my lab, which means that I'm a science geek."

Seeing Daniel smile, she felt her resolve strengthen. She could do this. "A few years ago I performed a study to identify the genome, or the part of the genetic string, that causes some people to seek control over others. The study initially had to do with crimes such as rape and domestic abuse where the crime was more about the power than the violence. The idea was that if we could isolate that genome, we could work to mitigate its impact. It was to be used as a rehabilitation tool. Simple. Straightforward. But two days ago, my study was in the newspaper along with the information that several of my test subjects had died of anaphylaxis, or, basically, a strong allergic reaction."

Gary interrupted with a question. "So the first you suspected that anything was going on was when your name appeared in the paper linked with the deceased inmates?"

"Yes," Sam continued. "And what made it even more unusual was that the story, in the Washington Post, specifically stated that I was unable to be reached for comment. However, no attempt to contact me had been made."

"Surely not," Gary sarcastically interjected. "Our mainstream media press would never print anything that wasn't true."

Sam laughed at this, "As dedicated as they are to telling the truth to the American people, this oversight was shocking." She was encouraged by Gary's laughter and so continued. "I wanted to verify that the names in the paper were actually part of the study, so I tried to access my files. I was denied. The security locked me out of my own study and I became frightened. I've never been particularly brave, so I did the only thing I could think of, I ran."

"You may not have been brave in the past, but coming on this show to tell your story shows that you are brave when you need to be. This is the bravery that America needs right now. The bravery of the people who will stand up and speak no matter what it might cost them."

"Thank you, Gary," Sam said, "But right now I'm scared to death. When I found out I was going to be on your show, I nearly hyperventilated. I'm not brave, though I appreciate the encouragement."

"Dr. Mallard," Gary continued, "Bravery is not the absence of fear, but taking action in spite of the fear. The fact that you are scared, as the public will learn you have every right to be, does not mean you aren't brave."

"Gary, you're going to make me cry and then I'll never get this story out. But thank you. So I ran. I ran to an old friend who I knew was or had been a reporter at one time. I thought he could help me and I was right, he has been a tremendous help. We met for lunch at a diner in D.C. and, before I could even bite into my sandwich, a bullet grazed the back of my head. It was only the quick thinking of my friend and someone in the diner -- who shall remain nameless for her own protection -- that kept me alive. As my friend hustled me out of that diner to safety, we found that there was a backup assassin at my car. I'd been tracked and followed, but we didn't know why."

"So somebody had tried to kill you, but you had no idea why?"

"Right, but the one thing I did know was that it had to do with my study. And that the research I had performed had been utilized to attack. The prisoners were used as test subjects by someone other than me."

Gary responded, "So how would they use your information to kill those prisoners?"

"Since I had identified the genome, an agent could be developed to attach to that genome and create whatever desired effect. In this case it appeared to be a lethal allergic reaction."

"But how do you know that the death of these prisoners was at all related to the study that you performed? What if they were all just allergic to something in the prison system? It wouldn't be unheard of."

Sam paused for a moment and looked to Daniel for encouragement again. "This is exactly the thought that the testers must have had. Who's going to ask about the deaths of a few rapists anyway? Good riddance, right? But somebody must have. And I was the diversion they offered up in order to protect themselves. I needed to be stopped from doing any more research into the matter."

"You know how this sounds, Dr. Mallard?"

Sam heaved a big sigh. "Yes, I know how it sounds. Which is why neither the newspaper I took it to, nor the Department of Homeland Security were in the least bit interested. But let me ask you this, if there is an agent that will cause a severe allergic reaction in anybody who thrives on having power for themselves or power over others, where could the biggest target be found?"

"Hmmm, let me think about that," Gary said with his trademark cynicism. "Where could a grouping of those consumed with the need to increase their own power be found? I wonder. Could it be -- might it be -- Congress?"

Sam laughed. His facial expressions were so interesting and so lost on a listening audience. He was so animated, using not just his face, but his entire body to communicate, and yet he managed to convey nearly everything with the changing tones of his voice. "That was the one that reached out and smacked me upside my head. What else could it possibly be? And based on their desire to eliminate me, they've tried twice now by the way, I can only assume that the attack is going to happen soon."

"You really believe that?"

"Yes, I absolutely do. If we don't find out who is behind this and what is going on, I fully expect to hear of the death of at least one congressman by anaphylaxis in the next few days."

"And the Department of Homeland Security wasn't interested in this?"

"Not at all. They said it wasn't a credible threat. Since I could not tell them the details of whom, when and how, they weren't willing to invest any time on it."

"So who could do this? Who would actually have the knowledge to pull this off?"

"I'm not sure," Sam replied, "I haven't exactly had the opportunity to do that kind of research over the last few days.

I've been just a tad bit distracted, but that kind of science is not widely known. There are only a handful of people in the field with the skills to create an agent that will attack a specific genome. We find out who those people are and the trail begins, but it's not a trail I'm free to follow at this time."

"You're just trying to stay alive." Gary turned his attention from Sam back to the audience. "Well, there you have it, America. This appears to be a case of Capitol Punishment. We'll be right back after the commercial break to take your questions."

Gary turned off the microphone again and patted Sam on the back. "You did great. We'll take some questions when we get back, and depending on how many calls we get, that may be the rest of the show." He paused. "And no matter what you think about yourself, you are incredibly brave for risking everything to get the story out. I admire your strength and dedication."

"Thanks, but I won't feel brave until the desire to vomit subsides."

Gary busted out laughing.

They returned from the break and the calls started rolling in. Some of them told her she was crazy, as she had anticipated, but seeing Daniel on the other side of the studio glass got her through these. Most of the callers wanted to know why we should try to stop the revolution. They wanted to know what Congress had done to deserve the protection of the people. The only answer that either she or Gary could come up with to this question was that, with no government in place at all, anarchy would reign.

The remaining hours of the show were taken up with the calls, and they flew by for Samantha. She was relieved that finally people other than those she knew and loved were privy to the information. With each call that came in, she felt more and more safe.

Chapter 10

Edward Jackson choked on his tuna salad sandwich as the voice of Dr. Samantha Mallard came through his radio. Coughing in an attempt to dislodge the tuna that he had inadvertently sucked down his windpipe, and subsequently dragging in wheezing breaths, he listened in dawning horror as the woman told all to the wide and expansive audience of the Gary Bright radio show.

After Congress had passed new FCC regulations in an attempt to silence the voice of the dissenters, the talk radio hosts had all moved to the satellite radio suppliers where they were no longer governed by the FCC, and it was amazing to him how many people, struggling under oppressive taxes and skyrocketing inflation, found the money to subscribe, himself included.

Unfortunately, the commissioner was also a subscriber. Edward prayed that the man was not listening to this show, and the absence of any angry bellow for his attention indicated that he was not listening, but the commissioner would have to be told -- eventually.

Edward had been sure that the couple hadn't really been going to Boston, but he had never even considered that they would end up on the radio telling their story. Edward himself had been pretty confident that they had them frightened enough to go into hiding and not come up for a while. He had been wrong. So very wrong, and he had to ask himself if she would have been so tenacious in her attempts to get the information out there if they hadn't been trying with equal determination to silence her. He thought the answer to that question would be a big "no". They had created their own problem.

Then came the angry bellow echoing throughout the cavernous home, and Edward pushed back from his desk, still wheezing, and hurried to the commissioner's office. When he had made it through the hallways, his heels hammering on the custom designed parquet floors, he entered the office to find the crystal decanter, which usually held the Glenlivit the commissioner favored, shattered on the floor with a stream of whiskey running down the now scarred mahogany paneling.

This was not going to be a comfortable interview.

The commissioner barely had his anger under control, the hurling of the decanter doing little to cool his ire. That woman was on the radio and she had figured out exactly what he had feared she would. By telling the whole world what she knew, Samantha had confirmed his suspicion that she was the stupidest smart woman on the planet.

Edward skidded to a halt inside the office and simply stared at the stain on the wall. The commissioner had to call his name to get his attention back where it needed to be.

Through clenched teeth the commissioner asked, "How is it possible that Samantha Mallard is sharing our plans on the goddamn radio?" His speech had started out soft and controlled, but rose in passion and volume so quickly that by the end of the question, he was actually screaming.

Choosing not to speak, Edward simply waited for the commissioner to continue with his thoughts. "You said they were on their way to Boston, so why is she in New York on the Gary Bright show?" More silence. "Answer me, goddamn it!"

Clearing his throat in an attempt to remove the last vestiges of the tuna salad, Edward croaked, "I'm sorry, sir," cleared his throat again and continued, "If you recall, I did suggest that the purchase of the tickets to Boston was a diversion."

This was entirely the wrong thing to say. The commissioner's face turned florid, his teeth clenched, and his fists balled up. Edward both feared and prayed that the commissioner would have a stroke in his agitation. "Yes, you said that, and you also offered no other idea of where they might be going. You absolutely did not suggest that they were going on a damn radio show syndicated to the entire nation." The commissioner solidified this point by picking up a glass, part of the set with the now destroyed decanter, and hurled it straight at Edward's head.

Although he managed to dodge and avoid the actual impact, the glass shattered on the wall behind him and Edward suffered several small cuts from the flying shards. This was it. This was the last straw. He was going to leave. He opened his mouth to tell the commissioner to take the broken pieces of the glass and the decanter and shove them right up his ass, when the commissioner's next words stopped him cold.

"We can't kill her now. If she turns up dead, it will only add credibility to her claims. So I want her brought here and I want it to happen now. Call the studio and tell her to come. Tell her it's for her own protection."

"I can't do that, sir. She doesn't know me. She won't trust me. Why would she believe anything I have to say?"

"Fine, I'll do it myself. I have to do everything myself." Edward actually snorted at this statement, and at the harsh look thrown his way, covered it with another coughing fit. The truth was, the commissioner hadn't done anything himself for months. Edward was just thankful that he hadn't been asked to wipe the commissioner's ass for him. That was about the only thing he still did for himself.

"I'll call her," the commissioner continued, not buying Edward's coughing fit, "But I want a team in New York ready to take her just in case. I believe I can get her to listen to reason and come here for her own safety, but we need people there just in case. Who do we have based in New York?"

Edward advised him of the resources available, becoming concerned when one particular name was mentioned and a slow, self-satisfied smile spread across the commissioner's face. Edward was about to leave to call in these reinforcements, something he didn't want to do, when the commissioner stopped him again.

"What is Samantha's cell phone number? I need it so I can call her."

Edward turned in stupefaction, "Sir, her cell phone is turned off. Had she been using it, we would have been able to track her through it." The commissioner opened his mouth to speak and Edward did the unthinkable and spoke over him, "And before you ask, Callahan's phone is off, too. If you want to speak to her, you're going to have to call the radio show like everybody else."

With this last bit of insubordination, Edward turned his back on the commissioner's apoplectic expression and walked calmly back to his office. He would give instructions to the new team, but he would give his own instructions, and those would be to handle her very, very carefully and to force her to do nothing. At least Edward knew where she would be. Even if they missed her at the radio station, if they could figure out where it was taped, the show repeatedly announced that she would appear on the Gary Bright television show on FNB News. The team could pick her up there.

The commissioner made the decision then and there that he could survive without Edward -- when this was over -- but for now, he still needed the blasted man, and he hated that fact. Listening to the radio show, he grew more and more agitated and almost missed the dial-in number when it was announced. He picked up the phone, dialed, and got a busy signal. He tried again, and again, and again, until finally he got through. After speaking for a few moments and telling them he was her father, sure that this would get him through, he was still refused access to Samantha. Slamming the phone down, he strode over to the wet bar in his office, picked up another glass, and hurled it at the wall.

Daniel was so proud of Sammie and how she was performing. She was doing great, sounding both professional and funny, which was just what was needed. He had been doing his best to support her by working with the screener to decide which calls to pass through. Most were acceptable, even those who believed she'd reached the wrong conclusion, but a few of them were obvious nut cases, and these were denied. However, one call in particular he took great pleasure in denying.

A call came through and Kyeshia Grady, the very competent phone screener, spoke to the caller for a moment and then placed him on hold. She turned to Daniel and said, "This man says he's her father and wants to talk to her. I just want to verify that he really is who he says he is."

Daniel smiled. "Her father is still living, so it is possible that it is him, but I can tell you that she won't want to speak to him. She is not on good terms with her father and putting him through will only upset her. She's already tense and it will do the show no good to upset her with his call."

Kyeshia nodded, she hadn't liked the tone of the man's voice anyway, took him off of hold and advised him that he would not be put through. She pulled the ear piece of the headset away as the man began screaming obscenities at her. She disconnected the line and turned back to Daniel. "Good idea. That man's an asshole."

Daniel just nodded in response.

Totally unaware that a man claiming to be her father had attempted to contact her, Samantha was feeling great. This interview had gone much better than she had anticipated, and she was even starting to look forward to doing the television show. At least there wouldn't be callers there, and Gary had been very kind to her; much kinder than she had anticipated. She hoped this worked as they expected it to and that the powers that be would find no reason to continue to hunt her. What they were trying to avoid had now come to pass, so what purpose would be served in killing her now? She prayed the answer to that question was nothing.

The time had come. Senator Highfall was due any minute and Pamela was so looking forward to this. She pulled the perfume bottle from her handbag, unscrewed the top, and removed the applicator. This was not a spray bottle, as they could not risk having too much of the agent in the air. If too many people were affected at once, questions would be raised, and right now questions must be avoided. Of course, for the full deployment they would release as much as they could into the air.

Using the applicator to dab the perfume behind her ears and on her wrists, Pamela watched for the Senator's approach. When she saw him striding down the hall, she removed the applicator again and, catching his eye so she would be sure that he noticed, she dabbed the applicator between her breasts. That would be sure to get the old letch's attention. She was not wrong about that.

The senator's eyes lit as he approached the attractive woman behind the desk. He loved a good looking woman, and especially one in a subservient position. Having the power and authority to give orders to women such as her was why he joined the Congress in the first place. Capitol Hill was one of the few places where a man could still treat women in the workplace as sex objects and do so with impunity. Senator Fisk would object to this treatment of her aide, but she couldn't refuse to see him. They needed each other, a fact of the Hill.

He really enjoyed making the women on the hill uncomfortable with his advances, and no matter how forcefully they rejected them, he still knew that they wanted it. They all wanted it. They craved his attention, of this he was convinced. Pamela's current behavior was just proof of this. The way she provocatively ran that perfume applicator between her breasts showed that she wanted him to look, she wanted him to notice, even wanted him to touch -- and she was supplying him with the perfect excuse, all but sending him an engraved invitation to fondle her breasts.

Pamela suppressed her shudders of disgust as the senator approached. There had always been something really creepy about the man and she couldn't understand how he kept getting reelected. He called to her mind images of that weird uncle that the kids instinctively know they should steer clear of. Complaints had been filed against him by many of the female staff on the hill, but no real investigation had ever been performed, he had too many friends on the ethics committee. Another reminder of why she was a member of the NACR.

Pasting a welcoming smile on her face, Pamela stood as he approached, doing her best to make herself accessible to him. She shook his hand in greeting and walked him to the closed door which led to Senator Fisk's office. Just as she was reaching for the knob and preparing to enter, he stepped forward and pressed himself against her back.

"Are you wearing a new perfume, baby?" he said.

Willing herself not to tense at the pet name which she found demeaning and insulting, Pamela reached up and back, pulling her hair aside and exposing her neck to him, much as a woman the spell of a vampire by whom she'd been seduced. Senator Highfall was a bloodsucker, that was a fact, but she was feeling neither spellbound, nor seduced. She was the attacker here, as he'd soon find out.

"Yes, sir. I chose it just for you. Do you like it?"

Senator Highfall pressed his nose against her neck, even darting out his tongue to lick, and inhaled deeply. "Mmmmm," he hummed. Pam stepped away from him and turned so she could see the reaction. His face was flushed, but she couldn't be sure if this was the result of his arousal, the evidence of which she had felt against her back, or a reaction to the perfume. She hoped the latter. The former was simply revolting. Turning back to her task at hand, she opened the door and ushered Senator Highfall into the office.

He couldn't breathe. His throat was closing, he was itching all over, and for some strange reason, his tongue suddenly felt too big for his mouth. He took the few steps into the office, cleared his throat, and attempted to speak a greeting. No sound escaped. The door closed behind him and Senator Fisk focused her disapproving and superior gaze on him. He really hated that woman. One of the only women on the hill he didn't want to dominate in bed. He was pretty sure that if he tried it with her, he would quickly find himself as the submissive in the equation.

He attempted again to pull in air through either his mouth or his nose, but nothing was getting to his lungs, and he began to panic. He began clawing at his throat, and judging from the expression on Senator Fisk's face, he wasn't looking good. He heard her call for her aide as his oxygen-starved muscles gave out and he dropped to the floor.

Pamela was waiting outside the door, attempting to hear what was happening inside, so she was right at hand when Mara called for her assistance. Flinging open the door, she rushed in and saw Highfall stretched out, face up on the floor, grasping at his throat and twitching.

"Call 9-1-1!" Senator Fisk barked.

Pamela complied immediately. She quickly relayed the information from Mara to the dispatch, and with that completed, knelt on the floor beside her boss. Mara Fisk was attempting to get air to the lungs of Senator Highfall, but nothing was happening, and the man was turning a horrifying shade of bluish gray. Kneeling as close as she could, Pamela tried to get Senator Fisk in range of her perfume. She knew she wouldn't be able to get her to inhale it now, but she at least had to try.

Mara was breathing heavily in her efforts to force air into the dying man on her office floor. She didn't like this man. Couldn't abide him really, but she had not wanted him dead -- out of Congress or any elected office, yes, but not dead. She needed some space and Pamela was hovering way too closely to her. It felt like either Pamela's wrist or head was always right in her face. Pulling in one more deep breath, she started to cough and was surprised as Pamela looked at her in fear, as Pamela could usually handle any situation.

"Give me some space," Mara ordered. "Both your tendency to hover and your perfume are giving me a headache. I need to be able to breathe."

Pamela moved out of the way and waited for her senator to suffer the same fate as the man she was trying to save; but other than a few seconds of coughing, no further symptoms appeared. Her senator appeared to be immune, just as she had suspected.

Sam sat back from the microphone, stretched her back, and sighed in relief. She was glad it was over, but also convinced that she had done the right thing. Gary Bright shook her hand, thanked her for joining him, and expressed pleasure at repeating this on his television show in just two hours.

She was grateful that the two shows were so close together, because it left her little time to overanalyze everything she had said and build herself up into a panic, although she also had Daniel now to counter her natural anxiety.

She had Daniel.

He was waiting for her as she exited the booth; he opened his arms in welcome and she stepped right in as if she belonged there.

Daniel squeezed her tightly and whispered into her ear, "You did such a great job. You were brilliant and I'm so proud of you." He just held her for another few seconds and then said, "And you look so sexy in that sweater."

Sam pulled back and smacked him playfully. It felt so good to be playful. Maybe this would all be over now. Maybe she could turn the responsibility for saving the world over to those more qualified to deal with it. Maybe she and Daniel could return to Sawyer's home and enjoy a vacation in the Big Apple. Maybe.

Daniel helped her into her coat while continuing to whisper encouragement and compliments; they then said good-bye to the staff at the show and headed out to meet Sawyer. They found him loaded down with shopping bags outside the studio building. Samantha groaned when she remembered what he had been doing while she had been regaling the masses with her conspiracy theories on the radio.

There were way too many bags in his hands. This didn't look good at all. Daniel had just the opposite view. He thought those bags looked quite promising.

Reaching out to snatch one of the bags from Sawyer, Daniel said, "What did you buy me?"

Sam pulled out of his arms and looked up at him, "Buy you? I only wish he had been shopping for you. You're not the one who has to wear whatever torture devices he has stashed in those bags."

Daniel wagged his eyebrows at her. "Nope. I don't have to wear them. I just get to enjoy seeing you in them. Don't think for a minute that Sawyer didn't have me in mind while purchasing those. There better be at least one thing in that bag just for me."

"You know me so well," Sawyer laughed. "Yes, there are one or two items that you might find interesting."

Samantha groaned. She would have preferred to continue to sleep in Sawyer's old t-shirt, but she didn't think Daniel would settle for that now. She repeated Daniel's movement to snatch the bags from Sawyer, and this time he gave up his possession. Sam grabbed the bags and opened one cautiously. It was filled with pink tissue paper, but once that was moved aside and she got a view of what was actually in there, she snapped the bag closed and looked up and down the street, horrified at the thought that a passerby might have seen what lay at the bottom of that bag.

The set was beautiful, she had to give Sawyer credit for that, but there wasn't much to it. The panties were as close to a thong as they could get while still adhering to her directive, but the bra appeared to have no cups. She didn't know what purpose it was supposed to serve with only about an inch of lace attached to a padded underwire used for support. She imagined her breasts hanging over that little scrap of lace and pointing towards the floor and groaned. There was no way she could wear that, but considering that it was in a midnight blue, she was confident that this was not the lingerie she would be wearing on the television show. Thank God for that at least.

Seeing her reaction, Daniel had to know what was in that bag and attempted to wrestle it from her, but she was not allowing it. Turning this way and that she managed to keep the bag out of his covetous grasp. This was no easy feat as he appeared to have suddenly sprouted several more arms and his reach was far greater than her own. Eventually they both erupted into laughter. Nobody seeing them on the street would have any idea that they were still being hunted.

Giving up the fight, Daniel advised her that he would prefer to see them on her as opposed to crumpled up in the bottom of a bag anyway, and he was gratified by the blush spreading across her face. Teasing her, he was finding, was both easy and fun. He couldn't wait until he could do so without this fear hanging over her head. He was also planning on holding her to the commitment of singing in public after this was over. He admitted to himself that he had been subconsciously making plans for their future since she'd burst into tears on the phone.

Sawyer shuffled the couple off down the street and in the direction of the news studio with Sawyer attempting, and failing, to waive down a taxi. By the time they arrived and won the argument with Samantha over wearing what he had purchased her, it would be nearing time for her to appear.

When a taxi finally stopped for them, the trio hopped in. With Sawyer's seemingly unlimited bank account, they could actually afford to ride instead of walk or take the subway, and they continued with their good natured teasing while seated comfortably in the back.

Feeling surprisingly light hearted, Sam allowed herself to be ushered into the studio and taken to a ladies room to change her clothes. The men waited on the other side of the door, and both burst out laughing as they heard her shriek echo off the tiled surfaces inside.

"She must have found it." Sawyer's statement was given an air of nonchalance as he brushed imaginary lint from his jacket.

"What did you buy her to wear under that suit?" Daniel asked.

Sawyer propped his shoulder on the wall and crossed his arms over his chest. "Well, it's yellow at least, so it does match the suit, and it's really quite appallingly conservative, so I'm not sure what she's freaking out about."

Now Daniel was really intrigued. "What is it?"

"It's an extremely tasteful matching bra and panties in a pale yellow lace. Quite attractive, and the panties do meet her requirements, not even close to a thong. The bra is a push-up to show off some of that wonderful cleavage that I could only ever achieve the illusion of with strategically placed make-up."

"And?" Daniel prompted.

Sawyer examined his nails. "Well, I suppose she might be a bit put off by the matching garter belt."

"You bought her a garter belt?" Daniel asked, a dreamy expression crossing his face. He had the image firmly in his mind now. Sammie standing there in a pale yellow set hooking her stockings to the garter belt. "Wow. Thanks."

"I thought you'd like that. I also figured she'd resist, so I only picked up thigh-high stockings which require a garter belt. None of that elastic top nonsense for her. And I do believe she's a bit too prim to go on the television with totally bare legs, not as fair as she is."

This was confirmed as Sam came out of the ladies room with stockings on. She looked lovely in the suit, but all Daniel could think about was the garter belt. Seeing his focus on her midriff, Sam placed both hands on Daniel's chest and shoved. When Sawyer laughed, he received the same treatment. "This is not funny! How could you do this to me? I just hope my stockings don't fall down. I've never worn one of these before and I'm not sure I hooked them right."

"Let me check that for you, honey," Daniel said as he ran his hand up the back of her leg to the top of her stockings.

Sam gasped, jumped away, and gave him another push. "Knock it off. And let me just tell both of you that when this is all over and I can use my credit cards again, I am going to buy you both the most outlandish male lingerie I can find. And you," she pointed at Daniel, "will be required to model it for me."

"I can live with that as a trade." Daniel replied.

"Oh, really?" Sam placed her hands on her hips, felt the garter belt underneath her jacket and skirt, and continued, "That's good, because I'm thinking of one of those g-strings with the elephant on the front. Do you think you could make the trunk rise for me?"

Feeling vindicated at his expression of horror, Sam smiled, stuck her nose in the air, and flounced off. Of course, she only progressed a few steps before realizing she had no idea at all where she was going.

Edward hung up the phone, thankful that he finally had some good news to impart to the commissioner. The pilot had succeeded. Senator Highfall had succumbed to the agent and died of an apparent allergic reaction, while Senator Fisk had survived. Edward was thankful for that.

They needed the right people still in place once the wrong ones were dead so that the country could still have a functioning government. Anarchy scared him more than the tyranny under which they currently lived. Time was ticking away until the ultimate goal was executed and, hopefully, succeeded.

He pushed back from his desk and started the trek to the commissioner's office.

Again.

Had he not previously decided to leave, he would have thought about requesting that one of those airport people movers be installed. The house was so large that it was quite a walk from his office to the commissioner's much nicer and larger one. He had begun to suspect that his office had been placed as far away as possible to drive home his status as a servant in the household, but he could live with it for another few days. He was sure he could. No matter how beautiful his surroundings were, a dank, one bedroom apartment was beginning to sound like nirvana.

Edward knocked on the commissioner's door and was granted entry. He stepped inside confidently and met the glaring gaze of the forbidding man behind the desk, thankful that at least this time he had good news.

With the way the last few days had been going, the commissioner was already geared up to hear that the pilot had failed, or that Pamela had been taken into custody. What he did not expect to hear was Edward telling him that the pilot had been successful. He was so surprised that he initially was unsure how to react.

"That's excellent," was all he could think of to say. "So we will proceed with the full deployment. Is everything set for scheduling and organization? Everybody knows what they are expected to do?"

"Yes, sir. We're in an excellent position at this point. No suspicion was thrown on Pamela at all."

"So Senator Fisk is dead then?"

Edward shifted his weight from foot to foot, dropped his gaze, and then straightened his shoulders and faced the situation. "Actually, Ms. Fisk was unaffected. The backup target, Senator Highfall, is the one who was impacted."

"So she's alive." The commissioner's voice wasn't angry; it was flat, totally devoid of any emotion.

"Yes, sir, she survived."

"Thank you, Edward, you can go now." The commissioner turned and faced out his office window. Lost again in the barren expanse of the garden, he questioned everything he believed about what they were doing. He had been so sure that Mara Fisk would be affected. So sure. Although he was glad that the agent worked on Sen. Highfall -- that man was a menace -- he had been so positive about Fisk. What if the others didn't react? What if the ultimate goal was an ultimate failure? Then there was the Samantha situation. What was he going to do with her once he had her here? She wouldn't understand or accept what they were doing, but he had to keep her silent and out of the public eye, and killing her was, sadly, no longer an option.

Chapter 11

Seated behind the desk on the set of the Gary Bright show, Samantha attempted to regulate her breathing. She could do this, she told herself. She knew she could. It was going to be nothing, a piece of cake, easier than taking candy from a baby. She searched her brain for more clichés to use in her pep talk, but came up empty. She was convinced that this would be much easier than taking calls from the public on the radio, or would be if it weren't for all of the people in the studio. Many more than there were at the radio station. There were people everywhere. Who knew that it took so many people to film a live show? Then, of course, there was that giant camera pointing right at her and leaving her a little unnerved, or a lot unnerved.

The microphone was clipped to her jacket lapel, her hair was fixed, and her make-up was done. She was as prepared as she could be and thought she looked pretty darn good, so good that she wished she could take the make-up girl home with her.

The teleprompter started rolling and Gary started speaking and Sam tried again not to hyperventilate. He went through much the same spiel as he had on the radio and then introduced her. She fidgeted slightly and then went through her presentation. Her voice was a bit shaky at first, but gained strength and stability as she went over the familiar information. Then Gary dropped a bombshell on her.

"So, Dr. Mallard, the studio got a call today from a woman who says she's your psychiatrist and that you are a very troubled lady."Sam was so stupefied with this statement that all she could do for a second was gawk at him and say, "What?"

"Your psychiatrist," Gary replied. "She said you're a very dangerous woman and we should not put you on the show. You can see how much attention I gave to that."

Gathering herself back together, she could see that Gary hadn't believed whatever the shrink had said to him, but he still hadn't made it easy on her. It was the way he had enunciated "dangerous", and the way he shuddered at the word, that indicated he didn't take it seriously. There was just a bit too much drama in the word. He was being sarcastic again. She should be used to that after their three hours together earlier.

"So what was my diagnosis?"

"She told us you have been in treatment for paranoid delusions for years and that you must be off your medication."

"Wow, I've become way more interesting over the last couple of days. Last week I was just a boring scientist and today I'm a dangerous psychotic."

Gary laughed and spoke to the audience about how this was the tried and true method of attacking the messenger, and then Sam jumped in again.

"I will need the doctor's name, of course, so I can sue my fictitious psychiatrist for releasing my private and protected imaginary medical records without my consent."

Gary chuckled at this one and then explained to the audience, "The fact that people are trying to discredit Dr. Mallard is reason enough to believe that she is on the right track. Who would bother to make such a call if there was no truth in her assertions?"

The show was going quite well, and Sam was beginning to believe that she might actually be able to sing in public one day. If she could do this television show, she could do anything. Then, suddenly, while on a commercial break, Gary's demeanor changed drastically. He became quite serious and looked at her with new eyes. When they returned from break she discovered why.

"America, FNB News has just received a breaking news alert. Senator Highfall of Nebraska died suddenly while in a meeting today. The cause of death was a severe allergic reaction, but authorities have been unable to determine the source. Does this sound at all familiar?" He paused. "Our prayers and condolences go out to Senator Highfall's family and loved ones as they deal with this sudden loss."

Gary turned back to Sam but she had gone completely white. It had happened. What she had feared. She came back to her senses when she realized that Gary was asking if he could have been the target all along. She shook her head and replied, "No. You don't do the type of research that this would entail for one person. There would be easier ways to accomplish that. This was a test run to ensure that the agent worked. Considering that it did, or at least appears to, we can expect something on a much grander scale, and probably soon."

Sam was grateful when she was no longer needed and Gary wrapped up the show on his own. She'd been too late for at least one man. She had hoped beyond reason that getting the word out would prevent them, whoever they were, from going forward with this, but she had failed, and that failure was weighing on her heart, her mind, and her soul. Thankfully, Daniel understood and enveloped her in a strong hug as she walked off the set and immediately started to shake. This was too much. She wasn't cut out for this. She wasn't strong enough for this. She just couldn't do this.

And then Sam looked up and saw the encouraging smiles of Sawyer and Daniel. She was sure that Jack was smiling from the production booth, as well. They believed that together they could do this, and if they believed it, so could she.

Sawyer, never one to consider discretion or tact, broke the silence by interjecting his own perspective, "Having that senator drop dead at just the right time added a real kick to the show, didn't it? And does that phantom shrink of yours give you any good drugs you'd be willing to share?"

"You always were filled with sympathy for your fellow man, Sawyer." Daniel replied.

"I'm also filled with sympathy for my partner, and the way this worked out, he might just win an Emmy for this show."

"Always putting things in their proper perspective, aren't you?" Sam added.

Sawyer just grinned. "You know I'm self-centered, and yet you love me anyway. And if I can overlook your flaws, such as white cotton panties, then you can overlook mine. Yours are far more tragic after all. Thank God you have me to save you."

They were trying to cheer her up, that was obvious, and so she pushed her fear and sorrow down deep and did her best to appear normal for them. It was one of the hardest things she had ever done.

What would happen now? Their main goal had been to get the story out. Well, it was out there, but now what? Did they just sit and wait, or did they try to figure out who was behind it. She knew the staff at the Gary Bright show would be investigating, but she wasn't sure if she should leave it up to them.

It took her only a few minutes to change out of the suit and the garter belt, and put her jeans and sweater back on. The one good thing about the announcement Gary had made was that it had succeeded in taking her mind off of that blasted garter belt. Not so with Daniel's mind, though. Not based on the longing look he gave first her middle and then the bag she carried as she made her way out of the restroom -- the letch -- but it did feel oh, so good to be desired.

They were a rather somber trio as they made their way out of the warm studio and into the cold winter air of Times Square. It was so busy, Sam thought, and it wasn't just the people. There was so much to see on all of the signs and the big screens, how could anybody actually process all the stimuli that was thrown at you just walking down the street here? Yet even with all of the visual and auditory stimulation, all of the motion of the people, the cars and the billboards, even with the two very tall men flanking her, she felt exposed. Had the people who were after her been watching, they would know exactly where she was. New York City was no longer even remotely safe for her. If they still wanted her, they'd now know precisely where to look.

Just one block away, a woman stood under the marquee for "Wicked" watching the FNB News Studio. The wind was kicking up and the woman, who had already been waiting for half an hour, was getting cranky. She was freezing her ass off and beginning to question what she was doing out there. She should be at work but had left the advertising agency where she was employed as a copywriter early so she could come out and stand on the square like a tourist or a hooker. She was dressed like neither.

Holly, a tall woman with brown hair and large brown eyes, was dressed in business attire that flattered her slim figure. She had great hips and the current pantsuit accentuated those nicely, though she didn't think that particular asset would serve much purpose in her current mission. She had to convince the Mallard woman to return to Kansas City, and this was not going to be easy.

On the up side of things, at least she didn't have to do it alone. Another member of the NACR, and her best friend, was there with her. Between the two of them they could accomplish anything; and if you had to stand on a street corner in Manhattan, you might as well do it with a friend.

Margaret stood next to her friend cracking jokes, humming the "Wicked" soundtrack and freezing her own ass off. But where Holly was wearing a stylish coat suitable for business attire, Margaret was in a parka. Where Holly was tall and dark, Margaret was small and blonde, but the contrast went beyond just the appearance.

As an athlete and an adventurer, Margaret had taken a job where both of those things worked to her advantage. She was a marketing editor for an extreme sports magazine, so dressing the part was acceptable and even encouraged. For this she was thankful as the cold seeped through even the thick down of her parka, as well as through her boots and thick wool socks.

The two women had just about decided to wait inside the studio and to hell with the instruction when, finally, there she was -- their target.

Margaret interrupted her own rendition of Defying Gravity to swear softly. The target had not come out of that studio alone. Instead she was accompanied by two very large men. Bodyguards? The two women both hoped not. Even though it was their job to convince and coerce, not to take by force – although they could -- it would be much easier if they were able to get close enough to speak directly to the woman. Should they fail, which they were determined not to do, there was another team on reserve prepared to exhibit force if needed. Both Holly and Margaret had declared that force would not be necessary. They did not want to see anybody hurt -- at least nobody other than those jackasses in Congress -- and the backup team wouldn't be concerned with being gentle, but would instead enjoy forcing the woman to do what they wanted.

Nodding at each other, the two women strolled forward in as unthreatening a manner as they could. The trio wasn't being particularly careful, but currently standing right out in front of the building, totally unprotected. Had the directive still been elimination, the woman would already be dead. As luck would have it, the trio turned toward the women instead of away from them. They would be able to walk right up as if they were any other pedestrians on the sidewalks of New York.

The women pasted smiles on their faces and headed towards their quarry.

Sawyer suddenly tensed at Sam's side. She could feel the agitation emanating from him. "What's wrong?" she asked, trying not to panic.

Sawyer pointed with his chin, "See these two women approaching us? There's something up with them."

Daniel, on high alert now, watched out of his peripherals; not wanting to alert them should they be a potential threat. "They're smiling," he said seriously.

Sam was a bit puzzled by this. "What's wrong with smiling? Why is that suspicious?"

Sawyer smiled. "You're so delightfully naïve, Sammie. This is New York. You don't stroll down the streets of Times Square with polite smiles pasted on your face. Those aren't tourist smiles. Those are smiles calculated to make you feel at ease. Nobody smiles like that in New York. Not on the streets. Not unless you want every weirdo and street vendor to start accosting you. Here you keep your head down and avoid eye contact when at all possible."

Daniel studied them more closely and had to agree with Sawyer's assessment. There was something just not quite right about the women. They didn't appear to be armed, but you couldn't really tell under winter coats; and they were headed right for them. Tightening his arm around Sam, Daniel started to turn her before the women got too close. The smiles dropped from their faces and confirmed their suspicions.

Feeling herself redirected, Sam was prepared to break into a run and was thankful that she'd changed out of the high heels and back into her sneakers. Then the women called out to her with a statement which stopped her dead in her tracks.

"Dr. Mallard," Holly called out. She couldn't let her get away. She just couldn't. "Please don't be frightened. I'm a friend of your father's. He's worried about you and asked me to find you."

Sam whirled back around to face the women. "What did you say?"

Both women were visibly relieved, but it was Margaret who spoke. "Your father heard you on the radio and is very concerned about you. He tried to call in to speak to you, but couldn't get through. He's very upset and frightened for you and wants you to come home where you'll be safe. He even has a charter waiting for you at JFK."

"He called the radio show?" Sam looked to Daniel for confirmation, and his guilt was written all over his face. "He did, didn't he? And you wouldn't let him through?"

"I didn't want to upset you. That's all. You were already so nervous and, well, after the way you'd talked about your relationship with him, I thought I was protecting you."

Sam sighed, but had to admit he was right. Had her father's voice come over the phone lines at the radio station, there's no telling how she would have reacted. She probably would have ended up as a stuttering idiot as she usually did around her father. Either that, or curled under the desk in the fetal position sucking her thumb. With the stress she was already under, having her father criticize her could have unexpected results. "I understand, and I appreciate that."

Turning back to the two women, she pasted on her own polite smile, "Could you give me just a minute to discuss this with my friends?" The women hesitantly nodded, and Sam stepped away with the two men. "Look, I already know that New York is no longer safe. These women finding me so readily is a testament to that, and if I'm going to find out who is doing this, my father is as good a place as any to start. He is at the top of the field and if anyone knows who has the skills to produce the kind of agent we're talking about, he does. I won't feel safe again until we know exactly who is doing the organizing and planning, and they are either dead or behind bars."

"Damn, Sammie, you're starting to sound like a real warrior. But you know you're not going anywhere without me."

"Just call me Xena, but Daniel, of course you're coming. I never would have made it through the first day without you and I'm not letting go of you now. You're my security blanket and I'm holding fast and tight to you."

"I'm going too," Sawyer added.

Sam's expression changed to one of serious regret. "No, Sawyer, you're not. I've put you in enough danger and you can't leave Jack here alone. Considering that he was involved with the show, I don't like the idea of leaving him unprotected. We don't know what these people are really capable of."

Sawyer looked fit to argue, so Sam continued. "I appreciate everything you have done for me. You will never know how grateful I am, but I can't repay your generosity by putting you into further danger. Had I really thought that my father's house was safe, I would have headed there first, but since these people know who I am, it stands to reason that they know who my father is as well, and could easily have tracked me there. I could be heading to the most dangerous place in the country for me, and I can't put you in that kind of jeopardy."

"So, Daniel's expendable and I'm too precious to risk? I can live with that."

Leave it to Sawyer to put it in a perspective flattering to himself, Sam thought. "Yes, that's it exactly."

Sam stretched up onto her toes and placed a kiss on Sawyer's cold, dry cheek and smiled her thanks. Then she turned back to the women, waiting nervously, and advised them that she would go, but only if Daniel accompanied her.

The two women, remembering the instructions from Edward, readily agreed and they hailed a cab to take them to JFK, leaving Sawyer to waive them goodbye from the sidewalk.

Holly and Margaret personally witnessed Dr. Mallard and her man board the plane, then waited for it to take off as they had been instructed to do. Once the charter aircraft was safely in the air, Holly pulled out her telephone and dialed Edward's number. It took no time at all to communicate that the mission had been accomplished and advise that there were two packages being delivered instead of just one. The commissioner's assistant accepted this information as though he had expected it, and based on his previous instructions, there was a high probability he had.

Flipping her phone closed, Holly slid it into her handbag and looked at Margaret, "How about a martini and some sushi?"

Samantha sat with a white-knuckled grip as the plane took off, and maintained that grip until the craft reached its cruising altitude. It was going to be a long flight and she didn't like air travel. She preferred the control of her own vehicle. People had told her over and over again that air travel was safer than driving; that there were fewer crashes in planes than in cars, and Sam agreed with that, the statistics were irrefutable. She understood that data, but the other side of that same data showed that the survival rate of a car accident was much higher than that of a plane crash. If you wrecked your car, there was a possibility that you would walk away unscathed. If you were in a plane that plummeted to the earth at a million miles per hour – only a slight exaggeration, she conceded -- you're toast. And this was a tiny plane, so every little bump, every smidge of turbulence, was amplified.

Daniel placed his hands over hers and squeezed gently. "So what are we going to do once we get to your father's house? Where do you want to start? Are you just going to jump right out and ask him if he knows anyone who would like to wipe out Congress?" A pensive expression crossed his face. "Wait, that won't work. We all know at least one person who thinks it would be a great idea to wipe out Congress. How about asking who he thinks actually could and would wipe out Congress?"

Sam tried for a smile, but it came out more like a nervous wince. He was trying to distract her, and she was doing her best to let him. It was probably a good idea to work this out before they landed anyway. Here they had hours in which to plan without fear of an attack; unless a missile was fired at them, but she wasn't going to think about that. She really wasn't.

The next few hours passed companionably enough, she was really enjoying Daniel's company and especially his much-needed affection and support, but as they approached the Kansas City airport, her fear escalated once more. She hated landing as much as she hated taking off, possibly more, but even her anxiety over air travel was overshadowed by the fear of seeing her father. She had not one single illusion that he would behave as a loving parent in this situation. She imagined how Daniel's parents would welcome him. There would be hugs, kisses, home-cooked meals, and an overall feeling of love and support. She expected none of that. She would be shocked down to the tips of her three-week- old pedicure if he even met her at the airport.

At the arrivals section of the Kansas City airport, Edward Jackson answered e-mails on his Blackberry while waiting for the plane to land. He had the sign with Dr. Mallard's name on it tucked under his arm and periodically glanced up from his handheld computer to check the gate. The flight wasn't scheduled to arrive for another quarter hour or so, and he was using that time to try to figure out exactly what he was supposed to do with the couple when they all arrived back at the house.

He admitted to himself that he was more than a little bit relieved when Holly advised him that the man would be joining Dr. Mallard. At least she would have some protection, which was important as Edward feared what the commissioner was planning to do to her. Whatever it was, it would not be as easy with Daniel Callahan watching over her.

It was a lovely day in northern Missouri. The sun was shining and the temperature was topping out at fifty-two degrees, but the weather could change at the drop of a hat here, which was proven by the prediction of an ice storm for the next day. Things could potentially get ugly, and they needed the ability to get to Washington, D.C., for the execution of the ultimate goal. However, knowing the commissioner, a little thing like two inches of ice covering the roads, the planes, and every other outdoor surface wouldn't stop him. The commissioner would be in D.C. and Samantha would be here, unable to impact anything. At least that was the plan.

The wheels of the Jetstream propjet connected with the runway, sending Sam and Daniel bouncing in their seats. This was almost over. As the plane taxied to the gate, Sam heaved a sigh of relief and gathered up the various bags that Sawyer had handed over when they parted ways.

As soon as the plane came to a full stop, Daniel stood and stretched. This was difficult for him, considering he could barely stand up straight on the small aircraft, but he bent back and twisted to the left and then to the right to loosen the stiff muscles of his back. This caused the olive green thermal shirt he was wearing -- a shirt that made the green of his eyes pop -- to ride up and expose a bit of his belly above the low-riding jeans. That bit of hairy belly had her transfixed for a moment and chased all other issues out of her mind. She continued to stare even after the shirt dropped back down to cover him, her mind on wild and erotic fantasies in which she saw so much more of him. She was shocked out of her abstraction when he grabbed the bottom of the shirt, pulled it up, and dropped it back down. He had flashed her. She blushed at being caught staring.

Daniel laughed as he helped her up from her seat and took the packages from her. She was so shy and so embarrassed by her sexual attraction. It was going to be so much fun to work at building up her confidence and helping her lose that timidity. When this was over, he would insure that she had plenty of time to explore every inch of him at her leisure -- as long as she was willing to return the favor, of course.

The two of them carefully descended the steep stairs of the aircraft and walked across the tarmac and into the airport, barely taking notice of the beautiful day. For Samantha it was the dread of seeing her father, and for Daniel it was Samantha's anxiety. He hoped he could resist the desire that was burning inside him now to firmly plant his fist in the face of Samantha's patriarch. With the least provocation, this desire may become overwhelming, and he fully expected to be provoked.

As the couple stepped out into the baggage claim area, the desire to throw a punch escalated as Daniel saw a man, not Samantha's father, standing with a sign with her name on it. So the man couldn't even come to meet his daughter at the airport in person. What a dick. Wild horses wouldn't have kept his own father from being there in this situation, which was precisely why he had not informed his parents of what was going on.

Edward held up the sign with Dr. Mallard's name, but he easily picked out the couple from the light, milling crowd. Even had Edward not already known Samantha's appearance, the resigned look on her face as she saw the sign, coupled with the clenched jaw and obvious irritation of the man at her side, would have given it away. It appeared that Samantha did not suspect that anything was amiss. She had not expected to be met by her father, which was a good thing. They did not want her on edge or becoming curious about her circumstances here. They needed her calm and accepting. She looked accepting, but not particularly calm.

Reaching out and shaking hands, Edward introduced himself, explained that he was her father's personal assistant and that he would be escorting her to the estate. He felt compelled to explain that her father had asked him to be the one to meet them in order to help protect her against any attempted attacks.

Daniel let his gaze absorb the characteristics of this man. He was short, paunchy, and balding. He did not appear capable of fending off a toddler, much less the types of attacks they had been subjected to.

Feeling this scrutiny, Edward added, "I'm in better shape than I look."

Daniel certainly hoped so.

Confirming that they had checked no baggage, that everything they had was currently in Daniel's arms, they exited the airport and headed to the short term parking.

The commissioner sat in his usual place behind his desk and considered how the coming interview should be handled. Had his original plan been executed as he wished, he wouldn't have to deal with the potential hysteria that was a definite possibility. It would have been so much easier to have her dead than to have her here, but sadly, that was no longer an option, at least for now. Once the ultimate goal had been achieved, he would be able to dispose of her. At long last.

Swiveling in his chair to face out the window, he brought the glass to his lips and sipped at the 18-year-old Scotch. He'd had to send Edward out to replace both the scotch and the decanter, but the minor inconvenience was worth the satisfaction he had obtained with shattering the old one. His only regret in that action was the waste of the excellent whiskey.

Samantha stared out the window of the black Lincoln in which they were being transported. The so-called luxury car was small and cramped and Daniel looked as if he were nearly folded in half in the back seat. As legislation was passed to increase fuel efficiency to higher and higher levels, true luxury vehicles had become a thing of the past. The most cost-effective way to keep fuel efficiency high was to keep the cars small.

Holding Daniel's hand as they traveled, her thoughts were focused neither on him nor on the depressing scenery of dead grass and bare trees. Her thoughts were running around in the memories of past meetings with her father. She searched for good memories, but they were pitifully few and very hard to find. The introspection served no purpose except to help her achieve the realization that she would much rather face the mastermind of the attacks than stand and listen to her father.

Daniel squeezed Samantha's hand in an endeavor to pull her from the dark places of her mind to which she hand journeyed. He knew her thoughts were not pleasant, as the agony and sorrow were clearly displayed on her face, and though she was turned away from him, he could see enough in the reflection of the window to know she was frightened at a time when she should be happy.

His own parents were so supportive and showed so much unconditional love that he could not imagine dreading a meeting with them. Even in his darkest times, when he was most ashamed of his own behavior, when he knew that their disapproval would be openly expressed, he did not fear a meeting with his parents the way Samantha obviously feared the meeting with her father. Daniel's fist clenched reflexively as the urge to punch the man in the face boiled to the surface once more.

So lost in her thoughts was she, that Samantha failed to register their arrival at the estate. Daniel had to shake her shoulder to bring her back to the here and now. She offered a weak and tremulous smile, inhaled a deep and stuttering breath, and opened her door.

This was her first visit to the house he had chosen for his retirement, and taking in the imposing edifice with the columned portico, she believed it suited him. It was just pretentious enough to satisfy him. She had not been for a visit in over five years.

The last time she had seen her father, he had been in Baltimore on business and asked her to dinner. Of course, that dinner had been spent criticizing the advancement of her career and her choices in everything from her clothes to her chosen city of residence, but most especially her continuing single and childless state. He repeatedly asked when his legacy would be handed down to the next generation. She'd made no effort to see him again after that, and that meeting was more than three years ago.

She barely even spoke to him on the telephone anymore, as the conversations were always about either him or politics; two subjects which had previously held no interest for her. Her interest in politics had changed. Her interest in her remaining parent had stayed the same. Were it not for the need to pick his brain on the leaders of her chosen science, she would not be here now.

Giving herself a pep talk, telling herself that if she could face down assassins then she could face her father, she waged an internal battle to find strength. She was pulling her courage kicking and screaming from where it lie cowering deeply in her psyche, when she felt Daniel's hand fall on the center of her back to assist her up the stairs. As soon as the touch was felt, her courage won the battle with her cowardice and rose to the surface. There was definitely something to be said for having backup.

Edward led the way up the few steps to the front door, swung the door open, and ushered the two people inside. He relieved them of their coats and their packages and then led the way to the commissioner's office. He was hoping he would be allowed to duck out of this interview, preferring not to witness the rough treatment that Dr. Mallard was sure to receive.

Sam stepped inside the house and was struck by how -- even though it was a relatively warm and sunny day -- the interior of the home remained dark and cold. The wood, the walls, and furnishings were all dark and unfamiliar. The parquet floor expanded out in front of her like the last mile walk of a condemned man.

To her right sat a Chippendale side table with an obviously expensive Chinese vase atop it. Everything was immaculate, expensive, museum quality, and totally lacking in any feeling whatsoever. She was glad that he had not furnished their home in such a way when she was a child. She had been a clumsy girl -- which had only irritated him -- and her fear of her father would have been amplified with such treasures waiting patiently to be broken.

Their heels echoed through the house as Samantha and Daniel followed Edward's lead to the end of the hall. The assistant stopped in front of two large and obviously heavy doors. The wood appeared old, though well cared for, with the recessed panels of another time. Sam watched, as if in slow motion, as Edward placed one hand on each knob, turned them, and threw both doors open wide. He then stepped aside and held out one hand, indicating that they should enter ahead of him.

Samantha stepped into the office with Daniel close at her heels, his hand still resting on her back, and felt her fear, so recently suppressed, rise up and nearly strangle her as she focused her gaze on the man sitting behind the massive desk. This man looked more forbidding than even her worst memory of her father.

Chapter 12

Rising to his full height as his guests entered his sacred domain, the commissioner did not smile. He did not step forward in greeting, and he did not allow Edward to escape, as he was obviously attempting to do.

"Edward, stay. Samantha, how nice to see you again, and who is the gentleman you have brought with you?"

Tempted to swear in his frustration, Edward turned back from where he had almost made it through the door to safety, and faced the commissioner.

Daniel felt the tension run through Samantha and chose to answer for her. "My name is Daniel Callahan. We met several times when Sammie and I were in school together. I'd like to say it's nice to see you again."

The commissioner raised a brow at this statement. The man's tone had made it clear that, though he might like to, he couldn't say that. Stepping forward, he ignored Callahan and focused solely on Samantha, his daughter. "Well, it appears that you've gotten yourself into one hell of a mess this time."

He received no response. "You're all over the news. I even heard you on the radio today. The mainstream media sources are talking about your paranoid delusions and quoting statements from your psychiatrist. And, what's worse, they are mentioning that you are my daughter. It is one thing to endanger your own career and reputation, but it is another thing entirely to call mine into question."

There was still no response. "Well, young lady, what do you have to say for yourself?"

Both Daniel and Edward believed that they could see Samantha visibly shrink under the weight of her father's disapproval and condemnation. Indignant, Daniel stiffened and prepared to speak in Samantha's defense, but she stiffened herself and beat him to it.

"Are you quite finished making the attempts on my life all about you?" Knowing that Daniel was prepared to defend her was all of the support she needed to enable her to defend herself. All of her life she had stood alone against this tyrant, but she was no longer alone.

The commissioner was taken aback by her offensive attack, but it took him only a moment to adjust. "Attempts on your life? Were they even real, or just part of the delusions from which you're suffering? Your psychiatrist was quite convinced that everything you claim to have experienced took place nowhere but inside your own mind. And I am disposed to believe her."

"Of course you are," Samantha snapped. "You were always disposed to believe everybody but me. But the fact is that I was shot and I still have the wound on my scalp to prove it. I was also shot at on another occasion. These events are documented with the Washington, D.C., Police Department and easy enough to prove."

"I don't doubt that the events took place, I only doubt your involvement in them. You must admit that you do have a propensity for anxiety and other neuroses. Why would it be at all surprising to accept that they have tipped off the edge of neurosis into full psychosis? You were always a troubled child, and I'm sure the time you have spent alone in a lab hasn't helped the situation."

The cajoling tone that he used, one appropriate when dealing with a deranged individual, nearly served to convince Samantha that she had imagined it all. He always did this to her. Whenever she had attempted to stand up for herself, he had twisted everything until she began to question herself; but she would not succumb today. This was too important to be manipulated again.

"The problem with your argument, sir, is that I was there with her both times, and I'm sure even you cannot deny that I am flesh and blood and not a figment of her imagination. Everything she said on the radio and on the television was true, and if this is what you had planned to say to her when you called the radio show, I'm glad that I denied you access to her."

Edward was so close to bursting into spontaneous applause that he actually felt his hands moving towards one another. He was proud of Daniel for standing up for Samantha, but it would be disastrous to let that admiration show. The commissioner's attempt to convince his daughter that she was insane had filled him with disgust. There was no cause that would justify sinking to these depths.

Edward had always believed that what they were doing needed to be done, that the ends justified the means, but now he could see that this was not always the case. The means mattered as much as the cause. You should not, could not, abandon your principles in order to achieve a goal. No matter how just that goal might appear.

The commissioner fought to keep himself under control at Daniel's revelation. The man stood there proudly proclaiming that he had been responsible for that debacle. He would have had his daughter here in his grasp before the television appearance if not for the man standing beside her -- a man who shouldn't be there at all. The commissioner threw a glower at his assistant, who shifted nervously under the fierce glare. He quickly pasted a neutral expression on his face and addressed the interloper in the room. "I apologize, of course. As a scientist it is much easier for me to deal with an illness, which can be treated or controlled, than with abstract threats from an ambiguous source."

Daniel was unconvinced. He had not missed the byplay between the good doctor and his personal assistant. Something very strange was going on here.

Sam was having the same thoughts. An ominous feeling of foreboding was creeping into her brain. "The source is not all that ambiguous, father. And the only reason I am here is in the hope that you can add some clarity to the situation."

"Me?" Dr. Horace Mallard, the commissioner, feigned surprise. "I don't know how I could possibly shed any light on this situation, though I am flattered by your faith in me. What can I do to assist you?"

"Considering the science that is being applied here, there can only be a few people capable of creating it," Sam stated. "It must be someone in our field, and though I don't follow who is doing what and who is being listed in the trade magazines, I know that you do. You must know who has the scientific knowledge and technological ability to create such an agent and put it into a deliverable form."

Horace smiled unconvincingly. "Oh, I haven't followed any of that since I retired. Science has advanced so much in the past few years that I must be way out of touch. I have no idea who would be able to perform such a task." He linked his hands behind his back in a casual pose, dropped his head, and began to pace. "Let me think about this for you. Of the people I knew who had that potential, although I have no idea if they ever reached it; too many people fail to live up to their potential, you know."

Sam felt the dig.

"There are only two people whom I believe could have achieved this type of science. One is Nicholas Wilmington, and the other is Maureen Hong. Perhaps you should start there."

Sam cocked her head to the side and studied the man. Something was off -- way off -- but she nodded in acknowledgement of his assistance. She purposely neglected to thank him.

"Well," the commissioner continued, "You must be tired. The main guest bedroom, the first at the top of the stairs, has been prepared for you." He turned to Daniel, "I was not aware that you would be joining her, so it may take a few minutes to prepare a room for you. I apologize for the inconvenience."

Daniel studied the man much as Samantha had done, and then took great pleasure in his next statement. "There is no need, sir. I'll be sharing Samantha's room with her."

"Excuse me? You plan on sleeping with my daughter, in my house, without the benefit of marriage?"

"Yep. The walls appear to be nice and thick, so we shouldn't disturb you, at least not too much. There's that whole "reaffirmation of life" riding us pretty hard right now, if you know what I mean."

Edward thought for a minute that the commissioner was going to have a stroke. He liked Callahan more and more every minute.

"I forbid it. I absolutely forbid it. Samantha, you will not sleep with that man in my house."

"Yes, Father." Samantha replied. Daniel felt the wind leave his sails for a moment until Samantha turned to Edward and asked, "Where's the nearest hotel?"

Edward bit his lip to keep from laughing. The commissioner had shown so much derision for his daughter, describing her as weak, stupid and unmotivated, but Edward could see now that, out from under her father's thumb, she was stronger than even she knew. Before he could open his mouth --which was good because he had no idea what to say -- the commissioner replied.

"That's not necessary, Samantha. If you absolutely insist, I will allow it."

"Thank you, Father." Sam felt as though she had been given a royal pardon. The bastard. She almost curtsied just to show how she perceived this interview. Aw, what the hell, she thought, and dropped low to the floor, bowed her head, then rose and exited the room with head held high.

Daniel trailed behind her, a proud and mischievous smile on his face. He was tempted to pat her on the butt and say "atta girl".

In her office in the Hart Senate Building, Mara Fisk was still reeling from the death that had occurred there. She stared at the carpet where Alan Highfall had collapsed and was overwhelmed by her own guilt. It had been in her office that he had died of an allergy that she had somehow exposed him to. She was taking this too personally, taking too much responsibility. Intellectually she knew that, but she always took responsibility upon herself. It was something that was seriously lacking in her colleagues and most of American society. Something needed to be done about this death, and she had a pretty good idea as to what.

Pamela sat at her desk and stared blankly at her computer. It had been one thing to want Highfall dead. It was one thing to plan for that death. It was another thing entirely to stand there and watch it occur.

Whoever said that death was beautiful must have been speaking theoretically, because the literal exposure to death was anything but beautiful. He had struggled to breathe, clawing at his own throat, turning first blue, then purple then nearly black. His tongue had protruded and his eyes bulged, and then he had gone slack. Pamela had never seen a dead body before and couldn't understand how somebody could come upon one and believe the person was sleeping, daydreaming or anything other than dead. There was a level of stillness that you never achieved in life, and no matter how relaxed you might be, your muscles never went as slack in life as they did in death. The image of Senator Highfall lying dead on that carpet would remain with her forever -- burned into her memory, into her heart, and into her soul. A soul whose final destination she questioned for the first time in her life. How could God ever forgive her for this?

The phone on Pamela's desk rang in a piercing tone more shrill than it had previously appeared. She picked it up out of habit and spoke in a voice devoid of all emotion. Mara wanted to see her. This was perhaps her opportunity to begin phase II. Could she do it? She had to. She'd come this far. If she did not take this opportunity, then the death she had facilitated could be deemed nothing other than murder, even in her own mind. She had to remind herself that this was war, she was a soldier and she had simply taken out the enemy – difficult, yes, but necessary in order to achieve peace.

Grabbing her notebook and a pen, Pamela moved the few steps to the office, took in a deep breath, turned the knob and entered. Her senator sat behind the desk looking shaken and disturbed, but this did not prevent her from getting right to the point. All business was Senator Fisk.

"We need to do something to acknowledge the life and death of Senator Highfall. I was thinking of a small memorial service or something like that, what do you think?"

Pamela had always liked the idea that the senator asked her opinion and really appeared to value it, but at the moment she would be happier to have been left out. This was her opening and she was going to have to take it, no matter how distasteful she found herself at the moment. "I think that's a brilliant idea, but the senator has," she paused, "I'm sorry, *had* been in office for many years. Perhaps we should hold a memorial just for elected or appointed members of the government and their staff. The public would, of course, be part of the official funeral services, but it would be nice be able to mourn one of our own without the circus that is sure to accompany the funeral." Pamela sat back, held her breath, and waited.

"I like that. Members of the press will have to be invited, of course, but I like the idea of including just those of us who worked with him." Senator Fisk leaned back in her chair and leveled a hard stare at the woman before her. The stare was not actually directed at Pamela, though based on the way she fidgeted, it appeared she thought it was. No, Senator Fisk was thinking about what kind of reaction this idea would get if it came from her. She was sure that rumors that she had personally assassinated Senator Highfall were already flying and reverberating through the halls of Capitol Hill.

She was not a popular woman on this hill because she pointed out the corruption of her colleagues and gave no quarter on those principles she knew defined the country. It was a safe bet that if she were the one to propose the service, nobody would attend. Playground politics ruled the nation right now and, at times, it made her physically ill.

She had thought high school was bad with the cliques and the popular kids, but not even the most extreme high school situation could come anywhere near the cliques in Congress, and she herself was not one of the popular kids. She was the geek that got thrown in the locker or had her face stuffed in the toilet. With all of the bullshit floating around on the hill, Mara often thought that it would be more accurate to call them sewage treatment specialists instead of legislators.

"Pamela, we both know that if I suggest the memorial, it will not serve the memory of Senator Highfall. Could you perhaps drop a word in the ear of the Speaker on this? He will be proud to claim it as his own idea. I believe that, with the passing of his aide, one of his interns has stepped up to fill that role. It would be kind of you to offer your assistance with planning."

"Yes, ma'am. I think that is wise."

The meeting wrapped up shortly and Pamela returned to her desk and called Clive Sledgewater's office. This couldn't have been more perfect. With Sledgewater organizing the event, meaning it would fall to his intern, meaning it would fall to her, everybody on the hill would be sure to attend. This was the perfect setup for their plan, but she felt no satisfaction in it; none at all.

Samantha nearly skipped up the stairs to the guest room. Daniel had collected the bags and she was feeling light on her feet. She had stood up to her father for the first time in her entire life and it felt good. No, it felt great. For the moment she pushed her concerns and misgivings aside and consciously worked to imprint the image of her father's face as she rose from the curtsy into her brain. She would cherish that look for the rest of her life -- and of course there was also Daniel's insistence that he share the room with her. That had made her feel even better.

She opened the first door at the top of the stairs and found this room much the same as the rest of the house. The room was beautifully appointed, the walls painted in a dark shade of sandstone which worked as the perfect backdrop for the ivory duvet on the king size sleigh bed dominating the room. There was also a Victorian writing table, three bookcases, and a vanity, all in the same style. In addition to all of that furniture, which would have in no way fit into either bedroom in her own small home, there was a wide, plush chair and an ottoman. If this was the guest room, she couldn't help but wonder about the master suite.

Daniel walked over to the lounge chair in this ridiculous room, dumped the packages, strode purposely over to Sam and pulled her body flush to his own. He gave her only a moment to gasp in surprise, and then lowered his lips to her still open mouth.

He was going to kiss her, at long last, she knew it and prepared for a hard kiss filled with passion, anticipating it really, but when his lips descended they were soft, teasing. His mouth was open on hers, then his lips closed, sucking her bottom lip in and then returning for full pressure once more. He lingered with gentle massaging kisses and teasing nibbles which did not push, did not demand, but coaxed, seduced, and with each new soft, teasing kiss she only craved more. More kisses with deeper and firmer contact.

One of Daniel's hands held her head, his hand buried firmly in her hair while his other stroked down her back and over her hip. He did not use the touch to pull her closer, but to feel her, explore her. This was not enough for Samantha and she pressed her body fully up against his, attempting to get closer. So close that she might actually crawl inside of him.

Wrapping both hands around Daniel's head, Sam endeavored to grasp his short hair and pull him closer still, but it was too short, slipping through her fingers. The blood rushed through her veins and pounded in her ears, drowning out all other sound, and her heart felt as if it would beat right out of her chest. She rubbed against him, pushing her hips to his, seeking something even if she wasn't sure what, but even that contact was insufficient, only serving to tease her more. She lifted one leg and wrapped it around his waist, seeking more, craving more, and then losing everything.

Daniel pulled back abruptly, his heart raging, his breath ragged. He'd had to end the kiss or this was going to go way too far, way too fast. And unfortunately, they really needed to talk.

"I'm sorry," Sam whispered.

Daniel brought himself back to his senses. "What are you apologizing for? And where did you learn to kiss like that? It was incredible. So much so that I almost lost my head, laid you out on top of the covers, and took you right here and now."

Sam's face flushed as she realized that she had not, in fact, been rejected. "Would that really be so bad?" She wasn't bold enough to flirt openly yet, so she had dropped her head. She now peeked up at him through her lashes, completely unaware of how coquettish she appeared.

Daniel groaned. "It wouldn't be bad, it would be great - phenomenal, actually." He reached out to stroke her face. "But you don't have four days to recover."

Sam gasped at the reminder of what he had told her in Sawyer's kitchen. She started to shiver and wanted more than anything for this crisis to be over so that she could spend the night with Daniel. Wait, scratch that. A night would not be enough. She intended to spend an entire week in bed with Daniel, maybe a month.

Her reaction was very, very promising as her body was still quivering with the need he had evoked. Oh, yes, it was going to be really good, but they had to talk. He had known that once they started talking, there wouldn't have been a good time for that kiss -- and he'd needed to kiss her. He had desperately needed to kiss her.

"Have you noticed that there's something really strange going on here?" Samantha had beaten him to the punch.

"Yes, I have. There was some interesting nonverbal communication taking place between your father and Edward."

"Yep," Sam replied, "And there's not a snowball's chance in Hell that my father doesn't know exactly who in the field has what knowledge. Retirement or no retirement, he would be up to date on the science, and he would certainly know that Nicholas Wilmington is dead and Maureen Hong has Alzheimer's. He deliberately fed me names of people he knew could not help me, thereby appearing to give assistance while supplying only misinformation."

Daniel sat on the bed, opened his mouth to speak, shut it and opened it again. "So there are a few questions that need to be answered."

Sam sat beside him and placed her hand on his thigh. "The answers are yes, yes, and yes."

Daniel raised his brows in question.

Samantha sighed. She knew the questions he had been going to ask as she had already asked them of herself. "Yes, it is possible, even probable that he has the scientific knowledge. Yes, it is possible that he has, or knows someone, with the technological ability. Yes, he does believe that Congress is the source of all of our problems. I've heard him say that often enough. But, most importantly, I believe he is psychologically capable of just about anything -- including ordering my assassination."

"I'm sorry, baby."

"No need for your hysterical woman tone. I'm okay this time."

Daniel managed to dredge up a chuckle in spite of how incensed he was on her behalf. "I have a confession." He laid his hand over hers where it rested on his thigh. "I don't have a hysterical woman tone. Baby is meant solely as a term of endearment."

At her rather watery smile, he leaned over and pressed a light kiss on her lips.

"Yes, Robert, I agree that the House Chamber is the perfect place to hold the memorial service. Very appropriate. We could suspend the discussion on the House and Senate floor, say, end of day tomorrow?" Pamela was doing her best to lead Robert, the intern- turned-aide for The Speaker of the House, down the right path while making him believe it was all his idea. On top of everything else she had been through today, it was sapping the last of her strength, energy and determination.

She fed him a few more critical pieces of the plan and, once satisfied that everything they needed would be in place and that she would be included in any further planning, she disconnected the call.

This was so much harder than she had expected it to be, but she wasn't finished yet. The NACR needed to be placed on alert for when this would take place and that the primary plan was a go. She rubbed her forehead, where a dull throbbing had progressed to a stabbing pain, and repeated to herself over and over that she was doing the right thing.

On the dark staircase of what they suspected was not just her father's but also the mastermind's home, Samantha and Daniel silently crept barefoot, their movement betrayed only by the stirring of the air around them. They had heard Sam's father retire to his room at least two hours prior, but there was no guarantee that he would yet be asleep. In fact, odds were good that he was still awake, but it was three o'clock in the morning and they couldn't wait much longer. They were unsure as to Edward's normal routine and they could not risk crossing his path as he performed his usual morning duties.

Having developed their suspicions, they had to confirm them before taking any action. They also still didn't know the full extent of the plan and needed to determine how and when this was going to be rolled out. They needed information, and they were going to find it. This is where Daniel's experience as a reporter was going to come in very handy.

Daniel had forgotten how much fun this could be. He had been doing the tabloid shtick for too long, and the Washington Press Corps before that. He'd forgotten what it was like to dig through an individual's personal papers looking for dirt, knowing that at any moment they could return and you would be caught and exposed.

Samantha grabbed the knob of the office door and met their first obstacle. "It's locked," she whispered. "I should have known that blasted man would lock it."

Daniel grabbed her by the wrist and led her silently down the hall away from the office. Once in the kitchen, strangely small for such a big, expansive home, he set Sam against the wall and motioned for her to stay. A slow grin spread across his face as he slowly and carefully opened each drawer, praying that nothing screeched or rattled.

He started out searching in the logical places, but finally found what he was looking for in the fourth drawer he opened. The silverware was not where it should be, he thought to himself. This entire kitchen could use a good reorganization. Who in their right mind would put the silverware drawer on the other side of the kitchen from the plates? Incredibly inefficient, no matter how small the room was.

Reaching into the drawer in the dark, he winced as the flatware contained there rattled. He felt around, located a fork, and slid it carefully from the drawer doing his best not to disturb the other flatware more than absolutely necessary. When it was finally free, he used his hip and gently pushed the drawer closed, turning to Sam and holding up the fork in triumph.

Sam was enjoying the drama but didn't quite understand what was going on here, so she just shrugged her shoulders and raised her brows.

Daniel rolled his eyes so hard that he ended up rolling his whole head, crept silently to her, grabbed her wrist and pulled her back out of the kitchen. He stopped at the staircase and looked up, holding her back behind him. He waited there for a moment, listening for any noises from the floors above. There was nothing. He then took the fork and bent three prongs down so that only one was left straight, then he moved over to the door and knelt down before it.

Inserting the sole remaining straight tine into the lock, Daniel leaned in close to see as much as he could in the darkness, but wasn't too concerned by what he couldn't detect. This was more an operation of feel than sight anyway. He wiggled and jiggled and wiggled some more and then stood up, a huge self-satisfied smile spreading across his face. Then with all of the drama and ceremony that he could generate, turned the knob and eased the door open.

He would have thrown the door wide, but the need for silence was too pervasive. So instead he had opted for easing it carefully open and welcoming Sam inside. When she was safely in the office and the door closed and locked silently behind her, he put his hands on his hips, placed a big smile on his face as asked, "Who's your man?"

Sam drew her brows down in confusion. "What?"

"You heard me," he said. "Who's your man?"

Comprehension dawned. "You're my man." She stretched up on her toes, placed her lips so close to his that she could feel his breath brush her and said again. "You're my man, and I'm so proud of my man." She closed the gap and pressed a soft, light kiss on his mouth, then turned and walked away.

"Tease," Daniel replied playfully.

"I think I'm starting to like it," Sam threw over her shoulder at him.

"Yeah, me too," he said under his breath.

His ego sufficiently stroked, Daniel decided they should probably get down to the business of searching. He moved to the desk while Samantha made her way to the expansive built-in bookcase that took up the majority of the east wall.

Knowing the desk would be locked, she left that to the man with the lock picking skills, but she also knew her father. He was a scientist so a bit anal retentive, but he was also secretive and a tad bit paranoid. Therefore, there was a high probability that the information they were looking for would be somewhere other than the desk.

Sam's attention was caught briefly by the wet bar, but only long enough to notice that the decanter and glasses that she had given him were not displayed there. She had purchased those the first year she was out of graduate school and gainfully employed and had searched meticulously and exhaustively for a set he would like. The one she had purchased was of the highest quality, but a simple design and had cost her an entire week's pay. His reaction to the gift had been underwhelming, to say the least. And now the set wasn't even being used. She pushed down the hurt and started scanning the spines of the books on the shelf to see if one would appeal particularly to the man she had the misfortunate to call father.

Daniel admired the desk and ran his hand lovingly over the leather writing pad inset in the top. The desk was obviously old, well cared for, and probably quite valuable. It must be nice to sit behind a desk like this -- but why sit behind a desk at all when you're retired? And why have a personal assistant? He didn't really think that the good doctor was spending his time playing video games, internet shopping, or virtual dating. Daniel grinned to himself as he considered what the man's internet dating profile would say. It would have to be something along the lines of "Megalomaniacal retired scientist seeks woman to bow, scrape and cater to his every whim." He wondered how many hits a profile like that would generate.

Eyeing the computer, Daniel debated within his own mind whether to start with the desk or the computer, and finally decided on the desk in the hope that any passwords required -- and he expected some -- would be in a log located somewhere inside it.

The desk itself was a twin pedestal design with nine drawers, and of course, a lock. Daniel lifted the swan neck pull of the center drawer and confirmed that it was, in fact, locked. He surveyed the items meticulously displayed on the surface of the expensive piece of furniture to determine if any of them could potentially be hiding the key, but everything was so obsessively neat that there were no real hiding places. No cups with pens, no change dishes, not even any knickknacks that the key could be hidden under.

Daniel's own obsessively neat side had him admiring the minimalist simplicity of the desk's surface, but the reporter in him was annoyed that the key would not be so easily discovered, and he didn't want to have to pick this particular lock. The brass plate around the keyhole would run a high risk of being scratched and their intrusion detected, and that must be avoided at all costs.

Looking up, he noticed Sam walking along the bookcase reading spines and was wondering if she was trying to find a good book to curl up with tonight instead of searching, but then he saw her pull one book free, open it, and check both covers and the spine before rifling through the pages. He smiled to himself and his misunderstanding. Of course, she was taking an analytical approach to the situation. What was the point of going through every book, looking for the proverbial needle, when you can first figure out where in the haystack the needle is most likely to be found?

Returning his attention to the desk, Daniel ran his hands up the outside of the pedestals and then crawled under the desk.

He was a big man and the desk was a decent size, but it did not have an expansive opening; it was already dark enough in the room without his body blocking what little light there was in the shadowy space. He managed to lie on his back on the floor and inch his way underneath.

Once in place, he ran his hands up the inside of the pedestals and across the top of the space. No key. He shoulder walked himself back out from under the desk and turned his attention to the chair. He ran his hands over it from top to bottom, but no luck. Then he flipped up the plastic mat which protected the floor from the chair coasters. Still nothing.

He was getting frustrated and coming to believe that he was going to have to pick the lock of this antique desk -- with a fork -- in the dark. He leaned over and rested the heel of his hands on the edge of the desk with his fingers curled over the edge, hung his head and swore silently to himself. He really, really, really did not want to go at that pristine lock with a fork. It wasn't like the doorknob which had a bigger target and was rounded, so free of the bent tines. On this lock those other tines would rub, scratch and possibly even gouge.

He leaned more heavily on his hands curling his fingers tight to the edge and squeezed in order to suppress the need to hit something. He was that frustrated.

That's when the leather insert shifted under his hand. Although it looked meticulously maintained, it was not completely secured. In fact, the whole left corner was free from the wood beneath it. Daniel carefully pushed at the leather to create a space, then grasped the corner between thumb and forefinger and very gently lifted. He did not want to pull more of it loose, but just to look beneath what was already free. And there it was. Shining in the dim light was a brass key. One of those full-faced smiles spread across his face as he pulled the key free, held it up in the air, and did an abbreviated victory dance.

Sam performed a golf clap when Daniel was done with his little performance. She had first wondered what he was doing, but then noticed the glint of the key in his hand. He appeared quite proud of himself, and he should be. She wouldn't have had the first idea where to find a hidden key. She was beginning to think that running to him was the best decision she had ever made in her life. She had received protection, support, expert assistance, and the best damn kiss of her entire life. Yep, definitely the best decision she had ever made.

Continuing her scan of the books, Sam noticed that very few of them had any creases at all in the leather bindings. Most of them, it appeared, had never even been opened, but were instead placed on these shelves for show. A great reader herself, Sam knew how the signs of usage showed on even the most cared-for books, and these had been so cared for that they'd never been opened. To confirm that this was the case and not simply an illusion created by the dim light, Sam pulled one from the shelf and opened it. The covers pulled apart stiffly, actually creaking a bit as they opened, and the pages stayed firmly pressed together. As she turned pages it was obvious that this book had never been held open for perusal. She shook her head at the waste of having a library of books whose wisdom, adventure, or history had never been imparted. It was sad really, but on the other hand, it would narrow the scope of her search. She began looking again, crouching and extending to get her face as close to the spines as possible. Each time she found a book that showed signs that it had actually been opened, she pulled it from the shelf and examined it further.

As Sam was pulling books from the shelves, Daniel was pulling files from drawers. Once the newly discovered key had been turned in the center lock, all of the drawers were available. He carefully eased drawers open and searched for information, any information that would tell them something about what Sam's father was doing with his time. As persnickety as the man appeared to be, it was vitally important that everything was arranged the same way when the drawer was closed as it had been before it was opened.

"I can't believe that as neat as your father is, you became a slob. How does something like that happen?" Daniel whispered.

"Rebellion," Sam shrugged. "Much as you became neat to control the chaos, I embraced chaos as an escape from the order." Doing her best Norman Bates imitation, which wasn't saying much, she continued, "We all go a little crazy sometimes."

"I gotta tell you, if you kill your father and start dressing in his clothes, there's no way I'll marry you."

"Good to know." Sam tried not to put too much importance on the marriage comment. It wasn't a proposal by any stretch, more of a joke, but the word was still out there. "I make no guarantees against killing him, but I promise not to dress in his clothes. Good enough?"

"Knowing your father, I can live with that."

Both returned to their search and their own thoughts and continued for a time frame neither could determine when Daniel heard something that put him on high alert.

Footsteps echoing on the parquet floor outside. They had no time. He waved to Sam, bringing the imminent discovery to her attention and motioning her to hide while he replaced the file, closed the door, relocked the desk and placed the key back in its hiding place. This was done neither as neatly nor as quietly as they had been removed, for there simply wasn't time. He'd just heard the key slip in to the lock.

Though bleary eyed with exhaustion and fatigue, Edward accepted that the recent losses of sleep were worth it. This was almost over and then he would be out of this house forever and could sleep for days, catching up on all the sleep he'd lost over the last several months. He would leave tomorrow, or technically, since it was already morning, today. He wouldn't even wait until he had found a place. He had taken two weeks of vacation from his real job and he was going to pack up his room and go stay with friends or family. He had to get out of here -- but the details for the big event had just been finalized and needed to be there waiting for the commissioner when he came down in the morning. It was all set. Their primary plan was going into implementation and he was thankful for that at least. The back-up plan would have been much more difficult to put in place and held a higher risk of discovery. The primary plan left little to chance.

Considering that he had been up half the night -- or more than half -- laying the final foundations and confirming the finalized plans, Edward was going to sleep in tomorrow and the commissioner could rot in hell if he didn't like it. Knowing that the information which he now held in his hand would be, not so much requested as demanded at the ass crack of dawn, Edward was going on the offensive and doing the unthinkable. He had put it all in writing. The where and the when were listed, but the how was not detailed. There was no need for it to be. The commissioner was already thoroughly updated and educated on the facets of the primary plan.

Jaw cracking with a yawn that was so big he was afraid he'd pulled a muscle, Edward took the last few steps to the office door. Pulling his copy of the key from his pocket, and still amazed that the commissioner had entrusted him with one, he inserted the key and turned. Another yawn hit him at that moment, squeezing his eyes closed as he pushed the door open.

Sam had looked around frantically, but saw nothing offering concealment. There was no table to hide under, no couch to duck behind, not even a strategically placed potted plant.

Nothing.

All she saw was the floor length, heavy damask drapes. She hated to be so trite, but had no choice at this point but to rush to the west window and slide behind the curtain. She waited there, afraid to move, fearful of giving her position away, but Daniel didn't join her, and she heard the key turn and the door open.

Sliding the corner of the leather back into place, Daniel started for the drape behind which Sam had concealed herself. He had considered hiding behind the drapes of the window behind him, but he would be far too close to the desk and a potential bump that would expose them both. Then the door had started to open.

He was too far from the window, but was offered some protection by the angle of the door. He did the only thing he could do. He slid against the wall and prayed with all of his might that whoever was coming would not close the door when they entered and expose him.

Edward let the door swing open and made his way to the east wall bookcase and scanned the middle section for the book he was seeking. He had located it in a matter of seconds, as this was not the first time he had searched for the book. This method of passing information had been in place for more than a year, but the messages were usually coded. Tonight was different. Extracting the copy of President Laughlin's "Reform, Rebuild, Remake, Renew" he slipped off the dust jacket, inserted the note face down against the book cover, and slid the jacket back into place. He then returned the book to the shelf, but left it sticking about a quarter inch out from its neighbors. That done, he turned to leave and lock the door behind him when a movement at the window caught his eye. He looked hard at the window for several seconds, studying it from top to bottom. When no additional movement was detected, Edward turned and left, pulling the door closed and locking it behind him.

Daniel spotted Sam peeking out from behind the drape and he urgently ushered her back. They didn't know if whoever entered would be returning, as neither of them had been in a position to see. Not Sam behind the drape, and not himself, fervently praying behind the protection of the solid door. He took a few moments to thank God for the answer to his prayers, controlled his breathing, and when he felt safe, called softly to Sam.

Her heart had been thudding behind that curtain as adrenaline pumped through her body. Samantha had been sure that whoever it was that entered, whether her father or Edward, could hear it beating, as she could hear little else.

They took only a second to smile at each other and then each returned to their posts and resumed the searching process. As Daniel approached the desk, he noticed that the leather was bubbled. In his haste he had done a poor job of replacing the leather and was thankful that it had gone unnoticed.

Retrieving the key from its hidey hole, Daniel unlocked the desk again and went right back to his search. In the sixth of the nine drawers he had searched, he found a notebook. Sending up another silent prayer, he opened it on the desk and there, on the very first page, was a list of passwords. Old ones marked out and only one showing as active. Giving himself a mental pat on the back, he fired up the computer.

Sam was scanning the spines again, and getting a headache from searching small details in weak light, when she noticed that one book was not flush with the others. Carefully pulling it from the shelf, she opened it as she had the others and began searching the inside of the cover. She did not see the paper as it floated to the floor, and had it come to rest anywhere other than the top of her bare foot, she might have missed it altogether. Bending down to pick it up, she flipped the folded paper open and, upon seeing the words, let the book drop with a dull thud to the floor.

At the sound of the falling volume, Daniel's head snapped up to see Samantha standing there white faced, a piece of paper held in her hands. It looked like the proof had been found. Daniel stood up, hurried over to Sam, and gently took the paper from her cold, shaking fingers. The words were simple, but damning.

> "Commissioner,
> The primary plan is a go.
> Everything is in place and the
> Memorial scheduled for 4:00
> in the House as planned."

Sam's shaking was getting worse. Much worse. So bad that Daniel wasn't sure she could stay on her feet. He walked her over to "the commissioner's" chair and pushed her gently down into it. He then went about righting the desk, much more carefully this time, shut off the computer and replaced the key to its hiding place once more. Only then did he turn his attention to Samantha.

The time he had taken had given her the opportunity to get herself back under control. They weren't done yet and it was even more critical now that their suspicions had been confirmed. Her father was behind it all. He even had a title in the organization - the organization which had been hunting her down and attempting to kill her, but she couldn't think about that yet. She wouldn't think about that yet. She had to stay together so that she could perform the same task on the bookcase that Daniel had performed on the desk. She had to replace the note and the book in just the proper way. Although she now realized that she didn't know where the paper had come from. Had it been between the books or inside that particular book? She hadn't seen the paper when the book was opened, but neither had she seen it when she pulled the book out. Shit.

Pulling herself back together took every single ounce of will she possessed, but she did it. Rising to legs that were still shaky, she half shuffled, half hobbled over to where the book sat innocuously on the floor. She bent down and picked it up, then took a few steps back to examine the bookcase again.

It was critical that the note be placed back where it had been, so she absolutely must determine where that was. Her brain was fuzzy from stress, shock, and exhaustion, but she forced it to focus. Her head began to pound even more, but still she studied. What would her father do? Where would he hide this kind of information? It couldn't be anywhere that the casual observer might find it, or even the casual visitor, though she believed he had few of those. It also should be someplace where a police search, which had to be prepared for, would not reveal it.

Not between the books then, too easy to find. Stashing it between the cover and the first page was out of the question for the same reason. Was it placed at a certain page in the book? She prayed the answer to that question was no, as her head would likely explode before she discovered which number he found most significant.

Sam had been slapping the book against her leg as she thought, not even realizing she was doing it, but as Daniel watched he became concerned. He laid his hand over hers and brought the book to a halt. "You're going to damage the dust cover." The smile she bestowed upon him was completely out of proportion to what he had said.

She pulled the book from under his hand, slid the paper between the dust cover and the book, and placed it back on the shelf. She even remembered to pull the book out ever so slightly from the others.

Once that task was completed, Daniel assessed the office but could see nothing which revealed their search or their presence. He unlocked the door and opened it, flipped the locking mechanism into the engaged position, followed Sam out, and pulled the door closed behind them. They crept silently back up the stairs to their room, and it was there that Sam's composure finally deserted her and she went completely and utterly to pieces.

Once back in the privacy and relative security of their room, Sam sat on the bed and burst into tears, trying so hard to keep them silent that she nearly choked on them.

Daniel sat on the bed beside Sam, wrapped his arms around her, and held her tight. She buried her face in his chest and let the tears flow and the sorrow overwhelm her.

It was her father. He wasn't just part of it, he was it. It must have been him who had called for her murder. All of this, everything that had happened in the last few days, all of the attacks, all of the fear, all of the anxiety, had been pressed upon her by her own father.

She had tried so hard her entire life to please him, to be what he wanted her to be, sacrificing everything in that attempt; and in spite of her efforts, he still held her in such low regard as to call for her murder. He hadn't even cared enough to do it himself.

The sun was just breaking on the horizon by the time her tears were spent. They must leave, she knew they must leave, but there was still more to learn and she was too exhausted to sneak out tonight. She also feared that this might be the safest place for her to be. As long as she was here, she wasn't being hunted. There was no need to hunt any longer because they had her right where they wanted her. Here, under her father's despotic and tyrannical control.

Chapter 13

Her hand reaching out to slap the snooze button out of habit and without ever opening her eyes, Pamela fought to pull her sluggish brain to full consciousness, when all she really wanted to do was roll over, pull the blankets over her head, and go back to sleep. Yesterday had been a long day, and today would be little better and had the potential to be a whole lot worse. Although she was not personally going to be assisting anybody to meet their God today, she was, in essence, helping them into their grave. She had assisted Robert with getting the basic plans for the memorial service set, but would spend most of her day today finalizing those plans and watching their effect on the nation. There were so many details to work out, so many final preparations to be made. Just thinking about them made her groan and flop back down on her bed.

This was normally just the type of organization at which she excelled and which made her an excellent congressional aide, as well as an excellent spy for the NACR. Had it not been for the anxiety and horror of the day before, she would already be executing the tasks before her with military precision, but the events of the previous day had happened. They had been required to happen to get them where they were.

Pamela only wished one of the other NACR operatives in Congress had been assigned the planning. But no, it had been her senator who had come up with the idea on her own before it could be planted in the head of another. Under the initial plan, this was supposed to be Mike Jameson's responsibility, and he wasn't happy that he had been cut out of it. If she had her way, she would gladly pass this particular torch to him, but she wasn't getting her way.

The time had come to get this proverbial show on the road, so Pamela threw back the covers and set her bare feet on the cold floor. She was awake now. Stumbling to the shower, all of the details that needed to be worked out were running through her head. She had to find a way to get as many members of Congress to the memorial as possible, and the easiest way to do that was to let them know that the press would be there -- old media whores that they were -- this would motivate many of them to make an appearance. They certainly wouldn't want to be listed as one of the people who didn't bother to show up at a memorial for one of their own.

Beginning to feel overwhelmed again, she stepped into the shower and let the spray cleanse her.

Horace Mallard inserted the key into his office door lock and twisted. He had risen early that morning with his daughter on his mind and his thoughts had not been pleasant. This all would have been so much easier if she were good and dead. Especially as she now appeared far more difficult to control. He blamed the Callahan character for that - definitely a bad influence. But he couldn't kill her. Not yet. As soon as the ultimate goal was achieved, after dispatching all of the power hungry, self-serving corrupt politicians polluting the political process, he would dispose of the other irritation in his life, his daughter. There would be no risk then, for the ultimate goal would already have been revealed in all of its revolutionary glory. Closing the door behind him to keep out the noise that his daughter was sure to make on her rising -- she had always been such a distraction -- he made his way to his desk and turned on his computer.

He had been working for over an hour, wondering where Edward was this morning, when he noticed the book out of line on the shelf. Cursing Edward for leaving a note instead of imparting the information himself -- what was wrong with the man anyway and why wasn't he here? -- the commissioner slid the book from the shelf and pulled the paper from under the dust jacket. He stared at the paper in his hand, examined the book, and then scrutinized the office as a whole.

With the paper, which had been face up under the dust jacket, still clutched in his hand, he moved back to his desk, picked up the phone, and placed the internal call to Edward's office. After letting the phone ring eight times, he swore, hung up, and dialed Edward's bedroom extension. If the man was still asleep this morning of all mornings, then as soon as this was over he was going to be fired. This was completely ridiculous and totally unacceptable!

In his room at the back of the house, Edward was dreaming that there was a phone ringing somewhere and he was desperately trying to locate it. He was searching and searching, all he wanted was for that noise to stop so the previous pattern of the dream could resume, and it had been a good dream, one where he was free from his despotic quasi-employer. Eventually it seeped into his consciousness that the ringing phone was a reality and not part of the dream.

Well, shit.

Forcing his heavy lids open, Edward tried hard to pull the illuminated numbers of the clock into focus and groaned. It was only 7:45. He had been asleep for less than three hours. This is so really not fair, he thought to himself.

Still half asleep, as he probably would remain on this most important of all important days, he picked up the phone, knowing quite well who would be on the other end of the line. "Yes, sir," he said, and then pulled the phone away from his ear to preserve his hearing as the irate screaming began.

"What the hell are you still doing in bed? In case it has escaped your notice, this is one of the most important days in the history of our organization, possibly the nation, so why in the name of all that's holy are you still sleeping? There is too much to do for you to be lying in bed like the lazy assholes our tax dollars support. Get your ass in my office in five minutes. We have things to discuss."

Speaking into the now dead phone, Edward simply replied, "Asshole." With that satisfying exclamation he rose from the bed, his eyes still gritty and his head aching from lack of sleep, dressed himself, ran a comb through the curly hair standing up all over his head, brushed his teeth, and headed to the commissioner's office. He did not rush, did not even attempt to do so, he even deliberately took longer than the directed five minutes. If the commissioner didn't like it, that was just too damn bad.

When, a full fifteen minutes later, he did finally walk through the office doors, he faced the enraged commissioner and simply raised his brows. He had done nothing wrong, he knew it, and he was done, finished, fed up to the proverbial eye balls with showing deference. The commissioner would receive the same respect that he showed; which was none at all.

Bristling at the insubordinate behavior of his assistant, the commissioner brandished the note in his hand and said, "Why would you leave this in writing with other people in the house? Especially those other people? Why didn't you get your ass out of bed this morning and convey this information to me in person?"

"Well, sir," Edward said, "Since I was up until three o'clock in the morning compiling the information and confirming it with the necessary parties -- all while you were sleeping snug in your king-sized bed on your 700 thread count sheets -- I thought that you might want to know it right away. Although I now realize how selfish it was of me to desire even half of the sleep that you yourself enjoyed last night."

The commissioner narrowed his eyes and spat, "I don't appreciate your tone, Jackson."

Edward smiled, "I guess we're even then, because I haven't appreciated yours for months."

"You're done, Edward," the commissioner snarled. "After tomorrow you will clean out your desk and your room and get out."

Again, Edward smiled, "I've already begun packing."

The commissioner was taken aback by this. It was one thing to fire Edward, he wasn't going to need him once this was over anyway, but quite another for him to quit. He could not, however, reveal his shock at this desertion, could not expose his dismay.

Then again, how dare the man? The commissioner's hands tightened into fists, crumbling the paper he held there and bringing his attention back to the issue at hand.

No longer making the least effort to keep the condescension and derision from his voice, the commissioner spat, "So what were the details you were working out while I slept?"

"The memorial service will be today at four o'clock and it will be for government officials and their staffs only; with, of course, a few members of the press invited to cover it. The details regarding who those members will be are still being worked out. I have chartered a plane for you which will depart Kansas City at noon, giving you ample time to arrive and watch the events unfold. Pamela has done an excellent job of leading Congressman Sledgewater's new aide -- losing Simon was such a tragedy -- in the planning. As a result, the prescribed delivery props have been requested and are, of course, already prepared for the event. Everything is in place."

Not bothering to commend him for his work -- he no longer saw the point -- the commissioner simply nodded and then glowered at Edward from behind his desk. "With that out of the way, we will now need to focus on what to do about my daughter and that man." Holding up the note and brandishing it before Edward, he continued, "She knows."

"Aww, Hell," Edward thought to himself. This was going to make things way more complicated.

Daniel awoke later than usual that morning. He had slept until 7:30, but wished more than he ever had before that he could go back to sleep. Though he was awake, he didn't rise, not wishing to disturb the sleeping woman pressed against his side, her head on his chest and one arm thrown possessively across his middle. He grinned, stroked her hair, and considered their situation. They were going to have to get out of there pretty quickly, but what to do next was unknown. If they ran, he had no question at all that they would be chased down and attacked once more, but they needed to do what they could to notify the authorities of who was behind it all. Perhaps with the name of the organizer, Homeland Security would finally listen.

Realizing that the usual morning need was becoming pressing and could be put off no longer, Daniel slid from beneath Sam, pulled on his jeans, and headed to the loo. However, when he opened the bedroom door, the peace and quiet of the morning were broken by the shouting voices below, voices which brought him to an abrupt halt. There was something going on down there, but as he tried to listen, the need to pee was overriding everything else in his brain. As he engaged in the adult version of the potty dance, he did manage to understand enough to know that he and Sam had somehow given themselves away and that a discussion on what to do about them was being waged. When the conversation dropped to the point he could no longer hear, he finally gave in to the needs of his bladder.

He rushed through the process as fast as it was possible to rush that particular function, headed back to the room, and shook Sam awake. This was far more difficult than he had anticipated. In other circumstances he would have been amused, but the situation was too urgent for that.

Barely half awake, if even that much, Sam swung her arm and felt it contact with whatever was shaking her. How rude could you get? Then the words intruded onto her sleep-befuddled brain.

"Sam, wake up, Sam. We have to go. We have to go now." Being as quiet as he could so as not to alert the men below, Daniel was also attempting to make enough noise to wake Samantha from the depths of her slumber. This was a delicate balance that he had not yet mastered, nor had he counted on her being so difficult to wake. Finally, out of sheer desperation, he threw back the covers, grabbed her legs, and swung them over the side of the bed. This did the trick. She was awake, and she was pissed.

"What the ---," was all she got out before a large, warm hand was slapped over her mouth.

"Shhhh, Sammie. We can't let your father know we're up. I overheard the men speaking downstairs and they know we're on to them. They know we found the note."

For possibly the first time in her life, Sam was instantly awake and alert. She nodded at Daniel, collected her clothes and few toiletry items, and eased out the door to the bathroom. She listened intently on the way, but could hear nothing but muffled voices below. She knew they were talking, but couldn't actually understand the words.

Although the normal morning need to empty her bladder was there, the real reason that drove her from the bedroom to the bathroom had been the idea of changing in front of Daniel, and him doing the same. She wasn't quite ready to strip naked in from of him, or to see him in the same circumstances, when there was no time to do anything about it. Plus, there was the classic fear -- expressed by most women -- of showing themselves in all of their flawed nudity to the man they love in the bright light of day. Even though the day wasn't that bright, she still wasn't ready for that level of intimacy.

These thoughts managed to only momentarily distract her from the issue at hand - her father's continuing plot against her. Daniel was absolutely correct, it was imperative to get out of there and get as far as they could, as fast as they could.

Sam would have preferred to find out more information about the organization her father led, like what the primary plan was and which house the memorial would be held in, but they just couldn't risk it. She had already concluded that the memorial was most likely for the senator killed in the test run, but where was the house that was referenced? And how would all of the people sure to attend such an event fit in a house? It would have to be a pretty big house. She and Daniel would have to work out some of these details together, and she was sure they could, as soon as they were safely out of this particular house.

She tiptoed her way back to the bedroom as silently as possible, eased the door open, and slipped back inside to find Daniel fully dressed, their shopping bags already packed and ready to go. She finalized her own preparations by slipping on her shoes and her coat, stuffing her pajamas into one of the bags, and then taking his hand as he led them both from the room.

Daniel was aware of only one way out of this house. There were assuredly more, but they had not had much of an opportunity to explore the house the previous day, so the stairs were the only known avenue of escape. Unfortunately, these were the stairs that ended right at the door to the office from which the voices emanated. They would have no choice but to attempt to slip past that open door. Daniel knew it was open -- he had first- hand knowledge of how solid that door was – and there was no way he would have heard the conversation had it been open. He paused on the landing, straining to hear what was being said, but could hear only the low murmur of voices. Still holding Sam's hand in a protective clasp, he pressed his back to the wall and eased down the last half flight of stairs, praying that they didn't creak. He was preparing to take that final step and peek around the edge of the door and into the office when he was stopped in his tracks; the pathway of escape blocked.

The commissioner turned his head abruptly, his ears straining. "Do you hear that?" he asked. He had heard water running through the old pipes, he was sure of it.

Edward shook his head, but in fact he had also heard the water running. There was somebody awake in the house besides the two of them. "But if you're worried about it, perhaps we should close the door."

"If we close the door, then we won't see them if they try to leave, you imbecile," the commissioner snapped. "Since they found the note, there's a high probability that they'll try to leave and we absolutely cannot let that happen. Surely even you can see that."

"I can see how you believe that, but then again you've been pretty determined to have your own daughter whacked for quite some time now. So I'm probably not seeing this quite the same way you are."

The commissioner looked at the pudgy, nondescript man before him and wondered where this backbone had come from. He had been given the job as assistant to the commissioner because of his efficiency and ability to maintain his day job from home, but the commissioner had always assumed he was weak. He looked weak. And he had always spoken to the commissioner with such respect and deference, only adding to that image of weakness and submission. Now the deference was gone, and the appearance of weakness with it as well. Although the commissioner was sure that this new attitude was nothing but bluster and that, if challenged, the man's internal jellyfish would float to the surface once more. He was completely confident that even with this new attitude, Edward could be controlled.

"My daughter will be a martyr to the cause, and she should be grateful."

"If she were going to be grateful, you would have told her how you were going to use her study in the first place, but you didn't. Could it possibly be because you knew she wouldn't agree to it, wouldn't condone it? That doesn't make her a martyr, it makes it murder."

"A murder you'll be complicit in," the commissioner replied. "You appear to be getting a bit self-righteous here, Edward. But don't forget your part in all of this. Are you saying you're willing to risk the ultimate goal to save one woman?"

"Of course not."

The commissioner smiled at Edwards reply. He had him now. The man was still a believer and that was all that really mattered. Any sacrifice, any atrocity was acceptable as long as the goal was not compromised -- as long as the country was saved and salvaged for the next generation.

Then he heard it again, the water through the pipes. This was an old house, a historic house, and the noise of the pipes was one of the things that had always bothered him. He planned to have them fixed as soon as this was over and it was safe to have workmen in his home. He was grateful for those noisy old pipes right now. Those pipes were serving as an alarm system for him, notifying him that his daughter and her lover were awake, and they were up, and based on what they'd read, were most likely attempting to leave.

He and Edward would have to figure out exactly what to do, or he would figure out what to do and make Edward carry out the plan. Keeping his voice low, the commissioner gave cursory instructions to Edward and they waited; waited to hear the footsteps on the staircase.

It was only a matter of minutes until the creak of the landing gave the pair away, so the commissioner had not had time to formulate much of a plan. Instead they did the only thing they really could; they stepped out the door and blocked the couple's exit. The commissioner grabbed his daughter's arm, leaving the man to Edward. He knew full well that Callahan would not leave without Sam.

Sam shrieked reflexively as she felt the hand clamp with painful force around her upper arm and drag her into the office. She struggled, pulled, dug in her heels, and fought with all of her strength, but could not break free. The grip was so strong that she was sure she'd have bruises, but she wasn't going to be docile. She'd been docile her whole life and look where that had gotten her. She was forced into one of the office chairs that faced the desk, and landed in it with a thud, sending a shock wave up her spine and rattling her teeth.

Daniel was trying to get to her, but Edward must have been stronger than he looked because he was managing to hold Daniel, which was probably a good thing. If freed, Daniel would probably kill her father and she couldn't allow that. Not yet. They still needed more information. Once they had that, then she'd let Daniel kill him. Or she'd do it herself.

She watched her father round the desk to assume his position of power behind it while Edward left the office, locking the door behind him, effectively securing them inside. God only knew what he was going to do - get a gun maybe. But instead of being frightened, well, instead of being *only* frightened, she was mad as hell. "So are you going to kill me, Daddy? Hasn't that been your plan all along? Eliminate the one thing in your life that you utterly failed at?"

The commissioner smiled at his daughter. Of course she was going to bring drama and emotion into this. She never could look at things with only logic and reason, maintaining that clinical and objective distance. "But you're not a failure, dear. You managed to perform a vital service for me. We would not be where we are with our current plans if not for the work that you performed. Your research was impeccable, and vital to the cause."

Jumping in to defend her, Daniel replied, "There's no question that Sammie is not a failure. The issue was your failure, not hers, for though you may be a brilliant scientist and the leader of whatever terrorist organization this is, there's no denying that you are one shitty father."

The commissioner clenched his jaw, but refused to dignify this statement.

"The most important role a man can ever perform," Daniel continued, "and you sucked at it. And I mean really sucked. You weren't just a bad father, you were downright dreadful. If you've done as piss poor a job of running the terrorist group as you did of running your own family, I would say that we have nothing at all to worry about."

Daniel leaned back in the chair in a relaxed posture and held up his hands. "I mean, how many attempts were made to kill your daughter? We know of at least two that failed, but how many were there actually? What do you think you can really accomplish when you can't even kill a woman frightened of her own shadow?"

Sam shifted her affront from her father to Daniel and turned to tell him that she was absolutely *not* frightened of her shadow, at least not all the time, but then saw him wink at her. He knew her father's temper. He knew how it could work to his advantage.

"The failure of my staff was unfortunate."

The shifting of the blame from himself to his staff was not lost on the two people before him. Even now he was taking no responsibility for failure of any kind.

"Had they succeeded, we would not be here now. It was also unfortunate that you had to go public with what you knew. It was an inconvenience for me to take the time to discredit you in the press, and even more of an inconvenience to bring you here. Not to mention the expense of chartering that plane. But, of course, we could not kill you at that point."

"We?" Daniel asked. "Don't you mean you? Or are you using the royal 'we'? Have you appointed yourself king as well as commissioner?"

Jealously maintaining his position of power behind the desk, Horace Mallard attempted to preserve his calm and composure. "The 'we', of course, refers to the organization as a whole. The National Association for Congressional Reform could not risk our plan to return the country to the people by eliminating the undesirables from public office. It is a lofty goal, perhaps, but an important one; one that you should both be proud to have assisted with."

Daniel directed his next statement to Samantha. "Do you know who he sounds like? He reminds me so much of Clive Sledgewater. The same condescending tone, the same idea that the people must be protected from their own choices. The same stink of elitist bullshit wafting from his every pore."

"And the same willingness to destroy another in order to protect himself," Sam nodded.

"We can't forget that."

The commissioner slammed his hands down on the desk, half stood, and leaned over to roar at them. "I am not like that man. I am better than him. I will do a much better job of leading this country than he ever did, ever could. That arrogant and corrupt excuse for a public official will be lying on a slab with a tag on his toe in less than twelve hours."

Edward chose this moment to step back into the room. He held a gun in one hand and rope in the other. He handed the gun to the commissioner and used the rope to tie first Daniel, and then Samantha to their chairs.

This brief interruption gave Sam some much-needed time to think. She had to stop viewing this man as her father and start thinking of him as what he really was; the leader of a terrorist organization. They had a rough idea of what was going to happen, but what she still didn't understand was why, and knowing why would help her understand the what and the how.

Think scientifically, Sam told herself -- get to the root of the issue -- work your way down until you know the real cause. She knew she couldn't fix the root cause, but she could definitely use it to understand the symptoms it generated.

Cocking her head questioningly to the side, she asked, "Why are you doing this? Not me. I understand why you've got me here, but why the ultimate goal? What's the rationale for that?"

With the two prisoners bound securely to the chairs and with a gun in his hand, the commissioner now felt secure enough to stand and pace. He always thought better while on his feet, and this had the added benefit of illustrating to the prisoners just how little a threat they posed to him now.

"I don't expect you to know or understand why, Samantha. You've ignored what was going on in the country, abandoned your role in the running of the nation. You abdicated your power as one of 'we the people'. You are, in fact, one of the millions of reasons that this action has become necessary. But Mr. Callahan understands, don't you?"

Daniel met the gaze leveled at him and responded. "Nope, not a clue. Enlighten me if you would."

"You of all people, Mr. Callahan, I thought would understand. After all, wasn't it the corruption and superior attitude of Congressman Sledgewater that ruined your career? Wasn't it the suppression of the voice of the press, the loss of our freedom of speech, and the criminal behavior of our elected officials that resulted in you losing your position as a member of the illustrious Washington Press Corps? Wasn't it your belief in the principles on which this country was founded that led you to pursue a story that brought the violation of the freedom of the press down on your head?"

Daniel had listened to this interpretation of events which had shaped his life and realized two things. First, that Sam's father, this lunatic, had a pretty good understanding of what had occurred, and two, that his voice rose as he spoke like a southern preacher attempting to rid his congregation of sin. It was all fire and brimstone from a man determined to bring those things down on his own head.

"You think I would," Daniel shrugged, "but I still don't. I've survived all of that and I've not been driven to murder, so you'll have to explain it to me, especially since you appear to be doing okay here." Daniel let his eyes wander around the excellently appointed office, making his meaning clear.

"Yes, I've done well. Quite well," the commissioner explained, "because I saw the direction the country was headed and made my investments in foreign markets. I saw the way the government was punishing success and driving the corporations out of the country, all while complaining and blaming *them* for their defection. They raised the taxes so high, added so much regulation and so many penalties that our companies could no longer compete in the world, and when they moved to greener pastures, the government, in their infinite wisdom, chose to levy even harsher punishments on those that chose to stay. They say they are working to fix the unemployment rate while simultaneously driving out the employers, and they use all of this, all of the problems caused by their own actions, to prove to the people how the government is the only answer; the only way to save them."

The commissioner was working himself up to full frenzy now, his pacing was becoming more frantic and he gesticulated wildly.

Edward had remained in the office, but had placed himself out of the way in one of the dark corners and listened with a different ear than he ever had before. He knew this speech, had heard it many times before. He understood the reasons behind the goal, knew everything that was going to be said, but this time he heard something new in the words, for in that moment when he had entered the room, new light had been shed on his commissioner's plans and beliefs.

"They've changed this country from the representative republic it was designed to be," the commissioner continued, "and have turned it into an oligarchy. Our leaders, those we elect to represent us, believe we are too stupid to know what is best for us. They not only don't listen to the will of the people, they view those who voted for them with nothing but derision. Whatever principles they may have when they enter the sacred walls of our Capitol Building, they quickly sell for a hefty contribution for their reelection campaign fund. They do nothing once they are in office but work to stay there, to hold their seats and their power. What they work towards is not the betterment of the country, the people, or the world, but solely the betterment of their own bank account. They seek office to serve themselves and not the people. And they must be stopped."

"And what gives you the right to make that decision?" Daniel asked. "They are voted into office by the people, no matter how misguided the people might be, so what gives you the right to take them out?"

The smile flashed by her father sent a shiver up Samantha's spine. She had never seen a smile so filled with self-satisfaction, and so devoid of any real feeling.

"I was given the right by the founding fathers, as were we all," the commissioner crooned. "The only difference is that I am willing to take up the challenge and the cause to preserve their ideal."

Daniel leaned over as much as he could and stage whispered to Sam, "Daddy's gone barking mad."

The commissioner heard this, as he was intended to, but what happened next was not precisely what Daniel had in mind. Striding forward with his arm stretched back, the commissioner approached and delivered a backhanded slap that sent both Daniel and the chair he was tied to reeling backwards. As he was unable to break his fall with his hands bound behind him, Daniel's head made solid contact with the floor with a sickening thud. The sound made Sam cry out in fear and rendered Daniel senseless. Horace Mallard nodded to Edward, who had remained in the corner, and beckoned him forward.

This was getting way out of hand, Edward thought to himself. He gently reset the chair and checked for blood, but found none. From the way Daniel's head hung loosely from his shoulders, Edward was afraid that the man had been killed, but was reassured when he pressed fingers to the man's neck and found his pulse strong and steady.

Struggling against her bonds, Sam fought to free herself, to help Daniel, and to then kill her father. She didn't know what she would do if Daniel were dead. She had found her strength through him, through his unconditional support. He had not tried to change her, but his very presence had helped her to change herself and start on the path to becoming what she should have been, what she would have been, had she been raised by any man but the one who stood before her.

"You sadistic piece of shit!" she screamed. "He's right, you're mad. You always have been, but I can see that it's just gotten worse over the years. But it's going to end, and soon. I'll kill you myself if I have to."

"No, you won't," the commissioner replied, rubbing the back of his hand where it had made contact with Daniel's cheekbone. You don't have it in you to take the life of another human being."

"You're not human," she countered.

"And I'm not mad," he continued, ignoring her last statement. "I was given the right to eliminate our government, as was Edward and every other member of the NACR. We believe in our Constitution and that it can be resurrected from its current place in exile, its reduction to memorabilia, and its relegation to an artifact, outdated and unnecessary. But what's more," he continued, the self-satisfied smile securely on his face once more, "we believe in the Declaration of Independence. Listen to these words and tell me that we don't have the right to do what we are doing. That we were not given that right by our founding fathers."

Samantha continued her struggles to free herself. She was imagining every way in which she could rid the planet of the insect before her. She had meant it when she had said he wasn't human and she intended to see him crushed.

"But when a long train of abuses and usurpations," he quoted, "evince a design to reduce them under absolute despotism, it is their right, it is their duty, to throw off such government and to provide new guards for their future security."

Oh, my God, Sam thought, he actually believes what he is doing is right and just. She scrambled to remember what he had once made her memorize and then responded, "But what about the bit about prudence dictating that governments long established should not be changed for light or transient causes? What about that?"

"You think the charges I have laid out are light?" he raged. "They have destroyed the very form of government they were charged with protecting and upholding. That is not a light or transient cause. What they have done is turn us into the very thing that our founders fought so hard to free us from. Those men pledged their lives, their fortunes, and their sacred honor to free us from an oppressive government, and we have repaid that sacrifice by systematically breaking down every standard of belief and code of honor that set us apart from the rest of the world, even the most sacred of all our principles - that the power should rest with the people. Thomas Jefferson once said that when people fear their government, that is tyranny, but when the government fears the people, it is liberty. Take a look at the circumstances of your lover and tell me where you think we fall on that scale."

Hating to admit it even to herself, Samantha could not deny that he had a point. What was done to Daniel and to others was tyranny in its finest form, but the people still had the right to vote. That had not been taken from them yet, and the people still had the ability to free themselves without this violence. The question was only whether or not the people would.

"So, why Congress?" she asked. She had to keep him talking. She was sure that if she could only keep him talking, she would learn enough to stop him. "Why not the President?"

The commissioner sneered at his daughter. "That's a stupid question, my dear. It does nothing but display the general ignorance of the people as to where the power actually lies. When it comes to domestic policy, the President is nothing but a figurehead. He can do nothing without Congress. He can suggest, he can have all of the ideas and all of the plans that he wants, but without the approval of Congress, he can do nothing. The President gets the blame or the credit for whatever situation the country is in domestically, but it is the Congress who is ultimately responsible."

"It was Congress who passed the bills that drove our corporations into bankruptcy or exile," he continued. "It was Congress who voted to take more than half of your salary and nearly three quarters of mine to support their own spending habits. It was Congress who approved the appointment of judges who interpreted our Constitution to allow what it was written to deny. It was Congress who passed bill after bill designed solely to expand their own power. It was Congress."

Sam shrank back in her chair as her father had progressed closer and closer to her during his speech until he was finally right in her face. So close that she actually felt his spit as he pronounced the word "power". She regretted the revealing movement when she saw his satisfaction at her withdrawal. "Goodness, Father, did you brush your teeth this morning? If you're going to get in someone's face like that you might want to consider some mouthwash."

Horace drew his arm back to hit her as well, but she made no movement to avoid it. She did not cower, did not retreat. She simply glared at him defiantly, her expression one of contempt, not fear.

Dropping his arm, he moved back and resumed his pacing and his litany. "What?" he asked, "You don't agree with my statements? Do you think the president has any real domestic power? Which is the first article of our Constitution, I ask you? Is it the executive branch?"

He waited for her response, but she gave none.

"No, it is the legislative branch," he continued again, enthralled with the sound of his own voice. "The writers of the Constitution did not want the power in the hands of one man, not even one branch. Their first draft of our governmental blueprint had no executive branch at all. The

Articles of Confederation had only a president of the Congress, part of the legislative branch, but no executive branch at all. Since it was added later, as an afterthought, only to fill a gap identified in their process, how much power do you think they would really have given? They did their best to protect us from a government of corruption by putting the real power in the hands of many and not the hands of one, and what did we do to thank them? We elected a corrupt many. No, my dear, killing the President is nothing but a symbolic gesture. But," a slow smile spread across his face, "that does not mean that he will be exempt from our revolution."

"And then what?" Sam asked, still attempting to gather as much information as she possibly could. She had to know exactly what they were planning, but he was doing nothing but preaching. Standing on his soapbox before his captive audience and attempting to regale one and all, or at least her, with his brilliance.

She had been his captive audience too many times as a child not to recognize the behavior now, but she had to bring him down from the pedestal on which he'd placed himself and back to the plan, that ultimate goal he had referred to. "What will the country do when our elected officials are all gone and we have no leaders at all? What will happen when we revert to anarchy? Is that what you want?"

The commissioner shook his head. "Did I teach you nothing? The state governments will still be in place and, should all of the Federal Government succumb, would have their rights -- those taken from them by the Federal Government -- restored to them. There will not be anarchy; the rule of law will be maintained."

"But why this way? Why with my research? If you wanted them all out, why not just attack the Capitol in the conventional way? Why not blow it all to hell in dramatic fashion and make a real statement? Go Independence Day on their asses?"

He opened his eyes wide in shock and held out his arms in a placating gesture. "We're not monsters, Samantha."

She snorted.

"Those of us at the NACR recognize that there are some, though they may be few and far between, who are in their positions of power to serve something or someone other than themselves. We don't want to see these people harmed. Of course we don't."

Samantha snorted again.

The commissioner ignored the undignified sound from his daughter. "But how to differentiate the good from the bad? How were we, so distanced from the happenings on the hill, to determine who was worthy to serve and who should be removed? It was you who gave me the idea."

"Me?" Sam questioned. "How on earth did I give you the idea to wage this deranged attack?"

"It was your study that first gave me the idea – your determination to find the genome that drove people to seek power over others and commit crimes in pursuit of that attempt. It was you."

"But I thought --"

"That I had paved the way for the research?" He interrupted. "No. You did that on your own. The government was more than happy to fund a study that would give them even more power over the people; research that could ultimately lead them to their dream of imprisoning people for crimes they might, at some point in the future, commit. I saw a different promise in your work than the government. I saw it as a tool to use, not against the people, but for the people, to free them from their oppressive government."

"So how ---"

"Will it be used?" He interrupted again.

She had him now, she thought. He appeared more than happy to share his pride in his idea, fully expecting her to marvel at his own brilliance. This must have worked on Edward and many others, but it would not work on her.

"We do not want leaders who seek only power, therefore anyone predisposed to that must be eliminated. But the question was how? A delivery agent was necessary, of course, but it went much further than that. Once we identified the agent, the extract of a plant -- just like so many of our medications -- it was only a matter of building it in strength so it would kill instead of just irritate. We genetically modified and enhanced it until it would not only work to destroy the genome, but would bond with the enzyme secreted by the destruction to generate an allergic reaction. How severe the reaction will be is directly tied to the strength of the genome and, therefore, the amount of the enzyme secreted by its destruction. In those where the genome is strong, the reaction will, of course, be fatal. Just as it was on the criminals you used in your study when we tested its effectiveness on them."

This much Sam had figured out for herself. It was the delivery of the agent she was interested in. "Fascinating," she replied sarcastically.

The commissioner continued to pace. "But how to deliver it became the question."

Here we go, Sam thought. Now she would learn the where and the when.

"We could not apply it one at a time or we would give ourselves away too quickly. If too many died, then questions would be asked and investigations would begin. We needed a way to deliver it to all of them simultaneously. But what could bring them all together? Our first thought was to deliver it during a major vote, but this was problematic as only one house of Congress votes at a time, and too many members don't show up to vote at all. So with that we might be able to get much of the House of Representatives, but the Senate would be warned, and we couldn't have that, so as tempting as it was to take out the House, that simply wasn't enough."

The House, Sam thought, was that the house from the note? Of course it was. Whatever was going to happen was going to take place today in The House of Representatives. "Senator Highfall," Sam whispered.

"Yes," the commissioner was really hitting his stride now, "He served a dual purpose. He was the main pilot, to ensure that it would actually work. The perfect target, as his corruption and need for power was no secret to anyone."

He neglected to mention that Highfall was not his choice. That, in fact, his choice, had she been the only one tested, would not have enabled them to proceed. This omission was not missed by Edward.

"So not only did he provide us the test, but he is also providing us a venue; the excuse to bring all the members of Congress together. They will gather to mourn the passing of one of their own. We have seen to that, it has already been scheduled, and should the President choose to attend, why so much the better. Though the executive branch is not our primary target, it will only help the cause to put the President to the test as well."

"You can't do this!" Samantha cried, struggling to free herself from her bonds. "You can't kill people because of a genome they have. You have no way of knowing if that is what's driving them to seek elected office. My test was on rapists and domestic abusers, how can you apply that to Congress? How?"

The commissioner raised his brows, his expression one of incredulity. "Do you think they're not rapists and abusers? They have been raping the American people for years, robbing them blind, talking down to them and convincing the people that they cannot succeed without Congress. No, Samantha, our elected officials behave in exactly the same manner as an abusive spouse; and today they will meet their justice." With that, he walked calmly to the office door, "Now, if you will excuse me, I have to pack. I have a plane to catch and an historic and revolutionary event to witness."

Chapter 14

Pamela sat down at her desk in the Hart Building, fired up her computer, and got to work. She'd already responded to fourteen e-mails from Robert via her Blackberry while on the Metro during her morning commute. Yes, this was definitely going to be a long day.

Congressman Sledgewater was exerting his influence, which was considerable, in order to suspend voting. Taking into account that most members of Congress would rather do anything than sit in chambers and actually work, this was not a difficult task to accomplish. So far everyone had responded positively, they all wanted to be seen showing their respects to their colleague. They could not miss the opportunity to display their compassion and concern for another to the American public. Pamela already felt dirty and the real filth hadn't even started yet. She had received confirmation that the candles for the service were ready and would be delivered to the Capitol for inspection by the Secret Service by one o'clock. Black arm bands were being pulled out of storage and would also be ready for inspection.

The list of speakers was nearly completed and currently being organized, but considering how many wanted to use this event to promote themselves, this memorial could go on forever. If it were allowed to, that is.

The seating arrangement was still being worked out. Robert, meaning Sledgewater, wanted to reserve the chamber seating for the members of Congress and relegate the staff and the press to the public area in the balcony, but Pamela wanted a first-come, first- serve situation. This was purely selfish on her part, as she wanted first hand, up close and personal exposure to the culmination of all of her plans and hard work, as did the other members of the NACR.

There were not many members who would be attending, only the fifteen remaining NACR-planted congressional aides. They were the only ones who would be able to communicate what really happened to the rest of the organization. The press would be there, of course, but they had not reported the truth for so long, she wasn't sure they even remembered how. She and her fellow aides would be on the informational front line as they always had been.

The news of Senator Highfall's death had been all over the newspapers and the networks that morning, but no mention had been made of Samantha Mallard. Last night, the main news networks had poked fun at FNB News for putting a delusional woman on the show and treating her assertions as true. They'd had a good time joking about how most of the people at FNB, and those who watched it, were kooks or nut cases anyway, but FNB would have the last laugh. Whatever damage that had been done to this last bastion of real reporting with the release of Dr. Mallard's fake mental illness, would be reversed when the ultimate goal was accomplished. It was only a matter of hours now. Exhaustion was giving way to excitement. Soon they would all get what was coming to them. It was going to be glorious to behold.

Elsewhere in the complex of congressional offices, the other fourteen aides were feeling much the same anticipation, all doing their utmost to ensure that their congressman and all others would attend the memorial. Each and every one of them was looking forward to the afternoon and the culmination of the plan, finding it increasingly difficult to focus on their congressional work.

Luckily, as with any other day, nothing of consequence was getting done on the hill in any case. The majority of Congress was not in chambers discussing legislation, but in their offices gossiping or on television doing interviews. This left the aides plenty of free time to plan and scheme and manipulate, and this they did with a vengeance, for it was vengeance they sought.

Slowly returning to his senses, Daniel groaned, he thought his head was going to explode. His mother had always told him that his smart mouth was going to be the death of him, and for a minute he thought it had been. Attempting to raise his hands to his aching head only served to remind him that they had been bound behind him, and his attempts to release them caused the throbbing pain to escalate to a point that he nearly lost consciousness once more.

Shit, he thought to himself, he was going to be useless. He didn't even know how long he'd been out. He turned his head to ask Sam for this information and found her still bound beside him. Her head was hanging down and her hair shielding her face. For a brief moment he thought she was dead, his heart clenching in fear, and then he heard her swear.

"Son of a bitch," Sam said under her breath. Her wrists had been rubbed raw and were probably bleeding from trying to work them free of the rope.

She'd had a rope burn in junior high school which she'd received in gym class, the only class she'd ever come close to flunking. She never had made it up that stupid hanging rope, as she lacked the upper body strength to pull herself up. A fear of heights had only made the situation worse. She had hung there, less than halfway up the rope, paralyzed with fear until finally her arms gave out and she slid back down, burning her hands on the way.

She'd remembered that pain ever since, and the humiliation of landing on her butt beneath it, but was willingly subjecting herself to it now in order to gain her freedom. It was imperative that she get to Daniel and make sure he was alright. His continued silence had frightened her, but that weak groan had scared her even more. She'd flashed him a brief look but had not been reassured, returning to work on her wrists even more fervently.

Her arms and shoulders ached from pulling and twisting, but at last the bonds were beginning to loosen, the blood on her wrists helping by acting as a lubricant. She gritted her teeth one more time and pulled, and pulled, nearly dislocating her shoulder in the process, but finally she had one hand free of the rope. With one hand released, the bond was loose enough to easily free the other. She shook the rope off, paused only long enough to rub her aching wrists, and in the strongest show of defiance she could think of, wiped the blood on the immaculate leather writing pad of her father's antique desk. Then she bent and untied the ropes that bound her to the chair itself. Once that was completed, she popped out of her chair, toppling it in the process, and went to work on the bonds still securing Daniel.

Sam pulled at the rope, but the knots were bulky and tight and she just couldn't get her fingers, slick with the blood dripping from her wrists, around them.

Becoming increasingly frustrated and desperate, she finally used her teeth and got the first knot untied, after that it moved fairly quickly, which was a very good thing because she had no idea how much time they had left. Edward had exited the room without saying a word and she was unsure how long he might be gone. He could return at any minute, but at least if he did, this time they'd be free. They'd have a chance to overpower him.

They must get out of here and the sooner the better, but this also went beyond them. They had to escape so they could notify the authorities of what was going on, and this time she would make them listen.

Daniel popped his shoulders, stiff from being pulled back to bind his hands, rubbed some feeling back into his arms, and stood; then immediately dropped back into the chair as a pain washed through him which was so intense it nearly made him vomit. He took several deep breaths and then tried again, managing to stay on his feet this time. He hated this. He was supposed to be there to protect Sam, and instead she had to take care of him. Willing himself to stay on his feet and keep alert, he followed Sam as she led the way to the door.

The need to escape was becoming increasingly urgent. Sam had no idea how long Edward had been gone now, but she did know that it had taken her way too long to free them and time was running out, but if they could only get out of the house, they'd have a much better chance.

They were so close. Just out this door, down the hall and out the front. They had no car for an escape, very little cash, and they were out in the country with no close neighbors, but she'd still feel much safer outside.

She reached out to open the door, the knob turning in her hand -- but she was not the one controlling it.

Concerned over what was happening and the plans of the commissioner once the ultimate goal had succeeded, Edward purposefully climbed the stairs to the master bedroom. He had questions that needed to be answered and he was determined to get those answers. What he would do once he had them, he didn't yet know.

Reaching the commissioner's private sanctum, he knocked and was bid to enter. Opening the door, Edward watched the commissioner as he packed, but remained silent. He didn't know where to start; how to ask the question that he needed to ask. His silence granted him the solution to his problem.

"How big of a plane did you charter, Edward?" the commissioner asked without even glancing up or acknowledging Edward's presence in any way.

Taken aback by the abrupt question, Edward answered automatically. "It seats eight. Why?"

"Excellent work. I've decided that we'll take Samantha and the man with us."

"Pardon me, sir?"

Annoyance making his movements harsher than they had been, the clothes snapping as they were shoved unceremoniously into the luggage, the commissioner, his voice dripping with condescension, deigned to explain. "We're taking them with us. We cannot dispose of them here. It would raise too many questions. We could explain it, of course, stating that she came here to hide and they found her anyway, but it would be much better for her body to be found in Washington. So we'll be taking them with us."

The commissioner finally looked at Edward and raised his brows, waiting for a reaction or an argument. When he received neither, he continued, "Once we land, you can take them somewhere and eliminate them in whatever way you deem fit." A truly evil smile spread across his face as he reached into his bag and pulled out a vial. "I even have a sample of the agent for you to plant on them. When they are found, it will appear that they were involved in the attack all along. It's perfect."

Edward eyed the vial in the commissioner's hand and agreed that it was perfect; the best possible solution for all. He had not known, but should have guessed, that the commissioner would have held on to one of the samples, using it as both a symbol of, and a trophy to, his brilliance.

His own plans solidifying in his mind, Edward took the vial from the commissioner, returned to his room, packed a small bag, and then headed back to the office.

The delivery truck pulled up to the Capitol Building, the driver's gaze focused on the Secret Service agents waiting for her. Bianca was accustomed to this procedure, having delivered to the Capitol many times before, but it never failed to ratchet up her anxiety. She nodded to the agents, a man and a woman, as they stepped toward her.

The cargo in the back of her truck would have to be examined before it could be unloaded, and especially before it could enter the building. The agents had equipment that tested for bombs, biological weapons, and pretty much any and every threat that could be imagined.

Following their normal protocol, one agent stepped forward and questioned her on her cargo; what it was, where it was coming from, who had ordered it, etc. This was all checked against a list of scheduled deliveries. Once it had been established that this was a legitimate delivery, that agent waited with Bianca while the other circled around to the back of the truck, opened her bay door, and hopped into the cargo section of the truck. This was always the most nerve-wracking part of the process. There was no conversation with the agent who watched her -- and she did watch her. The Secret Service had no sense of humor when performing their duties, their job was much too important. The role of the agent currently before Bianca was to ensure that she did not interfere with the inspection by the male agent in her cargo bay, and she was performing that duty really, really well.

After what felt like an eternity, with Bianca doing her best not to fidget or make any movement which would raise concerns in the agent before her, she received the all clear from the inspector and was instructed to proceed to the loading dock. Throwing the truck into gear, she pulled away from the agents, filled with relief, trepidation and exhilaration.

Sam snatched her hand back from the door and looked frantically around the room, putting Daniel on high alert. They had determined the previous night that there was nowhere to hide, and Daniel was in no shape to fight, but he was going to try. He couldn't leave her to handle this alone now, so he took the only action he could think of. He pushed her behind him in order to offer the weak protection of his own body.

The first thing Edward saw when he opened the door was the empty chairs. These two really were impressive with their ingenuity and tenacity.

The next thing he saw was Daniel's fist flying at his face. Ducking quickly to the side, Edward easily dodged the blow and then held up his hands and rushed into speech to dissuade another attempt. "I don't want to hurt you. We're taking you with us to Washington."

Daniel had already drawn his arm back for another attack when the words sank in. He felt Samantha struggling behind him to wage her own attack, an attack he needed to prevent.

Holding her back by using his larger body as a shield, he spoke to her over his shoulder. "If they're going to take us to Washington, what can we do, Sam? Think about that. Even if we escape here, and I'm not saying we could, we're still here.

At least if they're taking us to D.C., then they aren't planning to kill us. Not yet anyway." Daniel managed to communicate with his expression what he couldn't come right out and say with his words. He had faith that Sam would use her infinite logic to see how this could work to their advantage.

Giving up the struggle, Sam did her best to look defeated and replied, "You're right. I'm sorry I got you into this, Daniel. I'm so sorry."

Edward did not believe their contrition for even a second, but that mattered naught. Even their pretense of cooperation worked as much to his advantage as to their own.

Chapter 15

The predicted ice storm had missed Kansas City, allowing the plane to take off as scheduled. However, the ice storm was still in their original flight path, which meant that the flight plan had to be changed. There had been a delay while this was accomplished, which succeeded in causing the commissioner to become an even bigger jackass than he was before, which Edward had thought was impossible.

The flight had been scheduled to leave at noon, with a two-and-a-half-hour flight landing at Ronald Reagan International Airport at 3:30. This left enough time to get to the Capitol, but not much leeway. What little cushion there had been was now being eaten away, first by the delay in take-off and then by the changed flight plan.

The commissioner was not dealing with the delays well at all, and Edward had taken about all he could of the anger and blame that had been directed his way. Luckily for Edward's peace of mind, they had a strong tailwind and the flight time was decreasing with every mile. If the wind was maintained, they might actually land early instead of late. He prayed this was the case.

Edward was not the only one praying for the early arrival. Both Sam and Daniel had been upset by the notice of the delay. They needed to be on the ground before the memorial started -- way before if they were going to be able to stop it. Leaning to the right so he could see out the window, Daniel watched the ground below pass slowly by. He could not tell where they were, but he knew it wasn't close enough to Washington.

Their hands had been bound once more when they entered the plane, but the bonds were looser this time, enabling the blood to circulate and a bit more ease of movement, especially as their hands had been re-tied in the front instead of behind them. A concession for Samantha's wounds had also been made by wrapping some cloth around her bloody wrists so the ropes did not rub against her already-damaged skin. It was a concession which surprised her, but one which she appreciated all the same.

The new position would make things much easier when the time came to attempt another escape, and Daniel had been thinking of little else. He was pretty confident that they wouldn't be killed before leaving the aircraft. It would look more than a bit suspicious to attempt to unload two dead bodies – not enclosed in coffins -- from a plane, but once off the aircraft, the attack could come at any time, and from anywhere.

The biggest risk was that their adversaries would not be the aging scientist and the round assistant they currently faced, but more along the lines of the woman from the Smithsonian; a professional. Daniel could feel the tension and impatience emanating from Samantha in her position to his left, and he did his best to reassure her through his expressions, but he was having a hard enough time reassuring himself. Time was what they needed most, and it was quickly running out.

Time was crawling by for Senator Fisk as she sat behind her desk unable to focus. The voting had been suspended for the day in deference to the passing of Senator Highfall, and Mara was at a loss as to what to do with her extra time. She should be reviewing the legislation up for discussion or vote before the Christmas break -- she refused to call it the winter break -- but the legislation could not hold her attention. It was dull as dirt under the best circumstances, and these were far from the best.

Much as she had anticipated, the blame for Highfall's death had been placed on her. Gossip ran amok throughout the hill and the press corps, and the common theme was that she had deliberately exposed him to whatever it was that generated the allergic reaction. Although the trigger had not yet been identified, this did not stop her from being blamed -- especially by herself. She had checked her office over and over again, but couldn't find anything that would have triggered such a reaction; but there had to be something. She had a pervasive tugging at the back of her brain that told her something was wrong here, but for the life of her she could not determine what it was or where it was coming from.

Outside Mara's office door, Pamela was watching the clock and accomplishing even less than her boss. She had spent several hours on the phone with Robert this morning and everything had been confirmed. All the plans were set.

Similar to the day before, it now came down to waiting, and time was passing so slowly that she could actually hear it tick by. The ceremony was to begin at four o'clock. But they would begin entry and seating an hour before. This would give plenty of time for the members of Congress to show up, get their faces on the television or in the newspapers, and find their seats. The process would begin in earnest in less than an hour now.

Tick, tock.

A short distance away at the Longworth Building, where the Speaker of the House kept his office, Robert was feeling the stress of organizing an event of this magnitude and importance in such a short amount of time and was missing Simon Deefer deeply. Thrust into this position, he was doing the best he possibly could. He was eternally grateful for the assistance he had received from Pamela, but there were so many details and so much more preparation than he had expected.

The arm bands and candles had both been delivered and were sitting in boxes waiting to be unpacked and displayed. Lots of boxes. Lots and lots of boxes. He had requested that tables be set up to give this a more polished look, as they did not want to be handing the President or Cabinet members arm bands and candles straight out of the cardboard containers. Several other interns were now working to unload those boxes and lay the items out on the tables. This is a task that would continue as people arrived.

The tables would have to be replenished as quickly as they were depleted if the prestige of the process was to be maintained, but this was becoming potentially problematic as well.

The intern, with her face buried in one of the boxes, stood up and succumbed to a coughing fit -- again. Most of the interns had purchased bottles of water to deal with the scratchy throats that were resulting from their labors. This wasn't all that surprising, considering that the boxes for the arm bands were covered with dust and the candles were slightly scented. At least the votives in the glass holders were -- the tapers appeared to be unscented -- but even a slightly scented candle, in such mass quantity, could become a bit overpowering. Even Robert was beginning to get a bit scratchy.

The process was set up to have tables on each side of the three doors into the chambers, as well as by the stairs leading to the press galley above, with greeters in front of each table. As those wishing to pay their respects made their way to the chamber, they would be handed a program, an arm band, and two candles; a taper candle and a votive in order to hold candlelight service for the senator. It would be beautifully poignant and would play well with the press.

Robert was glad that he had thought of it, and the Speaker had been impressed with the suggestion as well; so impressed that he was taking credit for the idea. As interns, those assisting with the ceremony would not actually be allowed inside, but they would have the unique and coveted opportunity of bringing themselves to the attention of every member of the government, and few of the interns were overlooking this opportunity. There was not a chance that any visitor would make it through those doors missing any one of the four items to be dispensed.

Taking a swig of the water to dampen his increasingly scratchy throat, Robert congratulated himself on his work in organizing this event on such short notice. It was something that would definitely be remembered, and in the world of politics, being remembered was crucial.

They were making good time and would be preparing for the descent into Ronald Reagan any minute now. Edward rolled the bottle in his pocket over and over, using it much as one would a worry stone.

Little of any consequence had been said on the flight. Other than the commissioner complaining and ranting about potential delays, the flight had passed in near silence. Not even the man and woman had spoken, though what could they really say?

Sliding the bottle from his pocket and holding it concealed in his hand, Edward finally asked the question that had been burning in his brain all morning. "Commissioner, what did you mean when you said you will be a better leader than Sledgewater?"

"What?" The commissioner, distracted and absorbed in his own thoughts, had all but forgotten that his assistant was with him. Instead he had been checking his watch repeatedly, becoming more and more anxious as the time passed. He wanted to be there when it happened, needed to be there. He planned to be standing outside of the Capitol, watching as the events unfolded. It would, of course, have been better to be inside, but he couldn't take that risk - not with what his own genetic analysis had revealed.

Edward repeated the question, turning the bottle over and over in his hand.

"I don't know what you're talking about," the commissioner lied.

"I think you do," Edward replied, his face devoid of emotion and his voice just as absent of inflection. It was almost as though he were talking to himself. The importance of the answer to his simple question -- the answer which he believed he already knew -- was not revealed by him in any way. "You didn't say you *would* make a better leader, you said you *will.* It sounded like you intend to step into one of the seats vacated by the success of your plan."

Edward leveled a piercing gaze at the commissioner. "Is that your personal ultimate goal? To see yourself appointed as a senator or representative for the state of Missouri? Or are you willing to move in order to qualify for any position that opens?"

The commissioner was struck dumb. He attempted to cover this with bluster, but couldn't quite make it believable. "How dare you, Edward? How dare you accuse me of serving my own interests, when we both know that I seek only to serve the people?"

Samantha snorted and contributed her own opinions into the mix. "You haven't done anything in anybody's best interest but your own in my entire life. No matter how this may have started, it was always about improving your own situation."

She directed her next statements at Edward. "I caught that statement this morning as well, but it was no surprise to me. My only surprise would be if that was not his plan from the beginning. I find it laughable that an organization that seeks to remove the power hungry from leadership, appointed a power hungry, self-serving elitist as their leader. Ironic, don't you think?"

Edward nodded, but kept his attention focused on the commissioner. "Yes, that has occurred to me as well. Wouldn't it be a shame to remove the corrupt power seekers from Congress, simply to replace them with people exactly the same, if not worse? That would be a real tragedy for the people and the nation as a whole."

The pilot chose that moment to announce that they were on their final approach to the airport and should be on the ground shortly. Edward bided his time. In the interest of his own safety, he could do nothing until the plane had come to a stop.

Daniel let loose with a sarcastic laugh. "Wouldn't it be rich if your grand scheme to save the country actually made it worse? And if that ---" he used his bound hands to point towards the commissioner, "--- is what we're going to get as a replacement, the country is totally screwed."

This was the fear that had been creeping deeper and deeper into Edward's conscience all day.

Unable to justify any further delay, Senator Fisk was forced to admit that it was time to head for the memorial and face the nastiness that was sure to be thrown her way. She was grateful to have Pamela at her side, the one friend she had been able to count on in a world full of enemies. She grabbed her coat and purse, locked her office, and waited patiently as Pamela prepared herself. The two women walked out of the Hart Building with heads high, ignoring the murmurs that followed in their wake.

She should be used to this by now, Mara thought to herself, but of all the things she'd been accused of over the years, murder was a new one, and as much as she tried to deny it, she was hurt that people could actually believe her capable of that.

The two women stepped into the waning light of impending dusk on the brisk afternoon, pulled their collars up around their ears, and walked the short distance to the Capitol. The press was already amassed outside -- she knew there would be some members of the press inside as well -- and they were shoving microphones in the faces of the passing mourners. So much for the dignity of the occasion.

As tasteless as this behavior was, it was nothing compared to the behavior of the so-called mourners as they took the opportunity to pimp their ideas to the American public in a time of tragedy. The transitions from the subject of the memorial to their pet projects wasn't even particularly subtle. As Mara walked by the Speaker of the House, commanding the attention of the mesmerized press, she heard him discuss how much respect he had for Senator Highfall and how they had worked together in a bi-partisan effort on this piece of legislation or that, and how important the creation of the North American Union, a mirror of the EU, had been to the dearly departed. Mara snorted and said to Pamela, "Highfall would not have supported the creation of the NAU unless he was promised a position of power within it, just like the good Speaker there."

Pamela nodded her agreement. She was so nervous and excited that she didn't dare speak, too afraid that the tremor in her voice would give her away. She was concentrating so hard on not smiling that she was wearing a frown instead, however, nobody saw this as inappropriate for the situation.

It didn't matter that Senator Highfall had not been one of the more respected members of Congress, or that his behavior had made him all but a pariah among his own party; this was a performance for the press and everyone was playing his part.

Keeping her head down, Mara made her way through the milling crowd, running the gauntlet, doing her best to avoid the media crowding in on all sides. She heard questions such as, "is it true he died in your office?" and "did you know he had severe allergies when you invited him to meet with you?" She ignored them all.

That is, until one reporter went too far and asked, "Senator Fisk, don't you think it's inappropriate for you to be here today?" That was the very last straw. Mara had had enough! Stopping so suddenly that Pamela nearly plowed into her back, Mara turned to the reporter, a fresh faced, lovely young woman obviously attempting to make a name for herself, and froze her to the spot with a glare. "What did you just ask me?" Mara questioned. The ice dripping from her eyes and her voice made the chill of December in D.C. appear balmy.

The perky little reporter, pleased that she had grabbed the senator's attention when others had failed, placed an expression of somber concern on her face. She'd practiced it in front of the mirror for hours that morning. "Based on the rumors flying around the Capitol today, do you not think it inappropriate for you to appear at the memorial?"

"And what rumors would those be?" the senator asked, brows raised in a challenging stare.

The reporter, too inexperienced to see the pit she was about to tumble into, reveled in the scoop she was about to receive. "I'm sure you've heard the rumors and speculation which all indicate that Senator Highfall was helped into his grave - by you."

Senator Fisk smiled, and for the first time the reporter began to question what she was doing. "Oh, I see, so you work for one of those gossip magazines, do you? I didn't realize the Enquirer had been invited. I do apologize; you see, I thought you were an actual reporter - someone who does research and investigation and reports the facts. Had I known that you worked for a gossip rag, I never would have responded to your question." Mara then glanced meaningfully at the microphone in the hands of the reporter and continued, "You have either picked up the wrong microphone or GENBS has sunk farther than even I could have imagined. And everyone knows they haven't reported actual news for years."

Leaving the reporter speechless behind her, Mara stomped off, regretting her behavior immediately. She shouldn't let them get to her like that. It was just that type of interaction which had given her the moniker "the terrorist", but irresponsible reporting was one of her biggest pet peeves. How would anything ever change if the American people were not being told the truth? Objective journalism was a thing of the past. A politician was no longer judged based on his actions and his policies, but by whether or not the reporter agreed with their ideology, and many in the so-called press were bigger elitist pricks than those they reported on.

Pamela's hands were shaking with anticipation, which she masked as a chill as they cleared the press and stepped, at long last, into the Capitol and removed their coats. There was already quite a crowd and Pamela looked around in satisfaction. Scanning the crowd, she saw two cabinet members, three Supreme Court Justices and the Vice President. All of her hard work and tireless efforts, especially over the last two days, was about to be rewarded. They would be a nation of free people once more.

The plane bounced as the landing gear connected with the runway. Edward tightened his fist around the bottle he held, using his fingers to unscrew the cap. When that was completed, he let the cap drop and placed his thumb over the neck of the bottle. As the small plane taxied slowly and steadily to its gate, he decided the time had come to take action. He called the commissioner's name, and when he had his attention, uncurled his fingers and held the bottle up to display. "Do you remember what you gave me today? The item you instructed me to plant on the dead bodies of these two nice people, after I'd killed them in whatever way I deemed appropriate?"

"Put that down!" the commissioner snapped. He shifted his gaze to the prisoners, gauging their reaction to this statement. They were not surprised. They were not afraid. They were pissed off. "Be careful with that, Edward. It's dangerous, as you well know."

"Yes, commissioner, I know how dangerous it is. But I have the feeling that it's far more dangerous to you than it is to me. Shall we test that theory?"

Edward's tone finally penetrated the commissioner's arrogance, and for the first time in a very long time, he was actually afraid. He reached out to snatch the bottle, but Edward kept it out of his grasp. The aircraft seatbelt limited his movement and had him reaching across Edward, but all the shorter man had to do was switch it to his other hand and stretch his arm to the side. The commissioner continued to reach for it with one hand, while working to unfasten the belt with the other.

Yelling in triumph as the belt gave way, the commissioner leaned across Edward, grasping and clawing for the bottle. Nearly in Edward's lap and spitting with rage, he closed both his hands around Edward's and pulled, attempting to bring the arm in towards him and to unpeel the fingers from their death grip on the innocuous-looking bottle containing the deadly fluid.

Samantha watched the byplay, amazed at the behavior displayed by her father. Daniel's attention, however, was on the floor where, rocking back and forth with the motion of the plane, was the brass top to a small bottle. He attempted to get Samantha's attention without alerting her father to what was going to happen, but she was transfixed.

Unable to gain Sam's attention non-verbally, Daniel finally conceded defeat and whispered harshly in her ear, "Cover your nose and mouth. Now!"

The commissioner, hearing these words, pulled even more frantically, fear riding him hard, desperation overriding all logic and reason. He tugged as hard as he could, but the resistance was suddenly and surprisingly gone.

His hands flew back with such speed that he punched himself in the nose. Feeling moisture on his face, he immediately assumed that he was bleeding and turned to berate Edward for his behavior, but the malicious satisfaction that was spread across Edward's countenance made him check a second time.

The commissioner wiped his face, feeling the moisture, and brought his hand up to check for blood. There was none. In dawning horror, as his throat began to swell and his breathing became increasingly difficult, the commissioner held up the bottle in front of him for examination.

More than half of the contents were gone.

He had splashed the deadly agent directly into his own face.

He could barely breathe. Even his most desperate attempts for air pulled in only enough oxygen to keep him conscious as he fought to suck the live-saving molecules down a throat swelled nearly closed. He reached out for assistance, his eyes pleading with his daughter. She only turned away; her face buried deep in her sweater, and curled her legs away from his grasping reach. Next he grabbed on to Edward's pant leg, attempting to pull himself up, seeking help though he knew none would be coming. Edward did not turn away, but remained focused on the commissioner and watched his breathing become more and more labored.

Then Edward, too, began to cough -- and then to wheeze.

The commissioner, still fighting for breath and praying that this would ease, reached out again, turning once more to his daughter and finally snagging the leg of her jeans, attempting again to pull himself up.

Using her hands to keep her nose and mouth covered with her sweater, Sam had nothing but her feet to use as a weapon, and she employed them now. She raised her free leg and used her sneaker-clad foot to kick at her father's grasp on her pant leg. She needed to be free to run as soon as the plane stopped and the stairs were dropped, but his grip was still surprisingly strong.

With increasing desperation she kicked again, but her foot glanced off his hand and connected with something solid, and it was not the floor beneath her. She heard and felt something crunch.

Pain shot through the commissioner's face as his daughter's foot connected with his nose, but he could give no voice to this pain, for now an airway already dangerously closed was filling with his blood.

By the time the announcement came that they were free to exit the plane, the commissioner was dead -- sightless eyes in a blood-splattered face staring up at his daughter, forever locked in a pleading gaze — and Edward was hunched over in his chair, his coughing had evolved into wheezing.

Ignoring the dead man at their feet, Daniel raised the ropes to his mouth and worked the knot free, and then untied Samantha's as well. It was, after all, his turn. They then grabbed their belongings and walked as calmly as possible off the plane and onto the tarmac.

Edward Jackson cleared a throat made sore from forced coughing, checked his watch, and eased to his feet. He then called for the pilot and advised him of a medical emergency on the plane. Gazing down at the bloody, lifeless body of the commissioner, he checked his watch again. It was a quarter to four; the memorial would begin in fifteen minutes, leaving no time for Samantha and Daniel to stop the events that had been put into motion.

Perhaps they could have called the police or Homeland Security; that is, if their cell phones had not been removed from their bags. Edward himself felt no desire to witness what would happen and had found the commissioner's desire to do so macabre in the extreme. No, he did not need to see it; just knowing what would occur in the Capitol building would be enough to satisfy him.

Michael Easton handed out candle after candle after candle. His throat was going hoarse from repeatedly stating that the instructions for the candles were in the program, but his spirits were inappropriately buoyant. There were so many people here. He had been handing out these candles for over half an hour now, and it was going so quickly that the other intern, Vanessa, was working up a sweat trying to keep up with replenishing the table. The number of people who had showed up for this memorial was gratifying, to say the least. They would continue to hand out the props until the moment the doors were closed in preparation of the lighting of the candles inside the House Chamber.

After the candlelight portion of the memorial had commenced, no late comers would be allowed to enter the hall; it would, for all intents and purposes, be sealed. This, he had been instructed, was out of respect for the symbolic gesture. A gesture that Michael had learned would be introduced by the president himself. This really couldn't get any better.

Clive Sledgewater, having made his speeches to the press on the Capitol steps, now stood inside the House chambers and directed people to their seats as they entered; thereby making himself more the center of attention at this event than the recently deceased. He shook hands, schmoozed, conveyed his regrets and grief, and accepted the thanks for organizing this event.

He had done nothing in the actual planning, his current role the first he had undertaken himself. His new aide and remaining interns had done all of the planning, addressed all of the details, placed all of the orders, contacted all of the people, and done the printing and unpacking, but Sledgewater was more than happy to take the credit for this himself. He had even reserved himself a seat, front and center.

The very best part of this event, though, was the press coverage. There were two networks already set up in the chambers to record the president's speech and the remainder of the ceremony. There were also the additional press people outside interviewing members of the government as they entered, but here, inside the House chambers, aside from an occasional scan of those already seated, the coverage was trained on him. The only news currently being made was who would enter next, and they all had to shake hands with the Speaker of the House.

Yes, planning this event had been brilliant and would, he was sure, change his life and his career forever. This was just the kind of compassion and bi-partisanship that the people wanted to see in a president, and he would use it to his best advantage to secure that position and the power it provided.

Daniel and Samantha sprinted through Reagan International, weaving in and out among the blissfully unaware travelers. Daniel continuously looked back to ensure that Sam was still with him and adjusted his stride accordingly, but urgency was riding him hard. He checked the clock overhead, the time -- listed as 3:47 in digital red numbers -- mocking him. It was only a short distance from the airport to the Capitol, but first they had to get a cab, and that could take precious time that they just didn't have.

Sam wheezed through the stitch in her side and willed her legs to keep moving. She hated to run, and had repeatedly stated that the only reason to run was if she was being chased by something which intended to eat her, or if she was desperately late for something vitally important. This instance qualified for the latter.

Since theirs was a small plane, they had arrived at the very end of Terminal A and had to make their way down that long hallway to the ground transportation area, the clock ticking away the seconds with each step. Sam tried her very best to keep up with Daniel, but she knew he was slowing his long, powerful stride to enable her to keep pace. She wished now that she had taken up jogging, or even yoga.

Finally they made it to the ground transportation area and came to a halt outside. Sam pulled in much-needed oxygen, wheezing nearly as hard as her father had moments before, while shivering as the cold winter air hit her sweat-dampened skin. They scanned the area. There was not a taxi to be found.

Daniel swore vehemently, grabbed Sam's hand, and led them back inside. "We're going to have to take the metro. I didn't want to do this, but we have no idea how long it's going to take to get a cab. We could try to rent a car, but all that paperwork would take precious time, and with our luck there would be a wreck on the bridge."

Sam nodded, but didn't have the breath to speak. Recognizing this, Daniel did not break back into a run, but walked at a very brisk pace to Terminal B, where they could catch the metro. They passed under another clock whose red digital numbers, now displaying 3:51, caused Sam to pick up her pace even more. Nothing in the government starts on time, she reminded herself. They had more than the remaining nine minutes. She was sure of it. What she didn't know was how much more time they possessed. She feared that it would not be enough.

Pamela took her seat beside Senator Fisk in the House chamber -- black band secured on her left arm, both candles in her hands -- and scanned the crowd for the third time since she'd entered. There was going to be standing room only at this memorial, which was extremely gratifying. She saw the television cameras strategically placed around the room and the Secret Service agents flanking the podium.

The addition of the president was the perfect cherry on top of her metaphoric sundae.

The mourners were encouraged to take their seats so that the event could get underway, but many continued to mill around. This was fine with Pamela, she didn't need them seated for what was to come.

Then the real fun began. Two of her fellow aides, working for the NACR and not for Congress, began walking up the aisles with their own taper candles lit. They used those to light the taper candles of the people seated on the ends and instructed them to light the candle of the person next to them. As each new wick ignited, Pamela's excitement escalated. The symbolism couldn't be more appropriate. It was going to be so beautiful watching Congress go down in flames.

Daniel pulled up short as they reached the platform for the Metro Yellow Line. That smug clock showed that it was 3:54 and the next train was scheduled to arrive in one minute. Waiting even that single minute was grating on him and he paced in order to burn off the adrenaline pumping through his system, but there wasn't much room on the platform to accommodate his long and agitated stride.

This couldn't have possibly been timed worse, as they were hitting their travel at the beginning of rush hour. As a result, the platform was crowded with people and the trains would be filling up as well.

Seconds later as the train approached, Daniel was proven correct. The crowd swarmed towards the edge of the platform. Samantha struggled against the pressing crowd to stay with Daniel, but the masses of people and the noise of the train were rattling her already savaged nerves. She nearly sighed with relief as she felt Daniel's reassuring grip settle around her wrist again. He wouldn't allow her to be pushed aside or to miss this train, and that's all she needed to know. The doors of the Metro opened and the flow of people trying to exit crashed against the flow of those fighting to enter.

Feeling like a salmon swimming upstream in the desperate desire to reproduce, Sam pushed and shoved and fought to get on that train, not in an attempt to create life, but in the effort to preserve it.

Once safely on the Metro train, both Daniel and Sam remained standing to expedite the exit process. They would be getting off at the fourth stop on the line. Had this been a normal day and time not such an issue, they would change trains at that stop, switching to another line in order to get to the Capitol, but Daniel believed they could get there faster by walking –or running -- the remaining few blocks than by going through the maze of the D.C. Metro System.

Maintaining a death grip on the pole to which she clung, Samantha swayed and jerked with every stop and start of the train. She looked at the faces which surrounded her, average people going about their ordinary business of the day, and wondered how these people would be impacted should she and Daniel fail to arrive in time. What would happen to the city of Washington and its surrounding areas? Would these people still be on the trains when news was announced that their government was gone? The sheer enormity of the responsibility she had before her caused her knees to buckle as they jerked to a stop again.

Daniel reached out and steadied the woman beside him. She was such a trooper, so dedicated and determined. With everything she had been through the last few days, she was still on her feet, still fighting, still trying to stop what may be unstoppable. He loved her so much, but respected and admired her even more. She was stronger than she gave herself credit for being, and she made him strong as well.

He could not be sure whether he would still be trying if she were not with him. The desire to allow congress to reap what they had sown was roaring inside of him. The knowledge that Sledgewater would not miss such an opportunity and would be in attendance had him battling with his own conscience. He acknowledged, to his own shame, that if the Speaker had been the only target, he would have allowed the events to play out and would have felt no regret in doing so.

Their stop arrived after what felt like an eternity, and Daniel and Sam pushed and shoved their way out of the train and scurried through the underground to burst suddenly into the waning light of one of the shortest days of the year. They headed east at a near run, but not so fast that their approach would raise suspicions. They could not risk being stopped and questioned, creating a delay they could ill afford. All the while, both prayed fervently that God's will be done; that whatever occurred, whether they succeeded or failed, be based on the will of God and not the will of man.

Pamela was nearly bouncing in her seat as the president entered the chamber; the appropriately solemn expression pasted upon his face, he stepped up to the podium and called the chamber to silence. The glow of the burning tapers lent a spiritual air to the room -- an air that had been missing for decades, if not over a century. It won't be long now, she thought to herself, and couldn't help but wonder who in this room would live and, most importantly, who would die.

Secret Service Agent Steven Alvarez stood beside the podium, legs apart and hands clasped loosely in front of him, ready to bolt into movement should any threat arise. Normally, within these chambers he could relax as much as an on-duty Secret Service agent could relax, which admittedly was not much. This should be a safe room, and yet something had him on edge.

Deep in his gut he felt that something here was not right, and his gut had only ever failed him when he had failed to heed it. Perhaps it was the candles that were creating this general sense of unease, perhaps the impending birth of his first child, the rising costs of everything, or a combination of all of the above. But the candles were what he could focus on, and they were a disturbing distraction.

In the flickering light of one thousand candles, movement was hidden and strange shadows were cast. Were he not viewing the situation before him with an analytical eye, he may have been able to appreciate the beauty of it; or how it related symbolically to the President's statements on allowing the bright light of democracy to shine. He saw only the darkness of the shadows they cast - shadows made deeper as the house lights were extinguished, leaving the gathering illuminated solely by the handheld tapers.

The president wrapped up his lead-in with statements about what a great leader Highfall had been and how he had dedicated his life to the service of the American people. It was a speech so laden with bullshit that no one was likely to believe it, not even him, yet it was what needed to be said. It was unsuitable to tell the hard truth at a memorial service, and the hard truth was that Highfall had been a self-serving bastard unwilling to agree to anything unless there was an earmark placed in the bill for him. He sold not only important votes, but insignificant ones as well.

The President viewed the candles, not as the symbol of the lasting impact of Highfall's work as they had been presented, but instead as a ceremonial burning of the senator's memory. He spoke about the reason for the candles now, attempting not to drown in the shit he was shoveling.

The press was crowding the walk, blocking the path, as Sam and Daniel rushed as fast as their tired and aching bodies would allow them. The pair was pulled to an abrupt halt when one man recognized Samantha. At his shout, the reporters and cameramen pressed in on her, all asking questions simultaneously, questions she had neither the time nor the inclination to answer. She did the only thing she could. Screaming at the top of her lungs, she told them all to call for a Hazmat team, to call Homeland Security, the Secret Service, anybody. Daniel, on the other hand, just called for them to get the hell out of his way.

The response Samantha received from the press people surrounding her was limited to questions about her mental health. She had tried. That was all she could do.

Daniel began kicking, throwing punches, jabbing elbows and generally anything and everything he could do to move Samantha through the frenzied throng on the walkway and into the Capitol Building. Precious time and energy was wasted in this struggle, but at last they were inside and only a few steps away.

A cough echoed through the silence of the chambers, and then another, setting Agent Alvarez onto high alert. This was most likely due to the heat and smoke being generated from the candles, but it could also be something else. The candles were supposed to have smokeless wicks, it was a requirement for this room, but he couldn't be sure. He scanned the faces now illuminated solely by the light of the candles held before and below them, but he could see nothing that gave him reason to react. Yet every fiber of his being was urging him to get the president the hell out of here and to do it right now.

The Secretary of the Treasury cleared his throat loudly. He was being unforgivably rude to the leader of his party, but the pervasive scratching of his throat had to be assuaged and he had not a drop of water with him. His wife elbowed him in the ribs and handed him a hard candy from her purse. He popped it in his mouth and sucked.

This irritation in the back of his throat had started when he sniffed the votive candle to discover if it was scented; he had a low tolerance for any type of perfume, it made him phlegmy, it made him cough, and though he could detect only a slight scent from this candle, his throat was already itching. It probably hadn't been a good idea to sniff it in the first place. He should have had his wife sniff it for him. He counted himself lucky that it wasn't heavily perfumed, or he'd have succumbed to his coughing and missed the memorial entirely.

A few more coughs erupted in the chamber, which ratcheted up Agent Alvarez's instincts again. He was posed for action, just wishing that the president's plan was to leave when his speech was completed, but he had wanted to stay in order to show his support. Like everything else in this city, this memorial was all about appearances and nobody wanted to be the subject of negative discussions in the press the next day because they had chosen to skip it.

Continuing with his speech, the President said, "And now the time has come for the symbolic lighting of the special candles you each received. Upon my count of three, using your taper candle, we will as one, showing our unity at this time of loss, light the votive, which will be left to burn as brightly as our liberty in this great nation. One…"

Samantha's shoes, wet from the patches of snow outside, slid across the floor as she attempted a change of direction at high speed on a highly polished marble floor. Recovering quickly, she followed Daniel to the hall that led to the House chambers. Her feet pounding on the marble, her rubber soles squeaking, she and Daniel approached the doors, only to find them closed. Their path was blocked again, but after coming this far, they were not about to let a few kids stand in their way.

The interns had been turning all late-comers away amidst much grumbling and even shouting and swearing, but these two were really taking the cake. They were pushing, heaving, and fighting – fists, elbows, and feet flying -- one intern was lying on the floor with a bloody nose, another was still skidding on his butt down the long hall, and still another sat propped against the wall, knocked out cold.

Daniel was paying no attention to whom he hurt, whether male or female, something he never thought he could do, but their time was running out and maybe already gone. Hearing the President speaking inside, his speech leading up to the lighting of the candles, caused him to fight even harder.

Daniel's hand closed over the door pull just as he heard the word "three" spoken from inside. He called on the last of his strength and heaved the door open, using it to push those interns who were still standing out of the way, in time to see more than one thousand people lighting tainted candles. "Noooooooo!" he screamed.

Chapter 16

They were too late, Samantha thought, they had failed. All of the strength and energy she had been willing to her body in the attempt to prevent this catastrophe abandoned her in one fell swoop. She collapsed to the ground in exhaustion. The interns were still pulling at Daniel, keeping him from entering the room further, and through the still-open door seeped the sounds of coughing and the scent of the candles. Maybe it was not too late to save some, she reasoned. She negotiated with her tired body to force additional strength into her tired limbs for what she prayed was the last time.

She did not stand, but instead crawled around and through the legs of the interns until she had worked her way into the room. Then, and only then, did she jump to her feet and spring into action. She immediately started blowing out candles, pulling people from their seats, and hustling them out the doors. "The candles are poisoned!" she was screaming as loud as her strained and tired lungs would allow.

Daniel's scream had galvanized Agent Alvarez into action. This is what he'd been waiting for and all he had needed. Stripping off his coat, he threw it over the face of the president, wrapped his strong arm firmly about the leader, and rushed him from the room, all while calling in the report that a biological agent had just been released in the House of Representatives.

The president had first been confused by the coughing and the yelling, but knew better than to struggle when the Secret Service perceived a threat. Blinded by the coat over his head, he stumbled along in the hurried rush to remove him. He had not been given a candle, had not lit one, and had been several feet away from the closest of the ignited possible poisons. He was feeling no effects of anything, not coughing as those in the chamber had done, so he believed he was safe. What he could not understand was who would orchestrate and execute such an attack, and even more importantly, why.

The people struggling to exit finally succeeded in shaking the interns off of Daniel and nearly trampled them in the bid to escape. This left him free to join Samantha in the attempt to save as many as possible, though he did not hold out much hope that it would be many.

Pamela lit her candle with sinister anticipation, her eyes darting around the room, watching the action which would release the deadly agent into the air. The coughing began and unable to help herself, she smiled.

The man seated next to her lit his candle and the agent, carried through the rising smoke and heat, curled right up and into his nostrils. Immediately he began to cough. He inhaled deeply in preparation to blow out the candle, but was seized instead by a fit of gasping, wheezing breaths, sucking even more of the agent into his lungs.

His hands began to shake as he fought harder and harder to pull in oxygen and finally, both candles dropped from his hands. The votive landed squarely in the lap of the woman on his left who was herself struggling to breathe. Waving the taper in an attempt to extinguish it, she was sending wax flying, but she had not been the only one with this idea. Hot wax was sent hurling through the air from more candles than her own, showering the population in the flying droplets.

Even more wax pooled in her lap from the votive that had landed there, but it was so much worse than that. The candle had landed on its side with the wick still burning, and had set her skirt alight.

Dropping her own candles in her panic and sending them rolling across the floor with their wicks still ignited, she rushed to beat out the flames with her bare hands. Focused on her skirt and the fear of being burned, she became oblivious to anything else; even forgetting about the other candles around her, until she heard the whoosh and smelled the stench of burning hair.

Clive Sledgewater, in his position of power within the room, had an uninhibited view of the President being hustled away. Taking a page from that book, he held his tie up to his nose and mouth and used it as a filter, but it was too late, even though he had inhaled little of the poison before the filter, he had already inhaled too much of the powerful agent. The coughing was beginning, the allergic reaction had commenced.

The Speaker was managing to delay the full fury of its impact by breathing through his tie, but he recognized the symptoms. He'd been through this before. Allergic to bee stings, peanuts, pollen, and mold for most of his life, he had suffered through severe allergic reactions several times; so many times that his doctor had prescribed an Epi-pen which was to be carried with him at all times. He had it with him now. He could do this he told himself. As a man third in line for the presidency, he could do anything, he reasoned.

Reaching inside his jacket pocket, he pulled out the pen and then, through his peripheral vision, he caught a glimpse of Daniel Callahan at the back of the room pushing and shoving at people. He should have known that Callahan would be behind this. Not seeking vengeance his old wrinkled ass! He knew he had been right to suspect him in the death of his aide, and when this was over he would see that man crucified for what he had done. If only he could do that literally instead of just figuratively, he thought, it would be even better. Perhaps he could write legislation to resurrect the old Roman punishment. That was definitely something to think about.

Forgetting the Epi-pen in his hand in favor of pursuing the man who had the audacity to attempt to kill him, he began purposefully stalking up the aisle to the door, the tie still over his mouth and nose, but before he had gotten far, he was suddenly hit by a fit of coughing so severe that it had him doubled over.

The hand holding the forgotten pen was jarred as he was jostled by the panicked throngs of people rushing up the aisle he currently occupied. To his dawning horror, the pen with the life-saving epinephrine was knocked from his grasp and sent sailing to the floor, directly in the path of fleeing feet.

Waiting in her van for the memorial to be over and the attendees to exit, GENBS reporter Tanya Davis was getting bored. She'd already touched up her make-up, fixed her hair, and analyzed her appearance in her handheld mirror. Satisfied that she looked perfect, she searched for something to occupy her mind until this silly memorial was over, so she squinted out the side window at the Capitol Building in the waning light of dusk. Then she squinted harder and asked her cameraman, "Are people coming out already?"

The driver/cameraman squinted as well, but only for a second, and then burst into action. He jumped out of the van, threw the sliding side door open, grabbed his camera, and secured it to his shoulder. Something big was happening and he was determined that they be the first ones on the scene; the first to get the big story.

Still stinging from the gossip rag comment that bitch Senator Fisk had made to her, Tanya was determined to get this story and cover it like a true professional. She knew that she had been given this job because of her bone structure, her boobs, and her legs, but that didn't mean that she was a bimbo. She'd graduated top of her class at Berkeley University with a major in Journalism and a minor in Political Science, so she knew what real reporting consisted of.

Rushing forward, she stepped right into the path of a fleeing woman bringing the obviously frightened woman up short. "Ma'am, why are you running? What happened in there?"

The woman, an aide to Representative Schumacher of Rhode Island, was in full panic mode, her wide and slightly wild-eyed gaze staring blankly at the reporter before the cool fresh air of the outdoors helped her gather herself together. Then panting, sucking in the sweet untainted air, she replied, "It was a trap. The candles -- it was the candles."

Tanya was vibrating with excitement, but also with her competitive nature. Other reporters had left the warmth and safety of their vans and were rushing to other fleeing memorial service attendees. She had to get better information out of this woman and she had to get it quickly. "What was in the candles ma'am? What can you tell us about what happened?" She thrust the microphone in the face of the woman who was still trembling in fear.

"I don't know exactly what happened, but when we lit the candles everybody started to cough. And then a man and a woman burst in and started blowing out our candles and pushing us out of the chamber. She said there was a biological weapon in the candles."

"Who said?" Tanya was nearly drooling at this point. How often in her career would she have such an opportunity to shine -- to bring herself to the attention of the American people -- to secure a position as an anchor instead of working in the field in high heels and short skirts?

At that moment, a fleeing man collapsed and rolled down the Capitol steps. He was clawing at his throat, his chest heaving as he struggled to breathe. Tanya abandoned the first woman and ran to the fallen man. She did not wish to help him. She did not call for an ambulance. She wanted only to be the first reporter to capture his image. With her sprint down the sidewalk, she made it to his side in time for her cameraman -- she couldn't remember his name, had never really bothered to learn it -- to capture the swollen tongue protruding from his open gasping mouth as his struggles lost strength and his life slowly passed from him. "This is my Pulitzer," she was heard to whisper.

Small fires had broken out all over the chamber as candles had been dropped, thrown, or simply slipped from the slack fingers of the dying. Scot McClanahan was trapped in the center row of the press galley above, surrounded by the dead, the dying, the ill and the desperate. This was so much more than he had bargained for, so much more intense than he had expected, and he was trapped. He couldn't get out.

He tried to go to the left, but the path was riddled with people huddled over, collapsed in their seats, or dead on the floor. He turned to the right but it was the same, that path blocked as well. Desperate to get free, to get away from the horror, he climbed on his seat and took one step to the right, his foot landing in the lap of the man next to him, but the man did not complain, he was past the point where he was able to do so. Putting one unsteady foot in front of the other, he tried to make his way to freedom by stepping on the uneven surfaces of the lifeless bodies of people he had been complicit in killing.

When he could no longer keep his balance on the roiling mass, he dropped to hands and knees and crawled, grabbing fistfuls of clothing or hair in order to keep his balance. However, he wasn't the only one with this idea. As he raised his head and looked around, he found many others crawling, pushing, and climbing their way to freedom, positioning the dead and dying into the best climbing surface they could achieve. He was almost there, almost free, and then he was jostled by another fleeing individual; this one not caring whether the people she stepped on were alive or dead.

Scot lost his grip on the unsteady base of bodies and began to slide, his fingers grasping for anything to use as an anchor. He managed to close his fingers around the lapel of a young senator's suit coat and sighed in relief as his freefall was abruptly halted.

Struggling to get his kicking feet secured, Scot pulled himself forward with his arms and heard the fabric begin to tear, the sound ominously loud in an echoing chamber already filled with screams. He slipped by tiny increments as he kicked even harder, his feet desperately seeking purchase on the silk and linen clothing sliding underneath the leather soles of his dress shoes, putting even more pressure on the distressed coat lapel. The fabric finally gave way and Scot found himself going into a slide once more, the too low balcony rail approaching far too fast. He got his feet into position and they hit the rail with a force that sent a shock through his entire body, but he managed to stop himself, his feet braced against the rail keeping him steady, keeping him safe.

Exhaling in relief, he pushed with his feet as he grasped with his hands, grabbing and clawing in an attempt to remove himself from the perilous balcony edge. His fingers clutched the hair of the woman beneath him and he pulled, but this woman was not dead -- she was not even ill. She had been hunched over in shock, covering her eyes and ears from the agonizing scene which surrounded her. At the pull on her hair she jumped to her feet, the screams she had been too traumatized to express now given voice. Her quick movement threw Scot up and back, the momentum carrying him over the balcony in a graceful dive. A bare second later, he landed hard on another pile of bodies below, now as dead as those on which he rested.

Pamela watched her fellow aide fall to his death and the real consequences of what they had done began to sink in. The innocent were dying with the guilty. The very thing they had sought to avoid had come to pass.

The smell of burned hair still hovered, making her stomach churn; reminding her that she had to get the senator to safety. She had to protect her. She had to get her out.

Senator Fisk looked around her in alarm and dismay, while tears seeped from her eyes and ran down her face to drip on her black silk blouse. The coughs and wheezing of the affected, echoing and competing with the screams of the healthy, assailed her ears. She wasn't moving - she wanted desperately to help, but didn't know what she could do for these people that she had not been able to do for Highfall.

She watched the Secretary of Commerce wrap his hands around his throat and drop to his knees in the aisle. He was knocked to the side as people struggled to get past him to the exits, his own wife kicking him aside as she sought her own escape.

At first shocked into immobility, Mara next decided that it was much safer to stay in her seat and out of the frenzied chaos of the aisles. She was just turning to look behind her when she was punched hard between her shoulder blades, her upper body thrown forward, her head connecting solidly with the back of the seat in front of her.

Pamela screamed as she watched the scrambling elderly woman use Mara's back as a brace, unintentionally shoving her forward. The crack of the senator's head against the wood pounded in her ears. She pulled the senator back into a seated position, but the senator's head did not rise. Pamela then saw the blood running in a frighteningly thick flow from Mara's forehead. Searching frantically for anything she could use to staunch the stream and finding nothing, Pamela finally decided to strip off her own blouse and use that. Using the main body of the blouse as the bandage, Pamela secured it by wrapping the sleeves around the senator's head and tying them in a firm knot.

Now in just her bra and her skirt, she tried to get Senator Fisk in a position where she could carry or even drag her to safety, but more people were coming, clogging the aisles. Pamela had thought that sitting in the back would be a good idea, she would be able to see so many more people and be close to the exits, but now she was seeing too much.

The survivors were desperate for escape, pushing anybody and everybody out of their way, or when unable to do that, stepping on them whether they were dead or still alive. Pamela stood guard over her senator, pushing against anyone who came too close, beating them with her handbag and eventually even her shoes.

Grabbing her cameraman by his coat sleeve, Tanya pulled him against the flow of the wild-eyed mob racing down the Capitol steps. She had to get inside and find out what was really going on. She had to have this story - she just had to. Entering the Capitol, she elbowed her way to the front of the press throng and made her way to the hall where the House chamber emptied.

There was a crush of people trying to get out the now open doors, but the press blocked all exits as they battled to get in. Eventually, through sheer force of will and very bad manners, she made it to the doorway, the camera panning the crowd. Tanya stood her ground among the shifting masses, placing herself in the center of the doorway blocking the exit, and reported live to the studio.

Inside the chamber, many of the tainted candles still burned, the agent still being released and only slightly diluted by the fresh air coming in through the open doors -- but as fresh air came in, tainted air also seeped out. Tanya coughed, cleared her throat, and kept reporting.

Then she coughed again, and again. At first she believed the irritation in her throat was due to shouting over the cries of the ensuing battle, but then realized her throat was swelling and her ability to suck in air was decreasing. Eyes wide with terror and dawning comprehension, she shifted her gaze through the door to what was going on inside, finally recognizing that in her zealous quest for fame, she had exposed herself to whatever biological weapon had been released.

She dropped to her knees, the microphone capturing each wheeze and gurgle that escaped her swollen throat and transferring it back to the studio where the live broadcast continued.

The cameraman zoomed in for a close-up.

Still holding the tie over his mouth and nose, Clive Sledgewater searched the floor for his Epi-pen, but as his breathing became more ragged, more difficult, his search became progressively more desperate.

Finally he saw it lying in relative safety out of the crowd. He would have sighed in relief, but did not have the breath left to do so. He reached for the pen, his shaking hands nearly closing on it -- and then it was gone.

The woman who had kicked it in her attempt to escape slammed into Sledgewater; he threw her roughly to the floor, ignoring her screams as she was trampled under the feet of the fleeing.

He began his search again, though it was becoming more difficult as the lack of oxygen began to affect his vision. He would get that pen, he knew he would. He had to. He pushed and shoved and ran over anyone and everyone in his search, not caring whom he was hurting. He would have stepped on God himself to get to that pen, if he believed God existed.

"Out of my way!" he croaked through the tie as he threw a Supreme Court Justice and her husband hard into a bench and just kept going. Then, at last, he spotted it again. He would retrieve it and he would save his own life. He would escape this attack and be one of the few remaining, his power only increased. He reached out -- and lost the pen again.

It was kicked three more times before it landed in the open, in an area where the crowd had thinned as people were helped to their feet and herded in the direction of an unblocked door.

Sledgewater dropped to his knees, his chest aching as his burning lungs worked to pull in air through an ever-decreasing path. He crawled as frantically as his suffocating muscles allowed as he watched a foot approach his pen. The person was backing up, not watching where they were going, and coming closer and closer to his salvation. Sending up a prayer to the God he refused to acknowledge, he asked only that the pen not be kicked again. He just didn't know if he could chase it down again. "Please God," he asked. "Don't let him kick it."

Desperately he reached out and grabbed the pen – at the same time the foot took one more step back and landed right on the pen's tip, the tip which served as the delivery system for the life-saving epinephrine contained within.

Though his prayer had been answered and the pen had not been kicked, his salvation was gone all the same. He would have roared with rage, but he didn't have enough air left to do so. He looked up, cursing silently at the man above, and nearly roared again as he saw his killer.

The foot belonged to none other than Daniel Callahan – and he was still oblivious to what he had done. The Speaker collapsed on the floor, all hope gone, and turned his head to the side, his face away from the running feet that would kick it. There on the floor, directly in his line of sight, lay a Bible. The book had been dropped in the ensuing mayhem and now sat propped against the side of a bench, its pages open and displayed for the dying man. Sledgewater's eyes strained to focus on a verse before him, seeking a message in his last seconds of life. The verse was Romans, Chapter 12, Verse 19, but it was three small words in the verse which caught his attention: "Vengeance is mine." Clive Sledgewater closed his eyes against the Bible and allowed death to consume him.

Andrew Yarnell sat in the back of the government van in his Hazmat gear and advised his team of the process they already knew by rote. This was one of those situations for which they had all prepared, but prayed they would never have to experience. The van screeched to a halt in front of the Capitol Building as the team secured their helmets, jumped out, and split up. There were four more teams coming, but being the first to arrive, their main goal was to secure all of the exits. The massive building had countless exits, but this was something that had to be done. The biological agent, whatever it was, had to be contained.

Another team pulled up behind their van and began rounding up the people who had fled, taking the blows from the individuals who had finally escaped, only to be told they must return. One woman burst into tears, dropped to her knees, and begged the man in the Hazmat suit before her not to make her go back.

The problem was that if these people were out, there was a definite possibility that others had escaped, which meant that they'd have to lock down the entire city. Damn. Andrew called it in and knew that the instructions for grounding the planes and barricading the streets were already being communicated and put into action.

As Yarnell entered the Capitol, the sounds of screaming and fighting echoed through the cavernous building, bouncing off of the marble and carrying all the way up into the dome. The team headed to the House Chambers and paused for barely a second at the sight that greeted them there.

Advancing quickly, they immediately began pulling the press away from the door, sending several thumping into walls or skidding down the polished marble floors. Finally reaching the chamber, Andrew was stunned at the pandemonium that reigned as the leaders of the nation trampled one another in their panic.

Scanning for survivors, the team pushed their way through the small crowd and began rounding them up and vacating them to the Senate offices where the treatment center would be set up. Most went willingly, but one tall blonde woman was fighting and arguing with his people, insisting that they listen to what she had to say. He was used to this type of behavior from the desperate, but something about not only what she was saying, but how she was saying it broke through his professional detachment.

Sam nearly sagged in relief when one of the men in the big white suit pulled her aside and finally started to listen. Introducing herself first, she started giving him the facts of what she knew about the agent and how it worked.

Andrew listened intently, grateful that there was an individual on site who at least knew something about the poison so they would not be starting from scratch. It always helped to know what they were dealing with and the idea of an unknown biological weapon had disturbed him greatly.

The two stood to the side of the doorway, rocking in the wave of the masses seeking freedom and finding only redirection.

"It's not contagious," Sam yelled over the noise. Her nerves were on edge, her body exhausted, and her mind bombarded with guilt, anger, and fear.

"How can you be sure?" Andrew asked. "We can't take the chance of you being wrong."

"This was designed by my father to target the people in this room, and only those with a specific gene. It was never designed to go to the masses. In open air it will dilute quickly."

"Your father designed this?" Andrew asked in shock. "Where is he now?" If he could find the creator, he could get the real details and know exactly how these people and the others in the city would be affected.

"He's dead," Sam replied, her voice flat and devoid of emotion. "He was killed by the same weapon he organized the release of here."

"Damn!" Andrew swore. "Okay, so what do you suggest we do for these people?"

"It's operating like an allergic reaction. They need to be treated for that. Get some large doses of Benadryl and epinephrine. The Benadryl will work for most, but the epinephrine can be used for those severely, but not fatally affected. If they were going to be fatally affected by the agent, then they're probably already dead. We also need some kind of trauma unit set up for the other injuries. We have burns, abrasions, a few concussions, and even some broken bones."

Andrew called in for the delivery, but did not call off the quarantine of the city. They had to be absolutely sure first. He'd rather inconvenience a few people than kill millions - definitely best to err on the side of caution in this case.

Chapter 17

Gary Bright sat behind the desk on his program set, leaning forward, his elbows resting on the surface before him with hands clasped. He spoke directly into the camera, although he was really speaking directly to the American people. He had seen the footage coming out of the House chamber, the turmoil of the frightened people, the confusion, fear, and chaos. He had seen it, though his station chose not to air it.

His voice somber, Gary launched into his opening monologue. "Tragedy struck the Capitol Building today - a tragedy that we were warned about on this very show only yesterday. A biological agent was released at the memorial service for Senator Highfall, an agent that worked just as Dr. Mallard had warned us it would. A warning that was conveyed and either dismissed or ignored. For years we have been trying to make our members of Congress listen to us, the people with whom the real power is supposed to lie, but they refused, and that refusal brought about a revolution. A revolution waged by the unknown and in secret; a revolution that did not take to the streets, but went right to the source of the problem."

"It will be said by many in the mainstream press that I encouraged and advocated this revolution, but I did not.

Although I encouraged the people to speak out and fight for their rights given to them by God and secured in our Constitution, I repeatedly stated that violence is not the answer, and what actually happened is not what I expected. Reports are still coming in -- this is far from over -- but already we have 136 members of Congress confirmed dead and that number is only expected to rise. But along with those members of Congress, we also have their spouses, aides and even a few members of the press. What will the legislative branch of our government look like when this is over, the death toll confirmed? And who will we appoint and elect to replace those leaders now tragically deceased?"

Samantha and Daniel sat silently in the Senate Chamber, knowing they had done everything they could to help, but also feeling that they had saved far too few.

The Senate Chamber was filled with members of Congress and their staff receiving treatment for both the effects of the agent, and for injuries sustained in their attempt to escape.

The House Chamber was filled with the dead, body bags lining the aisles and laid out on the benches. Efforts were still underway to identify, record, and count the bodies. The damage to the grand chamber was minimal; a few small fires, easily contained, and some damage to the benches on which the Representatives had been seated. Other than that, the damage had all been human, and worse than even Sam's father could have anticipated.

Sam noticed one blonde woman huddled over the dark-haired senator she had seen on television just three nights before, her first night with Daniel. Had it really been so little time since she had fled her home in fear? The woman was crying and smoothing the brow of the senator, whose eyes were just beginning to flutter open.

Mara opened her eyes and saw Pamela above her. Only momentarily bewildered, the memory of what had happened flooded over her and she groaned. With the memory of the death of Highfall still so fresh in her mind, she could not help but compare his death to the others she had witnessed today. Pinning Pamela with a speculative and accusatory stare, she asked the only thing she could, "Pamela, what have you done?"

Bursting into tears, her voice rising to echo around the chamber, she replied, "It had to be done. I didn't think you'd be affected. I didn't think you'd be hurt. But they had to be punished, they had to be removed. They wouldn't listen. This wouldn't have had to happen if they'd only been willing to listen."

The shock and dismay of the survivors reverberated throughout the chamber. One of the perpetrators was in here with them?

One woman whose head was covered in bandages, severe burns covering her face and hands, stood and screamed, "You treacherous bitch!"

Other survivors followed her lead, most calling her names, screaming their hatred and demanding her immediate arrest, but three could not wait for traditional justice. Those three survivors, one a Supreme Court Justice, were on Pamela before the authorities could reach her.

By the time she was extracted and arrested, Pamela had three broken ribs, a broken nose, a busted lip, and various bruises and abrasions, and still she was protesting and crying that it had been a necessary action to save the country.

Behind her desk at Homeland Security, Agent Deckerd listened to the news of the release of a biological weapon within the walls of the Capitol building and told herself there would have been no time to stop it. She had found out about the attack only two days before and had none of the necessary information. It really had not been a credible threat, though she had little hope that this would matter to the powers that be.

As if she had summoned him with her thoughts, the director of the office walked in, climbed up on a desk and bellowed, "Does anybody here want to tell me why we knew nothing about this?"

His question was answered with silence.

Trying again he asked, "Are we or are we not Homeland Security? Isn't it our job to identify and prevent just these types of attacks?"

Again there was silence.

"Well, is it?" he screamed.

Finally, the whole office responded with an affirmative answer.

"Then why didn't we know? Why didn't we at least have some indication, even if no hard facts?"

Kissing her career goodbye, Deckerd rose from her seat. "I was notified of the possibility day before yesterday, sir."

In a rental car heading south on highway 395, Edward Jackson listened as the news of the attack broke on the radio. He felt no satisfaction at what was occurring, but was flooded with relief instead. It was over at last, and the people could appoint the new guards to their future security. He was headed to his sister's home in North Carolina, but wondered how long it would take for the authorities to find him there. Both the younger -- and far superior – Dr. Mallard and her companion knew him and how involved he had been, and he fully expected them to notify the police of that involvement.

For his last days of freedom before he was imprisoned for his efforts to restore the country -- efforts which would be viewed as treason, while the destruction of the Constitution was viewed as progress – he sought only the comfort of family. He would prefer to protect them from the fallout of his actions, but he knew this could not be done completely. They would be impacted, horrified, and shamed by his behavior, but in his soul he knew that what they had done was the right thing and would eventually be recognized as such. He had that faith. He had to have it.

As the coverage on the radio continued, Edward was thankful that he had beaten the roadblocks. His escape from the traumatized city was complete.

Maximilian Reginald Abernathy III arrived home from work to find his wife and his daughter glued to the television. The news of the events of the evening had burst through his office at the end of the day. Congress had been attacked by terrorists. A biological weapon had been released, but little else was known.

Max called out, but there was no answer, the women were too engrossed. He stepped up to his wife and laid his hand on her shoulder. She turned a tear-streaked face up to him and asked, "Who would do such a thing?"

Of course, Max not only knew who could, he knew who had. Sitting next to his wife, he watched the coverage of the event and for the first time was exposed to the actual results and not just the theory.

He watched as the leaders of the nation fought like school children to be the first to freedom. He watched as others succumbed to the agent and died on camera. He watched as one camera caught people falling from the press galley onto the people below. He forced himself to watch long after he wanted to turn away, ashamed of what he had taken part in, but even more ashamed of the press for showing it.

Samantha sat in Daniel's immaculately clean living room, still numb from what they had witnessed, and waited for Daniel to return with her cat. She needed Chloe. She needed something warm and soft and loving to cling to in order to chase the chill from her soul.

The door opened and Daniel stepped through, a wriggling Chloe in his arms. He set her down and she ran straight to Sam, climbed up in her lap and started to purr. This was exactly what she had needed. Daniel sat beside her and drew her in to his side, one arm wrapped loosely, but securely around her.

Samantha rested her head on his shoulder, stroked Chloe, and allowed the tears to flow freely. They did not turn on the television. They had no desire to see the news coverage of the event and suspected it was on nearly every station.

Daniel had seen Sledgewater among the dead. He had nearly stepped on him at one point, and yet he felt no relief or satisfaction at his death. It had all been too horrible -- the panic and desperation that had prevailed in one of the most sacred of all government buildings.

With all the fear of terrorists attacking the Capitol and the government leaders, the ultimate attack, the dreaded killing blow, had come from within. It came from people fed up with the direction the leaders had taken and a determination to make themselves heard -- and they had succeeded. People were listening now.

Daniel was dirty, the smell of the candles still clinging to his clothes and his hair, and he was suddenly desperate to get himself clean; to remove all traces of it from his body. He excused himself to Sam, idly patted Chloe on the head, and nearly ran to the bathroom.

He started the shower, making it as hot as he could tolerate, stripped and stepped in. He scrubbed his skin roughly and shampooed his hair four times, but still felt the grime. When his skin was rubbed nearly raw and his fingers and toes were pruning, he finally shut off the water and stepped from the tub. He grabbed a towel, drying himself harshly, and glared at the clothes on the floor; the clothes that Sawyer had purchased. Sending a silent apology to Sawyer, he wrapped the towel around his waist, bundled the clothes up, and carried them to the trash, stuffing them in the bag with more force than was necessary; with enough force that he almost shoved them right through.

"I'm so sorry," he heard Sam say softly.

"What are you sorry for, sweetie?"

Sam sniffled and rubbed her nose in Chloe's fur. "I'm sorry I dragged you into this. I'm sorry you had to witness all of that."

Daniel returned to the couch and hugged Sam to him again. "You have nothing to be sorry for, Sammie. The only thing worse than going through that is the thought of you going through it all alone. I couldn't have stood that. None of this is your fault, it's the fault of your father and everyone else in that damned NACR."

Sam stared up into his eyes and then dropped them, unable to deal with the intensity of emotion she found there. Unfortunately they dropped to the towel, the thin bit of terrycloth covering him. A thin bit that was parting as his legs spread in relaxation. The need to remind herself that she was alive rushed through her, pounding her blood through her veins and right to strategic and greedy places. The warm body she needed was no longer her cat, and the only purring she wanted to hear was her own, or Daniel's. In a flurry of movement she turned, straddled his lap, and kissed him with everything she had inside her. Daniel did not object.

Shocked only momentarily by her actions, Daniel wrapped his arms around her, stood, and carried her to the bed. As he sat her down and whipped off his towel, he smiled - one of those full-faced smiles that she loved so much. "What the hell," he said, "I think you now have four days free to recover."

"Do I really have to do this?" Sam asked.

A week had passed since the attack by what was being labeled as a "domestic terrorist organization," and Sam was fully recovered, both from the event itself and from the very energetic and completely wonderful nights that followed.

"Yes, you have to do this," Daniel replied. "You've always wanted to do it, and we both know you're brave enough."

The karaoke man called out her name again and Daniel pushed her from her chair and towards the stage.

Samantha walked up to the microphone, pulled it from its stand, and sent an admonishing glare to Daniel. If this went badly, she could guarantee that he wouldn't be getting any sex that night, although she'd be punishing herself as well. Now incentivized to do well, Sam listened to the beginning notes of "Someone To Watch Over Me", and softly began to sing.

Epilogue – One year later
Sam clicked on the news, the morning light bursting into color as it reflected from the engagement ring on her finger. She had moved to Arlington, Virginia, and purchased a small, craftsman-style home which she shared with Daniel. The main difference between this one and the home she had sold in Baltimore was that this one was clean. That, of course, was due primarily to Daniel.

She had automatically turned on the television -- now an avid news hound -- but immediately regretted that action. Today was the anniversary of the terrorist attack on the Capitol Building, and it was all being relived on the morning news.

The attack was attributed to the actions of a few disgruntled Americans, though Sam knew that it had taken a far wider range of people than the press indicated. However, since she and Daniel had advised the police that her father and Edward were dead, the only known member of the organization had been Pamela McCormack, and she wasn't talking.

Pamela was now in prison, but had never revealed the names of the other members of the organization. She still proudly maintained that what they had done was just and right and in the best interest of the nation. Her assertion wasn't completely unfounded.

When all was said and done, there were 324 members of Congress, three Cabinet members, and one Supreme Court Justice who died that day. The President and Vice President had escaped unscathed, mostly due to the quick action of the Secret Service, but the legislative branch of the government had been decimated. Now, one year later, it had been rebuilt and was stronger than ever, though far less powerful.

Members of the state legislatures had been appointed to replace the deceased members of the Federal Congress, and the new appointees were listening to the people. This had more to do with the fact that no antidote had been found for the biological weapon than with the people who were appointed. Not to mention that the general citizenry was not afraid to remind the new politicians of what had happened to the old ones.

Many of the laws and regulations that had crippled the economy had been repealed and new jobs were being created every day. The country was returning to its original design, though it still had a long way to go.

One thing was sure, though; the American people were once again free.

"When the people fear their government, there is tyranny; when the government fears the people, there is liberty." – Thomas Jefferson

Made in the USA
Lexington, KY
17 March 2010